BEIRUT BLUES

BY THE SAME AUTHOR

The Story of Zahra
Women of Sand and Myrrh

BEIRUT BLUES

Hanan al-Shaykh

Translated by Catherine Cobham

For sylvia
with Love
Hanan
-96-

Chatto & Windus
London

This edition first published in 1995
1 3 5 7 9 10 8 6 4 2
Published in Arabic as *Barid Beirut* in 1992
by Dar Al-Hilal, Cairo
Copyright © 1992 by Hanan al-Shaykh
English translation copyright © 1995 Doubleday

*The lines on p. 45 are from a poem by Yehya Jaber and are reproduced by
kind permission of their author.*

First published in the United Kingdom in 1995 by
Chatto & Windus Limited
Random House, 20 Vauxhall Bridge Road
London SW1V 2SA

Random House Australia (Pty) Limited
20 Alfred Street, Milsons Point, Sydney
New South Wales 2061, Australia

Random House New Zealand Limited
18 Poland Road, Glenfield
Auckland 10, New Zealand

Random House South Africa (Pty) Limited PO Box 337, Bergvlei, South
Africa

Random House UK Limited Reg. No. 954009

A CIP catalogue record for this book is available from the British Library

ISBN 0 7011 6303 8

Phototypeset by Intype, London
Printed and bound in Great Britain by
Clays Ltd, St. Ives plc

FOR NAJAH TAHER

Editorial Note

Readers who compare this translation with the original Arabic will notice a number of changes. These have been made on the basis of artistic criteria and it is intended that the next Arabic edition will incorporate them.

Hanan al-Shaykh & Catherine Cobham, 1994

My Dear Hayat

I'm thinking about you now instead of following Zemzem's example and inching forward on all fours so the gunman doesn't see me, or clutching the prayer beads like my grandmother and praying to God and His prophets for all I'm worth. I'm holding the new Energizer torch given away with four Energizer batteries. I shine it around the room, and there's the painting you gave me on one of your visits to Beirut because the woman in it looked like me. Does she? You can't see her face clearly. Perhaps the way she's sitting alone in the room with only a little light filtering in through the window reminded you of me.

I pass the torch beam over the cupboard and see the nails on the back of the door where I've hung my dress, and the washstand – one of those pieces of furniture with a mirror and drawers and a white marble top. I remember it has a bit of wire in place of a key and I shine the torch on it and then catch sight of the bag lying on the marble top with the abaya in it, waiting to be sent to you. Involuntarily I bring the torch down and over to the other side and see the quiet geometry of the mosaic. I think of the lengths I went to to acquire this and the abaya, and shake my head in disbelief.

I'm thinking of you and talking to you, and it's as if you're not far away, even though I didn't feel that closeness during your last visit to Lebanon. The thoughts and feelings born of violence appear very real, and you have what seem like final glimpses of those dearest to you flashing before your eyes. It's just as if I'm in love with you. I remember the first thing I used to see when I opened my eyes in the morning was Naser, and I knew he'd been there behind my eyes all night long, from the moment I switched out the light.

During my relationship with him, or at least at the beginning, I used to mention you all the time. You were my safety blanket. Every time I felt him cooling towards me, I would suddenly announce that I was going to visit you or that you were coming here. I would show him all the things you'd sent me, and realize that you really had been a part of my life like my father and Isaf, the family maid in my childhood. Loving him, I stopped missing you as much and grew accustomed to holding a conversation with someone other than myself, for with you it was just like talking to myself.

I know you're trying to contact me now since our telephone's been dead for a month. You're the first to call when there's fighting here, followed closely by my mother who's always crying and laughing at the same time. I used to know you were on the other end as soon as the phone rang. I couldn't believe how loud your voice was, as if you were somewhere in the house, and I found myself taking notice of life again, seeing the plants in their pots, being aware of the surface of the table, the veins on my hand.

You're trying to contact me, because the battles between Hizbullah and Amal must be all over the front pages in Belgium. Instead of feeling – as I normally do – that I don't want you constantly worrying about me during the fighting, I must admit that this time I'm comforted by the thought. I've only just stopped being guilty about our last conversation, when I let my incredible lethargy get the better of me, even though I knew you'd been sitting there hour after hour trying to get a line to Beirut. My lethargy could have surfaced before, but I used at least to pretend to be keen to talk to you, and if I exclaimed in annoyance because I had to go somewhere or had someone else with me, I would quickly change it into a sigh, as if I missed you. I don't understand why I behaved like this.

You always want to know my view of events and reassure yourself that I'm safe, while I'm absorbed with the trivia of love and sex – and the rat. How can I answer your questions about the state of the country, when my chief worry is the rat occupying our kitchen? We're beginning to have to ask its permission every time we want to go in there during the night, so we let it know we're at the door before we go in, then talk loudly and sing to it: "Come visit us, my beauty, come." But it's much cleverer than us and so far it's managed to dodge the traps: it actually knocked a plank of wood down on to the glue we'd laid to immobilize it while we bashed it on the head.

Can I really be irritated with Hayat whose name was so closely linked with mine that our two names were spoken as one: Hayat-and-Asmahan, Asmahan-and-Hayat? Is it because I'm never comfortable on the phone, while you love it, and seem quite at ease? You stand there looking your best as if you're face to face with the person at the other end. This wouldn't explain my aversion to your calls, for my indifference was rapidly changing to a kind of bad temper which I always tried to hide when confronted by your boring news and your eager questions: "Asma! What have you got to tell me? How are you?"

Isn't it ridiculous to summarize what's going on in one sentence? The war is this, or the war is that. People are dancing, people are dying. I don't care. Although I cared a lot yesterday. Then we're silent, then I ask you some questions and try to sound interested. But what shall I ask you about? What will you answer? What have you been doing? You've found a Lebanese cook who makes you kibbeh and moloukhiyya. And your son's playing tennis and is going to be a champion. And you miss home. Oh, how you miss it!

Meanwhile the life I've constructed in Beirut is only concerned with the heart of things. I get right to the bone now, no more floating on the surface, even in my conversations with Zemzem and Fadila. And they in turn have begun to look inside themselves. Since the generator went dead, Zemzem says to me, "I really miss the sound of that motor. It was like a human being."

Our friendship couldn't have survived as it was with the passing of time and the war; even the language has changed.

The war buried some people away and brought others to prominence. I developed thousands of different personalities all teeming with stories, as if I was an adolescent again, and because the war put an end to normal everyday life, people became odder. I began relishing this strangeness and was drawn to it once I'd opened myself up to the people coming and going; my grandmother used to compare my father's house scathingly to the village inn, and I began to think of my life like that. People began entering it in droves, and because they all generated their own noise and activity I sometimes felt constricted by them, but I was stuck with them.

Perhaps because in Belgium you can only establish marginal relationships, you've preferred to remain in our shared past, which we both began to draw on to preserve our friendship. We tried cobbling the past on to the present and succeeded at first to a limited degree, because we were both so curious to know about each other's lives. The strength of our feelings for each other helped but the distance prevented us from really entering each other's new lives and I sensed the past was gradually being buried under the rubble of the present, until you were no longer the person closest to me. I still don't know if you realized this on your last visit or if you justified my coolness as a pathological character change, and felt sad because your friend was no longer the person you once knew. Perhaps you forgave her and thought about helping her. For you couldn't comprehend how I could abandon you and leave the wedding party in the middle of the night, hand in hand with your brother's friend, who was years younger than me. We said we were going off to the convent to ask after Fadila's mother, but you must have seen me leaning against him or lying back on the stony ground, happy to feel him breathing close up against me. We came back to your parents' house at dawn, and all I wanted to do was sleep. When you asked me how Fadila's mother was, I laughed and said, "Happy with the nuns. I mean with the Prophet's family!"

I was worried from the moment I heard you were visiting Lebanon for your brother's wedding. I'd have to prepare, find Ali and go and meet you if you were coming by air. I sighed at the thought of it. This meant that you'd spend the first night with me so I'd have to get my room ready for you, take my things from here and there, cancel my meeting with Simon, try to persuade Jummana to come with me to your brother's wedding, and make you two more friendly with each other, as if I was responsible for the chemistry between you. The energy which all this required had long ago forsaken me.

Then I began thinking about what I should wear for the wedding. I remember I stood in front of the mirror for ages, imagining what you would see, hoping you'd be surprised. Although I've stayed in Lebanon I've still got some taste. I know what's going on in the outside world. I'm not standing still, and they haven't got me wearing a veil yet.

I tried on lots of different outfits but didn't manage to picture an expression of surprise or approval in your eyes.

I was sure you would be wearing the most beautiful clothes, and the art student you told me about would have designed your dress, because she's started designing everything for you, even weaves and dyes the material and finds someone to make your shoes and earrings. (I remember you telling me this while I was waiting to talk to Ali to tell him the generator had broken down.) I found myself standing in front of the open wardrobe as if I was confronted by a fridge crammed with food and could find nothing to eat. I no longer believed in buying expensive clothes or even admitted to myself that there were still parties and weddings taking place; but the garments I used to devise from scraps and cast-offs weren't right at my age. Suddenly I worked out how to make you gasp in admiration: I brought out my grandmother's dresses which I loved and couldn't bring myself to part with, even though they were going under the arms. They were velvet and silk brocade in colours of rust, green, blue, violet, and among them was one made of the finest black lace I'd ever seen.

In front of the mirror I lifted my hair off my neck with one hand and smiled, then I raised my breasts with the other hand and smiled again, as if I were facing a camera lens, or a man was looking at me. But I was alone with the broken mirror, and the sound of my grandmother's prayers drifting in through the open door. She was praying to God to protect me as I made the crossing into the eastern sector of the city. She was afraid for me, and I was nervous too, not only of crossing over to the east, but because I was meeting you. My uneasiness was still there the next day and I longed more than anything to wear the lace dress to give me courage as I crossed the sand and dead leaves to the other side, but when it came to it I folded it up and put it in an overnight bag.

I found fault with the way you moved and sat and talked. You were either insensitive or stupid. When you tried to be one of us again, the dominant expression on your face was pity, for everyone who'd stayed here. As you talked you clasped people to you, then touched their faces, then held them again as if you were saying, "I know what you're suffering." Why were you so sure that those who stayed were the only ones suffering?

The wedding ended and everyone said they hoped we'd soon find husbands. For the second time that evening. I said, laughing, that Jummana and I ought to marry one another. A woman remarked, "You're right. Where can you find normal men here? They're all crooks or fighters. The rest have left, or don't have a penny to their name."

Instead of going off somewhere with you to talk about what had happened during our time apart, I remained firmly in my seat, rejoicing that I hadn't gone back with the convoy of cars headed for the western sector. Those who had decided to risk the journey back at night couldn't possibly have enjoyed the festivities to the full.

I was happy to sit on the balcony listening to the crickets singing in the woods, a sound I'd never expected to hear again in my life, while the fireflies played blind man's buff among the trees. I sighed and Jummana understood why and responded with a sigh of her own. Without saying anything, we thought simultaneously that the easterners were the lucky ones because they had the mountains as well. You appeared to be rooting around for topics of conversation, and dismissing them as soon as they occurred to you, perhaps realizing they'd be of no interest because they were so remote from life here.

I put the blame on the noise and crowds surrounding us at

6

the wedding, and the constant interruptions: "How did we lose touch?" "How do we manage to live in West Beirut?"

A relative of yours remembered me and told me I should be married by now. To my astonishment you agreed with her. "You ought to visit me in Belgium. You'll be fighting off Lebanese men, there are so many of them there."

I wonder if you were lying to spare my feelings or really didn't know that the men who come back to visit Lebanon are either in their coffins, or actively looking for someone to marry. When I stared into your face I knew for sure I hadn't missed you. Was it your ballet-type shoes with blue flowers stuck on the front, or your blue dress which made you look like a girl in one of Gauguin's paintings? We couldn't be close when we lived such completely different lives, starting with your shoes, which wouldn't have survived more than a few steps over the uneven pavements and quagmires of mud. And that was just your shoes! So what about the expression on your face which said clearly that your leaving the country meant the war had ceased to exist? If we had rubbed your nose in it, you would have acknowledged its existence, but said it couldn't be helped if a few people had to live through it and be harmed by it. With the second glass of arak, I noticed I was enjoying the glances I was getting from your relations and especially from your brother's friends. There was one who was more handsome than the others. He was improvising poems to entertain the guests and every time he finished a verse he smiled at me.

It was Jummana rather than you who laughed and came to my aid: our thoughts have begun to coincide without any need for us to speak, just the way it used to be with you and me. You hadn't changed like this before, not even the year you came back married; in fact marriage seemed to make you extra-responsive to admirers, as if you didn't like the idea that a page of your life had been turned for good. And yet there you were, obviously annoyed by my antics with Jummana.

Your mother intervened, laughing. "Keep your eyes off the girls, you rascal! I know what you're up to!"

He looked into my eyes, and I felt he was kissing me, holding me close, in spite of the table between us loaded with plates and glasses and flowers. "No, honestly, it's Madame Yvette I want."

Everyone laughed. Do you remember when we were children, Sitt Yvette used to promise to make us a cake whenever I went into her shop with you? Sitt Yvette laughed and held out her glass, a piece of parsley stuck between her teeth. "Here's to you and all the young men like you."

"Knock it back, Sitt Yvette, and I'll give you a kiss."

She drank it in one go and covered her face with her hands. It struck me that the great divide really existed: I couldn't imagine this relaxed atmosphere in the western sector, in the city or the countryside, and the hopes for change seemed to have receded. Perhaps if the war hadn't happened we'd have had more chance.

I returned to the table. His warmth brought me back, his eyes saying to me, "Let me take you under the olive trees and kiss you."

I no longer looked him in the eye. I began to feel embarrassed every time he opened his mouth to recite a verse even though the females in his poems were always in the plural.

> The newly weds have gone tonight and left me
>   with the pearls
> My heart beats faster, but I tell it to be still.
> You could have had those pearls
> And now they're lost to you for ever.

I wished I could cling to him under the trees, rest my head on his chest and say to him, "My heart's beating too. If you hold my hands, I'll faint. Has it been a long time? Yes, ages since anyone stared at me and flirted with me like this. And even longer since anybody invited me to the cinema or a restaurant by the sea to walk and talk and be frivolous. Here there are cinemas and restaurants on the seafront, but tomorrow I have to cross back into the west, or if not tomorrow the day after, or in a week at the most. To tell you the truth, I don't feel as if I'm in my own country. I'm a tourist. It's too late. But I didn't always think like this. There were times before when I

8

used to say the war had given some meaning to my life. Now I realize that it's too late. I can't open my heart to you. Just for one night? It's not because you're a Christian but because tomorrow we'll be separated, and you won't be in a hurry to visit the western sector. Perhaps you've convinced yourself that I'm from here, because you've been drinking and I'm a friend of Hayat's and probably, like me and Hayat, you don't think of yourself as being from the east or the west. But I've grown full of suspicions. People are changing before my eyes. People I used to know when they were students have become professors and gone backwards a hundred years. They've taken sides. The time may come when I do the same! Who knows? Perhaps then I'll be happy. Belonging to some faction, however extreme or outlandish, might be preferable to this. If you make a commitment, however hard the consequences turn out to be, you can relax. The fanatic meets a lot of others like him, people he can operate with. Where I come from, they hate everyone from your sector, even the men at the checkpoint. But I always want to have a chat with them, make them laugh and flirt with me. I seem to need reassurance and affection from your people. I want things to be like they were years ago. But now I'm drunk. All I want is to rest my head on your chest."

His eyes bored into me, but thinking about what I would say in response to them made me miserable for a few moments, then I felt the warmth in his voice again, and admired his teeth which were revealed each time he laughed and joked with Yvette: "I'd give anything to hold your hand, to kiss you on the mouth. No, on second thoughts, maybe you've got no teeth. Okay, on the cheek."

"If you feel like it you can have a nice whiff of meat," she replied. "Come on! I've been pounding meat for kibbeh since early morning."

Everyone burst out laughing at her reply and the boy was encouraged to take this humorous flirtation further, so he asked her to have another drink with him. He held a full glass to her lips but she pushed it away. "My teeth are hurting me and my throat's burning."

He plucked a piece of ice from the glass, but she moved her

face out of reach, still laughing. "For Saint Maroun's sake, please, my throat's burning!"

"Look, Saint Maroun's asleep now," he answered. "See, he's got his eyes shut. So would you, if you had to stand up all the time."

Saint Maroun? I realized the illuminated statue down below us, which I had always thought was Christ, must be their Saint Maroun.

"Saint Maroun!" You drew in your breath remembering. "I was so afraid of him! My grandmother, Umm George, used to threaten me with stories of what he'd do to me if I didn't drink up all my milk!"

Suddenly I felt a longing for the old Hayat, but was distracted by the sight of a building which looked like a white silkworm at the statue's feet. "Is that the hospital attached to Saint Maroun's convent?" I asked eagerly.

Someone told me it was and my heart sank. "Poor Fadila," I whispered. It must have come out louder than I thought, for Hayat's mother asked, "Poor who?"

Enthusiastically, as if I'd been waiting for the opportunity to express my silent thoughts, I burst out, "Fadila's mother's in Saint Maroun's hospital." I had already guessed what was going on in the others' minds: "Fadila. That's an old-fashioned peasant name. Muslim."

Yvette asked curiously, "And her family's there in West Beirut with you?"

"They're always crossing over and visiting her here," I said.

Inevitably Fadila cut straight through the noise and the handsome youth's disturbing glances and was there with me.

I had an image of her in her high-heeled gold sandals, with her pale complexion and the black abaya thrown around her shoulders, begging me to let her come with me to the east, punctuating her words with movements of her plump hands and cracking the chewing gum between her teeth. I don't know how she manages to appear every time I decide to visit my friends on the other side, urging me to take her with me so that she can see her mother. I refuse, and this only makes her more insistent. I offer excuses and she doesn't listen, only groans and beats her breast, reproaching herself for not visiting her mother enough. She can no longer control the fear and agitation she feels when she travels alone in the eastern sector. Once she told us how, on a previous visit, she had opened a box of baqlawa and offered one to the taxi-driver in an attempt to stop herself feeling scared, but he refused saying, "Merci. No thanks."

She searched for the packet of cigarettes she'd bought especially for the trip to make her look like a powerful woman, and began blowing out smoke and coughing furiously. Then instead of cursing the devil as she normally did when she coughed, she began cursing Amal and Hizbullah, the "Party of God", trying to involve the taxi-driver. "I ask you, have you ever heard of anyone but us starting up a political party for the Lord?"

When the taxi-driver didn't reply, she set about opening up a plastic bag, checking to see that her black abaya was still stuffed in at the bottom, and took out a box of chocolates which she offered, only to be refused again. She told herself that he must think they were poisoned, and he was right to be wary, because they belonged to opposite sides of a divided city, which meant they were enemies and at war with each other, and stories of spies operating between the two sides were on the increase. She was nervous and uncertain how to behave. She held out the packet of cigarettes and when he reached for one she relaxed a little, but her fear returned when she suddenly realized that she could no longer hear the sound of car horns and that there was no other car in sight on the bumpy road. So she began describing the suffering which the people in the western sector were encountering in their daily lives, nearly weeping with fright, and because the driver's only response was a brief shake of the head, she began telling him again how much she liked and trusted the Christians, how she'd refused to put her mother anywhere but Saint Maroun's Hospital, regardless of the cost, which had risen to thirty dollars a day, or the distance, or the difficulty of crossing from the west into the east. "The hospitals in the western sector are chaos. They're all crazy there!"

The driver put his foot down and she was convinced he was

about to kill her. He would tear her limb from limb and throw the pieces into a ditch. She'd rather he raped her if that was what he wanted. She'd let him do whatever he liked with her, but not kill her. To break the silence and try to calm her fears, she said imploringly, "If only I lived here. I'd be respected and properly treated. This is how life should be. Not like it is with us."

To her horror, the driver suddenly struck the steering wheel with all his force, threw his cigarette out of the window, heaved a great sigh and almost swerved off the road. "Give me a break!" he shouted. "Life's shit there and it's shit here."

All the same, Fadila didn't relax completely until she recognized the hotel where the beauty queens used to stay in the old days, which was near the hospital. She thanked him for being so kind and helpful before she got out of the car, and again offered him a piece of baqlawa, a chocolate, a cigarette. "At least you've still got Samadi's patisseries over there," he said.

"Give me your address," she replied, bursting with affection. "Next time, I'll bring your wife the biggest box of baqlawa they've got, though nothing would be enough to repay your kindness, and your people are protecting my mother and guarding her as if she was one of your own."

As Fadila went to enter the hospital, she saw the mountains and valleys descending to the sea and exclaimed out loud to Allah. She clapped a hand over her mouth and looked around her, suddenly scared that someone might have heard her imprecation. All she could see were the nurses hurrying to and fro and she laughed, remembering the day she had brought her mother to the hospital. She'd been heartbroken, and had been nice to her mother all the way there, stroking her hair, asking her to forgive her for putting her in a hospital so far from home. "I would have done anything for you, Mother. But the combination of you and the bombs was more than I could take."

Then she began teaching her to pray to the Blessed Virgin rather than the Prophet Muhammad or Imam Ali and to invoke the name of Jesus instead of the name of God the Compassionate, the Merciful, so that everyone would like her, especially the nurses. Her mother repeated "Blessed Virgin" and "in the name of Jesus" after her in a normal, docile voice which was so unlike the way she usually spoke that Fadila began to wonder if she was mad after all. "Perhaps it's just the war," she thought.

But as soon as they crossed the threshold into the hospital, her mother refused to go another step, saying that the hens' wings were beating against her and that she was afraid of treading on the children's eyes if she went any further. When Fadila forced her to keep going and she found herself right inside the hospital, she gasped in wonder. "O God, bless the Prophet and his family and the pure women of his household," she cried, pointing to the nuns in their white habits.

I've never told you about all that before. It flashed before me and was gone even before I heard the handsome youth saying to me, "Come on. Let me take you to the sisters. They all know me. We changed the wiring in the convent a while back. Come on, get up. I'll take you. What are you waiting for?"

He wants to be alone with me under the trees. I want to rest my head on his chest. I'm not interested in telling him the story of Fadila's mother. I want to take hold of his hands and run them over my hair. I answer eagerly, "Let's go."

You interrupt, saying that the convent must be closed.

I stood up quickly, almost swaying from the effects of my third glass of arak which had settled in my knees and feet. I sensed, despite my third glass, that you were against the idea, but I went all the same, indifferent to your shocked stares. I knew without looking that Jummana was wishing someone else would drag her off to olive trees by the convent. The cold had spread to the car windscreen. Although I was in his arms, I had an image of Fadila's mother which I couldn't get out of my mind. She was resting both hands on the window bars while the nuns stood with their starched butterfly wings on their heads licking their moustaches in silence as they watched the young man enclosing me in his limbs. I wished we could have cleared all the tools out of the back of the car so that we could have lain comfortably together but the alcohol made me forget and focused my senses on one part of me. As I moved faster the butterfly wings on the nuns' heads moved up inside me, then I seemed to be entering the convent, going further and further in until I found myself in a room where one of the beds was shaking violently, although there was nobody in it.

When I went back to your house, dawn had broken, the gardener was digging potatoes and piling them up on one side and the door was open.

Instead of giving us new secrets to discuss as it would have done in the past, my night's absence increased the gulf between us, which I hadn't noticed so much while you were staying with me, especially when we went to the beach and the American University. Now it was getting wider again and as I listened to you criticizing me for going off with a man so much younger than me, then lowering your voice to tell me confidentially that this behaviour wasn't normal and perhaps I should see a therapist. Just like that, without batting an eyelid, or trying to understand how the pattern of life here has changed. I didn't take much notice at the time because I was praying that the clashes wouldn't start up again, since I was responsible for getting you and your luggage safely on the plane to Brussels. As soon as you'd left, I heaved a sigh of relief and went back to my daily routine.

It's strange how close you are to me now. I feel your voice, your anxious presence. I can picture you dialling my number. You must be worried about me because I'm worried about myself in the current battles. I feel scared at the very sound of the new weapons they've brought in this time.

Our street has begun to shake with the force of the bombardment. Twenty shells a minute. I'd just put olive oil on my hair when Zemzem came into my room. I noticed her voice had a new power and resonance, perhaps because she'd been out to gather the latest news from the neighbours and the shelter, whereas I and my grandmother had stayed in our rooms. "The women are going to hold a demonstration!" she cried, breaking in on my reverie. "They're going to carry Qurans and wear abayas!"

"One lot must have engineered it, because they want a cease-fire," I answered quickly.

"You've always been the same. If you haven't had a hand in

something, it means it's no good. They're demonstrating because the Syrian army's going to enter Al-Dahiya, seeing as Hizbullah's winning and Amal's nowhere."

Zemzem was letting out all her suppressed resentment. Since the fighting began she'd been trying to make us share her sense of panic. Not at all sorry for the commotion she'd caused, she added, "Why should the women need persuading? The boys are killing each other and they're all Shi'as – members of Imam Ali's party. Come on! Get up! They'll be pleased if you march with them. Get dressed! Your mauve caftan. Come on!"

The Syrian army. Hizbullah. What about Ricardo? Do you remember Ricardo? Yahya. Fadila's nephew. The moment you saw him on one of your visits your eyes gleamed in disbelief because you sensed there was something going on between us. He's on my mind now, even though I'm certain he won't be involved in the fighting. His aunt wouldn't have let him out. I'm scared for him, not because of the Syrians, but because of the despair he must be feeling. He'll discover now that he's fallen unintentionally into a void. And his comrades in the party? I only feel pleasantly spiteful towards them, towards the Modern Sheikh, and Kazim. Where are they now? Are they fighting? Is it their weapons we can hear, instead of the sound of them arguing and laughing? Kazim, who began coming round a lot and brought his brother and the Modern Sheikh to see me, to kill time but also to convince me of the exemplary nature of Hizbullah and the need for its existence. This was since Ricardo had been caught in two sensitive areas and been suspected of spying on them, for no one would believe that he wanted to join Hizbullah. Eventually Kazim came with him to our house at Ricardo's request, when his aunt Fadila was out. That was the first time I had seen Ricardo since he went back to Africa after staying ten years in Lebanon. He'd been a child of no more than four years old when he was brought here from Africa at the insistence of Fadila's father, his grandfather. The old man had somehow heard that his son had had a child by an African woman whom he had then abandoned for a Lebanese. Ricardo couldn't get used to living in a house mostly full of crazy people, isolated from other children, so he fled to the neighbours from the frosty atmosphere of his grandfather's house. But he was the son of an unknown African woman and as soon as he could make out his country on a map of the world he left Lebanon and only returned during the war, when he had changed his name to Yahya and believed totally in martyrdom, paradise and dark-eyed houris. He came back hoping to fly planes in the skies over Beirut and drop bombs on the politicians who were God's enemies. Today's allies are tomorrow's enemies, depending on where the arms and materials come from. But religion is above everything. Allies and enemies don't figure in it. "The leader has to be God, not a human being, because human beings are weak."

Kazim was listening to what Ricardo said but he rephrased it in more ideological terms; he said that religious faith was now the solution but this was a gut reaction after the failure of the other political parties. "We confronted Israel with weapons, nationalism, guerrilla operations. What was the result? If we'd fought them with our religion we would have overcome them. Look at them. Because they operate on the basis of a single religion they're the strong ones. Religion must become the authority."

The handsome Sheikh Nizar interrupted. He was the one known as the Modern Sheikh: he wore jeans, his beard smelt of perfume, he liked good coffee and admired the Persian carpet in the sitting room, tracing its design to a particular village in Iran. He praised Ricardo, saying that Islam had spread at the grass-roots in black Africa where the people didn't wear any clothes, and he denied the role of a sheikh there who was supposed to have fuelled the enthusiasm of African youth and been the link between them and the events in Lebanon. "One day the whole of America will turn to Islam," he added. "Gradually it'll take over in Russia, which is half Muslim already. God willing, Asmahan with her beautiful hair will return to the faith."

The word demonstration took me back to the sixty-seven war: the faculty is noisy with demonstrations, but an air of gloom hangs over it. You're asking me if I like your new eye-shadow and you bring your face nearer to me and close your eyes, so that I can see it. At the time I was thunderstruck by the inappropriateness of your question, but now I acknowledge that you were a seer and we didn't realize it. A prophet of the modern, looking beyond the coming days with X-ray eyes, predicting from a keen sense of reality what would have to be done. You were reckless and I have to admit that you were concerned with the individual rather than the fate of nations – going to the beach was an acceptable substitute for being involved in demonstrations. You gabbled away in different languages and always looked after your appearance even when it came to your choice of toothbrush. We thought of you as frivolous, uncommitted, although you were outstanding at your studies.

Now I find myself saluting you, acknowledging that when you left this country it was a prophetic act, as if you knew in advance that the war would never end in a matter of days, months or years as we believed, that life was too important to spend waiting, for we'd all forgotten why the war had started. Even those who ignited the blaze lost sight of their original aim. They fight, agree to ceasefires, make settlements, fight again, and their war achieves nothing, nor even their peace.

If I didn't have this piece of mosaic in front of me, I wouldn't believe I'd gone where I did to get it. Following your mother's instructions I went to a friend of your family's, an engineer who directed me to a man who sold old mosaic. The same with the abaya. If it wasn't for that bag lying on the marble top I wouldn't believe that I'd gone into the back alleys of Al-Dahiya for it. All these errands are simply devised by the mind to inject hope into the body, and energize the spirit that was there in the past.

First I went to L'Artisanat to buy you an abaya, but I couldn't find a colour which would suit you. I knew you would want one that looked ethnic and "original" in Europe, whatever the colour. But you know how much I love colours, and then there's this assistant whispering to me in a southern accent that in Al-Dahiya they sell genuine abayas just like these, all colours, for half the price. I notice she's trying to disguise her accent, and her hair's in the latest style, like her clothes. But she can't hide the way she talks, or the gold tooth in the front, typical of southern women, even though she puts her hand up to her mouth every time she smiles.

I went to the address she gave me. I've always thought I knew Al-Dahiya well since we're on its doorstep, but I wandered round aimlessly asking directions until I was at the end of my tether. I was disoriented, maybe because I had this sense that I wasn't in Al-Dahiya at all, but in some noisy alley in downtown Hong Kong on account of the sound of hammering, the whirr of sewing machines, the sand sneaking into my shoes, the animal carcases, the flies, the street vendors selling vegetables and bedding, the stagnant pools of water. Music played. People poured from all sides. Strange buildings sprouted extensions in every direction. Even the flat roofs had been converted into extra rooms, and basements hummed with activity. The streets served as markets to sell sheep, cigarettes, clothes and gold jewellery. Lorries blocked the entrances to alleyways so that people had to squeeze between the vehicles and the walls to get out. Porters were loaded down with wares produced by factories and workshops, big and small, underground, on rooftops, crammed between rooms. Clothes, mechanical tools, toys, ready to dispatch in boxes marked "Made in Germany", "Made in Italy", but never caring to admit that they were made in Lebanon.

This wasn't the first time I'd been here, but I always lost my way. I came to the area regularly for a while to help a psychiatrist friend who was doing a study of the effects of the war on Lebanese children. She worked in a school which used to be a stables and I remember how I lifted my feet like a horse every time I went in over the low step and how the smell of horse hit me in the face. Although the animals had been stolen long before, even the children's drawings smelt of them.

I really did find an abaya in the colour I wanted and at half the price. I went straight from Al-Dahiya to the engineer's, afraid that my laziness might get the better of me. Entering his apartment was an experience. The moment I saw the view from the wide balcony, I knew why he'd stayed in this building in the heart of West Beirut: he was remote from the war – the rockets in the air, the explosions on the ground had never touched him. Everything looked peaceful from that height; the people were small, the tanks and guns like toys and the fighters' weapons no more than big sticks. The war appeared to be an illusion, but so did the beautiful architecture, the unusual types of stone, all throwbacks to the past, which greeted me on the floor of the building.

The engineer welcomed me. As if he understood the effect of his home on his visitors he gave me time to look at the big leather sofa next to the piano, at the bed and the table-football. The floor was paved with slabs of stone with fish fossils in them. Then the mosaic: a naked woman was opening out a towel while a hawk, as big as her, was snatching the towel away in its beak. Around them were date palms, birds and four containers with flowers and vines trailing between them.

He apologized for not taking me to the mosaic dealer, but explained how to find him. I set off straight away and to my surprise he was in. His wife opened the door and greeted me as if she'd always known me. Her daughter came in with glasses of lemonade. The smell of gardenia pervaded the house, which was furnished in a mixture of gold Louis Quatorze and marble pillars and statues. The husband appeared shortly and held out his hand to shake mine, impregnating it thoroughly with his cologne. Then he led me to the workshop. If it hadn't been for his loud voice and his son's scooter parked there, I could have imagined I was somewhere in Byzantium or Canaan. Despite the damp and cold which hung about the room the statues imparted a strange warmth. The dealer had guessed I was an amateur; every time I asked him about a statue I liked he pointed out that it was an imitation. He touched a foot made of marble and slapped it playfully as if it was his own or his children's. "For example, this one's genuine. But it's sold."

We left the workshop only when I asked about the mosaic. As we went out into the garden, a man got to his feet and followed us. The sound of shots rose in the air. We didn't pay any attention to them, but it made me wonder what would happen to the mosaics if a rocket landed on them. I felt a surge of dislike for the man, but his open smile and honest manner made me think I was being too hasty. A piece of mosaic lay at the garden gate. I paused to look at it and he remarked immediately, "The bastard cheated us with that one."

He opened a door into another workshop and I saw pieces of mosaic lying everywhere. My feelings of dislike flared up again as I watched him walk over the fragments scattered on the floor. "What's the situation with these women?" he asked his assistant, gesturing downwards.

"I really don't know!" replied his assistant. "We've tried to put them back together but it's very hard, because of the bunches of grapes between them."

Then the dealer started to tell me how beautiful this mosaic had been before it was spoilt. I crouched down to look at it. A woman's face was visible in the middle. Her neck, her hand, a goblet she was holding, part of her breasts. Then she broke into a random assortment of little coloured stones where ants and other insects had taken up residence. "Someone must do more work on it. You should get someone from Syria," I said firmly.

"It's the glue they've used on the face to pull it out whole," replied the assistant. "They've obviously been trying to economize and they haven't put on enough, or else they've used a cheap brand."

The dealer grew tired of me squatting there, but I was concerned that the three women would be destroyed, their goblets, faces, breasts pulverized under foot after surviving for centuries. Here they were, dying on the dirty ground, walked over by men in trainers, in a room whose walls were regularly rattled by explosions. Nearby lay a Pepsi bottle, empty except for an inquisitive cockroach, and a crumpled picture of a well-known singer which made her look like a monster in a nightmare. I suggested to the man that I could try restoring it myself.

"It's difficult. Like sweeping up salt with your eyelashes."

I ignored his reply and asked him impatiently if he had a picture of the mosaic. He looked as if he couldn't take much more of me, and had begun to wonder if I was serious. Still hunched over the mosaic, I attempted to justify my request, by giving him the impression that I knew someone who could return it to its original state for nothing. "Money's not the problem. But it's an impossible task, unless you find someone with the patience of Job. And you know, Madame, what people are like these days."

Then he went over to the table, pulled open a drawer and took out a bundle of pictures. He leafed quickly through them and handed me one of the three women looking just as I'd imagined them: their hair was flying out behind them with an ethereal quality, their breasts were small and beautiful and the bunches of grapes between each one made an almost physical impact. I admit that I had decided not to buy a mosaic at all when I saw them piled up there. I thought it was a crime for them to adorn strange, foreign walls. From time to time I find myself criticizing everything that Lebanese expatriates do, and you're one now. In an attempt to escape from the mosaics without buying one, I forced myself to recall an episode which upset both of us.

Do you remember the pretty mother with her husband and children getting out of a car to choose some ancient stones from the fort at Beit Mary? The children were pointing and shouting. "That one, Mum. No, that one," as if they were on an Easter egg hunt, while her husband stood there, pleased to see his children enjoying themselves and waiting for his wife to decide so that he could lift the stones in his strong arms, as if they were children's toys.

You shouted at them to leave the stones or else, but the woman didn't look in our direction, even when we rolled some little pebbles down towards them. The husband finished carrying off the stones, deaf to threats. You took the number of their car as they brushed the dust off their hands and drove away, with part of the fifth century in their boot next to the can of oil and the spare tyre.

I defended you to myself as I remembered the episode, recalling your face with affection. I thought of them selling stalactites like ice creams at the cave of Qadisha. Then I decided that if I bought you a piece of mosaic it would have been saved from damnation as far as you were concerned and I'd be doing a service to history and art.

The mosaic and your abaya have begun to play games with me. Every time the fighting stops for a while I can look at them in a normal fashion again and imagine Ali taking them out of the door, once I've packed them and written your name and address on them. But as soon as the fighting starts again, I wonder what those unfamiliar objects are and what they're doing there. This has been going on for three days, during which time I've hardly left my bed and refuse even to hide in the passage or the neutral seclusion of the store room.

Despite the calm which has descended on me I confess the explosions have dislodged my head from its moorings. I lie down a lot of the time and begin to postpone everything, even going to the lavatory, and am thinking of getting a portable one like Fadila's uncle. He sold flowers in the street, and didn't move from his corner in her house all night, insisting it was too cold. At dawn he would hurry down to the entrance to move his flowers out into the street, his improvised chamber-pot hidden behind him. "Flowers need sun and they have to breathe," he would mutter.

"Your pisspot needs sun and air too," Fadila would shout after him.

Lying down eases the ringing in my ears, helps me put up with my grandmother and Zemzem and makes night blend into day so that time slips by. But it no longer interests me to follow the warring factions and put them into categories. So while I'm in this state, or rather the city is, it's hard for me to work out my feelings with any degree of clarity. "We might as well be dead. The Syrians are entering Al-Dahiya," says Zemzem, although her words no longer make much sense to me.

She looks like a cyclamen. Do you remember those flowers? I was so embarrassed when I called them "hunchbacks" as we do in the south. I rushed to pick one and crushed it in the palm of my hand, exclaiming as it excreted its yellow juice, "It's got diarrhoea!" You looked quite taken aback at my way of talking. As far as you were concerned the flower was called a "shepherd's crook", and the word diarrhoea and other words I've forgotten now shocked you at first, until you grew accus-

22

tomed to the fact that there were people who'd been brought up differently from you.

I wish Zemzem would get an ulcer on her tongue so that I wouldn't have to listen to her nervy conversations all the time, and maybe some on her feet too, then she couldn't pace about in that agitated way. I've changed my mind: cyclamens are beautiful and Zemzem isn't. Her eyebrows are thin and constantly twisting into expressions of surprise and fear.

"Come on. Let's go down to the shelter across the road," she shouts.

"I'm putting oil on my hair," I reply.

2

Dear Jill Morrell

The story of the hostages has only started to figure prominently on the news and in people's thoughts again over the last couple of days. Before that it had been submerged by day to day events.

The violence going on at the minute has prompted local and international radio networks to keep mentioning them because the area called Al-Dahiya where they're being held is ablaze now: Amal and Hizbullah are pointing the finger at each other; Hizbullah says Amal are traitors for calling them troublemakers, and Amal says that Hizbullah's turned Al-Dahiya into a no-go area. Our house is near Harj Beirut, close to Al-Dahiya. We always maintain it's on the outskirts but actually it's part of Al-Dahiya these days.

What scares me is that they'll be forgotten and as the kidnappings mount up people will grow accustomed to the idea. I used to think of you every time his name cropped up, or I saw your picture, or heard you talking on the news, hoping for a glimmer of information about him. I wished I could help you. I thought of you as I went through the back streets of Al-Dahiya and saw alleyways like mazes, never-ending like a shaggy-dog story, or dark like the inside of a whale, and when I heard rumours that the hostages were in a certain apartment or garage. But what can I do about the forgetting, the acceptance bred of repetition and habit, the thinking which leaps barriers and leads us inevitably back to ourselves?

I must admit when I first heard the report about your lover

McCarthy, I thought of Paul McCartney and the Beatles and wondered what I'd done with their records. I began recalling the sleeves, especially the one where they're all leaning against a door, next to a bust of a woman wearing a black cap. I always wondered who owned the cap. John or Ringo? And who thought of putting it on the bust? I remembered the gloom of the loft where my old possessions were stored. Zemzem never dared to throw them away, even though it wouldn't have made any difference, for once we threw them in there we forgot all about them. I felt nostalgic for the loft and our old house, where I was born and lived until my father died, and my mother burnt all his things and nearly burnt the house down. The moment his corpse had been turned to face Mecca and the wailing had begun around him, my mother rushed to gather up the belongings he had accumulated over the years and fed them to the fire. Tongues of flame beat against the walls and ceiling and the wood crackled. The funereal wailing was punc- tuated by screaming and coughing, as they tried to extinguish the fire, and the clatter of pots, jugs and Nido milk tins added to the uproar. In their haste the women accidentally drenched each other, then dissolved into laughter. "If the old man came back now and saw us like this, and his things going up in flames, he wouldn't hang around for long," remarked my mother.

Our loft was much frequented because it was like a treasure trove. Jars of oil, fat and olives were stored there. My mother loved them for a secret reason even though she didn't cook, and if she ever tried she burnt the food and the cooking pots. Unknown to my father, she sold these jars to her friends and with the money bought anything that was in fashion, especially if it was plastic, a material banned from our house. She also sold her jewellery and swore that she'd lost it or had it stolen. She lived in a world of movie stars like Asmahan and Anwar Wajdi, reliving the dialogues of their films, and singing their songs. I would probably have remained in the house where I was born but when my mother chose to remarry and move to the States, it didn't occur to her to think about me, or to consult my grandmother about what should happen to me; but everyone knew instinctively that I would live with my grandmother and her maid Zemzem or our maid Isaf, no matter where, in a great variety of houses, playing with the children round about. In our family, decisions were not taken; instead things were simply left to take their course.

I realize that what I'm talking about doesn't concern you, and that includes Paul McCartney even though he's English. He may not have heard of your friend's kidnapping and if he has he probably isn't that interested. But I can't get the record sleeves out of my mind, or the rhythm of the Beatles' songs. I used to imagine that I'd save some money, go to London, and end up marrying John Lennon.

You see how people revert to thinking about themselves. Even the fact that you're going through my mind now is a result of my being wrapped up in myself. I feel as if all I possess at this moment is my body and this bed. My mind is no longer my own and if I force myself to think about it, I know that I possess my body but not, even temporarily, the ground I walk on. In short, I'm a hostage just like your friend, lover, fiancé. What does it mean to be kidnapped? Being separated forcibly from your environment, family, friends, home, bed. So in some strange way I can persuade myself that I'm worse off than them. They rode in a comfortable car which dropped them off by mistake in a city of horrors, but I was abducted to a city which resembled the one I'd lived in originally with its clear skies, changing clouds, and some small details of life, like thyme and sesame pastries and the black soot which always clings to the outer wall of the baker's oven. For I'm still in my own place, but separated from it in a painful way: this is my city and I don't recognize it.

I'm a stranger here. Not because the streets have changed physically, and the signs are no longer illuminated, the lights don't work, water doesn't come flowing out of the taps as it used to in ancient memory. Not because the paint is peeling off the cars and their workings are visible, or the seasons have become different from one street to the next, or a forest of trees has risen up where there used to be cement, while in gardens and open spaces there are plastic-bottle trees. Not because stagnant water glistens from the swamps which have formed across main roads, buildings have collapsed and half collapsed, and even those built recently are falling down before they are finished. The façades of shops are not only unfamiliar, but they actually transport me to another country. There are Iranian signs on the shopfronts, on the walls, posters of men of religion, of leaders I don't know. I no longer understand the language people use. I know it is Arabic but it has become a series of riddles, its letters mysterious symbols, and it's not the language we learnt in childhood and practised in youth. It has different meanings which are unfamiliar to me. I tried looking in a dictionary but didn't find equivalents of the words I heard spoken, even though I attempted to observe how they sounded and the contexts in which they were used, so that I could understand a little at least, but it was impossible for me to follow the logic.

I tried to use a map as the street names and the recognizable landmarks began to change hour by hour, even minute by minute.

The world is trembling, breaking apart, turning upside down, and the people are being transformed. Instead of my friend's beautiful face, I see a sheep looking through the iron railings of her balcony. Refugees have come to Beirut, which used to be a dream city, their sentiments have exploded into music and song and they have put up loud-speakers in the heart of the residential and commercial areas. I walk as if I'm in a big soap bubble, rolling along, not touching anything around me until I meet up with other bubbles and my friends emerge from them. How can I recognize a city which tolerates fanatics who search for blond hair and light eyes to kidnap as if they inhabit a crude fairy-tale world, or allows a date palm which has been there for a hundred years and grown close to the sky to be uprooted to make way for a rocket which can even dissolve dental fillings?

How can I recognize a city which only lets me hear a faint echo of what it thinks as it dances and fights, fights and dances? I hear the sound of its breathing mingled with Arabic and western music from the clubs and televisions screens, with explosions, sirens and the smell of death. Like your friend, I've grown used to the dark and I no longer see shadows or reflections. They blindfold him every time they take him from one place to another, even from his cell to the lavatory. I've made friends with the darkness since there's no escaping it. Sometimes I light candles and sometimes I delude myself that I can draw light from the darkness, which has begun to hide faint wrinkles on my face and some little grey hairs which have found their way on to my head.

My daily routine is uncomfortable like theirs: do a few exercises, wash my face, brush my teeth, analyse my situation in whispers, eat a little food. The hostages have stopped enjoying food, and my appetite has gone too. Eating requires hands adaptable to the morsels of food, teeth for chewing, a tongue that can taste. I must be suffering from anaemia. Whenever I reach out my hand, my wrist muscles go limp. Do I think about doing sport? It seems remote. Something that goes with mountains, wide safe roads and rooms where the sun comes in.

Part of the daily routine as well as exercises, washing your face, brushing your teeth, analysing, whispering, is the sensation that time has stood still. A minute passes slowly, stretching itself out for as long as it can before it gives way to the next. This makes me stop believing that I'll escape from my abductors, and my resolve fails, for I find myself adapting to them, starting to try and be like them as a last resort, hoping that perhaps they'll take it upon themselves to release me, and my city will be restored to me. However, like the hostages, I don't really resemble those around me nor do I come to depend on my abductors as kidnap victims are supposed to do after a while. In fact my relationship with them is based entirely on increasing hatred and revulsion and the conviction that my guards are shoddy, immature characters, who have suddenly found themselves in positions of strength thanks to their wild hair, thick moustaches and beards which cover large expanses of their faces, gold chains round their necks with spent bullets dangling from them and unnecessarily loud voices. I recognize the voice of a young lad from a local shop, who used to sell water melons before the war and spray the pavement in front of the shop on hot dusty afternoons. The owner played backgammon with his friends while the boy bobbed between them, obeying orders, adding more embers to their hookahs, and making their coffee.

Like the hostages, I can't find any excuses for my gaolers, even if some of them are rootless exiles. They change continuously as if there's a factory producing new versions all the time. They're like nouns and verbs ungoverned by rules, indeclinable, or arithmetical problems where numbers and logic interweave and every time the teacher and the student think of solving them together their brain cells hit a concrete wall, so they despair and leave them unsolved, for today's enemies are tomorrow's allies and vice versa.

Even though my only solution is to feel resentment towards everyone, like the hostages, I have no alternative but to follow the uncomfortable daily routine. I read, play cards, grow bored with reading, puzzle over chess moves. I play cards alone, seeing a pattern emerging from the numbers, which I both believe and disbelieve.

Again I shake my head as the hostages do, finding no rhyme or reason in it all. Who kidnapped them? Who's kidnapping me? Is this a civil war, an international war or a capitalist war? It's odd how I grow accustomed to this routine, how they do, how hope remains that times will change and new life return.

All the same, I'm always thinking about death. It's there, and sometimes it's coming towards me. I open my eyes or keep them closed, depending on whether I'm interested in seeing and eating and staying alive or indifferent and without hope. In this game of mine, when my eyes are open I see the crumbling walls of my room, the new window pane, which is actually a thick plastic bag, and the marks left by the mirror which splintered and scattered on the floor in an earlier round of fighting. So far I haven't thought of painting over the place where it hung. For now people don't even renew the façades of their houses. I leave everything as it is. Like the hostages I don't think about trying to achieve anything.

If I wanted to recall exactly how I was kidnapped, I'd have

to go back a few years to the time I took cover in the shelter and the shock of realization that hit me as I crouched there. I'd only gone down there for the sake of my friend Hayat, who'd arrived on a visit to be greeted by a flare-up of violence. She was terrified, like a passenger in an aircraft which was about to explode in mid-air. She hid her head in my lap, and I tried not to think about the stale smell of the shelter. As I huddled there motionless, looking at the rank walls, I knew I wasn't free. I swore to myself that I would never willingly let this feeling take me over, that I had to confront it.

Looking back, I think I was kidnapped twice. The second time, I was driving through winding streets, some partly cordoned off to protect an embassy, a hospital, a party head-quarters. Among the cars, which were missing paint and headlamps, I was queen of the road and I nudged and pushed and kept my hand on the horn until I reached Simon's building. The trembling in me surged ahead of me as I ran to find him. I was happy. My meetings with Simon gave me a feeling of warmth and excitement, snatching me right out of the city as it surged back and forth between uproar and fragrant calm. For Simon was the noise at the heart of events and at the same time he was like me, outside them. Our eyes shone and our breathing grew faster whenever we were close to one another. I waited until we lay down naked on the sofa. Then the drugged sensation and the love took over and the feeling that I wanted to have my pleasure whatever happened. It was only when we got up and dressed that I knew I didn't love him.

I was still indulging in pleasant fantasies of what lay ahead of me when the traffic came to a halt. There was a sound of firing, and people vanished, abandoning their cars so that the street was transformed into a frightening, noisy garage. As I hesitated, trying to decide whether to go back home or keep on to Simon's, a gang of youths fell on the car and hauled me out, and drove off leaving me alone there, dumbfounded at the sight of my beloved car submitting to someone else's touch and deserting me. I took refuge in a nearby building in the end, but only when I saw a bomb landing in the distance, and people were calling to me to take cover. I wandered over to the building and was dragged in by a family gathered together in a bare concrete room. My first thought was that they were prisoners, especially the children, who were sprawled in a dejected heap in a corner. Then I wondered if they'd abducted the children from their playgrounds, which were devils' territory these days. Their faces were corroded with fear.

I must be like the hostages. I no longer think about life outside the place I am, and I even stick with the other hostages. Despite the regularity of the routine I can't concentrate. I keep reliving the shock of my kidnapping and I shall never be free of it even if I'm released. I know I'll always be like a kidnap victim and the bitter memories will haunt me. I no longer think about life outside. Even the existence of other countries seems like an illusion. I've forgotten what it's like to walk around at night, looking at the stars, hair flying, a muslin shawl draped around my shoulders. The only world that exists is in this room, this house. So I have no aspirations. In fact I grow more and more used to being lazy and irresponsible and can no longer read newspapers.

I've abandoned myself to the notion that I am not responsible for my fate, and I allow those closest to me – Hayat, my mother, other friends outside Lebanon – to wonder whether I'm alive or dead every time the battles rage. You must know how they feel.

I admit, Jill Morrell, that I thought more than once of staging my own kidnapping. That was several years ago when I was abroad, and some power must be having its revenge on me now for those thoughts.

The first time I was convinced that as soon as Naser and I had been reunited for a few moments and he had held me close he wouldn't be able to let me go back to Beirut, and he would abduct me. I smelt him, as I always did when I thought of him, and he embraced me. The warmth settled around us, but I couldn't see him. I waited for him on the beach in Tunis, burning like a hot coal with the sun and longing. My craving for him made a fool of me, and I kept lying there, deluding myself that he was watching me from a distance, enjoying the sight of me waiting for him, that he would jump out on me any moment and throw sand over me, and I smiled. I went on harbouring these illusions for days, just as I did while I was waiting for him in Port Said and Alexandria. Always on beaches, as the tide ebbed and flowed. Anyone listening to me now would think I was a dreamer. Of course, otherwise how can I explain my great love for Naser and Beirut?

All the same I threw myself at a Spaniard and tried to make him like me enough to kidnap me and keep me at his country estate. The idea of settling there for good had slowly taken hold of me as I stood with a friend of Naser's and his wife Asya on the edge of a Spanish road, surrounded by almond trees covered in snowy blossom. The sight of the plains stretching to the horizon gave me a feeling of pure contentment and peace. We arrived at a big house with cactus plants bordering the drive, bearing flowers like coral, and I envied whoever lived there.

The car turned along the drive and stopped at the broad sweep of gravel in front of the double door, which stood wide open. At the noise of the car's brakes a plump, balding man came out to greet us, distracted temporarily from his solicitous welcome by a huge dog which suddenly appeared from nowhere. Then he led us through his ancient house on to the balcony, where I sighed deeply hoping he would feel sorry for me.

The yellow plains, the cultivated terraces, even the cool breezes, all seemed to emanate from the red sun, enveloped now in a pink and violet haze. The sounds of sheep and cattle being driven home from pasture were clearly audible even though they were still far away. I stood at the balcony rail watching them, remembering my village. The shepherd, unconcerned by the barking of his dog, seemed to be rolling a cigarette and lighting up. The Spaniard approached me, holding out a glass of wine. Then he stood next to me resting his hand on the balcony rail, lord of all he surveyed. I pictured my grandfather dressed like him in a coloured shirt and jeans, a cigar in his hand. My grandparents probably thought I would marry a man such as this and stand with him on our balcony, except that instead of the returning flocks we would have been surveying our fruit trees.

Darkness fell gradually. The noise died away and calm settled over the place. It was as if the whole of nature was re-emerging from the mouth of the night. Blackness engulfed the surrounding country, transforming everything into shadowy noiseless shapes. Even the cricket in the wood was taken by surprise at the coming of darkness and poised silently, not moving its wings.

Footsteps sounded behind us, preventing me from telling the Spaniard that I too was a daughter of the land. They turned out to belong to an old man with a scowl on his face, who muttered a few words and then left. Our host smiled and invited us to go in to dinner. Minutes later a woman called Vera came in and kissed us all and asked which of us had just arrived from Beirut.

I collapsed on to my seat. Beirut came back to haunt me, paralysing my hands as I tried to eat, making me forget how relaxed I'd been here, in a country which still existed, and was free from the chaos of warfare. I was used to the idea that there were places where people led normal lives and, although the reality made me uncertain and jealous, it had helped me forget what I'd seen and heard in the times of violence and siege. Now I wanted them to lower their eyes and listen to me, and I was desperate for the polite details to be done with. The old servant no longer had any excuse to come in and out with the dinner. I retreated into silence, waiting for their questions. They weren't questions, but statements. The emotion in them was genuine but they were in a hurry to let the trivia take over the evening again. We rose to do a tour of the house. Big rooms. Big spaces. A big past. Then a small chapel. The Virgin Mary wide-eyed. A small theatre and a small cinema with a huge screen.

We paused in an enormous room which was empty except for a large antique bed. The Spaniard picked up a book from the window-seat, opened it and pointed to a photo of the bed. I nodded my head admiringly, not bothering to work out what he meant. I was wondering what effect this bed would have had on me and Naser. Would we have laughed, and thrown ourselves down on it, or taken the mattress off and put it on the floor as we always used to when we were moving around a lot and didn't like the look of a bed?

I touched the gold and silver ornamentation on its four posts, which rose like the columns of a ruined building. We wouldn't have liked its outlandishness, and its mattress was sure to be infested with damp. We would have fled the empty room, fearing a trap.

I drifted away from all these people to the rooms where Naser and I used to meet and relived each room, one by one. I met him in an ever-increasing variety of rooms: in beautiful houses with jasmine on their balconies, in buildings swarming with inhabitants, in foul houses which never saw the sunlight and where even the flies didn't venture. The last room had no electricity, and the room before that was in a hotel where a friend of his lay in the other bed with a high fever, so that periodically he shouted out streams of nonsense which we found amusing at the time. Sometimes they weren't bedrooms at all but luxurious sitting rooms full of Palestinian artefacts in large empty apartments. Then there were rooms in the houses of his married friends, and I used to be filled with disappointment, because I knew I wasn't going to be alone with him as soon as I heard the noise from inside. But this feeling was replaced by a surge of renewed pleasure at the thought that he was drawing me in to him, whatever the circumstances, and I watched him playing with the children before he ate, then noticed them observing him uncertainly as he chewed and swallowed, and when one of the children reached out and touched his Adam's apple I had the urge to do the same.

I tried to guess what the place would be like as soon as he contacted me and gave me the new address. Was it an apartment, an office, a house? Would we be by ourselves? I began to picture the place. The unknown chair waiting for me to sit on it. A room in a hotel which I could pretend was in a seaside town, unaffected by the war. Despite the tension, I blessed this Aladdin's lamp which whisked me from one world to another, once from dry land to the ocean in the form of an undulating water bed. I sprawled delightedly on is soft dark-red cover like a film star and felt faintly nauseous. "You mean we can't travel by sea?" remarked Naser in a mock-serious voice. Travel? When we are meeting fleetingly in the waves like the ebb and flow of the tide?

But I knew he used to think about marriage more than those men who led ordinary, normal lives. He needed to. Even when he walked along the street he was aware of what he was doing, conscious of his feet as they struck the pavement. The idea of marriage removed the uncertainty he felt about his commitment. When sometimes he lost faith in his revolutionary activity, he regained some enthusiasm if he could think that his struggle was also for the sake of protecting his family and creating a better, more stable future for them.

"I hope you have lots of children, Naser," Asya had said in Beirut. He had just presented her with a female kitten as a consolation for giving birth to a son instead of the daughter she wanted.

"Both of you, I mean," she added, turning to me.

I was pleased she saw our relationship as serious and liked us meeting in her house while she was away, but he was scornful. "What?" he scoffed. "Do you think I want to drag my children from one house to another like you do? I'm not that crazy!"

"The garden?"

The Spaniard didn't appear to be as enthusiastic as Asya.

"O Asmahan, you're going to be wild about it," she whispered to me.

If she knew where I am and what I'm thinking of. I don't want to hear any voice but Naser's, sit anywhere but beside him. Nothing I see interests me. In fact, I scarcely see anything, and I don't notice what I am eating. I follow them to the iron gate, kicking stones like a petulant child, wondering how I'm going to get through the rest of the evening.

I went a few steps along a narrow path. There were a lot of trees surrounding a lake. I was thinking how Asya exaggerated, but then I caught my breath in wonder. It was paradise, as described in holy books, or pictured in flights of the imagination. Underground rivers, cataracts, waterfalls, willow trees, and other trees I'd never seen before either in reality or in books. Their branches reached out, intertwining. Only a sliver of moon was visible, or perhaps it was the sun.

"How beautiful!" Naser's friend cleared his throat as he spoke, and the sleeping birds stirred a little then settled down again. The tree roots had emerged from underground, curious to see how their daughter trees were growing, what shape their branches were, what colour their leaves; roots like Tarzan's ropes, some descending into the water which tumbled among the rocks. A round clearing in the sky between the treetops left us silent, awestruck. The Spaniard rushed to pick up flat stones and skimmed them across the water. The music rippled out into the silent night. The birds ruffled their wings again, and only settled down as they grew accustomed to the sound, and calm returned to the trees. When we began to be able to see each other, we realized that a portion of the moon had appeared in the round clearing in the sky to light up this paradise.

To my right was a sort of natural staircase of ascending rocks and I went up it on to a narrow pathway.

"Where are you going?" asked the Spaniard.

"Up into the sky," I answered, embarrassed.

I realized that by answering like this I wanted to appear different from how I was, coquettish. He walked along beside me, telling me that this was a dead end, smiling at me. His concern was real, as the path narrowed suddenly and we were on a spur of land overlooking a sheer drop down to the tree-covered black paradise. He took my hand as if to protect me from danger, and to my surprise I came to like this plump warm hand round mine, forgetting that it was attached to a face whose features I couldn't recall and a person I didn't know. I walked along with him, and with each step I was thinking about this castle-house, this paradise-garden, Beirut, and my life in general. I was thoroughly confused about where I should live and whether I should go back. It wasn't the touch of his hand awakening these thoughts in me, but the silence, and the fact that I was a stranger to everything. This place was neutral and the language, the people and their secret thoughts and desires were all alien to me. As far as I was concerned it was the beginning of the world and all I had to do was take the empty glass and enjoy the illusory potion. The idea of staying there loomed larger in my mind with every step down the rocky staircase.

In a place like this I won't be expected – or even expect myself – to keep a hold of the thread of the past which has made me and try to weave it into my present. It will break automatically when I isolate myself here without my things. I have a brief, radiant vision of myself picking up the letters which the morose-looking old man has brought me on a gold tray as I lie on the antique bed, unable to stop slithering around on its silk sheets. The letters touch my heart and so I have another brief glimpse of myself showing the paradise to my friends and embracing Naser there. I stop at this image. It doesn't fit with my sense of estrangement in this house, nor with the life I'm supposed to have left behind.

But I'll transform it into a house that's half Arab. I'll go back in time, have children and call them old Arab names: Belqis, Tarik, Layla, Ziyad.

I looked hard at the Spaniard and from his smile I guessed he knew his house was bait for the houris, but there was no sign that he had any inkling of what I was after.

I claimed I'd had too much to drink and my head was hurting. For the first time I found myself thinking that if Naser called and nobody was at home to answer him, it wouldn't be the end of the world. The Spaniard brought me some Alka-Seltzers and suggested that I had a lie down somewhere. Vera, who was a plump blonde with slightly bulging eyes, tried to be concerned but she didn't manage to hide her annoyance as I had monopolized the attention of her friend all evening, talking about Beirut during the siege and occupation, describing how I'd left it and how it used to be before the war. Meanwhile, I could feel Asya watching me, unable to believe that I was the sad, abstracted woman she'd invited to wait in her house in case her lover contacted her there. Every time the caller was somebody other than Naser, I would say the same thing: "He's forgotten all about me . . . or perhaps nobody gave him my message."

37

And here I was trying to win the Spaniard's favours. I kicked off my shoes and laughed loudly. "I'm drunk," I said, and lay back on the sofa.

As I dozed off to the sound of the guests taking their leave, I felt a hand on my forehead, then on my hair. I sat up, pretending to be alarmed. Making out I was reassured once I knew it was him, I closed my eyes again. All he did was wrap a blanket round me, then bend over me breathing heavily and reaching out to touch my face. I opened my eyes and smiled at him and let him put his lips on mine. The only sensation I got was the smell of wine and cigar but I submitted to his lips and kissed him back and let him put his tongue in my mouth, although I'd already decided I wouldn't let him go any further. But all he did was put his hand on the blanket where my breast was, then he heaved a deep sigh, stroked my hair and said goodnight.

Morning in the castle-house was even more beautiful than night. From a distance came the sound of cocks crowing, animal bells jingling, voices talking in Spanish. It was just like dawn in our village when the farm labourers rose to start work. Day arrived, concealing the damp scents of the night. I wondered if the bush they called Queen of the Night had stopped giving off its intoxicating perfume of the night before. The sounds came drifting up to me again, and I pictured myself rising in the morning once I had become mistress of this place.

I rose and went strolling through the vast high-ceilinged rooms and noticed that now instead of swallowing me up they seemed to draw me in. I wished I could speak Spanish so that I could ask the way to the paradise-garden. The voices exchanged banter and it was like being at home. The labourers greeted me. They must have been used to the sight of women of different ages and races in this house at all times of day and night. But they didn't know I was different: I didn't want to throw parties, acquire money or jewels, but just to exist in the midst of this beauty, start a new life.

But the Spaniard was in a hurry. He was a lawyer. He picked up a leather briefcase like any man going to work, and the illusion that whoever entered this castle-house severed any connection with the outside world vanished. But it didn't matter.

It was all the better for me. Most of the time I'd be alone in this paradise.

In the car I learnt that not only would I never be alone there, I'd probably never see it again. Because Vera had started to have doubts. The man offered me lunch in an apartment he owned in town. I knew I'd been thrown out of paradise and Vera had him in her clutches. I'd never been as sad as that day. It was worse than when I was waiting for Naser to call day after day. I'd been happy to bargain with my body and emotions for the sake of that house and a new life, and still I'd been refused.

I can feel you growing impatient, Jill Morrell, but that's what hostages are like. Reliving the past. Conducting a constant dialogue with it. We should return to the question of the kidnappers and their victims. You want comfort and rapid information, but perhaps I've opened your eyes to something you hadn't taken into account before. Now I'll tell you how senseless kidnappings have become a commonplace of this war. There are no rules. The war is changed by a shift in accents and uniforms. Sad things have become laughable, funny things sad, kidnapping a legitimate practice.

A relation of Hayat's who was held for a few months woke up one morning to be told, "Congratulations. We're going to let you go today."

He was terrified that they were going to kill him. He was taken blindfold to a car and driven to some other building, but before they dumped him they removed the blindfold. As he struggled to get used to the light, the din of voices, the screech of cars, the strident call from the muezzin, he thought how someone in his situation focuses entirely on himself and his five senses. He pushed open the door and heard his first sentence on the outside: "Good to see you. Come on in. Your family's expecting you."

The speaker shook his hand. He was a youth dressed in ordinary street clothes. The released man was still in a state of shock. The room was packed with young men, all in ordinary outdoor clothes. One of them picked up a water pitcher and drank from it, while he stood there open-mouthed. Then he began to cry as someone handed him his trousers and he put them on over the striped flannel pyjamas which they'd given him the day after he was kidnapped, even though he'd always worn silk pyjamas before.

Where were his kidnappers? Had his wife paid the ransom?

Well, the affair didn't end with the return of the hostage. His kidnappers turned up on his doorstep a few days later.

They walked in and greeted him like an old friend. "We've missed you!"

They chatted easily for a few minutes, intimating that a close bond had been forged between them and their prisoner. One of them remarked to his wife, "Really, Madame, we thought about you all the time. Your husband's a fussy man. This was too salty. He didn't like that. This wasn't properly cooked. We used to say, 'How does his wife put up with him, God help her!'"

Then they got down to business. They complained they had incurred losses which they hadn't foreseen when they kidnapped him. They'd spent lavishly on his food, bought indigestion tablets and medicines for his stomach, bribed people living nearby to keep quiet, even the good woman who'd cooked for him had asked more than they could afford. They'd barely finished their complaint and drunk their coffee, when Munir disappeared and came back with an envelope containing money which he handed to them, begging them not to forget the cook. He used to hear her asking the guard if the Christian gentleman had liked his food. She cooked whatever he wanted and she was a good cook even though she added a lot of garlic and coriander, which made him drowsy. He'd been surprised at the care she took over his food and her concern that he should enjoy it, despite his circumstances. Then he asked them how they were free, as someone had informed him that they had been disciplined by the party for kidnapping him. It turned out that they had consulted a sheikh, who had issued a fatwa pronouncing him a legitimate target because of his American connections, and so the party had been forced to release them. As he digested this thunderbolt, he assumed an air of indifference, but he was shaking with anger and fear. His wife wanted to throw what was left of the hot coffee over their heads, snatch the money back and scream that they weren't her fellow countrymen. The same night the couple decided to emigrate.

Don't worry, Jill Morrell. Your boyfriend won't come to any harm in these battles. Things will change. The current deranged bombardment of the city will stop, they'll gather up the bodies, the Red Cross or the Red Crescent will take the wounded to hospital, and they'll announce a ceasefire, temporary or long-term.

This is the problem. That things go back to being exactly as they were, and all they've done is added a great deal of salt to the wound. What's going on now has no connection with anyone but the fighters. Who's going to take a war of the streets and alleys seriously, and care about its outcome?

I don't believe I'll think about anything beyond the confines of my room. But I have to stop myself sneaking a glance through a gap in the garden wall at a house which is said to be occupied by party members. The night was calm, and every-one was asleep. I saw the fighters sleeping with their families. I could almost hear them snoring. I lowered my head and wondered if I had really been kidnapped. Perhaps I was still having a bad dream. People sleeping peacefully couldn't be kidnappers. Then I reminded myself that evil sleeps too.

3

My Dear Naser

You're on my mind again, and if I hadn't been distracted by the tank parked outside, I'd have been worrying that you were going to fall ill or die. Something always seems to happen to the people I have strong thoughts or dreams about and I hear of it sooner or later. I know these ideas have been ingrained in me since childhood by the women around me, and if I really believed them nobody I knew would still be alive. I've often tried to curb my premonitions but then I think that they might sometimes turn out to be for the good.

My mother not only dismissed such beliefs but made them a subject of ridicule in the cassettes she regularly sent to Fadila: first, her gentle voice sings a verse of a folk-song, then there are some gasps of laughter, then she says, "What a miserable life it is here! Everything's so proper, we've even stopped being superstitious!" After that she tells the story of her brother-in-law who runs a hotel laundry and washes the sheets as the guests depart; so far none of them has fallen out of an aeroplane, or met his or her end under the wheels of fast-moving vehicles on the way home.

I've told myself it's just the circumstances making you surface in my thoughts again, although I was crossing my fingers or touching wood at the same time. My head's like a book whose characters fade and disappear from one chapter to the next then re-emerge in all their clarity to inhabit the pages again. Except that in the really bad times and when I fear for my sanity, I tend to think about things that are remote from events round about me. For example, when the battles were in full swing and the girl next door came round in the hope of some moral support, I asked her why she didn't knit me a shawl, then I fetched the brass pestle and mortar so we could grind chickpeas and make something nice to eat. She was amazed by my suggestions and panicked every time she heard an explosion, but once I'd convinced her the shelter was deadly and staying in the house could be pleasant she settled down, despite Zemzem's constant shouting: "They're all crazy! Thugs! Savages! Hell, we're going to die."

I'd even begun to find the sound of Zemzem's footsteps intolerable, so to relieve my feelings I tried to annoy her: "Hell's a lovely word," I teased. "You can imagine devils or bad angels prodding people with big forks, their eyes blazing, their faces yellow and thin."

I'm used to Zemzem being confused or uncertain, but I couldn't stand her wailing, beating her chest, shrieking, and turning round in circles like a dog chasing its tail. Since the battles had started up again she had been imploring us constantly to leave the city not for the village, but for Egypt or Syria.

"Do you want people to feel sorry for us," my grandmother would remark, "and say how dreadful, they've abandoned their houses and are wandering here and there like vagrants?"

"Listen to her! You think people would pity you if you went abroad? They'd be jealous."

Gunfire shook the house. We were each in our separate rooms. Zemzem's wailing preceded her as she came into my room; when she saw a book in my hands she backed away as if I was pointing a deadly weapon at her: "In the name of God the Compassionate, the Merciful!" she exclaimed.

She hurried in to my grandmother who was reading a prayer-book by candle-light, and asked her if there was a special prayer to stop the fighting. My grandmother was suddenly tired of Zemzem and told her to find a family who'd take her abroad with them.

Zemzem quivered as if she'd touched a live socket. "You mean you can do without me," she said tremulously, "now that you've drained all my strength? When I first came to you I was as fresh as a head of basil."

I began to feel sorry for her. "My grandmother's talking like that because she's upset," I called. "She's scared you'll go away and leave her."

Suddenly I see Zemzem as a stranded fish on a dried-up river bed trying to find a little pool of water among the weeds and pebbles. Her backbone has begun to curve and she's crying out for oxygen. Without my grandmother and our way of life Zemzem couldn't survive. But perhaps I am wrong, for the days have long gone when Zemzem was proud just to sit next to my grandmother in the car, or at home when she was receiving guests.

We heard the door rattle as she slammed it violently shut behind her. "If only we had taught her to cry, 'No Amal! No Hizbullah! Imam Ali is God's chosen one!' " said my grandmother. Then she began to repeat softly to herself, "No Amal and no Hizbullah. Iman Ali is God's chosen one."

A demonstration! Was it possible? Even the word had an alien ring for it was a reminder of more normal times. Was Zemzem taking part in a demonstration wearing her house slippers and caftan? I heard my grandmother coughing a little in her room. How weak she has become. She's no longer a djinn. Perhaps it's because she's stopped wearing her big flowing dresses and white silk kerchiefs as if she's just returned from the pilgrimage to Mecca, and these days she doesn't powder her pale face in the theatrical way she used to.

For the previous three days we hadn't moved from our rooms; then we heard a dreadful explosion. We all screamed and rushed out calling to each other. When the three of us almost collided in the landing, we burst out laughing. Flames were coming from the storeroom and I raced my grandmother to the door. A metal object lay innocently on the floor there in the midst of the destruction. It resembled a thick, dry branch. "Come on, let's cook it," I said to my grandmother.

Laughing, she said fondly that I had my mother's sense of humour so I felt obliged to tell her that it was plagiarized from a book of poems I'd been reading:

My mother decided recently
That if a rocket came into our kitchen
She would hollow it out
Drop it in the dish she uses for stuffed courgettes
Cook it with shrapnel rice
And a handful of our pine-nut fingers
And we would invite the fighters
To the most delicious feast
They'd ever tasted.

I looked around me again and felt a sudden hatred and revulsion for our house. How could it have conspired to let the bomb penetrate its concrete walls and land in this unlikely place between the store cupboards and the sacks of cracked wheat? I had believed in common with many others, including those who manned the guns, that I was protected by some magic armour and the violence couldn't touch me.

Zemzem returned with the news that the Syrian tanks were about to enter the area; Fadila had locked her nephew Ricardo in the house and gone on the demonstration too. She had shouted at the Syrians and beat her breast, drawing attention to herself, so – as Zemzem remarked grimly – they would be sure to remember her face when they were searching for Hizbullah fighters. Zemzem was like a monkey in a banana store, uncertain where to begin. She kept telling us again and again that the whole neighbourhood was preparing to leave. In the days that followed, we discovered how right she had been, for the savagery of the combat had reached our doorsteps and the noise of the bombardment pounded in our ears non-stop.

I was thinking I had to escape this battle-noise outside, and inside was no better: my grandmother dreamt of picking cherries in green orchards, or standing on Mount Arafat, or floating on a marble sea, and Zemzem begged aloud, "For God's sake, someone take me away from here! Even if it's the Angel of Death shaking my yellow leaf off the tree, that'll do, if it's the only way I can get some peace."

So I suppose I was ready for the knocking on the door. We were amazed that there could be someone there all the same, and it made more of an impact than the mad cacophony in the street. My heart lifted and I hoped it was a brave knight who had heard of the princess-who-never-sleeps and brought his sword to cut through the bullet-thorns. I heard Ali's voice, "Hurry up and open the door."

I smiled and opened the door eagerly to him. "Did you really think Ali had forgotten you?" he cried.

"We would never think such a thing!" I replied, overjoyed.

This affectionate reception seemed to embarrass him, for he said quickly, but not without pride, "Come along. I've come to take you to the village. Hurry. Get yourselves ready."

My grandmother called out to him, as usual wanting to hang on to her role even in circumstances like these. Like a minister of war questioning her front-line commanders, she demanded, "What's the news? Who's winning? What's going to happen?"

"You've only got a few minutes," answered Ali impatiently. "It's dragging on. They'll be wading in blood up to their knees."

"It would be all right if it was only to the knees," answered my grandmother.

"Nobody's asked me how I'm going to get you there," I heard him shouting from the sitting room. "I've brought a tank for you. You heard! A tank!"

It made no difference to me whether it was a tank or the blessed horse Buraq of the gilded wings which transported the Prophet to Heaven. What mattered was that I went somewhere where I could be out of range of Zemzem's voice and my grandmother's laboured breathing. I called back hypocritically, "A tank, Ali!"

He interrupted me, proudly. "Yes, that's right, Miss Asmahan. A damn great tank."

I gathered all my Billie Holiday records into a plastic bag and put them with my underclothes, a couple of skirts, some blouses and a packet of sanitary towels. I knew that was the one thing the village shop often didn't have. Once when I was complaining about there not being any when I needed them, Zemzem remarked that people in the village were sensible, unlike people in the city, who wasted their money on bodily filth.

I heard a shout from my grandmother and then an anguished cry from Zemzem. Zemzem was in a state, "trilling up her own arse, no better than a tinker", according to my grandmother. Her desire to leave the house and take refuge anywhere as long as it was away from the violence was matched only by her inability to leave when it came to it. She went round in circles, not knowing what to take with her, what to leave behind, frightened for the house and reluctant to abandon all the things she had cherished.

Although I was glad to be going, I hesitated and didn't follow Ali straight out to board the tank. It seemed as if I was running away and was afraid of criticism, even though I had anticipated it. Was it your reaction which concerned me, or the neighbours'? But they were in the shelters. I dawdled along, trying to reassure myself: was I scared of the cats who had begun to know what the war meant, or of the twisted street lamps?

Ali tried to hurry us along. His saliva sprayed the air. His tone had grown more commanding and decisive in these last few years, since he left our service. He had been our driver and acted as general handyman to the family in Beirut until the war came.

I wanted to take my time leaving, but I heard Ali shouting at Zemzem because as well as the suitcase he had allowed her, she had brought the quail in its cage. I hurried out. My grandmother was shouting at Zemzem too.

"Let's go. A rocket's going to hit this tank any moment now," said Ali.

He watched Zemzem running to a neighbour's house to leave the quail, swearing that he wouldn't take her with us and she didn't deserve any sympathy. My grandmother was in a state of wonder because Zemzem had become a human being in her eyes: she had left the Moulinex and brought the bird.

Zemzem's voice rang out again, letting us know she was on her way. As she came up Ali reproached her for not leaving the bird at his house. "Why should I? I don't know you," she retorted. "For all I know you'd quite happily slaughter it and pluck it and eat it raw."

My grandmother asked her if she had left it with Zakiyya,

but Zemzem didn't answer her, merely muttering regretfully, "God forgive you all."

Then my grandmother asked her if she had turned the key in the lock. She had already asked her the same question as we were coming down the short flight of steps into the garden, and Zemzem had answered that she had fastened both locks. Although everybody was making such a noise, I couldn't help noticing the smell of the frangipani still growing in our garden, its branches hanging over the wall into the street. But this time it was mixed with the smell of the gunpowder which had turned the purple bougainvillaea black. The buildings around us were pockmarked by bullets, immense leopards with their spotted skins. A room in a nearby house had no outside wall. It was still painted blue with a dining table and chairs in the middle of it. It looked beautiful, as if it was suspended between heaven and earth. "Ali, what happened to those people?" said my grandmother. "They were so nice."

"I don't know," shouted Ali. "Get in, for God's sake, can't you?"

The neighbourhood was quiet, as if it was resting after yesterday's rowdy party, when fireworks had flashed and sparkled in the sky for hours on end. A building hung its head wearily, its water pipes like coiled black snakes. A lamp-post leant over as if it was trying to kiss the ground. Smoke continued to rise in the air and hung there like a black cloud in spring. A red tile lay like a child's toy waiting to be built into some forgotten palace. The huge metal door of the shop was like a Chinese fan with its folds pressed out. The balconies tottered on broken legs. The tank stood waiting for us with its radio blaring. We climbed in. The last thing my eyes fell on before I entered its hidden world were the posters of martyrs and religious leaders, peeling off as if they had been scared by the fighting and tried to get down from the walls.

My grandmother addressed the youth who was closing the hatch on us without a word of greeting. "Thank you. We're grateful for the trouble you've gone to."

Zemzem didn't seem to like the solemnity of my grandmother's thanks, and hastily took up where my grandmother

48

left off: "God preserve you for your families. God keep you from harm, wherever you go."

Only then did the youth glance quickly in our direction, saying carelessly before he vanished, "You're welcome."

I must have stopped being attractive. He hadn't responded to my smile. Actually he'd ignored me. I put it down to the tense situation. I wanted to look in the mirror. My appeal, even my normal liveliness must have deserted me. This continued to bother me until the vehicle started away. When I grew used to the constant rumble, I began to study my surroundings. The tank resembled an ambulance, its seats like short narrow iron beds. I noticed the roof, like a steel hedgehog. Ali got to his feet, looking towards the driver, who was only visible from the waist down. Ali banged on the side of the vehicle as if it was a horse that had just won a race, then tapped the driver's feet. I could picture the driver surveying the street, ready to fire. He ducked his head in, smiling broadly at us and addressing himself to Ali: "What do you want?"

Ali raised himself up until his head vanished through the aperture. A few moments later it reappeared and he shouted, "Come here, Miss Asmahan. Come and see."

The tank came to a halt as he bent lower, stretching his head towards me, repeating eagerly, "Miss Asmahan, please come. Come and see the Red Cross pulling people out."

He held out his hand to me. He was so insistent that I stood up in the end, although I had grown to like my cosy retreat. From the opening I could see the sky and earth with their contents strewn far and wide. I saw myself too in the midst of this destruction, and a building still standing, then there was a resounding explosion and my head was shoved down inside the tank and the two youths were struggling to close the hatch without success. Ali pushed them out of the way and struck all the buttons ferociously. One youth did his best to restrain him. Suddenly it was dark inside the vehicle, and they turned on Ali with mounting annoyance. I began to think that we had been too quick to agree to travel this way. Anxiety gnawed at us all. I knew plenty of stories about people who in their attempts to escape the bombing had been lost at sea instead of being killed

49

on land. It only became clear to me now that it was these boys' passion to be in command of a tank which had induced them to oblige Ali, rather than a concern for our safety. Then I felt desolate as the three of them tried to master their new toy, and longed suddenly for the house. I saw it somehow reduced, its contents without life or colour. They used to be animated, even talkative, and had gradually become an inseparable part of me, witnesses to the slightest changes in my thoughts and feelings. Now they were represented by a bunch of keys in Ali's pocket and instructions to water the garden. I suddenly felt weary and wanted to lie down on my own bed. Every time I was away from it, I pictured it waiting for me, assuring me that the danger would soon pass, asking why I had abandoned it, and I saw plainly that danger was everywhere, even in this tank. As if my grandmother wanted to rid herself of tension she said, echoing my own thoughts, "If only we'd told Zakiyya to water the marjoram and basil and watch that the boys didn't hit the bitter orange tree.'

"Here we are about to die and all you can think of is the marjoram and basil," said Zemzem crossly. Then her features relaxed and she muttered to the plastic bag beside her, "I knew you'd be a credit to me."

She'd hidden the quail in the bag and brought it with her. We laughed, and my grandmother commented that she'd heard a noise like someone's stomach rumbling. Ali laughed too and told the youths in the turret but then my grandmother seemed to tire of the subject and began to talk about Ali looking after the house. "I'll order an iron door," he replied. "Anyway your house is empty. There aren't any treasures in it. But nobody likes the idea of a stranger getting into their house, even if there isn't anything valuable there."

He winked at me and I realized that he was making sure the boys commanding the tank didn't get any ideas. Everyone continued chatting amicably and exchanging jokes; Ali wished there was a camera so that he could have his picture taken in the turret, while my grandmother began reciting the throne verse from the Quran and prayers for our safety.

You're in my mind now because I'm travelling in a tank, and

I feel you in my body because I'm sweating slightly and it reminds me of the times we managed to be together, in spite of the fighting all around.

The noise the tank makes is a kind of loud whine. What causes it? Contact with the road, or the engine itself? The tank makes me think of a bracelet of my mother's with thick gold links like its tracks. Now I understand why it's the tank that is the most important land weapon in wartime. The sound it makes is enough to inspire terror wherever it goes, a giant roaring before he picks up the city like a bowl of fruit. Now I understand why when they're in a tank soldiers feel they can crush cars and trees in their path like brambles, because they're disconnected from everything, their own souls and bodies included, and what's left is this instrument of steel rolling majestically forward. I feel as if I've entered another world. No destruction. No streets, no people, no long years of war; they've gone, as if I have been in a submarine the whole time. There is no window where we are, and the feeble light comes from a bulb, or filters through from the small windows in the driver's area.

I know you wanted to leave Beirut five years ago in a tank like this, unseen and unseeing, alone with your disappointment, which was like barbed wire unravelling everywhere. Whenever you tried to outsmart it, dispute with it, ignore it, it snagged you and entangled you in its coils, made you aware of its weight bearing down on you with every breath you took, and so you went beyond it. You tried to exploit its danger, to have your revenge by staying alive. Your body represented freedom now: if it remained free, so did your mind. You'd never allow yourself to be a prey for those entering Beirut, the Israelis or anybody else. Israel would enter Beirut. What was happening was the reality. She would not only take airports and ports and establish her bases; she would enter houses, offices, nightclubs, subterranean passageways, the crevices between thoughts written and unwritten, and the whites of people's eyes. Was it conceivable that Israeli soldiers would be in the streets and alleys where people lived, see washing spread out to dry, bunches of onions and garlic bulbs hanging on balcony walls, and witness the changes, from the pots of roses and basil dead from lack of water, to the mountains of rubbish which had become such a familiar feature? Would they sit in chairs where we used to sit, around the same café tables, walk where we used to walk? Would they notice the gates of the universities and admire their spacious gardens and quadrangles, where we used to criticize them in the sixty-seven war?

Being evacuated in a civilian ship, standing in front of a soldier who barked out "Name? Age? Country of origin?" snatched away the last remaining vestiges of your spirit. You compared yourself to a mad bull removed because the matadors were unable to kill it. But you really saw yourself as a young ewe or nanny-goat bleating at the sight of the butcher, stamp in hand, coming forward to brand a number on you. You had never envisaged this withdrawal, especially in the early intoxicating days of the resistance when you started going to the camps and searching among the trees and names and camouflage uniforms for Salim, your neighbour's son. He had disappeared and it was said he had joined the resistance. You didn't know why you volunteered to travel to Syria and Jordan to ask about him, but the enthusiasm with which you left your engineering office and your drawing board took you by surprise. For the first time you forgot the buzzing in your ears which had become chronic after you'd worked digging roads in Kuwait.

Why this enthusiasm? Was it because Salim's family was so anxious and automatically assumed their son had been snatched away from them, seduced by the soft words and harshness, the promises and dreams known as the Palestinian resistance? Or was it because you didn't want to believe that you would never see your uncle's house in Arab Jerusalem and you had to do something to stand up to a person who built a wall around the West Bank, locked its door and put the key in his pocket? You thought you wanted to work for the resistance, but in a different form, although boys like Salim were the focus of your interest. You would never carry a rifle or a revolver or join up with others; you'd work alone outside the official circles. If you preserved the individuality of your thinking, you'd be able to open doors which they hadn't even thought of trying. But what lay on the other side might be dangerous, and there was your profession, your family. You hesitated, mulling over the complications, but, seeing the tub of flowers on the threshold, reflected that you ought not to let the situation influence you adversely, that in fact you should turn it to your advantage. You could go on being an engineer and working for the resistance. Then without being asked, you told the official in the camp in Jordan that most of your family had stayed in Palestine, and your mother and father had only followed you out in forty-eight because they had missed you so much.

Seeing you for the first time in three years, I hadn't expected our conversation to take this turn. When I stopped my car in a back street and asked for directions to the building where your office was, I was surprised to find sandbags concealing the entrance. Inside, the porter painstakingly took names, asked to see identity cards, examined the contents of carriers and handbags. When I gave him your name, he said, "First floor on the right."

And I hadn't expected to see you behind that tiny table in a bare room with a feeble unshaded light and a sofa such as you might find in the stationmaster's office at a remote railway station, with a faded woollen rug thrown over it, and a tiled floor looking as if it had never been swept or washed since it was laid. Against the wall you'd stood a wooden vegetable crate, full of rusty nails, with a thermos, an electric kettle, a jar of coffee and a bag of sugar on it. Then books and more books and papers and files were heaped up on a wooden shelf, spilling over on to the floor in a corner of the room.

Where had I come from, what did I think? My car seemed out of place here, the ribbon in my hair even more so. I glanced around, concealing my embarrassment, and caught sight of an apricot stone in the ashtray. I couldn't help looking at it again as it seemed important, the only reminder of life in this dryness. You must have changed, and shed everything but the shirt and trousers you were wearing so that you could become as pure as the tea-glass in my hand. However, from where I was sitting I could see the red blooms of the poinsettia through the window and it took me back to the bustle and uproar of Beirut, the day we met in the sixty-seven war in your big apartment, with its colours, green plants, fish tanks, your striped shirt, the record player and records. I suppose you must have left it behind you, something conjured up to dispel the feeling of despair which came over us all in sixty-seven. Those days came back to me in a rush with such force that I felt a warm blast of air hit me as I sat facing you on the uncomfortable cane chair, looking at your feet in trainers under the table and finding it hard to believe they had any connection with the feet which had played with mine a couple of years before. Meanwhile you sat there asking how I was, and awkwardly, feeling as if I had my head stuck in the park railings, I tried to explain to you what was going on in my head, and making a mess of it. I tried to say I was out of place in that office, wholly out of place in my white floor-length coat and white leather boots, but you stood up as if you were dismissing what I was saying, and asked, "More tea or coffee?"

You stood watching the water come to the boil, while I tried unsuccessfully to express something other than my embarrassment. As I drove off I felt an abyss had opened up behind me.

But then Beirut was plunged into its own war and I found I was pulled down into the abyss with you from the moment I saw you again sitting in a newly opened restaurant in a residential street. Because of its position this restaurant was unlike any other of the city's multitude of restaurants, and strangely out of keeping with its surroundings: the war simply vanished from all our minds as soon as we stepped over the threshold. We piled on to the seats near the window watching the passers-by, convinced we were somewhere safe, inviolable, even when the world outside was rocked by explosions. The circumstances of war coloured the personality of the regulars, whether they were intellectuals who had stayed on in the country, ex-combatants or those still actively engaged in the fighting. Powerful relationships were quickly formed in those circumstances, and disintegrated at the same speed, but the curiosity to find out what lay behind new names and faces remained undiminished as social circles in the city became increasingly restricted.

You rose to your feet as soon as you saw me and reached out your arms to embrace me like a father reunited with his long-lost daughter, but I suspected that the turmoil of this new war had changed you. I could distinguish that special smell, which I must have retained in my memory since the sixty-seven war, accompanying the kiss which I had planned in advance. I expected some burning emotion to be rekindled between us, but the kiss ended quickly and there was no aftermath.

Another few years have passed and you knock back the whisky as I sit watching you, and seem tense and out of sorts. I wish you would go back to being your old self. I don't mean full of optimism, convincing yourself that the war is bound to take conflicting paths, that those guns are just noises, the fires colours, the black red, the dead merely statistics in newspapers. I just want the old Naser.

I sit watching you, knowing that I am your newspaper and bringer of bad news. I have become your only link with the outside world, an owl screeching with foreboding, looking at you with unblinking eyes. I tell you about the people who have taken refuge on the stretch of beach off the Corniche between the British and American embassies, and about the rifles abandoned on the sands at the knees of a mother or wife in case a fighter comes back from the sea, about the backgammon tables, about how people are scrambling to get food, water, generators and paraffin lamps. When I go on to describe an international football game you explode: "I know. Do you think I'm deaf? What do you think all the radios in the neighbourhood are for?"

I grew to hate this task of mine, and so I didn't tell you how committees and fronts were being formed to administer food supplies, baking, welfare clinics, publications, for you would have taken this as an indication of just how futile your efforts had been. I stopped going into detail about what I'd seen or felt. Your presence was a dead weight: every time I wanted to stay with you, you shocked me by your desire for your own company, and whenever I stayed at home I had the idea you

55

were clutching on to me, even at a distance, so that I'd transmit some of my freedom to you. I wanted to be close to you, my longing for you flowing from me and coming to a halt in my fingertips. But your silence inhibited me from approaching you and I sat dumb and distant, reproaching you inwardly for not accepting me and sticking with me. I saw you as a grass-hopper, never still, alighting here and there. I used to take off your shirt, which you hadn't changed for a week, your trousers, your underpants, feeling your breathing on my neck. As you paced up and down like a panther shut up in a birdcage, I felt the weight of your body on mine. The words spilled out of you like foam and I nodded my head and closed my eyes.

I was naïve to think I had become responsible for you. I used to keep quiet about what I'd heard and seen: the crowds out on the streets reminding me of feast days in my childhood; the games of chance people were playing. Are you staying or leaving? Are you going to live or die? Who will be the unlucky one this time? Or is this a lottery everybody loses?

But you seemed to have been blessed with X-ray vision, for I arrived one day and sat on the couch, breathing heavily, closing my eyes, pretending to be tired and instead of asking what had happened, you poured paraffin over your papers in the middle of the room, set light to them and stood back and watched them disappearing in the flames. You remained motionless until the fire began to spread a little. I wanted to tell you about the fire my mother had caused at the time of my father's death. I wanted to make you feel well-disposed towards me so that you would forgive me for what I had thought on my way to see you. As I raced through Harj Beirut I had been confronted by tree stumps and charred embers instead of the dappled green canopy of pines. Sobbing, I continued on my way over the blackened road, thinking that perhaps the Palestinians ought to go; then the sky would not be full of Israeli aircraft leaving their mark on everything. I know. I know that if they went, you'd go with them. But I didn't want Beirut to change so much that we no longer recognized it. Its skies were being transformed by the coloured leaflets the Israelis dropped, danc-ing in the air instead of paper aeroplanes and clouds. But were they Israeli planes dropping leaflets from the sky, or "flights of birds striking us with stones of baked clay" as if we were Ethiopians threatening Mecca in the Quran?

The pavement was riddled with holes, big and small, but it was still a Beirut pavement. People still walk in the streets of Beirut; their eyes register the wrecked buildings, the broken glass, the burnt trees. The toy shop has become a roast-chicken takeaway. The barber's is closed for ever, boarded up with sheets of metal. But do they want Beirut to disintegrate completely?

At this point I stopped thinking, still watching the fire with you as it died down and the papers turned to ashes. Among them lay the hopes and wishes which had accompanied the words; the days and nights which were no longer any use for encouraging the spread of logic and faith and conducting internal debates; the arteries which blocked any attempt to inject new life into them, or even to restore life to how it used to be in the past. You see your friend shutting his door in your face, apologizing for being unable to give you a roof for the night in case the building becomes a target, because he knows you're on the run. This shocks you because your friendship wasn't based on talking and going to the cinema together, but on a shared vision of the future which you were committed to realizing together. And you must have noticed in my eyes the pressure I anticipated from your continuing presence in Beirut. Is it possible that you could become a burden to me and the city, as if you were not the Naser who has been my consuming passion for so long? I need your heartbeat to keep me alive. I have to be so close to you that our limbs intertwine and our breath mingles and forms a single protective layer against an unknown terror. You must remember that night, three or four days before you left? You sighed and said, "I've got a craving for ice, a lot of ice, with my whisky."

We walked out of the Commodore Hotel, swaying slightly from the whisky and red and white wine we'd drunk, trying to work out whose apartment you had arranged to spend the night in. Then you asked me to get back into the car and drive us to the clinic. I drove as if I was in a dream and parked and got out, still half dreaming, for the city was dark and peaceful, despite sporadic bursts of shelling. We entered a room where the nurses were playing cards with doctors and a few patients. We exchanged jokes with them, then you asked for some ice for your whisky. It was reserved for cooling their instruments, but they sliced a bit off the slab for you. We didn't bother looking for the apartment where you were meant to stay. Instead we went to visit an artist friend. The door of his house was open, as if he knew he would have a lot of visitors. We walked into the sitting room, which was overflowing with young people, especially girls sitting in untidy groups on the floor with their belongings scattered around them, making it look like a school common room. You sat sipping the iced whisky you'd brought with you, while I talked to someone who said it was suffocating in there and why didn't we go out on the balcony. It was as if our arrival had re-ignited dying embers, for the music blared out again and the girls got up to dance to it and some of them danced where they sat on the floor. The very moment that the youth reached out a hand to feel my breast through the opening of my shirt, I happened to glance through a doorway and see your friend's daughter resting her head on your chest while you stroked her hair affectionately. Was she crying? She must have been afraid. The boy's hand played with my nipple while Beirut lay under siege and watchful eyes stared intently through telescopes at weapons attacking the city from land, sea and air. Everything faded as the music died, except the boy's hand squeezing my breast. I was aware of nothing except the blackness encircling the city. Once again the sitting room looked like a room in a girls' boarding school. As you came back in, I saw you patting the girl on the shoulder. You heaved a sigh of relief when you caught sight of me but you made sure you held her to you, touching her face affectionately, gathering her hair up on either side of her head, and then you said to me in a whisper as we went down the stairs, "She's scared."

You told me how her hand had gone around your waist and you'd stopped her and told her to put her head on your shoulder. I was silent. I didn't tell you about the young man touching my breasts. We never discussed things like that. The sound of Israeli guns reverberated from battleships out at sea as we climbed the stairs to an attic room in one of the buildings we knew. The darkness was intense, perhaps because so many people were sleeping on the staircases. The children were sound asleep or too tired to make a noise, so the only sound was the grown-ups mumbling to themselves; some seemed to be in the depths of despair, and others were philosophical. A woman hung on to your leg and I thought you had tripped over her and were bending down to apologize. But she lifted her face up to yours and her moist hand clung round your neck. As soon as we were back inside the room you began to talk and talk, never stopping to listen or ask a question or reply to one of mine. I was happy you were favouring me with your confidences, as you punctuated your sentences with "See what I mean, my love," but equally I doubted if I really was your love and not just part of the Beirut scenery. I felt you were addressing the city because you would be pulling out any time. Still, I let you talk and listened to you as if we'd only just met, as if we had days and nights of intimate conversation ahead of us. I had the sudden painful sense that the frenzy and noise of Beirut had dominated our lives, never leaving us time to talk as we were talking now. I reached out my hand to yours, but I knew it was like a borrowed hand. I looked at my watch. You were annoyed. "Are you going somewhere?" you asked. Actually I had been unable to believe how quickly the time was rushing past. You knew and I knew that it would soon be time for you to leave the country and that with it you would be leaving the warmth you had felt since your first night here in a village guest house heated by the sleeping animals.

You had come with your uncle's family in 1948 on a trip from your village to a place called Lebanon, which you had thought was just another of the many orchards you had passed through, walking, running or taking turns on the horse with your uncle's wife and son. When the trip showed no sign of coming to an end, you were convinced your father had sent you away to escape the revenge of two British soldiers whose resplendent uniforms you had accidentally splattered with mud.

But the journey went on through these lands called Lebanon after the rest of your family had joined you and your mother had kissed you and pressed you to her, repeating that she had come after you because she'd missed you so much. Then you began to live in a room with running water instead of the guest house and the convent, and you went to a new school and acquired a new name: "Naser the Palestinian".

"I'll have to kill myself. No, I must keep going. It doesn't matter which I do, since both will have the same result: surrender. Keeping going doesn't mean that I present any threat to the Israelis. It means moving on, leaving all my hopes behind me, forgetting everything that's happened. Suicide is a gesture of pride which I'm not fit to make."

This monologue of yours went on unabated, although I sometimes thought you were wanting me to participate. But as soon as I opened my mouth, you went on talking as if you had just been pausing for breath. Meanwhile I began to conclude for the first time that dialogue had died, not just between you and me, but of itself. I had an uncanny sensation that you had already been snatched away from me and I was sitting with someone else who resembled you and had taken over your name and way of talking, and it was this other person who was thinking of fleeing to a country where they had never heard a word of Arabic and changing his name, or settling in a Gulf state surrounded by wealth. You confused the words for wealth and revolution which sound similar in Arabic and I said it was not a slip of the tongue but a slip of the soul. You didn't laugh but looked up into the city sky as if you were bidding yourself farewell, having given in to your other half. For you had split in two, one part of you wanting to know what was going on outside, the other resigned to the routine of this solitude which hardly touched you. You had cut yourself off from your command and no longer tuned in to hear your instructions or find out what had happened to the others. The veins throbbed in your temples. "Are the Lebanese afraid Israel will finish them off, or have they lost faith in us?" you asked, as if you were thinking aloud. Although Beirut looked like a shadowy network of narrow streets and alleys from the balcony, it was exposed as minutely as if it was under a microscope. Overnight it seemed to have changed from a beautiful friend, whose boundaries were the sea, the sky and the trees, to a magnet which drew out even the pins hiding in nooks and crannies.

Was this really the same Beirut which has always been like a ball of many colours rolling along? Bronzed faces, immodest bathing costumes, cars bearing splendid names, theatres and cinemas, cafés and sports clubs; women with dark eyes ringed with kohl, world-famous singers, artists, girls on motorbikes. Modern apartments – some shuttered, others with their windows wide open – in tall buildings like capsules, floating in a vacuum, whose inhabitants only ever saw the blue sea. And the old quarters too, where familiar cooking smells hung around the staircases, and from the balconies came the sound of carpets being beaten. The contradictions made the inhabitants of Beirut seem eternal.

I used to watch the high life breathlessly from a distance, not daring to move in close. I was too well aware that I was not comfortable with it. I didn't want to stop being critical, despite my fascination, so I expressed my disapproval of the wealth and at the same time coveted the material which reminded me of pictures of palaces in Venice, and dreamed endlessly of having an emerald-coloured lamp for my dressing table. What stopped me approaching the glittering Beirut was the crush of people around it; women and girls who seemed like princesses with their hairstyles, clothes and haughty calm – a way of moving which betrayed self-confidence and experience – and men who went in for foreign culture whether they lived abroad or stayed in Lebanon. I used to ask myself why I hesitated and didn't plunge in like them and pounce on everything new that came from outside, whether it was to my taste or not.

Was it the same place I discovered through you? With the outbreak of war it was as if the country had announced it was staging an international fair, and representatives of various organizations, fighters and journalists poured in the moment the celebrations began. Their ideas and muscle power flowed over its open borders, and a relationship which began in the heart and mind sometimes extended to the pocket. Also those who thought of Lebanon before the war as a rich tart living off immoral earnings, because of the gleam of money and gold and the luxurious hotels, and thought that she must be heading for ruin, came to see Beirut become more human; no longer sparkling like a jewel, it started to suit the likes of my grandmother and Zemzem.

My father should come back to life now: the city would understand him better, understand why he used to go around the restaurants and bring back the leftovers. The popular cafés that cling to the mouth of the sea belong to a city with soul. Even the alley cats have become real cats, catching flies, lacking an eye or a leg. You took me around and introduced me to my city which had begun to pulsate with life like cities with long histories, Cairo for example. Characters emerged who seemed eternal and had some kinship with the half-collapsed walls; apartments which previously dreamt only of the smell of food and the rustle of soft dresses became houses for convictions, ideas, where people could breathe freely and make love. You sat me in front of people peacefully smoking hookahs, or selecting fish and savouring the air, and this great serenity seemed to pass between them and the waves. I was like a bee, discovering the honeycomb city with you. I sat facing the sea, the hookahs bubbling around me, and found I was not distracted by the images of devastation and dead bodies the way I used to be before.

Later that day we descend the stairs from your room eagerly; you introduce me to the porter, asking him about a dog hit in the bombardment. We go into a patisserie and you draw my attention to the colour of a piece of pistachio in a baqlawa, sing "aah" along with Umm Kulthum on the radio, sip sugarcane juice. You take me to a club in Zaytouna where the singers are tired, the dancers drunk and the band given to surges of enthusiasm interspersed with long interludes of apathy. Each player in the band seems to have settled on a woman to favour with his attentions. He winks at her or licks his lips suggestively or passes a hand over his hair in a sort of greeting.

You loved that club, which was almost deserted, and told

me it was real, more real than any other nightclub. There is a constant popping of champagne corks and the girls empty the remains of their drinks under the tables or in among the dead plants, unable to drink any more. You dance the tango with me, your eyes on the sea. In your jacket pocket you have some papers which you take out and study from time to time, while I watch the other customers and the musicians, embarrassed because the sight of us dancing like this must give them the feeling that we don't take them seriously. You dance looking out to sea even though with the darkness outside and the light inside you can't possibly see it, and in any case the glass is dirty and misted over. You close your eyes euphorically, drawing me so close that I am almost swallowed up in your breath before your body envelops me and you are whispering into my ear and my neck that you want to eat me. "You Lebanese want to destroy us. You want to drive us out."

Were you exaggerating? Because it seemed to me at the time that the sea of Lebanon, stretching away for ever, was only for paper boats and the sky was for clouds and the sun; that the snows and the birds of prey were the only spies on the mountain tops; and the hunters watching the little birds skimming over streams and plantations and declaring war on them with small shot, the only observers.

The same sea became your obsession in the final days when accounts of what was happening in Hamra reached you at last: the fighters were preparing to leave and the back streets had been transformed into a vast departure lounge full of luggage; all the shops had started selling bags and cases, and lawyers were everywhere, transferring ownership of cars and apartments from the departing fighters obliged to leave them to those who remained. They were like pupils in the school hall on the last day of the year, saying goodbye after the prizes had been distributed, signing autographs, writing lines like, "Everything passes with the passing of time except the memory which lasts for ever."

Did I tell you that I wrote that once to a boy in the village? I was so proud, mainly of my handwriting, but also of the fact that I knew this line by heart. He struck his head against the wall saying that I didn't love him, and I wept in disbelief. Everyone was exchanging addresses and giving convoluted instructions. "Get in touch with so and so and I'll get in touch with him as soon as I find out where I'm going to end up. Or I'll write to your address in Lebanon. The Lebanese post is bound to start working again soon. In any case I'll definitely write."

Everything was in uproar in the city's damp heat. In one place the departing fighters were covered in flowers; flowers were stuck everywhere: in gun barrels, button holes, jeeps and civilian cars. When you boarded the ship, I was lying in bed thinking of a way to smuggle you out across the mountains past the houses with red-tiled roofs and green-painted windows, and the pine trees and laurels; I had absolute faith that all these things would stand with us and prevent anyone trying to drag you from your hiding-place. I believed until yesterday that you would never escape by sea. You would continue to trust that the city and its labyrinths would love and protect you. I had thought about getting you a forged passport, or taking your case to the UN, or driving you out in my car. You had shaken your head; perhaps you saw another reality: that this country was no longer open to all who descended on it, with customs officials who stamped passports and didn't look too closely. Your intuition was sounder than mine, even though you had been shut away in that room. My car with us on board, heading for safety, looked about as secure as a cardboard box carrying two feeble wraiths bowling towards the gates of hell. I thought that my struggle to learn to drive despite Zemzem's dream, which my grandmother interpreted as a warning to abandon the idea, had been a waste of time. For when I needed it to escape on to safe roads, it gave up in the face of the roadblocks all along the coast as far as Sidon. You told me that Alexander the Great was never so moved as when he had to take his leave of Sidon, with the colour of its sea and the smell of its orange blossom, and I remember thinking at the time that this no longer meant anything when its asphalt was being pounded by huge Israeli army boots.

When you didn't open the door to me, I stared at its blank

64

surface, listening to the hollow sound of my own insistent knocking. I swallowed and it felt as if my tongue had dropped into my guts. I guessed you were on the high seas on one of the ships with hundreds of other fedayeen and I seemed to taste the sea's salty water and choke on it. I rushed to the nearest sea I could find. Its water was colourless. I stared hard at it and looked along the horizon but all I found there was heat and indifference. This is something that irritates me about the war: nature fulfilling its function without missing a beat. The waves continued to crash on to the same rocks, the spray boiled up and subsided. Only the sky was not its usual colour because so many bullets had been sown in it and it still bore the acrid traces of the farewell rounds fired on your behalf. You must have cursed these little hailstorms and ridiculed them, your eyes alighting briefly on the boys eagerly collecting the spent bullets, or a boy alone catching baby fish in a plastic bottle, or another clutching a faded bouquet which he was trying to sell to the departing fighters or their friends and relations. But why do things appear more serious when we read about them in history books: "They were surrounded, so that the sea was the only escape route left to them"?

I rushed to the football stadium, the collecting point. The ululations had stopped and grains of rice and broken flowers strewed the ground. I went home dejectedly. A picture of you sitting fiddling with your papers for ages before you burnt them loomed large in my mind. I was beside you, pretending to read the newspaper, and you said to me, "I'm stupid. Have I really not learnt my lesson yet? Not learnt that things change? There were so many people strangling this place, and suddenly they find other hands at their own throats."

Perhaps because of your sudden burst of confidence in the future, you didn't want to know what I had to say or let me try to protect you, and were reluctant to accept the idea that behind my eagerness to accompany you everywhere was also a desire to be with you alone, close enough to smell your smell. Who would use such logic but a woman: to think of finding an opening in that busy, noisy mind of yours which appeared to be governed by a demonic force, and extract some grains of affection and desire?

I could think only of going after you, although I realized what an absurd notion this was, for all the routes were blocked except the sea. Once more I could see nothing but the sea, nothing but the colour blue.

I had to go to you as quickly as I could. The fever to leave West Beirut had begun to spread among its inhabitants like a contagious disease, while the eastern sector reopened lines of communication and pulled down the roadblocks for us. Everyone who knew someone in the mountains, or who could afford to stay in the hotels there, left the west of the city. At night, from hotel terraces or friends' balconies they watched it burning. They would pretend to ignore it, enjoying the quiet of the trees, but blame themselves inwardly for leaving, heartbroken at what was happening. They were upset by the indifference of the people in the east to events in the western sector and realized that their flight to safety was an illusion.

Then I met a taxi-driver who took me back to Hayat's house from the port, where hundreds were searching for a place in a steamer or small boat. He launched into an anguished, unstoppable flow of words when he knew where I had come from. The journey was not very long, but he told me the story of his life, expressing his longing for the other side of the city. There was no pressure on him to go fast, no honking horns or traffic jams to negotiate. I wished he would be quiet, and found myself almost quivering with impatience. However, he adjusted his mirror so that I could see his face, or so that our eyes met. This made me feel awkward at first, but then I couldn't help listening.

He was from Ain Mraisseh in the western sector, from a shack opposite the Ondine swimming baths. If his father caught a fish, that was their meal. They were poor: "A fishing family. Ah . . . if I could just see that room . . . The wood and earth floor, the wooden ceiling. The fishing gear hanging in the entrance. I can smell it, I know the feel of it. If only I could see the frying pan, the sink, the gutting knife."

I stopped trying to ask questions because when I did he just went on talking. "If only I could see the little table, the bath, the loofah. The fisherman and his wife fostered me at birth: there were ten of us and my mother couldn't feed us any more. She used to draw the sign of the cross on the flour when she was baking bread, and my aunt the nun made the priest bless our house on his parish visits. I lived with my adopted father – the fisherman – and called him Baba Nikola, and his wife I called Mama Layla, so that people didn't get mixed up, especially as I used to visit my real family every Sunday and felt like a stranger among them. Ah, Mademoiselle . . . Madame . . . Mama Layla died in the war and Baba Nikola before it began."

I left Lebanon in an army helicopter: a relation of Hayat's, an army officer, had pulled strings for me and so it was that anonymous hands, impersonal orders transported me like a delicate fig and deposited me on board. My fellow passengers included several children, who made a noise the whole time, despite their mother's constant threats, the previous president of Lebanon and his wife, and one other passenger whom we recognized the moment he appeared as the Shia émigré said to have given financial support to the political parties in our sector. These parties and their allies of course had nothing but criticism for the eastern sector whose forces were now responsible for ferrying out their benefactor.

The émigré approached and shook hands with the ex-president and his wife, then glanced around. Smiling, he let his eyes rest on me for a moment then sat down, lighting a cigar. The children waved the smoke away from their faces, and one of them shouted, "Mama, it smells awful. I feel sick. Mama, mama."

I noticed that they spoke Arabic when they wanted to argue or complain; otherwise they could have been a family of for-eigners. The country was as hard to grasp as beads of mercury: the mother of these children, judging from the way she spoke and dressed, wouldn't acknowledge the existence of the western sector; she would be quite sure that the name Lebanon only applied to her part of the country, and yet she did not appear at all surprised that an important representative of the Shia community was on board the helicopter.

If they had known what I was thinking and why I was here they would probably have stopped and thrown me out. I hadn't felt any gratitude to the army officer as he took my arm and said, "At your service, Madame," and accompanied me to the steps of the helicopter. He was the reason why you had to flee the stifling summer heat of the city on board a steamer. I checked my anger and thought again. No, he wasn't the reason. It was Israel who had taken you away, or at least it was because of Israel that you'd gone. If you had escaped with me to Hayat's house, you'd have been with me, proof to the political analysts that they would never be able to grasp the beads of quicksilver. Being completely bound up with one side in this war, you were against this ex-president whose thick neck bulged over his collar, against what he represented. He was against these children, who were shouting in French, "We're bored. We're hungry. Where's this Cyprus? Make it hurry up. This isn't like James Bond's helicopter. You're a liar, Mama."

These kids will grow up to fight all the things you're committed to. Or perhaps one of them will fight on your side. And if the ex-president is blessed with children and grandchildren they'll make war on these children in a few years' time, because they don't want competition and perhaps because they want to unite the country, which I could see from the air lying like a fallen acorn.

From Cyprus I followed you to Egypt to the beach at Port Said and sat on the sands unable to believe that I was by the sea, by the blue sea, waiting like a sailor's wife or a hungry cat for the return of the fishing boats, watching the waves breaking one after the other in eager anticipation. I could hardly believe I was there, that I had only left Beirut yesterday. I felt as if I had spent years between Beirut, Jounieh, Cyprus, Cairo and Alexandria racing against time just to see you and hear you say goodbye to me.

My friend Muna was with me, impatient for my news, or rather for news of Beirut and the siege. She had left Lebanon for Cairo at the outbreak of war, and felt guilty, but I didn't want to stir up emotions, and felt like a traitor myself for escaping.

I thought the ships would stop the minute they saw us, but Muna ran towards them and her daughter chased after her crying. She plunged into the water and waded forward until it reached her waist, her daughter still trying to follow her, both of them waving and shouting, but the ships slowly disappeared from view although some people on deck waved at us. Muna's daughter was wailing, "Pick me up. I want to see the fedayeen."

The ships disappeared like passing clouds, leaving me with an image of hands raised in victory salutes. I didn't believe that ships could go by so fast. Aircraft are visible for longer and you still hear them when they're out of sight and see the white vapour trails. The ships seemed to surface for a moment like submarines, then plunge back down to the comfort of the sea bed.

We waited impatiently for other ships. The sun had moved off our faces and off the cold drinks for sale on the beach. I began to be afraid that we might be waiting in vain, and a tiny part of me hoped we were, in case it hurt your pride if I saw you standing dejectedly on deck, or rolling your sleeves up to prepare your grilled fish. I longed for all the commotion to stop, the pop and fizz of bottles being opened and the mothers shouting in fear and annoyance each time their children went near the water.

The sun was almost submerged in the sea and the Egyptian officer came up to assure me there would certainly be other ships passing, no doubt remembering the horror on my face the previous day when they had vanished in a flash.

The ship appeared. It was coming closer, dropping anchor, or was I mistaken? The officer pulled me by the hand and I caught hold of Muna and her daughter. Others followed us to a small boat which ferried us out to the ship. All the bottled-up waiting seemed to breathe out again in that little rowing boat. I thought of what I would say to you when I saw you; the conversation I had worked out before, the way I had imagined us looking at each other had vanished into thin air. It wasn't until I was on board the ship that I knew I had been deluding myself. You must have been on one of the other ships, or else still in Beirut. Muna was weeping bitterly as she embraced the fedayeen, and this made her daughter cry. The young men and women fighters tried to calm her down.

The older men, their faces creased with fatigue and hopeless-ness, succeeded in quietening all those who were weeping. A young woman with a deep brown skin and eyes full of life and mischief came up. "Put my mind at rest!" she said. "Is it true that in Sudan and Yemen the sun is scorching? I'm scared I'll go even darker than I am already."

"Don't worry," said Muna reassuringly. "A month, and you'll be back."

The wounded men lay on deck wrapped in civilian clothes and keffiyehs over their battle fatigues, shivering with cold. They asked the Egyptian officer for blankets and he promised to do what he could, but did not move from where he stood. I thought I could hear Greek music, Greek voices. It was a Greek merchant ship; as far as the crew were concerned, they were just carrying a different cargo from usual. That fact shook me more than the dried blood on the deck. Isolated by having the sea as their constant companion, these sailors appeared to look harshly on everything connected with dry land. Voices called, "One dollar. Two dollars. Coffee, tea, sandwiches."

I was astonished when the youths reached into the pockets of their combat gear and brought out dollars. Some stared out to sea and the others gathered around us giving us keffiyehs and flags, live bullets, and some letters to post.

I realized I was no longer thinking about you, forgetting you in the chaos, aware only of the ship's decaying timbers and the voices of those around us. I clutched the letters, promising to post them the same day. Muna and I were trying to catch her little girl who had begun to wail loudly, refusing to leave the ship, when I heard a voice calling me. "Asma, Asma."

It was Rana, your friend's daughter, in black shorts. She pulled me to her, embracing me and asking if I was going with them. She looked around for you and asked me about you. I recalled her room where you had stayed for a few days and how I had refused to lie down on her bed, and remembered her whispering to me one night, when you called me into the room claiming you had something to give me, "Perhaps he's going to kiss you."

4

My Dear Land

We're making for you, but we still haven't reached you. I can picture you lying under the sun and rain; you are the only thing lost in the war which is still physically present.

I haven't visited you since you were occupied, since your trees were cut down, and they changed your features. How hard I tried to make my grandfather leave you! But he preferred to expose himself to kidnapping, even to death, in order to stay close to you. How can someone be so attached to the inanimate? But I suppose you're alive: you bear fruit, grow thirsty and cold; you're changeable and not always compliant, for with your great open spaces or a small handful of your soil you've modified and shaped humanity; you've produced my family and been privy to the minutest secrets of their souls. You whispered my family's name and the echo picked it up and went shouting among the mountains and valleys, across the plains and round the telegraph poles, until it reached Beirut; you stayed where you were, but kept close to us even in Beirut.

I expect to feel pain at the sight of you and the unbelievable changes in you; what I see now as we drive past ruined buildings resembles fragments of crossword puzzles, made out of cement and wood and gaps where the sky shows through, or which people have filled in with plastic bags. Nevertheless a secret feeling of happiness creeps over me, as I catch a glimpse of a tree and picture a bird singing in its branches or flying off into the lovely wide open sky, and feel convinced that there are still colours and life in the world. The driver stops in a queue at a checkpoint and I hear him say to the car drawn up next to him, "I've got some jars of honey here for the father of a mate of mine, from his son in England."

This normality, even though it gives a skewed picture, brings peace to my heart, making Beirut seem far away. These days the city is awash with coloured plastic water containers; the word dollar dominates the conversation, drowning out the sound of the generators; moneychangers follow the price of the dollar, headsets clamped to their ears; Fadila mistook these for Walkmans. "Is that a new model?" she asked one of them. "How much did it cost you?" They even have mobile premises these days: a plastic bag which they carry around with them. People have grown accustomed to seeing the dollar and the picture of George Washington, instead of the blue of the Lebanese hundred lira note. Even the gipsy who sells thyme and chicory asked Zemzem to pay for her purchases in dollars. "Why not? Just for you! In dollars it is!" Zemzem replied spitefully.

She left her sitting on the staircase, her sack in her lap, and came back with a bundle of newspaper clippings. When the gipsy objected, Zemzem laughed. "I bet you've never seen a dollar in your life," she said.

Beirut is far away now, like a blazing ember which we dare not approach even in our thoughts, for fear of being burnt, but the echo of exploding shells persists inside our heads. We get out of the car by a flourishing orchard to rest from the potholes and the roadblocks, which show no sign of diminishing in frequency as the journey progresses. There are still many hours to go to our village and the driver suggests lunch and begins lighting a fire and taking potatoes, eggs and chicken from a bag. "Ali's orders," he declares.

My grandmother objects, muttering that we aren't hungry. "I am," cries Zemzem. "So's the driver. We all need to eat."

Many other people had already stopped their cars and were scattered in groups around the orchard, some lying on the grass, others chasing after their children. The smell of roasting meat crept into my nostrils and I suddenly felt hungry, and flung myself down on the grass like them. At once my grandmother asked me not to, explaining that I was different from them.

I sat up, clasping my legs and resting my head on my knees and my grandmother reprimanded me again. I wandered over to watch the driver who was still fanning the fire with a newspaper. A group of boys had gathered round him, including one who had lost his hand. He seemed quite lively even though he still had spots of blood on his shirt. I must have been staring at him as a woman came up to me and said, "The bastards he worked for did it." Before I could think what to say, she went on, "He went to work as usual, reached out to pick up a shoe and there was an explosion which blew his hand off."

Could he really be a garbage collector? He looked about ten. "Why? What does he do?"

Her face lit up at the prospect of someone who would take an interest in her troubles. "He goes to the tip and sorts everything into separate bags. Sorry, it's a bit disgusting. Glass, plastic, empty tins. It's better than being scared out of his mind, which he would be if he went to look for gold teeth in the graveyard at night like some of them do."

I felt embarrassed at my failure to grasp all the implications of what she was saying. "What does he do with the things he collects?" I asked her.

She stared, and looked me up and down, appearing to become convinced in the process that she couldn't form an opinion about my material status on the basis of my clothes. "He takes it to the scrap dealers."

I replied quickly, as if wanting to exonerate his employers, that it wasn't in their interests to blow his hand off.

She did not challenge me immediately and say, "Why not? Where have you been?" She just looked me up and down again, and nodded her head assuring herself of my naïvety or the truth of her words: "Why not? Everybody knows about it. When respectable men and women start looking through the rubbish, the dealers get annoyed, as if it was specially reserved for their own people. God will see justice done. Big tough men are losing their dignity. Never mind. We're going to ask Al-Hariri and they'll make him a new hand."

She fidgeted a little and looked down at the ground, then asked me where we were going and whether the driver was my brother or my cousin, and if Zemzem was my mother. Then pointing to the big lorry she said, "Our neighbour took pity on us. I wanted to go and see my mother and he gave us a lift."

Why did I not believe the stories Zemzem told, and yet I believed this woman? Was it because there was always a ring of grim satisfaction to what Zemzem said, a tearful note, a hint of exaggeration? Whenever she told us tales like these I found myself saying it was the victims' fault or feeling indifferent towards them, and I noticed my grandmother did the same. Had Zemzem not told us about explosions in the rubbish dumps which had taken people's fingers off and we had dismissed the subject, saying these were just rumours designed to spread fear and chaos, so that people like her would get scared?

"Somebody's mother sold her wedding-ring so that she could make bread salad and meat loaf. Somebody else bought a wedding dress for her daughter off the family of a bride-to-be who'd died before her wedding day. Zakiyya took her son away from school because he wasn't very bright, so that she could afford to send the rest."

It was true every household was feeling the effects of inflation, even ours. My grandmother decided that it would not make us live any longer if we ate qashqawan cheese, so she stopped buying it. Zemzem roasted one chicken at a time instead of two, and white-collar workers and people with average incomes started doing without basics. Our next-door neighbour no longer brought a pot of coffee round in the afternoons when she came to hear our news; instead she would bring mulberry juice from her village.

We go back to the car and drive off, only to be pulled up at another checkpoint. I've become familiar with the variations and am learning how to deal with them. A show of seriousness is required if they are manned by the militias; pleading or looking frightened doesn't work; it is best to be patient with the Syrians, as their soldiers seem tired, and fed up with being away from home. In the past I had overreacted at checkpoints: they seemed to open my eyes to the plain truth that Lebanon had been divided into statelets and zones, that there were people working to specific agendas and that the present situation had not been anticipated in advance by the fighters.

We stop. "We'll have to go back. We'll take the upper road: the low road is full of bandits. Mr Ali's orders."

"What's the world coming to?" sighs my grandmother.

I understand what she means: Ali has become Mr Ali. The low road is nearer, easier, but the trees grow so thickly on either side of it that it is overrun with ordinary robbers posing as militiamen, and holding up cars on the pretext of checking drivers' ID cards. If only the driver would take a risk and go by the low road so that I could see its trees in all their abundance, have a look at the bandits and relish the sight of Zemzem fearing for her quail.

Some of the villages were razed to the ground and looked like historical remains or part of the natural scenery, but I was pleased to see washing spread out to dry and smell smoke rising from a valley where they were burning rubbish and dead leaves; I was even glad to hear a donkey braying: it all reminded me of the past and you. But the roadblocks reminded me of the present, and my fear for you.

We used to visit the village from time to time in the early years of the war. As the country grew more rocky and mountainous, the vines would appear, and the orchards, full of gladioli like yellow and white lollipops; the village seemed untouched by the fighting and the sound of rockets and mortars there was unimaginable, but some buildings had obviously been hit. In peacetime we left the sea, drove over the mountains and plunged downwards on to the plains until we reached the outskirts of the village. I used to wonder why it was there in that particular spot. The blind shepherd was always the first to hear my grandmother's car, and recognize the sound of its engine; he would hurry towards it, feeling his way over the stones with his stick and as soon as he came to the asphalt, he would shout at his flock to wait. Ali stopped the car and dismounted to fetch him and lead him up to the window, restraining him from hitting it too vigorously with his stick. When the shepherd heard my grandmother's voice, he kissed his palm and put it to his forehead in a gesture of gratitude. She opened her black handbag and took out a bundle of lira notes, folded them in two and placed them in his hand. When she closed the bag again, it always made a loud, self-important click.

On this occasion we were not greeted by my grandfather's orchards as we had been in the past, but by a sign for Samira, Coiffeuse. "A hairdressing salon here!" I exclaimed. "Incredible!"

I could not imagine any of the women in the village having their hair done except Ruhiyya. I smiled at the thought of Ruhiyya with a cigarette in her hand and a cup of coffee on her lap.

"A chocolate factory! A bank! A chicken farm. A family restaurant. The Nabaa Café – Three Floors. Villas. Is this really our village? A bank. Another bank."

"Do you put cotton wool in your ears?" answered Zemzem impatiently. "I told you before that a hairdresser's had opened in the village, and when Kawakib went to get her hair done, the first time the hairdresser told her that there wasn't any hot water, the second time she was making stuffed vine leaves, and the third she said she was tired and couldn't do it. And I told you that Hamad Jaafar got his money out of Kuwait and came and opened a factory, and his brother opened a restaurant, and they couldn't believe their luck!'

I had heard it all before, but I couldn't picture it: tables with cloths and a waiter with a pencil and paper, instead of one of the estate workers on the little patch of desert where we used to buy melons which were still green, and cucumbers.

"Half a kilo," we used to shout, and he would put down his hoe and come over to us carrying a cucumber wrapped in newspaper, or in a scrap torn from his bag of earth. I think I can still hear the flies buzzing, but it might be the hum of the machinery in the chocolate factory.

My grandmother clears her throat more and more frequently. She can't look at her orchards for any length of time, while I can't tear my eyes away from them. The trees have mostly died and the wild flowers no longer grow in such profusion. The colour of the earth seems to dominate the other colours, then our house appears, and I hear the sound of the water cistern. I feel as if I have never left this place. Everything is as it always was. Naima runs out, followed by another girl, and my grandfather. The unknown girl examines us, then rushes off in the opposite direction and disappears. Everybody kisses us, my grandfather clasps me to his chest, lets me go to kiss my grandmother's hand, then holds me tightly again and behind him I see the line of washing dancing in the breeze. The pine trees are as they were, the pear tree right beside the water tank. I free myself from his embrace and stretch up until I can see the tent on the roof, where one of his relations used to take his siestas and compose poetry, so we nicknamed him Abu Tammam.

The windows still appear to have no function and stand permanently open. I always used to compare them to the city windows which were closed when it was cold or wet, and could never remember it raining in the village. Nobody ever looked out of these windows with their intricate wrought iron bars. When a car horn sounded or tyres crunched over the sand and gravel, we would rush to the wide-open door.

My grandfather puts his strong arms round me again. "You had me worried. You could have contacted me. Why didn't you leave right at the beginning?"

Of course Zemzem seizes this opportunity for revenge and tells him that although she went on and on at us croaking like a frog, it had not done any good, and when a rocket landed in the house, we had actually started to laugh and talked about hollowing it out and stuffing it with rice.

Now my grandfather is pulling me by the hand out beyond the house. The sun has set on your orchards. I hear voices and laughter coming from them and my heart gives a jolt of surprise. I breathe faster. In the middle of the orchard is a small stone building with a zinc roof. My grandfather points. "See the poison planted there."

But I can see nothing except some unidentifiable plants, motionless in the darkness.

"See what they've planted. Poison and filth."

"Even if they've planted apes and monkeys, who cares? They'll soon be gone," I say consolingly.

Then he starts cursing loudly, and when I implore him to be quiet, it seems to fuel his agitation. "Why should I be quiet?" he shouts. "So they'll think I'm afraid? All I've got left is a voice. I just want to make them hear. What can they do? Kidnap me? They've already tried."

When they hear him shouting, Naima and my grandmother come up to us and, without saying anything, try to drag him inside. He refuses to go and Naima gives vent to her feelings. "He's like this every day. Morning, noon and night. As if he has fits. I'm glad you've come to see with your own eyes what the old wretch is like, and how much we have to put up with from him."

The porch gathers us in once more. All that is visible are the stars and the chain of high mountains. My grandfather sits down heavily, for he carries you on his back and in his heart. Then he looks about him and asks where Juhayna is. "Juhayna! Juhayna!" he calls. He turns to me and, as if I'm a little girl, promises that she will be a pretty and intelligent companion for me. "Where have you gone, Juhayna?" he calls again. Then he mutters to himself, "She's vanished like a djinn, God save us."

When he was a boy he wanted to learn to read and write, even though his father and other members of his family had banded together to try and dissuade him. "Your family has everything and you want to sit down in front of a teacher who'll order you about and tell you what to learn? The 'a' has nothing on it and the 'b' has a dot underneath it. Get servants who can read and write for you. Why go to all that trouble?"

But he insisted on having an education: the Ottomans and the French read newspapers and wrote with pens. He had seen them as they relaxed after hunting parties.

He began going on horseback to the sheikh's school in the nearby town and his mother and aunt recited charms to protect him on the way. But when the time came for him to leave you and go to college in Beirut he couldn't do it. The little sparrows and the big birds of prey were the first to call him to you and eventually my grandfather became an expert hunter like his father; but unlike him he did not ride around as if he was lord of all he surveyed, ordering the horsemen and the beaters and their dogs to follow him. He didn't prevent others in his party from shooting so that the local people would talk about the number of birds hanging from the master's saddle as they had done in his father's day. He began instead to share this hobby of his with the men and youths of the village and anyone from round about who liked to hunt. He went on hunting parties with the Ottomans and the French, until gradually he became aware that he was bound to you heart and soul. He drew life from you and expressed his concern for you with every breath, and came to discover that you, and not reading and writing, were the constant; you would stand firm in the face of disasters and crises, and the solutions to them would be in your hands. The villagers found themselves drawn to you. Their importance came from belonging to the person who owned you. You refused or accepted; roared in anger or gave your blessing, and you accepted my grandfather and allowed his roots to extend deep inside you.

You knew it was your duty to find him a bride, and you found her for him one day when he had gone for a long ride on horseback. My grandmother-to-be had cried until her father agreed to let her and her mother go out of the house with him, swathed in black from head to toe. He had waited until sunset so that no one would see him, and had chosen a remote spot where my grandmother sat on a rock talking silently to the departing sun, demanding to know why her father was so harsh and autocratic. She was a prisoner in the house; nobody heard her speak, not even the walls, nobody saw her except the women who came to bring her and her mother news of what was going on in the world and the neighbouring villages. In the end she became famous as some kind of demon princess, invisible to all but her father and heaven. Time and time again she asked her father why he didn't allow her to go to the female sheikh to learn to read and write and he would reply that he didn't want a living soul to catch a glimpse of her, for besides being a girl she was his daughter. So she asked him why in that case he didn't allow the sheikha to come to the house to teach her, as their family's name was associated with religion in people's minds, because it had dispatched its sons to learn the basics of Islamic law. To avoid being beaten conclusively by his daughter, he said he hadn't known that the sheikha could read and write and thought she recited the Quran from memory, and in any case she only left her house for religious ceremonies. When his answers failed to achieve the desired effect, he finally admitted the truth: "I'm afraid you might read novels and stories, and learn to write letters."

"Surely reading and interpreting the Quran correctly only teaches you how to be closer to God and His Messenger?"

My grandmother won and books and writing became the most important things in her life, rather than women's talk restricted to the tree producing fruit, or the cow miscarrying, or the latest wedding. She began studying late into the night, turning up the paraffin lamp, and discovered that being able to solve the riddle of words gave her power; she refused to eat sitting on the mat and put her food out on a little table. When her father threw his huge, worn out shoes away, she rescued them and put them on and felt the power springing from them.

On my grandfather's land, she lowered her eyes from the sky and fixed them on her father. She wept, saying she needed to see the sky and breathe the air every day, not just on rare occasions. But his thoughts were elsewhere, as he looked all around him ensuring the spot he had chosen was quiet except for the sound of loneliness and the horse shifting restlessly between the shafts of the cart which he had stopped on the level ground. When he was certain nobody could see his daughter, he heaved a sigh of relief. But there was someone there, and he was watching her. My grandfather could see part of her face as she spoke and he sighed to himself, and fell in love with her.

My grandfather's name eventually became known in Beirut, having become part of the fabric of the country like the Beydouns and Sursuqs and other families with areas named after them. His name was given to varieties of apples and pears and a new kind of fruit he produced by grafting an apple on to a guava. The feel of it was somewhere between the sweet smoothness of an apple and the rough porous texture of a quince, and it tasted like a mixture of orange-flower water and cherries. I heard its name everywhere, especially on the lips of street vendors.

Although my grandmother travelled away from you, you had taken root in her, and so she only half gave herself to the city: one eye, nostril, hand. Everything connected with Beirut was temporary, or if not temporary, always peripheral.

She did not express her taste in furniture, as she did in clothes, and bought it haphazardly, remaining in the car and delegating Ali to buy whatever was available. She never tried to mix with her Beirut neighbours or even to accommodate to the city itself. We continued to live as if we were close to you, eating off an assortment of dishes with brass spoons which were turning rusty. We consumed large raw pieces of meat and offal, unconcerned about the liquid floating in the tureen and the flies hovering around the milk, sometimes falling in.

I adapted to Beirut in the same way as she did, but you were there in front of me every time I came home and saw wooden crates piled up in the entrance, or rode in Ali's car and sat next to a box of eggs, a heap of slaughtered chickens, or a pail of milk.

As soon as the war spread outside the city, it penetrated right inside you, where you were moist and bursting with life, and when the seeds were fertilized they produced the fires of battle.

The Palestinians were the first to occupy you, taking over a rocky, uncultivated area known as the wilderness, and my grandfather made sure that anybody with the remotest connection to the Palestinians knew how he felt about this. Eventually he went to the man in charge, who had been to visit him on a previous occasion to ask permission to use the area for manoeuvres. My grandfather had refused, not because he feared it would give the Israelis an excuse to attack but because he and my grandmother were possessive to the extent that if a bee or a butterfly moved on to one of their trees they believed the creature automatically became their property. They wanted everyone, even the cattle, to know that a particular stone marked the beginning of their land, and not a single cow would reach its head out over this boundary to graze. There was no barbed-wire fence or wall surrounding you. Anyone was free to look at you, but there was a solid mental boundary which sent an electrifying quiver through those who crossed it intending harm. The fear was not of the two of them, but of all they had: the house, the trees, the car and its driver, the house in Beirut and the guests who called on them; the pilgrimages to Mecca and the holy places, the prayer beads they had brought back from Mount Arafat, the water from the sacred well of Zemzem, and the limitless supplies of food which appeared to be the source of their power.

My grandfather began making for the "wilderness" to observe the fedayeen night and day as they carried out imaginary operations, rolling down the slopes, taking cover, practising firing and letting out exuberant cries as they roasted a snake for their evening meal. He used to imitate them dancing, waving his hands in the air and bringing them down to his sides, and produced a centipede from a jar and went through the motions of crunching it up in front of them. He would ask them from a distance, "What do you want? How many lira to see the back of you?"

He had no faith in politics or the struggle, and they finally lost patience with him, for every time he heard a shot he would call out, "It sounds as though somebody's had too many beans."

If you were my grandfather's reason for living, then mankind was my grandmother's. It was not that she loved her fellow human beings, but she felt that she derived her lifeblood from dominating them. When she lost the wilderness, it was as if she had lost the wings which enabled her to fly. She tried to preserve a certain permanent image of herself, my grandfather and his ancestors in the Palestinians' eyes, by convincing my grandfather that he should agree to lend them the wilderness, even curry favour with them, so that when she sat cross-legged in gatherings she could say carelessly, as if waving away a fly, "We gave them charity, so they have to do as we say."

The Palestinians left the wilderness after an Israeli reconnaissance aircraft was seen circling above the village and the surrounding area on several occasions, acting on information received from a spy in our village, it was said at the time. My grandfather went to survey his territory joyfully, hurling the whitewashed stones which had been used to mark out the camp boundaries on to the rocks below. With my grandmother, he considered whether to plant fields there and cultivate the wilderness or to burn off the wooded slopes and leave them fallow for a time. But the village youths did not leave him undecided for long, as they occupied it one dawn, at the moment when the watchful eye dozes, confident that the night and its dark terrors are dispersing, because the first signs of morning and clarity are only a hairsbreadth away.

My grandfather rushed from the house, shouting, "I've been raped by my sons! I've been raped by my sons!"

He raced along, his shirt hanging over his trousers, and my grandmother ran after him, holding out his belt to him and crying, "A man without a belt has no restraint, and a man who runs gives the impression he has no sense and no dignity."

When my grandfather saw Mustafa and the rest of the youths in the wilderness, a blood vessel burst in his eye.

"Mustafa? Abu Mustafa's son?" he was shouting as he came round from the anaesthetic. "His mother was packing fruit when she went into labour and they brought her to our house to give birth to this thug."

He wouldn't be quiet even though the doctor warned him that he'd burst another blood vessel.

He thought he had sorted the matter out with the young men's families, some of whom had promised to help and been extremely upset about what had happened, but their sons made plans to leave the wilderness and occupy the orchards: the idealists among them thought the orchards would be a source of income; then they would not need to be committed to any political party, individual or state, and the cash would enable them to start up a new party, independent of all those round about. Meantime my grandfather, who still had one eye bandaged, swore to have his revenge, not only on them but on you – the earth and the trees that had accepted another master. He vowed to set you alight, but he was like a little child crying in pain, and needed someone to calm him down all the time in hospital; my grandmother and his brother only made things worse and he began to scream again, like the child refusing to play any of the games suggested to him. "An eye for an eye and a tooth for a tooth," urged my grandmother. "We should form a militia. A gang of thugs – or fighters as they call them – who look ferocious enough to make a lion stand up on its hind legs and beg for mercy."

"A militia?" shouted my grandfather, overwhelmed. "Shooting and getting shot? What's the matter with you? You're the wisest, most sensible, most intelligent woman I know. How can you think about having a militia?"

"My body is on fire!" she screamed. "I feel as if somebody's hung me up by the eyes on a fish hook. You think it's reasonable for some thugs to push us off our land? Off our ancestors' land? Reasonable that we should let godless people surround this house, whose walls have been purified by all the prayers I've prayed in it?"

"They're all communists, with no religion, no breeding," put in my great uncle soothingly, "but a militia, Umm Fatima? Are we thugs too?"

"You're right, we're not," she answered contemptuously, "but one has to change. If we protect our lands in the only way open to us and they call us thugs, then perhaps we are. If the politicians are, then, yes, so are we."

The idea of starting up a militia had been like a seed planted in her heart in the earliest days of the war. She had watered it and slowly it had grown and matured. She stood there defiantly. "What do you say?" she demanded, deliberately addressing the question to my grandfather, because she knew that his brother would not give him any encouragement, and also because she felt, as she always had done, that the family consisted solely of her and my grandfather.

"Whom would you want to carry guns, my dear?" inquired my grandfather. "Abu Karki and his wife, Hussein, Abu Mustafa, father of the ringleader, or Fadil?"

We all burst out laughing, as my grandfather had chosen the oldest, the most decrepit, the most naïve of the local people, or else those who were still loyal to our family purely because their sons were abroad or in Beirut.

My grandmother stopped laughing abruptly, regretting her frivolity. "No. Do you think I'm so short-sighted and stupid? No, not at all. Did no one hear me saying that the militias were bullies and thugs who love the colour of money and the taste of power? They're vigilantes, bullies, but you just agree to what I'm saying and I guarantee you'll have everyone under your feet like cockroaches."

My great uncle spoke this time, prepared for the storm his words would provoke, but feeling there was only one solution to the problem and he would state it whatever happened: "You have to have an agreement with the family you won't name."

"My wife has gone mad, and it looks as if you have too," said my grandfather, "but luckily I'm still sane. Drag our name through the mud for the sake of a lot of wild hooligans who've rebelled against their families because it's time they got married?"

"It seems the years have played tricks with your mind," remarked my grandmother to my great uncle, not looking in his direction. Then, disregarding his proposal and returning to her original train of thought, she went through the families she knew who had militias. "Even the Albino has a militia. That makes about twenty in all."

"So who have you got round here?" reiterated my great uncle. "Listen! Talk to the family you won't name and they'll put some of their bandits at your disposal to protect your land. You won't lose as much as an onion skin. On the contrary, you'll stand to gain – when they've recovered your land for you, they'll be glad to work with you."

I don't remember a time when we ever mentioned the name of the unnamed family. We called them the Birdseeds, the Shitshovellers, the Nasties, the Unmentionables, the Nameless.

The animosity towards this family was not because they smuggled hashish and cocaine (one of their sons had a degree in mechanical engineering from a leading university in the States, and when he came back he designed a small wooden aircraft for the family to use for short runs into Syria). It was

85

because they had risen to prominence in the course of the war and had a lot of influence, although my grandparents did not publicly acknowledge their existence.

My grandfather could not forget how this family had expanded and become one of the richest in the area, when their forefathers had been reduced to living on their wits, transporting sand and gravel on their pack animals until, thanks to their shrewd instincts, they became big tobacco smugglers, graduating to hashish in the war. In no time at all they began to throw their money about, acquiring big American cars, new villas and gilded furniture. They forbade their women to collect camel and cattle dung to feed the fire and actually gave up the outside oven and the tin sheets for bread baking when they had an asphalt path laid and planted flower beds on either side of it.

One of their sons married a much-married actress who had posed in a bathing costume with a bottle of perfume held up to her breasts and the caption, "It's good to be warm even in a heatwave." Instead of criticizing them, local people admired them more than ever, proud that they came from the Bekaa, and were particularly impressed when the family became involved in politics, took hostages and kidnapped those who got in the way of their business activities. Bullies and vigilantes gathered around them, until eventually they had a militia protecting them, their routes and their men, whose methods of communication with the outside world had begun to command the greatest respect. They had acquired walkie-talkies and a private international telephone line stretching above the sunflowers and telegraph poles and running by the streams. They had even introduced new methods of preparing hashish, processing it and making it ready for shipment. All the young men in the village and the surrounding area had aspirations to join their circle, enticed by the private helicopter overhead, their Presley haircuts, the gold and diamond rings on their fingers, their genuine crocodile belts.

The confusion inside my grandmother's head increased as she understood that, for the first time, she was powerless to act. When the armed men gathered and advanced right up to her boundaries, she hurried to visit the houses in the village, one by one, houses where she never set foot except when someone died or gave birth. It escaped her notice, she who never failed to notice even the colour of someone's eyelashes, that the people were scared of her visiting, scared that their children would be as rude to her as they had been to them. For they had already tried to persuade them to leave the land, either by shouting and threatening, or by recounting stories of our family's generosity in an attempt to win them round and make them see sense. Their talk was weighed down with the past, unlikely to strike any chords with their children, who knew nothing of the time before the war, who had learnt about nothing but the different types of arms in circulation, and who wanted nothing more than to dress in combat gear. Their families' intervention only served to make the children more alienated, more irritated, for they had never understood why their parents were so well disposed towards a big landowning family like ours, and they accused them of fearing the past and continuing to be dominated by it.

My grandmother sent Naima out to reconnoitre, and gleaned from her hesitant reports that the people would rather she visited them in the morning. My grandmother swallowed as if her mouth was full of pins, recalling the past when she had never had to inquire about the best time to visit, because their houses were open to her all year round, and they were pleased at her interest in them. However, she smiled at Naima and said, "Never mind. The morning is a good time to go."

She toured around listening to the echo of her words, for the rooms were almost bare except for cupboards and mattresses, and the pin-cushions and woven straw mats on the walls. She guessed that people were no longer as upset as they had seemed in the past when they heard that the land had been occupied, even though they cried in front of her and bent to kiss her respectfully on the shoulder, disowning their children or swearing to punish them, promising to do whatever they could. But my grandmother sensed that a change had occurred in these houses: it was the feeling of tranquillity, as if the parents had become subservient to their children. She reproached them for abandoning their authority.

She was wearing a dress she hadn't worn for ages which was beginning to cut into her a little around the waist, but she loved the velvet trimming on the sleeves. Over it she wore the coat whose colour had faded, but which she still liked all the same. She smelt of amber essence and had remembered to put a few drops on her prayer beads. Despair had no power over her: it was as if she had given her mind a protective coating, reinforcing it with arguments taken from history, from received wisdom, even from the daily papers, and it had started to creak because she had polished it so much. Her listeners were ill at ease, watching the door. My grandmother deliberately put off leaving, deciding that she would get more out of the sons than from these evasive folk who swayed from side to side, tutting and repeating, "There is no power or strength except with God," and "We can't do a thing unless we put a knife to their throats! We're willing to do it, we'd do anything for you."

She finally stood up when Mustafa entered. He must have heard about her visit when he was in the orchard and have come, not to see her, but to make peace with his father who had rejected him publicly from the minaret of the local mosque. My grandmother had pinned her remaining hopes on her final visit to Mustafa's father's house; despite his frail build, his eyes gave off sparks. Your trees only seemed to bear fruit when he touched them and your soil only responded to him watering it; however, the folk song which his father had bawled out as a kind of oath of allegiance to my great-grandfather was the sole reason he was as pliable as dough in my grandfather's hands.

> My lord, O my lord
> You are the cow and I am the fly
> Consider me a fly under your tail
> I'm going to keep a close watch on the peasants
> Who see you as provider and protector
> And tell you what they're up to every day
> And if you ever find I'm lying
> Then you must beat me, beat me
> Until I shit a mountain
> And give up all my secrets.

Mustafa knew that only in my grandmother's presence could he make an incursion into his father's logic, if his father was to hear him having a discussion with her, blocking all her chances to make skilful interventions or use her powers of eloquence, and leaving her fumbling for words. As he spoke to her he was acutely conscious that he must not make the same mistake again: he was not going to open his heart to her and tell her as he had told his father months before that he wanted to be a guerrilla, to stand ready in combat gear, give orders, feel the heat of a weapon; Bruce Lee films were being acted out in your orchards and he was aware of it, but instead of fulfilling his ambitions he was obliged to run errands for his mother, give her his blessing whenever she spat at the bands of youths and go along with her as she emptied the bowl of dirty water after the wash and cursed them: "God willing they'll become like the black scum in that water."

Mustafa said, "The fathers don't understand the rage of their sons. Yes, they were in the orchards and so were the boys' mothers, hoeing, planting, harvesting and packing, while the sun beat down on their children all day long, and they were left to scream unattended when insects stung them. Wherever they looked they saw land stretching to the horizon and knew that it all belonged to the blond man sitting in the hut, the one with a resounding laugh who rode around on horseback. Did he have a right to these lands simply because his grandfather imported wheat and slabs of ice to the villages during the First World War and took land in exchange when the people had no gold liras?"

Mustafa was disconcerted when he realized that despite these historical arguments he was unable to defeat my grandmother. She was more knowledgeable than he had believed, and brought religion into the discussion and quoted the sayings of the imams and the prophetic traditions in front of his father, who was a believer. My grandmother kept a hold on religion by way of its prophets, its imams and its female personalities: Fatima the Prophet's daughter, Our Lady Zaynab, and the Prophet's wife Khadija. She knew all the stories about them, their sayings, the prophetic traditions they had themselves related and the ones told about them. She argued over their biographies, giving her own stubborn interpretations of the texts, not shifting an inch from her declared position, even when her opponents were sheikhs and religious scholars. At the same time she was well informed about the late President Nasser and his land reforms, and about the Israeli enemy. In desperation Mustafa quoted from his own experience: "I can still remember my father and mother on the threshing floor in the very hottest part of the day," he shouted, "and my big sister shaking a tree to bring the fruit down, and holding out her skirt to catch it."

My grandmother gasped in disgust at the hypocrisy as she stood up to leave, drawing her coat around her and gripping her sunshade. "How did we oppress you? Your mother and father were agricultural workers, not the king and queen. Did we take them down off their throne, steal their gold and force them to work? See! We're making you remember. Isn't that better than being in the dark?"

That was the last visit and my grandmother and Zemzem came back home, my grandmother holding the blue sunshade so low that it was almost touching her face, for fear that the sun would damage her snow-white skin. She sighed deeply, hoping to provoke a response from Zemzem. For the first time in her life she wanted her opinion, although she knew that she would only select a word or two, a sentence at the most, from what she had to say. Zemzem did not take the trouble to choose her words as she normally did, but simply sighed herself too, and said, "It's boiling hot."

When my grandmother pressed her, she remarked indifferently, "Working on the land is like a job. Now their children have got other jobs and some kind of status. Not only that, but they've started to bring money home and spend it on themselves. If you'd put five piastres in their pocket they'd have understood what you were saying."

My grandmother looked utterly downcast, like a young girl who had discovered on her wedding night that her sweetheart was marrying somebody else. "You're right. Money talks. Kalashnikovs bring power and power brings money."

She was very depressed because you were no longer hers.

You no longer needed her. As she walked along, at the mercy of the sun's single eye with no shade to protect her, she felt dwarfed by you. She was certain people were watching her from their windows and porches. She had to think of a way to grow taller instead of shrinking. What had happened to the wooden box lined with green and mauve velvet which used to be beside her father's bed? She wished it still had gold in it: English sovereigns, Ottoman gold liras, and Egyptian guineas, all shining and jingling. She had seen inside it when she was little. Where had it all gone? If she had thought about it before when she was younger, perhaps she would have found an answer. If only the profit from these orchards had been turned into money and paid into bank accounts instead of being used to buy more land; if only she had bought comfortable furniture.

My grandparents never thought that you would return to them until the Israelis were actually inside Lebanon. How they both hoped that the Israelis would reach the village! They followed their operations on the radio and right at the beginning my grandfather asked Naima's son to go to the Unmentionables to find out what news they were getting on their walkie-talkies, while my grandmother in Beirut relied on the news from Radio Monte Carlo. Each time my grandfather deduced from the news that Israel was making progress, his face grew redder and rounder, and whenever he heard that America and other world powers were cautioning Israel and trying to halt her advance, his eyebrows stuck up in all directions. And my grandmother used to turn her pillow every evening and every morning, addressing my grandfather: "I'm thinking of you. God willing, they'll reach you."

Zemzem heard her and laughed to herself. She told me that although my grandmother was old she had not given anything up and was still dependent on my grandfather as a man.

There were rumours that the Israelis would soon reach our villages with their airborne weapons. Early one morning helicopters hovered in the sky above and the armed men who were occupying my grandfather's land fled like frightened chickens from a predatory fox and scattered far and wide. My grandfather was overjoyed and let out a whoop of delight, then rushed to your orchards, kissing the earth and raising his eyes to the sky, whether to pray to God or Israel we didn't know. When two days went by without any further activity in the air, my grandfather was afraid the occupiers would return, and wished at that point he had a militia. For a few moments he thought of throwing himself on "that family's" mercy but discounted the idea and considered other possibilities. However, the events of the next few days gave him confidence again: a helicopter landed, with a Star of David emblazoned on its side, and men in civilian clothes jumped out, asking about Mustafa and his companions, who had fled from the village and its environs into the tangled network of trails among the streams and fields which connected the villages to one another. In spite of some fear and caution the children and adolescents gathered round curiously and followed the men. They spoke Arabic fluently but with an accent. They made straight for Mustafa's house and went in without any warning, searching for weapons. Mustafa's aunt, who was almost stone deaf, welcomed them enthusiastically: "Hallo, come in, we're delighted to see you. We're always glad to see handsome lads like you. What can I get you?"

Then she called out to Mustafa's sister, Amina, who was gnashing her teeth in fury. "Why are you standing there like some graven image? Get something for these young men. You're most welcome. A cold drink. Or perhaps they haven't eaten yet. Put out a dish of rice and lentils for them."

At this Amina's patience deserted her. "Sit down!" she shouted at her aunt.

One of them came up to the aunt and clapped her on the shoulder. "You're a kind woman. Where's Mustafa?"

She didn't hear what he said. "Aren't you hungry?" she asked. "Now why are you standing up? Please sit down."

She talked incessantly, and kept apologizing that Mustafa wasn't there. "He's off with the bandits firing guns. He's not tidy and clean and well-mannered like you."

She said goodbye to them, waving until Amina struck her hand to make her stop. "Someone should gag you," she yelled in her ear. "They're Israelis and you go welcoming them."

Her aunt gave a cry and beat herself on the face. "What? Oh, no!" She rushed up on to the roof, grabbing her slippers as she went, waving one threateningly in the air and striking her cheek with the other. "Oh, God, I'm so stupid! They were Israelis and I was trying to give them something to eat."

The soldiers in the helicopter saw the friendly woman waving and waved back, not noticing the slipper in her raised hand.

My grandfather saw the arrival of this helicopter as meaning that a dark page had been torn out and destroyed so that life would go back to normal in his orchards. Almost instantly his old worries were replaced by new ones. Should he give Mustafa's father and the other lads' relations their jobs back or replace them with the Pakistanis and Sudanese who were knocking on doors all over the area looking for work? Then Israel started to worry him, flooding the market with cheap vegetables to tempt the Lebanese merchants; he called Israel a snake, while my grandmother ended all her prayers with an entreaty to her Maker to destroy Israel's houses and fields. After a while she changed this to a prayer for the destruction of the strangers and thugs who reoccupied the orchards and distorted your features without a thought, transforming you deep down as well as on the surface so that now you have a different spirit.

I seem to hear sounds as if there's a fight going on but it's a strange sound, which even drowns out the tap on the cistern. I get out of bed and discover that it's the wind rising. I try to secure the window and succeed in deadening the noise, but find I'm wide awake literally writing this letter in my head, even taking care to put in all the commas and full stops, and open and close the inverted commas, but I notice that I no longer use question marks and exclamation marks. A fly buzzing around on the low ceiling, despite the darkness, stops me sleeping.

My grandfather's voice roused me: "My mule's better than yours. My saddle's better than yours," he was calling.

The veins running through your branches and each particle of your soil still seemed to be charged with his voice and simply repeated his words in reply. But other voices called back, "Let's get some sleep tonight. How about letting your family have a bit of peace and quiet too?" Then I realized that I had only just woken up.

I heard the sound of footsteps on the porch, then this barking or weeping or singing or laughing: my grandfather again. No one responded this time and I twisted over to the other side of the bed, trying to forget what I'd heard and go back to thinking about you and about my mother and this strange world. But then I sat bolt upright at the sound of glass breaking on the porch and my grandfather shouting, "Where can I hide my face from my family, and my father's bones, when the land is planted with this poison?"

I ran to the porch. The neck of the empty oil bottle was still in his hand. I took it from him gently and steered him away from the scattered glass. "Were you asleep, my dear?" he asked me simply. "Since those wild boys took the land I haven't been able to sleep like normal folk."

I realize now why the occupiers ignore him: all his strength has left him. They tried to kidnap him the day they occupied the land; he was armed and on horseback. Following their instructions, he dismounted and gave himself up. Their faces were covered and they blindfolded him and made him walk with them. Then he managed to escape and raced away from them, hurling himself from rock to rock. It seems that even acts of violence are governed by laws agreed in advance and that if a kidnap victim knows the identity of his kidnappers and can escape, he will never be kidnapped again. To their astonishment, my grandfather called his abductors by name.

"He died with a hoe in his hand and only the cow to mourn him . . ." sings my grandfather, disparagingly.

"But, grandfather, Mustafa's not with them any more," I say.

"Who cares? It's all his fault."

I laugh and he laughs with me. I try to pretend to myself that he's cheered up and go inside, but he starts shouting again. "Your mothers and grandmothers thought my father's car had dropped from the skies. They touched it as if it was the holy Kaaba. And didn't they think photographers could take their pictures without seeing them? So don't come telling me about your walkie-talkies and driving around in front of me in your flash cars."

Yet again I hear the sound of footsteps on the porch outside the door of my room and a faint chuckle, but I don't consider getting up this time. I wonder why the deep red tiles give a feeling of great warmth and delicious coolness at the same time. I can't believe I'm really here: although we took so long on the journey, it seems like magic.

I open my eyes and close them again, delighting in the mild, dry air, and the noises which remind me of normal life and mingle with the steady beat of my letters. I thought these letters fell asleep as soon as I closed my eyes, but they are still awake like me. I hear a different laugh, then Zemzem's voice, then the new voice more loudly. From Zemzem's uncomfortable tone, I know the newcomer is cramping her style. Zemzem makes an effort, but the new voice grows louder, full of laughter. I listen hard to it, trying to make out who it is. My grandfather speaks but is drowned out. "I don't want anything to eat or drink. Ruhiyya has been waiting for Asmahan since the crack of dawn."

At this I sit up sharply. Am I losing my mind? I haven't thought about Ruhiyya since we drove past the hairdressers, cafés and chicken farms. My grandfather lashes out again, saying that today is ideal for spraying the fruit; he curses the bandits, the young tearaways, the bearers of grudges, the beggars and pimps, shouting that their women are whores, that they pimp for their mothers and daughters and wives. The newcomer tries to silence my grandfather, but his voice, which makes a sound like a gramophone record played with a rusty needle, is not easily silenced and its rasping echo continues to reverberate all around the porch. I hastily put on my clothes so that I can go and join in, frustrated by my inability to hear properly because of the thick stone walls and the emotion distorting the voices. Is my grandfather weeping? No, he's laughing. Laughing and singing a folk song. The loud female voice silences him.

I came out, overwhelmed by the feeling that the day was almost over, that they had all got there before me, and monopol-

95

ized events down to the tiniest detail, so that there was no longer a place for me. The owner of the voice flung the tongs she was holding into the washbowl and swooped down on me. Ignoring Zemzem's expressions of disapproval, she pulled me close and kissed me, saying, "Thank goodness you're safe. Thank goodness."

She was the girl who had stared at us from a distance the day before when we arrived, who had seemed uncertain whether to approach us and then vanished. The smile never left her beautiful face and her blue eyes almost bored into me, so that after a bit everything seemed to be tinged with their blueness. Obviously mystified because I wasn't more friendly, she introduced herself as Juhayna and said that I had given her my hairslide when she was a child. I remembered her as a little girl, red-eyed from some allergy, and she said she still suffered when figs were in season.

I laughed in spite of my annoyance at being so much older than her.

"I put a bunch of flowers in your room," she said. "Naima and all the rest of them tried to stop me."

"Stop gossiping," interrupted Naima. "Perhaps Asmahan wants to have her breakfast."

"Why do you call her Asmahan?" asked Juhayna bossily. "Her name's Asma. Asmahan sounds so old-fashioned. She's not eating. Ruhiyya's been waiting for her for hours." Then she turned to me. "What do you think? Would you like to go to Ruhiyya's?" she said ingratiatingly. "When she knew you'd come she was over the moon. Really. She's crazy about you."

My grandfather returned from the small part of you below the porch. Dusting the earth off his hands, he said, "Today's perfect. No frost, not too hot, and there's a heavy dew. Just the day for the apples to get a colour on them. Ah, these poppies will break my heart, if Juhayna hasn't done it already."

Juhayna was still talking loudly and she seemed to want to provoke me, but my attention was distracted by the opium poppies swaying in the gentle breeze, flashes of white and scarlet in the sunlight, a vast expanse spilling out darker, deeper colours on to your yellow and green. For the first time I felt I had come face to face with my grandparents' tragedy, and I was deeply struck by the idea that this no longer belonged to us. The labourers' noisy shouting, the trucks and barrows no longer kept you company like before, and our house which looked out over our lost possessions was an empty shell. My thoughts strayed to the other houses in the distance. How had they all come to accept this change as normal? Why hadn't it made more of an impression on them? I watched their cars making their way through your orchards. Sounds of laughter and voices floated down, and the words of a song were audible on the breeze: "Come on in here with me for an hour, I want to play with you under the shower."

"It would have been better if they'd burnt it. Opium's like poison. It sucks the water from the soil, takes out the vitamins."

My grandfather is afraid for your well-being. Now he is comparing you to a snakeskin sloughed and shrivelling up in the sun, while I am wondering why Juhayna's voice annoys me. She must have snared my grandfather in the coils of her long, light hair.

"If only I'd had some sons. I would have let them loose on them like a pack of dogs, and watched them tear them apart, I swear it," he said dejectedly.

"See, it's your fault," I joked. "You should have married again."

"But you've got half-brothers, so Naima told me," interrupted Juhayna.

"Three of them."

"Is it true that your mother stole Afaf's shoes when she was staying with you in Beirut?"

"What if she did?" put in my grandfather with a laugh. "I remember them. They were red and shiny."

Juhayna came towards us and pulled me away from him. "Come on, let her get dressed. Ruhiyya's waiting for her."

My grandfather put his other arm around her, and drew my face close to his again. "Take me with you to see Ruhiyya," he begged. Then he asked me in a serious tone, "Please tell me, apart from you and your mother, have you ever seen anyone as beautiful as Juhayna?"

I turned my face away. "Grandfather, you're suffocating me."

"Let go of me," shouted Juhayna. "Do you want me to bite you?"

I was surprised at the way she talked to him, and had the sudden feeling that they were like two people of the same age. Old or young? I went into my room to change, overwhelmed with joy at being in the village and not in Beirut, and felt a rush of longing because I was going to see Ruhiyya in a little while. I went out into the passage and stared into the familiar old mirror. It was covered by a layer of dust, and seemed to have abandoned its role. I couldn't see myself properly. When I wiped it clean, grey semicircles remained like little birds here and there. In it I saw your calm reflection, looking as if you were still ours.

5

My Dear Billie Holiday

I think about you, once I am used to walking and can no longer hear my heaving breath as I try to keep up with Juhayna.

It could be that I haven't walked as far as this for a long time. I watch my feet as they hit the ground.

The war stopped us from walking with our arms swinging freely: instead we clutched them to our chests. We thought about whether what we were wearing would be suitable in the eyes of the passers-by and the armed men; as well as the actual visible barricades there were barricades in our minds which were far more powerful.

I am feeling relaxed and happy. Nothing can touch me now, not the occupiers of our lands, nor my grandfather's anguish. Your face appears, smiling at me, and I think about how you were no longer able to walk properly towards the end of your life. The drugs activated your mind and made it float and fly but left your body behind and made your legs useless. I no longer walked in Beirut; it wasn't because the pavements were almost non-existent, the streets all potholes and refuse, but a street should take you into a different atmosphere, to see different people, and the places where this was likely to happen nowadays could be counted on the fingers of one hand. Thinking about being able to walk doesn't remind me of you now but of Ruhiyya, because I'm going to visit her, and of what's growing in front of me, behind me, to my right and to my left: the green cannabis plants whose pungent aroma fills the air. If you had used hashish you would have ridden the horse and still been alive, but the horse of heroin controlled you instead and you stopped understanding where it was taking you.

Cannabis and opium poppies grow on the plains in the sunshine as far as the eye can see and even at the sides of the road; green, scarlet and white plants swaying gently, looking for all the world like tomatoes and beans. A hose winds over the earth and dry grass like a snake; an earthenware jug lies by the road next to a tin can. A dog begins to howl, and others join in. "That's all we need," snaps Juhayna impatiently. "Filthy mongrels watching everything we do."

She bends down and picks up a handful of stones and throws them at the dogs, swearing.

We see some cows drowsing at the roadside, nice and calm, and Juhayna comments that they have developed a taste for cannabis.

Again she bends down, picks up some stones and throws them at the cattle. They merely stare at the horizon, moving their heads from side to side. "They'd have a job to stand up."

The smell of the cannabis had begun to have an effect on me. Juhayna laughed. "My little brother wrote in his essay on spring that it has a beautiful perfume and looks like a lovely carpet of green silk brocade."

It had started to grow everywhere in the village. Juhayna pointed out the house of an old woman who had died without realizing that her land had been planted with it right up to her front steps. "It isn't like broad beans, bless its heart. Wherever you plant it, it springs up at once. My sister planted a seed and it had come through within a day. It's like a ball bouncing up at you. It's wicked stuff! It would even flourish on the coast."

I looked towards the horizon and the rocky hills stretching as far as the eye could see. They were almost bare of vegetation, and so was some of the agricultural land. I could make out a narrow track going up the mountainside. My grandfather used to point to it, insisting that it was going to become a tram-line, and I believed him. As we walked I saw the peasants' one-roomed houses, always white, whitewashed walls, with vine trellises at the side clinging to the window bars. At the entrance to one house was an American car parked next to a gigantic cannabis plant, as big as a tree. A woman standing with her husband asked about my mother and Beirut, and wanted to know if the people had electricity. When she withdrew her hand from mine and placed it on her chest I saw that her fingers were blackened and dry. This was Umm Kamil who had developed a passion for growing cannabis and was always regretting the past. "If only we'd found out about hashish long ago. We were crazy to grow courgettes and aubergines."

I smiled at Juhayna, wondering where she got her self-confidence. She behaved as if I was no older than she was, apparently unimpressed by my family and my education, not to mention the way I dressed. Her confidence undermined my own. I must seem old to her; she thinks I've missed the boat, which means my family must have missed any number in her eyes.

Inspired by my grandmother, who would get her own back by holding forth on any subject that occurred to her, I remarked, "It's the dry weather that makes the opium and cannabis grow so well."

"As if the Almighty's deep in the heart of them."

Her answer silenced me and I turned aside and picked a white poppy. I was surprised by the number of butterflies and bees on the flowers. To my astonishment Juhayna pounced on them and began picking more. "One flower! What's one going to do for you? But watch out for your grandfather, for God's sake. If he saw this, he'd eat you alive."

There seemed to be new villages on the horizon, and the paths had changed. I saw black patches on the earth and rocks. Juhayna noticed where my eyes were focusing. "That's what the Palestinians left behind."

"What about the other parties?" I asked her.

"They went to eat in people's houses, or their families brought them food," she answered, laughing.

When we climbed up on to the plains, heading for the higher parts of the village, the colours sang out to us. Although Juhayna was still walking fast, I found myself slowing down, enjoying what I saw, even the Syrian tank with its soldiers drowsing on top of it. I wondered how yesterday I could have wanted to return to Beirut, instead of being grateful that I was far away from Hizbullah and Amal and could bathe in water warmed by the sun beating down on the pipes, and take deep breaths of fresh air.

The moment I was in Ruhiyya's arms, I saw your face smiling at me again. Since I first became addicted to you, you have reminded me of Ruhiyya. It's not only your skin and teeth and your eyes with their permanently reproachful expression, but your personalities and voices. Both of you seemed to have been created from deep in the earth. Cotton plants and thistles grow in your land; Ruhiyya's is made of rocks and stones and red sand. You were nourished by sun and moisture, Ruhiyya by dry blazing heat, and both of you were shaped by the earth's tumult and grief, by your longing for sweet rain and the light at the surface, and then you both discovered the reality there, loving men passionately from an early age. You heard the blues played again and again on records rising and falling and spinning like globes in circular seas, and Ruhiyya heard them from minarets and in the songs of the Shia martyrs' passion plays.

Neither of you resorted to the pen, to writing your thoughts about your thoughts. Dealing with the surface and all that goes on there is hard, and instead you both sing the reality you live.

Sometimes your voice rises drowsily from your throat when every other part of you is asleep. And Ruhiyya's voice? I won't repeat myself. It's the same as yours.

Ruhiyya let out a welcoming trill of joy even before she opened her battered wooden door. She seized hold of my face, called me her beloved, light of her eyes, her beauty. I felt embarrassed at being the object of so much genuine affection and struggled to look at her. I saw her intelligent eyes, soft as if a transparent mist covered the surface of them, her deep brown skin, her thick lips and then her teeth which had changed dramatically. She turned to Juhayna: "What did I tell you? Didn't I say that Asma's different from anyone else in the world? There's no one like her. People talk about her family, but she's the one for me. O, Asma, my dearest. Why have you been away so long?"

Apparently this effusive welcome made her want to smoke. From her pocket she took a small tin containing cigarette papers and tobacco, rolled a cigarette, lit it and inhaled deeply. "There's nothing left but cigarettes. God's taken everything away from me, but He's left me them. Do you want a roll-up?"

"No. A pomegranate," I replied laughing.

Ruhiyya roared with laughter. Like you she used to be beautiful, and now she no longer was. Her teeth were the colour of tobacco and some of them were missing. Her lips were still full and brown, with a dark blue tattoo on the lower one like a gipsy's. Blowing out smoke, she asked me for news of Beirut, my grandmother, my mother, Fadila. But she changed tack when she realized I was reluctant to answer. "Never mind. Everyone's fine. It's tiring to talk. Everyone's fine. If they're not six feet under, they're doing great. But where's lover boy?"

Before I could smile in response to her remark, she turned away to talk to Juhayna: "I knew when Asma came you'd keep quiet about what you're up to. See how you've turned into her little pet dog." She laughed loudly, gasping and coughing, the cigarette clamped firmly between her lips the whole time. "Never mind," she managed to splutter out. "It's natural for people to want a better life, to want to sip tea and eat biscuits!"

I didn't understand immediately what she meant, although I sensed she was telling Juhayna off. But Juhayna was yelling back at her and her tone of voice made me think there was more to it. Before I had time to take it all in she was at the door, accusing Ruhiyya of being crude.

Seconds passed, and Ruhiyya seemed to regret upsetting Juhayna. "Where are you going, my beauty?" she said affectionately.

When Juhayna showed no signs of coming back in, Ruhiyya got to her feet to go after her, with me behind her, but Juhayna hurried out. "Come back in here," called Ruhiyya. "Come on, let's be friends. People like a joke every now and then, for heaven's sake."

But Juhayna was gone. "She'll come round after a while," remarked Ruhiyya, closing the door.

"It's her and my grandfather, isn't it?"

Ruhiyya laughed. Her mouth looked enormous and all her teeth and the veins in her neck were visible.

"You're priceless. You smell things out like a dog, even from a distance. You knew what they were up to from the very beginning, you sly thing!"

I was sweating all over and my heart was beating furiously. Ruhiyya talked so simply about my grandfather's relationship with Juhayna, as if it was a reality. Maybe she wouldn't have if she could have seen my grandmother as clearly as I could and pictured the effect this would have on her. I put the image out of my mind. I knew my grandfather better than Ruhiyya and Juhayna did. What was between him and Juhayna was nothing more than a bit of fun.

Ruhiyya was trying to remember the last time we met. "It was ages ago. He started teasing you and I had a go at him and told him he was bothering you. Do you remember? I feel ashamed now. I was like a police agent. Or Ataturk."

I nodded my head. I knew at the time she was cross with her husband because she was jealous when he flirted and wanted to touch my hair.

"I deserve to be punished! How cruel I was to him. And now I'm suffering for it."

She stood up suddenly, one hand high in the air. Waving it to left and right, she chanted,

"We are widows and our sorrow's deep inside
We are widows and our sorrow's deep inside."

Then she stopped abruptly as if doing so cost her some effort. Wiping her face with the palm of her hand, she changed the subject. "What's the nicest thing I can give you to drink, apart from my lifeblood?"

I laughed, but she wailed, "Didn't I shed my last drop of blood over him when he died? If it wasn't for these cigarettes I'd have been abstinent for months out of respect for him. I even took tablets so that I didn't have periods and could fast constantly. But I can't give up these damn things."

Looking at her cigarette, she stood up and went over to the door and bolted it on the inside.

"He knew he was dying. That's what was driving me crazy. Every time he took one of his anti-drink pills, he'd say, 'You're killing me, you're killing me,' and his eyes bulged like a frog's."

Taking her face in her hands, she wept.

"It was his brother that upset me. He wouldn't agree to have the funeral at his place. He said his son was at university and people would give him the evil eye. What an awful mentality! We held it here. Some people sat in the garden and some stood out in the street. You just hope for the best. You know how people feel about death. Not about life, though. My mother was right. She always said, 'Put your trust in God and your store cupboards.' She meant your cupboards have things in them which are worth cash."

Ruhiyya's husband was addicted to alcohol: arak, beer, cognac, whisky, then meths and cologne, any time of the day or night. This addiction of his made her shut her mouth and draw her head in like a tortoise. She couldn't bear being in a dark well, no longer performing her unbridled laments for anguished mourners, increasing and assuaging their suffering in equal measure. She didn't think that she had a right to sing in the Passion of Husayn, once everyone knew about her husband. For every year she used to re-create the tragedy of Husayn's martyrdom in her sad, tremulous voice, recalling humanity's eternal thirst, yearning to moisten the dry mouths. Her voice was the light in her life. She had discovered that she could do more with her mouth than eat and exchange trivial gossip, and that it distinguished her from all the other women. It was her genitals, her sex. And yet she had to curb it now, because she was no longer free to speak out and have her revenge. Thorns pricked her tongue every time she tried to sing.

"God, it's my fault! It was me who gave him a taste for drink. You know, I used to drink arak secretly. From the time he found out that I'd turned him down because I was in love with my cousin he went crazy. He no longer wanted to come near me. I said, 'Have a glass of arak.' I thought it would make him high and relax his mind so that his body would get moving.

Ah! There will never be anyone else like him. His mouth tasted sweeter than the sweetest fruit juice."

Then her face brightened again and she laughed at me: "I ought to keep my mouth shut. Why am I singing love songs to someone six feet under, when you're right here in front of me?

"O, Asma. O, Asmahan. Your name's always on my lips
I love you blindly, I pray my wishes will come true
And I'll see you here in a wedding dress
Before the oil in the lamp runs out
I want to ring the bells for you
And fire a round of bullets in the sky
In celebration."

Laughing in embarrassment, I tried to change the subject. "Have you planted hashish or opium?"

Her mouth opened wide as a cave again. "Do you want some? It'll be ready for you tomorrow."

I had kept up my friendship with Ruhiyya in spite of the difference in our ages. It made my grandmother and Zemzem jealous, and confused the local people. Whenever she visited me in Beirut the whole village knew about it as she made different kinds of bread and cream cheese balls in oil, picked pomegranates and practised her new songs. I was always delighted to see her, took her with me to the university, the cinema, the café, and made her spend the night with me rather than going to one of her relations; I even introduced her to Hayat and my university friends, and then to Naser in the war years. I had been attached to her since childhood, when I used to sit beside her while she did the washing and wish I could stay there for ever watching her hands rubbing and squeezing the clothes in the big bowl as she sang. She talked to everything around her, including a passing lizard. Drinking coffee in preference to tea, she would sit beneath the pomegranate tree once she had sprayed the earth with water to cool us down.

Year after year Ruhiyya kept me informed about her life; as a result I found out unconsciously why I had been drawn to her when I was nine or ten years old. How did she work out that I was worthy of her trust and friendship when I was so young? How did she put up with my daily visits when she had so much to do, and her mother was still alive, being awkward and demanding? I had been fascinated by her since I watched her singing the Passion of Husayn at the feast of Ashura, in particular the part where she wept as she depicted Husayn's thirst. I had tears in my eyes too; I really believed it was Ruhiyya herself who was thirsty and I wanted to fetch her a glass of water. The dust of Karbala which she sang about seemed to have settled on her lips and temples. I began to sob out loud. The girls of my own age sitting near me thought I had a fit of the giggles, as one of us usually did when we were squashed in with the older girls and women at the passion plays. To us these occasions were a night out, like a visit to the cinema. We regarded the women, especially the old ones who wept and wailed, as comic characters, and would giggle hysterically, our faces buried in our hands. Most of the time there was a break in Ruhiyya's voice, but she usually suppressed the tears and kept control of her vocal chords. Her sad image would not leave me and I decided to visit her the next day to prove to myself that she was a normal human being who did not spend her daily life on the verge of tears but sat eating fried aubergines off a wicker tray like everyone else. But I was right; she was not like the others: she hadn't been putting on the sorrow. She was suffering. She had lived through painful experiences which had scarred her soul. When they found a husband for her she was in love with her cousin and had tried to resist marriage in a song:

"O, mother, mother! Look at my red and swollen eyes!
How can you let me go?
Who will grind the wheat for you and make you
    macaroni?"

"I don't need anyone to grind the wheat, and I don't like macaroni," answered her mother. "The biggest favour you can do me is to go away and find yourself a husband. Then I can eat faraka made with the best meat."

"Tomorrow you'll sigh and complain and only the walls will reply. It's all over now. The mother raises the child and grows old and the daughter flies the nest," chanted Ruhiyya.

She tried to escape from her husband, hiding in the vineyards, behind the water cistern, in her uncle's house, and she managed to evade him for a whole month. But one morning when she was going out, her mother and her uncle's wife blocked her path and grabbed her by the hands and feet. Although Ruhiyya was strong she did not put up much of a struggle, believing that her husband would never throw himself on top of her with her mother and aunt there, and so she waited calmly with them. When she saw him approach her like a hungry dog who had found a bone she felt both curiosity and desire.

"When he rode me I didn't know what had happened to me. I began to call out, 'Get him off me. There's a fire burning me.' My mother and my aunt turned their faces to the wall, crying because they thought I would die from the pain of refusing him. They had got used to me shouting, 'No. No. No. I don't want to marry him. I don't know why.' Then I began to scream that I was being stung by a hornet."

I asked her what she meant by the hornet and the fire when she first told me the story. She had burst out laughing and laughed until the tears ran down her face. Then she clapped her hand to her mouth. "God! I ought to put pins in my mouth. You're still a child and I'm corrupting you. The things I tell you! But we mustn't tempt fate! I forget you're still a child. I talk to you as if you were twenty."

In the end she was glad she had married him. She discovered that he liked her voice, her forceful tongue, the way she always argued, her sighing, her moods. He told her he preferred her smell of cigarettes to the smell of newly washed bodies or perfume, and admired her because she was the only woman in the village who dared to smoke in public. She didn't automatically answer the door to everyone who came knocking; sometimes she claimed to be tired or under the weather, preferring to be alone with him and distract him from his work so that he would come and sit beside her. But he kept goading her to tell him why she had refused him at first and she acted coy, lied and avoided answering, until one day she came out with the truth – that she had been in love with her cousin in Beirut.

When I visited her she would smell me and say, "Please let me smell Beirut, the place, the people." I asked her if she knew it and she sighed. "It's where I lost my heart."

She had known the city since she went to her maternal aunt's there to help with the housework in exchange for board and lodging, while she learnt sewing with a seamstress who turned out to be more interested in making her peel garlic than teaching her a trade. She put up with it all because she had fallen in love with her cousin, who was aware of how badly his family was treating her and had whispered in her ear one day, "It's a shame this body only wears clothes from the market and those lovely legs don't have better quality shoes to set them off. You should use a toothbrush and toothpaste on those pearly white teeth instead of rubbing them with salt like my mother does."

To hide her emotion, and because he had pinpointed her weak spot, she burst into tears. "Where would I get the money to buy a toothbrush?" she wailed, striking her face.

The next thing she knew he was holding out his handkerchief to her and saying very tenderly, "I'll give you one. Never mind. Don't cry." Then, as if he regretted his tone or was scared of what it meant, he went on in a louder, harsher voice, "I'll get you a toothbrush. That's enough now. Stop crying."

He bought her a toothbrush, and a notebook and pencil; and he began teaching her how to tell the time, dial a telephone number and other things.

She was in love with her cousin but she perceived as she studied the words he dictated to her that there were things keeping them apart: for example, the huge books he carried under his arm, whose pages he delved into at night. She took some of them with her one day when she was delivering her uncle's lunch to him at work. Holding them in her lap on the tram she felt different from all the other passengers. She was certain that these books, and his tennis racquet, white tennis balls, thick white socks and especially his white tennis shoes were what divided them. That same evening she told her aunt that she wanted to enrol at the state school near the house, and she could see herself coming home in her black school overall with the white collar on which she had embroidered a green cedar tree.

But her aunt startled her by immediately broaching another topic: that of her return to her village. "Beirut's a heap of ruins," she began. "You know how to hold scissors and a needle, and there are men queuing up to marry you back home."

Ruhiyya blocked her ears and carried on dreaming. She begged her aunt to enrol her in the government school and her aunt replied, "You're seventeen years old and you'll be doing the elementary certificate. How can you study with girls younger than you? The girls here are clever. They'll laugh at you and say you're old and stupid, the biggest moron they've even seen."

Ruhiyya didn't give up. She even thought her cousin would help her prepare for the certificate exam, but he was not consistent in teaching her or buying books for her. He was changing. There was no longer the same tenderness and he did not seize the opportunity to be alone with her when she told him his mother had gone off to visit a relative. He only showed up in the evening, when she'd been sitting there all day waiting for him, thinking thoughts that made her pulses race. Ridiculous thoughts crowded in on her and images flashed before her eyes. She saw herself stretched out in front of him with no clothes on, pulling him to her, taking him by force and becoming pregnant by him. Then she saw the sheikh performing the marriage ceremony and herself sitting in their new home with a white telephone at her elbow.

A few months later her aunt was reading her coffee cup. "The person you're thinking about is going to marry his friend's sister. I see a truck taking a Singer sewing machine to the village, and money in your pockets and my sister buying meat and having faraka for dinner."

Ruhiyya simply shrugged her shoulders, pretending not to care, but she felt as if she was choking at the meaning implicit in her aunt's words.

"Why don't you go to the village on Friday, and I'll come too?" said her aunt.

Ruhiyya began to cry and beg her aunt to convince her son that he should marry her. Her aunt sighed deeply. "There's nothing I'd like better. You're like a daughter to me, but force doesn't work these days."

Ruhiyya did not know how another two years went by. She waited so long that time ceased to exist. She was waiting for him to look tenderly at her. She occupied herself with sewing and her aunt bought her a sewing machine and she made curtains and a cover for the radio and another for the television, chair covers, bedding for the family, underpants and shirts for her cousins. As she moved her foot up and down on the pedal, she sewed sentences in her head, all ending up in the same melody. Every time she sang it within earshot of the neighbours she heard them laughing and realized she had not stitched her words together well, especially the time she screamed them at the top of her voice:

> "I love you to death, my family
>   Pray God to grant you prosperity
> But why did I forsake the ABC
>   Just because of you?
> My joints seize up whenever I remember
>   How you did me wrong
> And all I have to say to you is
>   May God forgive you."

Ruhiyya didn't give up hope even when he finished his studies, graduated and was engaged and then married to a Beirut girl. She danced at his wedding to the song, "Beat the tambourines, good people, come," and in her head she changed the words to "Beat my head with stones, good people, come."

All the same, she never stopped thinking up verses and songs and when she recited them she felt close to him and her sorrow increased, but afterwards it abated. She did not return to the village until he took up a highly paid post abroad and travelled away. For the first few months she talked about Beirut as if she knew it like the back of her hand, dressed smartly and wore high-heeled shoes which got holes in them when she walked on the stony ground. The first thing she always looked for in the newspaper, which she still bought from time to time when she went down to the village square, was news of the country where her cousin was. She refused all the men who asked her to marry them. Most were schoolteachers in neighbouring villages and one was a man from Beirut whom she had already met while she was living with her aunt. But she wanted someone like her cousin, or at least someone with the same kind of job. After a while people stopped asking her. Her voice took on a huskier note and she sang folk songs and laments, rolled cigarettes, coughed and hawked up phlegm like a man, didn't care what people around her thought and laughed and joked with people much younger than her. In particular there was her younger cousin Jawad, who discovered when he was an adolescent that his cousin Ruhiyya, who used to dress him in his school overall and buckle his shoes for him, had made a lasting impression on him. He began coming to visit her in summer vacations and hanging around in her house with his friends.

So her house swarmed with adolescents who were fascinated by her. She joked with them, criticized them, advised them, and sometimes found herself caressing their hair and singing to them.

"A firefly kept me company one night
I thanked the Lord for sending it
Even though it was bite-size
At least it lit the darkness
But when I got thirsty
And had a drink
Tarzan the firefly swung down
And leapt into my mouth."

Ruhiyya opens the wooden door into the garden and the light floods in revealing her furniture, looking the same as ever. I follow her over the doorstep down into the hanging gardens as she calls it, or alternatively "my little patch of earth", in the middle of which is a single pomegranate tree with fruit growing right to the tips of its branches.

"Food from God, Asma. You sit on the step and I'll peel some for you."

She laughed and reached out her hand and rested it on my knee. "What's going on, princess?"

I answered like a polite schoolgirl. "Nothing. Everything's fine."

"Come on! You can't tell me you're looking so nice for nothing!"

Thoughts of Simon, the press photographer, even of Ricardo went through my mind. I shrugged my shoulders. "Everyone asks. Marriage and all that stuff. But who wants to fall in love or get married? I work only one day in ten. So I oil my hair, wash it in camomile, put courgette ends on my face, coconut milk in the bath. That's all."

She laughed. "I know you're waiting for my cousin Jawad. Why don't you go and visit him abroad? When he sees you he'll go wild. I swear my name's not Ruhiyya if I don't get you two together."

I felt embarrassed. I knew how Ruhiyya's mind worked, and she was looking at my breasts.

We heard Juhayna shouting from the street. "What's this? Danger? No entry?"

Ruhiyya hurried delightedly to unlock the door. "It's all right. It's someone perfectly respectable."

Juhayna came in full of confidence, laughing too. "Of course it is. I came back for Asma's sake. Come on, I want to take her for a walk. To show her the hairdresser's and the café. She asked me about them this morning. Didn't you, Asma?"

Having left the hilly parts of the village behind us, we walked along down on the plain, the hot air striking us in the face. I liked the feel of it and wished we could have a long spell of hot dry weather. In place of the winding arid streets were villas, apartment blocks and big cars standing out in the sun. All that in the space of two years? The café-restaurant had a neon sign which probably flashed on and off at night. A delicious smell of grilled meat floated up our noses. Smoke drifted over the tables and chairs and hovered above a line of washing which was visible in one corner despite efforts to hide it with an arrangement of dried grasses. I suggested to Juhayna that we should have lunch there. She hesitated, then said that most of the customers at this time of day would be men; the girls came later on in the afternoon. We went on round the café towards the door and saw Samira grilling meat over the stove. She rushed to kiss us both, and urged us to eat with her in her house. When Juhayna indicated that I wanted to sit in the restaurant, Samira shook her head dismissively. "I couldn't possibly let you," she said.

I tried to convince her that I had difficulty believing there was really a restaurant in the village at all and was curious to eat there to prove it to myself. She seemed to be the only person in the whole place apart from us, but then we heard the sound of a car pulling up. "I hope that's my husband," she said. "I could do with some help."

But it was an enormous black Cadillac and Juhayna rushed out, calling to the driver to give us a lift. Samira waved the smoke away from her face, smiling, and said Juhayna had been a good girl and taken care of my grandfather while we were away. "You came back yesterday, didn't you? I really must go and say hallo to your grandmother."

Juhayna rushed back in. "Come on. Shauqi's going to give us a lift home."

Samira didn't object; apparently she'd forgotten inviting us to eat, and I fancied a ride in this monstrosity of a car. I could hardly believe that girls had become bold enough to take lifts with men. When I was in my teens ours had been the only private car around here, and then the family without a name had bought one. I stopped myself thinking like this; it brought it home to me that I'd truly left the village behind and become thoroughly immersed in life in Beirut.

Shauqi opened the nearside door for us, and I followed Juhayna into the car. I said hallo to the round face brimming with sweaty well-being. The chaos which prevailed in the luxurious interior did not surprise me – plastic cartons, cigarette packets, a keffiyeh – but the high-quality paintbrushes attracted my attention. I asked who the artist was, certain it couldn't be the driver. Juhayna seized the packet of brushes and opened it. "God, does the martyrs' painter really use a brush like this?"

"Why? Do you expect him to use a broom?" Shauqi retorted.

I laughed loudly. Pleased at my response, he repeated the joke. "What does she expect me to say? Do people normally paint with yard brooms?"

His solid head shook with laughter.

"Yes. Painter to the martyrs. He gets down and does these paintings as if he's working the land. He goes from village to village. Comes back with these photos, and starts painting any old how. He's finally got lucky. He was never any good at anything. And now his paintings are hanging in every house."

It was his brother Abdullah who was the artist. He got to know the fighters in Hizbullah and Amal before they died, and painted them after their death. I expressed a desire to see these paintings and Shauqi said I was more than welcome.

"Now? In the heat of the day?" gasped Juhayna.

"It's not as if you'll be outside," he retorted. "We have air-conditioned rooms these days."

Then he inquired after my grandparents' health. "God give the old man strength," he added, making me tremble with rage. As if they were ill or frail! Suddenly I pictured them through the eyes of the villagers who used to come to the house to ask after their health or discuss work in the orchards, and then sit tongue-tied in their presence.

This luxurious car and the gold keyring must make him think he was superior to me. But my anger vanished when I saw the "air-conditioned rooms", whose furniture still amounted to no more than a few mattresses and cushions around the walls. His mother was very welcoming, and couldn't believe it was really Asmahan getting out of her son's car and coming into her house so informally. She went into the other room and I heard her swearing by Imam Ali that I was here in their house. Three women and a man crowded into the room. I was shocked by the man's appearance as he came up and shook my hand. I remembered him as the youth we used to call the elephant man. "You're the most famous person in these parts," teased Juhayna. "People are coming from Beirut to see you. Asmahan only arrived yesterday and she's come rushing to look at your paintings, you sexy thing."

I was annoyed by Juhayna's loud voice, and the way she tried to act as if she was in charge of me, but I acquiesced.

"Just for you, then," replied the artist.

If I hadn't been used to his facial tics and twitches, I would have thought he was making fun of us.

His mother shouted that he should bring the martyrs into the sitting room rather than taking me to that garbage dump.

The artist replied defensively that artists' studios were always in a state of chaos and I should know that. He spoke with a pronounced stammer. I stood up encouragingly. "If we may?"

"It's the ladies that gi . . . gi . . . gi . . ."

"Give the orders," his mother finished for him, as he led us into his studio.

We heard a loud noise coming from the room where the baking oven was. Juhayna stopped at the door. "You're working hard! Abdullah's going to show us the martyrs."

"I hope you don't have my nephew's photo there, Abdullah!" a voice called.

"Yes, here it is," he answered derisively. "In my pocket. What do you think I am? The Angel of Death, come to snatch away s..s..s..souls!"

I stood in the middle of the room, not believing what I was seeing around me. Was it his bad eyesight – he wore two pairs of glasses like compresses over his eyes – or did the paralysis in his left hand affect his right, or was it his mouth being down on one side that made the words falter between his thoughts and his tongue and interfered with the discourse of his paintings too? His mouth remained open as if he might be going to say something else. He separated the paintings from one another, spreading them out before us in this rubbish dump – I thought his mother's description was fairly accurate: there was a plate with the remains of a meal on it which looked as if it had been there for a year. Were these faces or incoherent scribblings? Had a tin of tomatoes been spilt and turned rotten in the hot air, or was this an attempt at colour? Did these lines end somewhere outside the painting because he hadn't seen the edges of the canvas? Was this a man's eye, or woodworm?

Painting was Abdullah's release in this war, and why not? He was like the people who had never picked up a pen in their lives except to note down their expenses, and then began pouring out their sorrow and anger on to paper as if they wanted to hold a conversation from the grave. Abdullah interpreted my lifeless response as follows: "Nobody sees these paintings without being st..st..stunned."

Juhayna had disappeared. I heard her voice coming from the room where the oven was.

"Everyone says, 'If only I could die a martyr so that you'd paint me.' Before the lads go out on missions they come knocking on my door. I know, but what can I do? I have to control my emotions and with a couple of strokes I get the face. Then I put the canvas aside, and whoever's martyred first I go back to his portrait and start filling in the details."

I asked him if they saw the rough drafts before they died.

"Of course. There was one who told me his moustache should be bigger. He took the painting home and had his photo taken alongside it the day before he was killed! Now anyone who wants to know if his son's in the party comes and asks me if I've got a photograph of him. As if I was Sherlock Holmes!"

I stopped examining the paintings and turned away, pretending to look for Juhayna. The place was swarming with midges, making it even more like a garbage heap. I caught up with Juhayna at the back door where Abdullah's mother and another woman were boiling quinces. The second woman, whom I couldn't identify, had her hand up to her face because of the steam rising from the pot and was muffled in a white headscarf, but her voice was clear enough: "Well, Asmahan, did you see those madmen's pictures? See how stupid they are. They're the death of their families. Their mothers put up with all the pain of giving birth to them, sweep up cow-shit for their sakes, and raise them. The fathers die a thousand deaths to keep their mouths stuffed with food, and go out begging to make sure they have an education. As soon as they're old enough, they say, 'Bye bye. We're off now.' "

Juhayna picked up the song. "Bye bye. It's time for us to go. Forgive us for what we put you through."

"You've got a lovely voice, you bad girl," interrupted one of the women.

"That's enough of your st..st..stories," shouted the artist.

As we stood there, we heard someone calling in the distance. "Juhayna!" Then laughter, then "Hey, gorgeous! Come and see us."

Some girls in brightly coloured dresses were standing in the yard of a building up on a nearby hill. "Who's that with you, gorgeous?" they asked.

Their manner worked like a charm on Juhayna. She began to laugh. "Eat your hearts out!" she shouted back.

She dragged me away, saying goodbye to the artist's mother who tried to make us stay for a meal.

The artist walked along with us and Juhayna turned off towards the building on the hill. "Wasn't that where Abu Ahmad's house used to be?" I asked Juhayna.

"You're right. But it's changed so much," she said. "They've added a warehouse, a factory, and rooms for the workers, and the house is beyond them."

The artist realized eventually that we were intending to visit the house on the hill and took his leave of us. The girls were still joking with Juhayna: "Walk straight, sexy! Stop swinging your hips. Do you think you're Madonna, you slut!"

She shrieked and giggled back at them until we were face to face with them. They recognized me at once and kissed me. I hadn't even remembered there were three girls in the family. They begged us to come home with them, tugging at the keffiyehs wrapped around their faces; Juhayna protested, telling them not to leave their work, then asked them if they had anything cold to drink.

We should have come to welcome you," one of them said to me, "but we were up to our eyes in work here."

We went into a vast room full of women and girls. One of the girls with us opened the lid of a large container and a blast of cold air rose up from the slabs of ice where water bottles, plastic bags, and an earthenware pitcher were being kept cool.

An old woman came up, kissed me on both cheeks and asked after my grandmother. Her face was hidden by a white scarf, leaving only her eyes visible. "Have a rest, mother," said one of the girls, but her mother insisted on helping us to a drink. Then muttering, "In the name of God, the Compassionate, the Merciful," she began to pick up withered bundles of cannabis from a small doorway through which they spilled in profusion. Another woman, sieving the shredded leaves as if she was sprinkling dried mint on a cabbage salad, said abruptly, "The Palestinian woman asked if mothers and daughters are paid at the same rate."

The older woman, by now intent on her own sieve, didn't answer for a few moments. "I don't know," she said eventually.

My eyes had grown accustomed to the darkness in the warehouse and I could see a boy hanging on to the window bars outside, calling his mother. Then he started to imitate every word the women said. It appeared his mother was one of two women bent over a workbench with a perforated strip running down it. With wooden implements like planes they ground the plants vigorously into pieces small enough to go through the perforations in the table on to the tiled floor below. The other women gathered it up to sieve it or carry it elsewhere, muttering, "In the name of God."

They carried the ground cannabis in shovels and sieved it by hand in progressively finer sieves until it was like powdered coffee, coloured green. The mother of the three girls went from one table to another, examining its consistency, murmuring "In the name of God, the Compassionate, the Merciful", under her breath. On each occasion the other women repeated this invocation after her and I felt as if I was in a temple observing some paradoxical ancient ritual.

Into the dusty shadows to the sound of the music playing on the radio came a young girl carrying a crying child. A woman went up to her, her brightly coloured dress trailing along the ground behind her, and seized him from her. "My baby's here! He's come to see his mother!" she exclaimed delightedly.

She took her breast out from the opening of her dress, concealing it with the black scarf around her shoulders.

Juhayna flitted from one woman to another, laughing, gesturing, and looking at me from time to time. A man appeared, obviously not from the village, and spoke to the mother of the three girls, mainly communicating by moving his head in one direction or the other.

"Please, Juhayna, take the baby for me," called the woman feeding the child. "I'm scared he'll be stung by a scorpion if I put him down. I want to pray the noon prayer." Then she turned to the girls' mother. "Come on. Tell the man to go. We must have a break and pray."

On our way back we saw the man who had been talking to the girls' mother. Juhayna said "Salaam alaykum," to him and he returned the greeting. "Does he understand anything else?" I asked.

"He's beginning to understand everything."

She told me how he had been the focus of sympathy when he first arrived in the village from Afghanistan, everyone asking him if he missed his family, if he ate enough, if he had enough blankets.

"He's from Afghanistan! What's he doing here?"

"What's so funny about that?" she answered critically. "They come from South America too. They're the ones who taught us about coca. Nobody knew about it before. And from Nicaragua. They want to trade arms. We've got it all. Did you think they were better than us? If you could see what the Afghani collects! Everything! Even Pepsi bottle tops and big empty tins."

I fingered the opium flowers which had died and felt like shreds of silk in my pocket. I did not speak until we reached home when I had to reassure Juhayna, who was starting to blame herself for being late back and not helping Naima with the housework. I heard her recounting the day's events to my grandfather and remarking what a nice person I was.

"She's really intelligent," responded Naima. "If she was a man, nobody would dare to take a scrap of land off her."

I went to my room and threw myself on the bed. I heard my grandfather's voice and Juhayna telling him I was tired, then Zemzem's voice, then Naima's. Finally the door was pushed open and my grandmother came in. "What is it, my love? Why are you so tired? Do you want them to heat up some water for you so you can have a bath? It's dark outside."

I replied that I wanted to close my eyes for a while. When she went on sitting there I knew she wanted to say something else. I shut my eyes. She picked up a towel from the end of the bed and covered me with it. I knew for sure the words were fidgeting inside her, but I kept my eyes closed. Clearing her throat, she sat back down on the bed and asked me if I'd gone visiting the grand folk with Juhayna.

"The grand folk?" I repeated scornfully, yet full of sadness. Who was she talking about? Shauqi, the artist's brother, who told his prayer beads with food stuck between his teeth. Or did she mean the house on the hill and its supervisors who could be heard everywhere singing out orders and threats, then agreeing docilely on the price of a load with two men who had ridden up in a huge car, two wheels down in a dip and the other two scraping and bumping along the side of the slope? The two were said to have links with Interpol so they knew about anybody who came to the village intending to spy on the dealers. The grand folk? Musa's son and his donkey? The fighter and his gun? The paraffin seller with his big can? I closed my eyes again, thinking that my grandmother's era had withered away like the crops on her land.

"Did you see the trees? Nothing but bare sticks! And opium growing instead of fruit? Everything's changed."

I made no comment on this but went on lying there with my eyes closed until suddenly she asked my opinion of Juhayna. Was she an angel or a devil? I opened my eyes and said, feigning innocence, that I didn't know. I was thinking of putting on one of your records; I would have liked to roll a joint and close the door and withdraw into another world.

I smiled at the thought of you and Ruhiyya, realizing more than ever why you two are similar: you both preach a religion of your own.

6

My Dear Grandmother

I know that my grandfather and Juhayna have an understanding. To describe it like that, rather than saying they are lovers, shows there is some confusion. We were used to him falling in love, lying in bed complaining loudly with his hand on his heart; and we were used to you assuring him with a smile that he'd get over it, predicting that before long he'd fall in love with someone else like he always did: for the heart is always on the move, looking for somebody else to love. When his torment persisted, you consoled him as if you were taking a sword to his delicate feelings and cutting them down with a single blow: "Everything changes. That's the way of the world. The fruit ripens. The branch becomes like a bare stick. The leaves fall off and new ones grow."

The shocking uncertainty hit us like a thunderbolt, and we could no longer make out what was happening between my grandfather and Juhayna. She was young but accepted his behaviour, while we were used to seeing him chasing women and being turned down by them. What we heard secretly from the twisted tongues of old women, was that the unmarried women only turned him down out of respect for you. Marrying a man who already had a wife was not a disaster; on the other hand it couldn't be regarded as an ideal marriage. This wouldn't have stopped them: my grandfather's vast lands, his way of laughing, and the fact that the exploits of his ancestors were engraved on the foreheads of newborn babies gave him untold power.

I remember that I blamed you inwardly for accepting this state of affairs and when the feeling became too much for me, I asked you about it. I can see you now dissecting the question, going into intricate detail to give substance to your arguments, until I was helpless with laughter.

You had a strange view of things; you looked from a particular angle, responded to a random vibration which nobody noticed but you. Your pale face was unmarked except for a few blue veins in your forehead. You said, "Nature, my precious, doesn't sit there doing nothing. It presides over us, observing, plotting, sniffing out information, and it knows I didn't have any more seeds after your mother and the child I lost. But it knows your grandfather has oceans of them. Every time he sees a beautiful woman they get busy and desire her and say if only we could get to know her seeds so that we could have fun, instead of being crammed into this dark body among the flesh and fat and blood and sinews. But the problem is that in your grandfather's body there are also eyes, a mouth, nostrils and more still in his head. Every time he goes too far with a woman these all send him stern warnings: 'What are you doing? Why? Does anyone else in the world have eyes like Sulayma's, speak like her, smell like her?' His mind functions separately, detached from him, as if he's put on a loose shirt which won't bother him when he gets hot. But it intrudes all the same. 'It's no concern of mine. If you want to fall in love with some woman, get an erection and sleep with her, that's your business. But I've got a special affection for Sulayma.' So this war between your grandfather's seeds and his mind, eye, mouth, and nostrils goes on all the time, as you can see. And then don't forget, my precious, that your grandfather's in a wretched position. On top of the seeds that sneak out through the window all the time, and attack him from all sides, when he turns his attention to me unfortunately he doesn't find even half a seed."

I listened to you and I wasn't surprised, as I've been used to your particular way of looking at things since I asked you one day when I was nine years old, "Do we come from she-djinns, granny?"

Then my eyes met Zemzem's and I added hurriedly, "You and me, I mean."

You noticed this and rushed at me like a whirlwind, smothering me in your embraces. "Come and listen, everyone," you called out at the top of your voice. "Asmahan's asking if we're descended from djinns."

Then you put your face close to mine. "How did you know?" you said, so I thought it must be true.

"We're not like other people," I replied. I turned to Zemzem. "But Zemzem doesn't come from she-djinns, does she?"

You burst out laughing. "Come and listen, everybody," you cried again. "Of course, you're right. Zemzem's not descended from the djinns. She's only learning."

This seemed to annoy Zemzem. "In God's name," she said, getting to her feet. "Really, Madame, that's blasphemy."

"She thinks we're not like other people. She doesn't really mean djinns. God forbid!" you replied in a superior tone. Then you asked me very earnestly, "Why do you think we two are descended from djinns?"

I thought about it for a while: it was difficult to explain to you, for I had never seen another grandmother like you. I found myself saying, "My mother isn't."

You held me close so that I could smell the rosewater you rubbed on your face and neck and breasts every day. "You're right. Only me and you," you whispered.

I thought I had neatly avoided explaining what I meant, but you started pressing me for an answer again. Images flashed through my mind which were too complicated to put into words. I heard your voice accompanying them. "My soul is like smoke and clouds in a chest at the bottom of the sea," you murmured.

At night I used to see you coming up to my bed in your long white nightdress, your pale oval face framed by curly black hair. You approached on tiptoe, pulled the covers up around my neck and kissed my face all over. But I couldn't describe what I felt. When you kept insisting, I answered that I didn't know another grandmother like you. Then I realized that being a grandmother didn't mean anything to you, since you were always saying, "Asma's not my daughter's daughter, or my own daughter. She's me when I was young."

You were still looking at me expectantly, and I wanted to appear extremely intelligent. I reminded you again how you had cured me of an illness by squeezing the juice of an unripe lemon into some broth for me, and rubbing my nose with a clove of garlic.

At the time I didn't tell you that while you were roaming restlessly around in the night I was awake as well, tossing and turning in my bed. You were like a character from the historical novels which we both read. I thought of Elissa, founder of Carthage, and Shajarat Al-Durr, Queen of the Mamlukes, because your curly hair sometimes looked like a luxuriant green tree. The long turquoise dress you sometimes wore reminded me of a Persian miniature. You were the Yemeni queen Arwa who went around the narrow streets of the hill town of Jabala interrogating the stones, with one big difference: you cruised around in a car which had faded crimson upholstery. All the same you never seemed settled there: your true place was in these somewhat shadowy regions of the past.

But I have described your face to you years ago. How it flashed like a djinn in a thunderstorm when I had lice, as if I had announced to you that there was hidden treasure in my hair. Zemzem said, "Maybe you caught them from Hajja Nazr's daughter. You and she were like sweethearts, perish the thought."

"Is that how they talk to high school girls?" you answered scornfully. "What sort of logic is that?"

When Zemzem declared that I must tie my hair back while I was eating, you scolded her again and added reflectively that man was about to land on the moon and so far no one had managed to wipe out head lice. Once you had said that, I no longer felt embarrassed about having them and went and sat in front of you while you rummaged about in my hair. There was a period of silence, broken by occasional mumbling. "This little lady's strolling along as if she fancies herself. She doesn't stray from your parting. She's keeping to her route like a soldier on the march."

Zemzem hurried to examine my head. "Yes, it's true! God forbid!" she exclaimed.

"If you could see it, Asmahan," you continued. "It's lost in the waves of your hair now. Enjoying the shade, the softness and the perfume of mastic."

I noticed how very cheerful you seemed, although I couldn't understand why. Then you started trying to pick out the eggs. I squirmed irritably. "I have to get them out before they hatch," you said, "or you'll have a whole army of lice there and they'll march you off wherever they want to."

"Is that true, granny?"

"You know it's not, but it might be. Who knows?" Then you went on, "Praise the Lord! How did He manage to invent lice? Creatures that live on someone's head, lay eggs, feed off the scalp and thrive in its heat; and then when they've had enough, off they jump on to someone else's head. I believe in you, Lord!"

When I thought about what you said, my head felt like a forest full of creatures living together and multiplying.

"You forgot the paraffin," began Zemzem.

"I'd rather cut off my hand than pour paraffin over her head," you shouted.

"Because of the smell?" I asked.

"That's right," you said, clicking the bones in your neck. "Because of the smell, and the soft skin on your head. It's not like a sponge that'd just soak it up. The smell might make you sick and addle your brain."

I sat on the bathroom table as usual, only this time I covered my lower half because of the little hairs starting to grow there. I knew you studied my body and knew it by heart, and felt proud whenever there was a change in it as if you were the one responsible for stretching it up and out. You lifted me off the table and told me to squat down in the washbowl. I couldn't see what this had to do with the lice, but you fixed a spray on the tap and sprayed my head as I crouched in the bowl. "There's one! And another!" you cried, as you spotted something black on my back or floating in the water, and caught it on your fingertips and wiped it on the edge of the bowl. "Out you come. We're trying to give Miss Asmahan a bath."

I examined the lice and counted them. Nineteen. You were still muttering. "Come on. Got you!"

You didn't stop until you'd finally given up hope of finding any more. I couldn't see your face but I could imagine it concentrating, concerned, like a shepherd with his sheep.

"That's the end of them!" Then you peered at the comb, and sang gaily, "O eggs, you're stuck in the teeth of the comb! All you'll give birth to is devils' dandruff!"

I entered your house as Asmahan who didn't talk straight. My tongue seemed disconnected from the rest of my body; I spoke in jerky uneasy sentences, and told lies, because I was used to having to justify myself, or cover up for my mother and sometimes even for our maid, Isaf.

You understood this and tried to return my tongue to my mouth and made it subordinate to my ears, eyes, and mind. You made me speak more easily and fluently.

I was pleased and annoyed in equal measure by the attention heaped on me. I felt like an unfamiliar metal which had to be tested with various substances before it would reveal its true nature. Sometimes I just wanted to turn out the lights and take refuge in sleep. When you hurled yourself over the porch wall at the sound of me, Naima and Zemzem all shrieking because I had fallen out of the fig tree, you were overreacting. But another time I remember you stopped me going to the bathroom when I was ill and brought a white chamberpot to my room instead. I asked if you were afraid of me being exposed to the air, since you had a fixation about the air, as well as the sun. But you waited until I'd finished and then examined the contents of the vessel with a twig you'd brought for the purpose, to determine how ill I was and whether you should call the doctor or wait a day. Then you raised my eyelids and counted the veins in the whites of my eyes, examined my tongue and told me to spit so that you could gauge my state of health. I didn't mind that at all.

When you took me away from my old school and sent me to a lay school you were peeling away the layers of skin until my core was revealed. I began to understand how to read and write for the first time. I carried my books and Ali took a cushion for me to sit on, in case the seats were too hard for my bottom. He drove me in the car in my clean overall as if I was Cinderella going to the ball.

I wasn't the only pupil brought to school in a private car. There were plenty of us, while in my old school there had only been one girl who didn't come on foot: she was driven in a horse-drawn carriage by a soldier in khaki uniform. At lunch time I used to hurry home to eat; the food was not always ready and I had to listen to my mother and Isaf cursing and swearing. Here I began going to the school dining room. Zemzem would arrive with my food shortly before the bell went and start heating it up on a primus stove she had brought with her from the house. She would sit facing me to make sure I finished my plateful, then clear everything away into a leather satchel and push a bar of perfumed soap and a small towel at me. The other girls gathered around me in amazement. Coming to this school, having new shoes and a mother in America seemed to put a gleam on my mind as if I had polished it with almond oil.

To return to the seeds, which seem to be different on our side, for they don't always sprout like maize as they do in my grandfather's case; sometimes they fall into a deep slumber. Take your mother: after your father had slept with her she hurried off, not to pump the primus stove, boil water and wash as is the custom, but to put the seeds in a glass jar and bury them in the darkness under the apple trees which surrounded the house. Your father was setting off on a long trip at dawn the following day, and if she found she was pregnant in his absence, she wanted to be able to exhume the proof of paternity.

I remember the rites which surrounded these seeds in our family. Everyone in the house knew that it was proper to wash straight after sex, but you used to wait in bed to give the seeds a chance. You called to Zemzem to boil water as soon as my grandfather went out of the door. I think you were showing off, letting everyone in the house know that he was constantly in your bed. Even Zemzem colluded with you and squatted down to pump the primus energetically until it roared as if to announce out loud why it was boiling water.

Many times I've wanted to get my grandfather away from Juhayna, but restrained myself out of love for you. This isn't the first time I've noticed I have some things in common with my mother. I don't mean those characteristics which are an exact copy of my mother's. For example, her impatience: she poured oil straight into a bottle without a funnel so that half of it went down the sink and the other half on her clothes, threw out all her keys because she couldn't be bothered with them, left drawers open, squirmed as if she was on the rack while Isaf or I did up the zip on her dress for her, pulled the buttons off her shirt if they didn't come undone easily, tugged at my hair ribbon with her teeth and if it was obstinate took a knife to it, ignored the salt cellar and took handfuls of salt from the bag. I've suppressed this part of me and fought against it for your sake. Once I was laughing unrestrainedly in front of Zemzem. You took hold of my head, pressed it against you so that I was no longer aware of anything but the smell of your dress, and raised your face to the sky. "I am your obedient servant. The older one's past help and now here's the little one. Open her mind, Lord, make her heart blind – tie the veins that make her want to laugh. Block her ears for ever against her mother's ideas and her grandfather's jokes."

When my grandmother married my grandfather and realized what he was like she became very depressed. She thought people who laughed all the time and had gregarious natures were suffering from a chronic disability. She became convinced she could change him, but all her efforts failed. Then she blamed herself for marrying him. She should have been on her guard: when his grandmother was brought to his father's funeral on a donkey, his mother had hidden her face in her hands and started to shake. The other women pulled her hands away, thinking she was convulsed with sorrow, and discovered she was laughing uncontrollably at the sight of her mother-in-law.

My grandmother was afraid she would have a child like my grandfather, with a frivolous personality, and prayed God not to bless her. When several months went by and she wasn't pregnant, she decided God had answered her prayers because he knew in advance that any baby she had with my grandfather would be laughing when the midwife pulled him out, instead of shrieking with the shock of the birth. She didn't want to ask God for anything more, and gave up opposing my grandfather and criticizing his temperament. She began to ignore the things which annoyed her about him until she no longer saw or heard them. When she eventually became pregnant she didn't give a thought to the newborn baby laughing, because she was too busy thinking aloud how she would bring him up to be lord of all he surveyed, by ensuring that he was intelligent, well-educated and wore sober ties. She would teach him to walk and talk in the first few months and to count and recite the letters of the alphabet when he was one. She would take him to live in Beirut, because although there were highly educated people in the village, they lacked manners. Hasan, who had studied in Najaf and even consulted the sheikhs of Al-Azhar in Cairo, wiped his nose on the sleeve of his jacket, and swallowed his drink in one go.

My mother finally arrived, and my grandmother claimed that she had dreamed these dreams for her child irrespective of its sex. However my mother showed signs of having a frivolous nature from early childhood. She hated learning and preferred to laugh and look at the world from under lowered eyelids and gossip with the girls who worked on the land. When she was fifteen she wanted to marry a wholesaler who bought from my grandfather, because he looked like a well-known movie star. She used to escape from her room; my grandmother had given her a room of her own, something rare for those days, but my mother felt that she was a prisoner in it, cut off from the village girls and their laughter. My grandmother wanted her to sit and read biographies of famous women and the translation of A Tale of Two Cities, since she had given up trying to persuade her to stay on at school. She didn't put pressure on her to read prayers and the traditions of the Prophet and the Quran with her, for my grandmother was a realist; she had known what kind of child she had from the time my mother first walked and talked.

I don't remember sitting and talking with my mother once I was grown up; on the other hand she used to tell me funny stories about herself or other people. She didn't want to know anything about me. Her way of showing interest in me was to say, "Watch out for your pussy! It's gold."

Quite often she'd point right at it and say, "It's lovely. God preserve it! It's a gold mine!"

I don't think I heard her talking seriously about anything to do with either of us, except once, although I didn't believe what I was hearing at the time. I introduced her to Naser on one of her visits to Beirut. She was chewing gum like a teenager, which seemed out of place, given the glamorous dress she was wearing, her long painted nails and her gold watch. Nevertheless, she spoke suddenly in a calm, measured tone, and it could have been my grandmother: "God guide Asmahan and set her on the right path. She won't meet anyone like you, but let's hope she'll meet someone else. I know you're going to make her happy sometimes, angry many times without meaning to, and force her to sleep in a different place every day. She'll be frightened about what happens to her when you have to go, and frightened for you even when you're still with her. She's going to lose all her friends because they'll be scared to visit you. The time will come when you have to run for your life and leave her behind."

Naser gave me a look which I understood to mean that my mother was not the person I'd talked to him about. Nor was she the person whose laughter I'd shared even before I understood what her stories meant. I had seen her slapping her thighs with mirth, putting her hand over her mouth, clapping Isaf on the shoulder and laughing, laughing, laughing, until I was convinced laughter was something which accompanied all human activity: eating, praying, even grieving.

When my mother found out about me stealing from a family who lived in a neighbouring street, she laughed. She turned my father's prayer-times into a comedy, fixing an improvised tail to the back of his pyjamas. When he went on for too long *she hovered about him, asking questions which he steadfastly ignored. She even managed to give the Quran recitation for my father's spirit a farcical dimension. When she got bored she interrupted the sheikh's performance and offered him a glass of water. Then she pressed food on him and advised him to take a break. The moment he resumed she suggested he should go to the mosque to recite in the company of other worshippers, and gain every possible advantage for my father's spirit. He refused, and then she actually begged him to stop, claiming unblushingly that the memories were too painful. If there were no women visiting to offer condolences, she asked me to make a lot of noise to distract him while she took a nap, or else went to see Fadila. Before the mourning period was over she stopped opening the door to the sheikh, but made fun of him as he stood outside, telling him point blank that he had never been to this house to recite the Quran for her dead husband. By shutting the door in his face, she opened the way for the soul to return to our house, energetically setting about re-arranging it until it no longer bore the slightest trace of my father's memory.*

I am behaving now exactly as my mother behaved when one of her friends took my grandfather seriously and began to make plans, in the belief that nothing could be easier than dominating a man who cracked jokes and laughed as he did, and had a daughter with a similar affliction. What the friend didn't know was that my mother had eyes as sharp as a hawk. Now I want to find him another woman whom I can control, which is exactly what my mother set out to do. I must keep my eyes open, get hold of the girls in the village and pick one who, if nothing else, has freshness and youth in common with Juhayna.

For my grandfather has grown accustomed to the fragrance of a moist, dewy mouth. He won't be satisfied with pinching flesh which is not soft and juicy, as he used to be in the past, or paying compliments to a mouth containing gaps and gold fillings. I know that it would only take a new female joining the household to make him happy again, even if he had to content himself with watching her talking, walking and doing her work. Before Juhayna he used to like to joke with a new girl, maybe pinch her, and play the game of cat and mouse, but Juhayna has corrupted him, and we must teach him to play harmless games again.

Juhayna consciously exploits her hair and figure, making their presence felt in every room and every nook and cranny. Her voice is omnipresent; it trembles in the air around us and permeates everything we do, even weaving itself into our pillows at night. She washes her hair and dries it in the sun, and it looks like shining falls of honey. She washes her clothes very carefully and slowly, and as she rubs them she's reminding us that they'll be on her body as soon as they've dried in the sun. She hangs them out as if to say, "These are my clothes. This is me hanging free in the sun and wind so the old man can touch me and desire me."

The sound of her footsteps and the echo of her voice batter our senses constantly. The smacking and cracking as she chews her gum reverberates in our ears and fills us with bitter thoughts. She has no inhibitions about turning the taps full on, as if she's saying to us in the rush of water, "I'm free. I don't care about anybody or anything."

I know my task is difficult, like my mother's before me. She managed to persuade the woman we knew as "Masabhi's wife" to agree not only to come to the house, but to smile at my grandfather, let him flirt with her and accept his gifts. My mother wouldn't have chosen her if she hadn't been sure that there would be instant benefits: my grandfather would forget Layla, who wanted to make him forget himself and his family, while Masabhi's wife was like a rose on top of a pyramid of thorns or a pressed flower in a book, addicted to the thrill of fear which went through her at the thought of her husband. I never knew her first name and still think of her only as Masabhi's wife.

I know it's difficult; it's not just a question of choosing the most suitable candidate – find another girl, and that's it. There won't be another like Juhayna, for Juhayna is as rare as Lolita. In case you don't know, grandmother, Lolita was a child who saw the desire in a man's eyes and played with it. She chewed it like a piece of gum and sucked all the sugar out of it, then blew a bubble with it and popped it and rolled it in her fingers, playing with it and watching it disintegrate in her hand. That's what Juhayna wants to do, so that she can eat biscuits, as Ruhiyya said. Not only biscuits, but the occupied land, the house, and even our souls.

My task is difficult because you know that there are no longer streams of girls as there were in the past, desperate to work in houses to escape the monotony of tending the fruit trees.

When you asked them to leave the land and come up into the house to help Naima, they were delighted and thought their luck was in. To them the house was like an enchanted castle. It had cool water in an earthenware pitcher; the aroma of meat grilling floated down to them as they worked in the sun, and they heard the radio playing, and the boss laughing on the shady porch. But now, if they don't fancy working with hashish and opium, they can go to the maternity hospital run by women who will train them to become nurses, or the schools and institutes set up by the Iranian Embassy, who have begun to distribute free exercise books with Imam Khomeini on the cover, and there are the Islamic cooperatives and pharmacies and all the other businesses run by the young men of Hizbullah.

Before Juhayna, you declared confidently to us that his liking for other women wasn't serious, otherwise you wouldn't have moved to Beirut. When my mother married again you had me to live with you in your house there, where you'd rarely spent more than a week at a time in the past. You sensed a germ of intelligence in me and realized that the fact that I didn't do better at school could have been due to the abnormal atmosphere at home. In fact there were two atmospheres pulling against each other, with me in the middle: my father's praying on one side, my mother's singing on the other, and if they were in agreement over the act of weeping they disagreed on the reasons. My father wept out of fear of God every time he lay face down on the prayer mat, and my mother because the film she'd been watching hadn't turned out the way she wanted.

Nobody knows if your move to Beirut was just for my benefit

or for yours as well. As time passed, I began to understand why you visited the village less and less often. You grew to like city life. Everything you did was of such delicacy that it appeared to be wreathed in drifting smoke. You woke up in the morning, revelling in your bed, which looked as if you hadn't slept in it, unlike the violent turmoil of the bed you shared with my grandfather. Even your pillow appeared untouched. You did your ablutions, prayed and drank your tea before I got up, and I marvelled at the calm enveloping the house.

You rose full of pleasure in the morning and I heard you addressing the sun or the clouds from your window. Then you looked in the mirror and murmured to yourself, "Perhaps I didn't sleep well. My eyelids are swollen."

You fetched a bottle of rosewater, poured some on to a clean piece of gauze, and placed it over both eyes and lay down. "Bless the Prophet and his descendants. Rosewater is fragrant, like the gardens of Paradise," you murmured.

Afterwards you went around the house as if you were walking on eggshells, swaying gently from side to side. You listened to the news and songs that made you happy, read translations and the traditions of the Prophet and walked in the garden every afternoon. You received neighbours or women who came visiting from the village; after a while you felt that they were an interruption, as the boredom began to outweigh the pleasure. The conversations you had with them were ordinary. You preferred talking to yourself or to young students. You liked eating alone, explaining, "God forbid that anyone should see me chewing my food like a cow."

You sat looking as if the dishes of food were beneath your notice, taking even your favourite things slowly and daintily, and eating in abstracted silence to convey the impression that, rather than eating, you were thinking about important matters. You chose the moments when everybody was preoccupied elsewhere to go to the lavatory for we never even heard the cistern flushing. Only when you performed your ritual washing did you pray in a loud voice. You prepared for the night, for your tidy bed again, picking a jasmine blossom or a sprig of honeysuckle to put in a coffee cup on the little table by your bed, calling to Zemzem to make green tea and sipping it as if it was the elixir of life. "The smell of it gladdens the heart," you murmured.

Then you changed your long white dress for a nightgown and sat in your room listening to the radio, leaving Zemzem to watch the television news in the sitting room because it disturbed the calm waves around you, even if you turned the sound down. You didn't like the way the people looked, letting fly at an overdressed female news reader and describing the programme's suave male presenter as tedious.

If I came back from school and saw you with your head bound I knew you had a headache. You would wrap it in a piece of red cloth and say, "Red. Like the blood pounding in my head."

When you called me to lie beside you, convinced that your pain would vanish as soon as I was close to you, you would lay a piece of gauze on the pillow so that I wouldn't be infected by your sore eyes. But having done that, you would take me in your arms and kiss me all over my face, head, hands, neck, chest, back and even on my mouth, telling me how much you loved me.

When I saw your vanity case, my curiosity got the better of me, even though its contents never changed; nothing new in it, nothing missing: hairpins shining in their little packet, various kohl jars, dried grasses in a paper bag, a sheet of paper folded inside another one in an envelope, a ring with a dark blue stone set in diamonds. I took the box to my room and sat cross-legged like you poring over it, leaning forward like you did, and took out a kohl jar. You made up your eyes, looking in the little mirror in the lid without blinking like my mother or Zemzem, your gaze wide and steady, and I tried to imitate you. Then I took out the box of face powder and opened the lid which had a picture of a woman like a Roman empress on it. What colour was this powder? How was it I'd never seen any like it before although I was quite familiar with different types, including what my mother and Fadila kept on their dressing tables?

One day I asked you about this strange colour, and you smiled proudly and assured me that you didn't follow others blindly like a sheep. You told me how you mixed three types of powder together to produce it. I asked you how you'd come to invent it. "When the spring comes, I'll show you," you answered.

I looked into your eyes. The big greenish-brown iris almost dominated the white which was so white as to be nearly blue. Then I looked at your strong, slim fingers, your short nails and the sleeves of your dress which hung down, almost covering your slim wrists. You were like a queen bending over to pick a flower.

The spring had come. "Please forgive me, little one," you said, prising open a flower bud and showing me the colour of the powder inside, pink, browny-red, peach and even white. I also remember you showing me the "shy plant" and you said I mustn't let anyone else know the secret, to protect the plant. You struck it gently as if caressing it. "Come on. Be shy," you said and the plant responded at once by going limp. After a while it stood up as straight as before. "You see. A woman must be shy like that sometimes too," you told me.

I'm sure I've said before that I've never seen you shy, but I've seen you humble when you read religious books and say your prayers.

You live in Beirut without my grandfather whose idea of a serenade is:

> O your pretty red panties
> Aren't half as pretty
> As what's inside them
> And their fringes and lace
> Drive me crazy.

He flies into a rage if he's hungry and there's no food on the table, wants to be able to tell his jokes, say what's upsetting him, recount his dreams whenever he feels like it, even if it's the middle of the night. Everyone criticized you for living between Beirut and the village, not staying with my grandfather.

None of them guessed that you were happier doing that because you had worked out that when you lived with a man you needed to have an airing from time to time like clothes in your wardrobe.

I realized that you weren't happy with a lot of things to do with my mother and Isaf and our house, even though at the mere sound of your name my mother listened intently to the conversation and stopped laughing and joking. She was afraid of you, and always tried to see to it that you didn't know all her business. She wanted you to approve of her. It seems I too needed to hear your reaction to what went on in our house, and I told you things that I knew were supposed to be kept from you. As a result I was the cause of your final break with my mother. You took me in your arms, asking me if I loved you. "I want to stay at your house," I said, preparing the ground for your next question, "Why, my love?"

I knew full well that I was going to regret what I said. "Because Mum and Isaf argue about you and my grandfather, about my Mum's friends that grandad loves," I answered, my heart pounding.

You told her in a voice gentle as the breeze that you were afraid for me because of the way she carried on and it was wrong for a child like me to live in a house that was more like Khan Toomain than a family home. You grabbed my hand without discussing the subject further, and led me towards the door. I looked back at my mother and Isaf, upset at being the cause of their distress. They wouldn't let me go with you. They swooped down on you, trying to pull me away from you, and you suddenly let go of me, your chin trembling, swearing that you would never set foot in this house of ill repute again as long as you lived. "Unless there's an illness or a death," you added as a parting shot.

My mother screamed after you that you wanted to bring us bad luck; you were hoping for our downfall; you'd never loved her.

You stopped visiting us after that. My grandfather still came, in spite of that day's events, which I tried to blot out of my mind. For a long time I even suppressed my curiosity about the place called Khan Toomain because I didn't want to remember my bad feelings. A long time afterwards I found out it was where the peasants rested themselves and their animals on long journeys. For two piastres they bought a ticket which allowed them in, then they unloaded their donkeys and lay down on their blankets wherever they could find a space.

To this day I've never told you exactly what happened when my grandfather visited us. I was frightened that you would accuse me of betraying you. And I was betraying you, even though I was so young. My mother's face used to light up when grandfather appeared. She would exclaim delightedly at the good things he brought with him and hover around Ali like a bee around nectar as he unloaded the car. Grandfather said to her, "For heaven's sake, you don't have to be so pleased about a bit of flour and cooking butter! Be more serious. You're married to an important merchant."

My mother laughed in reply, rushing to see to the boxes and bags in case Isaf hid them somewhere and she couldn't find them.

My grandfather tried to tell her in a light-hearted way that it wasn't all for her: he'd brought presents for the women who pampered him and gave him their affection. He had a reason for everything he brought. He'd give them a bag of almonds and delicate little green plums, saying, "To make you drool like I do when I see you!"

He even told my mother that whoever had the biggest breasts would get the lion's share. "To be eaten raw without salt or spices, just like you!" he would say as he set a piece of meat before them.

They snorted with laughter and struck him playfully on the shoulder until Isaf came and snatched it away from him and began to beat it to make kibbeh.

They waited impatiently for his visits, taking it in turns to pray that he would soon be there. He took them to summer resorts and invited them to dine in famous restaurants where they relished being among the beautiful rich women who dominated the gossip columns. Sitting there with garlands of jasmine around their plump necks and plates of food in front of them they were exultant; not that they were desperate to eat, but it was just so enjoyable to have someone waiting on you while you smoked a cigarette or a hubble-bubble, and it made you feel important.

Did my grandfather bury his face in Juhayna's breasts, or was he content to touch them? Did he ask her to take off her clothes for him? And was he bowled over by the parts of her which he had only pictured in his mind till then? Or did he just like chatting, and find that affectionate talk, which was sometimes honest too, made him feel masculine?

And what about desire?

I can't imagine my grandfather doing anything less than planting a kiss on both cheeks, reaching out a hand to the shoulder and the thigh, and then as he touched the breasts, saying, "God bless you! You're getting very strong and healthy. God bless you!"

Zemzem and Naima were like two lionesses eager to hunt Juhayna down. They were afraid that her stomach would swell up and bring shame on our family, and my grandfather would be forced to marry her. It didn't seem to occur to them that he might not have any seeds left, as they were certain that the men in the villages didn't age unless they were ill and approaching death. Zemzem was eager to stay awake till first light to catch them alone together, but I refused to join her, although I was curious, and I deliberately put the idea out of my mind. He must think he's entitled to his relationship with Juhayna, that it's fate. If we asked him about it and mentioned her age he'd probably say that he hadn't forced her, and she often seemed older than him.

I must admit I stopped bothering about what was going on between my grandfather and Juhayna after a few days. When I saw him looking happy from time to time I even thought their relationship was a blessing. His cheeks were pink, his hair looked less grey, he was in love again and forgot the pain, for a time at least, although it must be like pincers in his flesh every time he turns his head and sees the orchards.

Until I found myself listening to her, perhaps because it was night time, and at night conversations become real. She was in

140

her nightdress, with no gold, no chewing-gum or blue hair ribbon. She usually kept the ribbon in to protect her from the evil eye, since her sister – who was veiled – had tried to cut off her hair while she was asleep. To my surprise she seemed innocent, sitting on my bed with her chin propped up on her elbows, and I could see nothing in her face but a young village woman's naïvety, as she asked me if I had been in love with one of Yasser Arafat's comrades.

I had no doubt she had brought up this topic in order to talk about my grandfather. But she didn't talk: she undid the buttons of her nightdress and I wondered what she wanted me to see. Then she peeled off her nightdress and bra while I sat there dumbly, too shocked to react. I saw mauve bruises made by teeth or fingers. My grandfather's? Her nipples were big, round as moons. I pictured my grandfather's hands on them, his teeth, and shuddered in disbelief. I looked down at the floor. For the first time I calculated that he must be in his seventies. I didn't think about why this had happened, but I felt annoyance rather than the sympathy she seemed to want. I was still dumbfounded by what I saw and disconcerted by the fact that I couldn't imagine what was going on between them. Had I encouraged her without realizing it? Had my silence been taken as acquiescence?

It was as if he didn't care about keeping their relationship secret. As the dark bruises grew larger before my eyes I wondered if he intended to marry her because everything around him had run dry. Marry a girl and become young again, turn a new page and bury you, me, the land and the past.

I remember Ruhiyya warning me against having Juhayna as a friend because she was scheming to get control of the land, especially if she could give my grandfather a son. As soon as the old man died she'd be off in a fur and diamonds to a famous composer; he'd write a song for her and she'd be a star. She'd progress from tea and biscuits to Nescafé and gâteau. "Listen, Asma, my dear," Ruhiyya had admonished me, "everyone wants something from someone else. The ant wants a grain of wheat. The wheat wants the soil. Why they want it isn't important. It's what they want that matters. I wanted my

141

husband to love me without being out of his head. He wanted drink. Death wanted him. It's not that difficult to figure out!"

I looked hard at Juhayna. Was she being extremely clever when she chose my grandfather? Whatever the reason, in choosing him she was merely choosing the past which had proved its authenticity compared to the bearded leaders, the conflicting voices, the clash of arms.

Juhayna sighed as if she understood my silence. "I don't know what I'm going to do. If I left your grandfather, I swear he'd die."

Then she was silent in spite of herself, but there was eloquence in her silence too. She fastened her bra and put her nightdress back on. How had it happened? My grandfather seemed like a sick child with you, looking at you with a lost, tearful expression, his eyes begging, "Please God I die in your arms."

You put hot vinegar poultices on his head to try and bring his temperature down, read to him from your book of prayers and invoked the great leaders of the faith one by one. Did he make dark bruises on your body, or didn't he dare? I can't picture you closing your eyes in shyness or ecstasy when you're in bed with him. I know how you're always full of thoughts and feelings, and I'm sure you've never abandoned yourself in his arms.

I didn't know why Juhayna was showing me these bruises or how to respond. Then, suddenly angry at myself for this uncertainty, I was you in a flash, answering her with practised hypocrisy. "You're young. He's old enough to be your grandfather. Don't bother about whether he lives or dies. Think of your own situation. You're the important one."

"I love him. You won't believe it but I do. He's like a little boy. He's no older than me. He's not like my grandfather. I love him with all my heart."

I let my eyes rest on her for a while, on her hair streaked with gold, and wondered why she wanted him. Why she was planning to become mistress of this house and these fields, allowed an old man's hands and false teeth to roam over her body, let his rough vests and underpants rub against her? Or were mine the feelings of people with possessions, while those who had none went through their lives like thirsty travellers blind to everything but the trickle of water they had glimpsed in the distance? What did she expect when she showed me her bruises and talked to me like this? That I would arrange their marriage? She had stuck to me like a shadow before finally telling me her secret. She wanted me to be a witness to her love and give it my blessing. She must have told him that I'd guessed what was between them and yet had done nothing to break it up, and that my failure to say anything meant that they had my agreement. And here she was waiting for a sign from me so that she could tell him that his family had no objection, as if she assumed that you and I were the same person.

I knew she distracted him, a little at least, from brooding about the land. She involved him in all her gossip and this became their own private world, their source of entertainment – how Zemzem looked at her, what you said and whether you were aware of their relationship or not – and in the end this world also became a protective armour for her when she had to confront people's criticism.

I started pretending to be asleep whenever Juhayna came into my room at night and saying I was tired if she came to see me in the day. I refused to go out with her, talk to her, or even look her in the face. She must have begun to feel that the dreams she had woven when you and I were far away, and believed that she could realize with patience and guile, had collapsed as soon as we returned to the village.

She talked to me about it one more time. I looked straight at her and chose the words you would have used, saying that I loved her and that was why it hurt me to see her having a relationship with my grandfather. She shouldn't destroy her future, he was close to death and she was in the prime of her youth.

She shouted back that we were heartless, leaving my grandfather to suffer as his lands were occupied under his nose, while we stayed happily in Beirut, and that we should be grateful to her for preventing him from landing in trouble with the occupiers.

It didn't end there. It seemed more as if this fired her up; I heard her arguing with Zemzem, and my grandfather, and stamping her feet in anger. Then she came back into my room, even though I was pretending to be asleep, and wouldn't go away until I opened my eyes and listened to her. She said accusingly that everyone had changed towards her, that she had done nothing wrong and hated all this spite and ill humour. I saw her as a burden, like the occupiers, and couldn't feel any pity for her even when I saw she was crying. Instead I reflected that things had really changed in the course of the war, and I must get her out of the house. I thought of a cat being dumped in the wilds and making it back home in time to greet its owner, miaowing loudly, as if to ask what had kept him. How could I prise my grandfather out of her claws if I didn't find a substitute? In the evenings the girls walked around singly or in groups chatting and laughing together in front of the fighters whose eyes were fastened on their hips. The fruit in my grandfather's orchards was no longer picked by girls breathless with the heat of the sun and their longing for men, marriage and motherhood. Where were they, these girls who used to descend on the fields after the harvest to gather the fallen grain in their bags? I remember asking you what they did with it. "Grind it and eat it with sugar," you said.

Especially on Easter Sunday at the beginning of spring after February had passed, lashing the trees and sky with its fierce winds, I used to go with them to look for wild flowers.

We looked for balsam flowers to make our faces whiter and our eyes larger. Zemzem put all the flowers we had picked in a pot on the porch. Early next morning Yamama and Khadija slipped in and woke me quietly and we washed our eyes with the liquid from the flowers steeped in water overnight mixed with dew, until one day an adder got there before us.

Juhayna started disappearing, but not completely, like a beautiful bird vanishing into a cranny in a building and leaving the tip of its tail visible, until one night, bird and tail disappeared altogether. My grandfather waited for her, sipping camomile, coffee, tea, with noisy slurps and belches, smoking, throwing stones at the invaders' tents. He laughed wildly. "I should have learnt to play cards and drink forbidden liquor, instead of being obsessed with the land and female flesh. I wasted my time hunting, or falling for brown eyes and blue eyes. But now the land's gone and all I've got left is that brat, and she's disappeared. I wish I was dead!"

He was not the only one waiting for her. We all were, especially Zemzem, who was convinced she was planning her revenge on us. Zemzem began looking for someone to go with her to visit Our Lady Zaynab's tomb, so that she could pray to her to protect us from harm. My grandmother accused her of inventing these fantasies because she wanted to go to Syria and buy gold cloth, eat Syrian pastries and bring back some mastic.

My mother used to make vows to Our Lady Zaynab, the gold earrings and liras which she intended for the offertory box held firmly in her hand as she prayed and pleaded. She would back away from the tomb, whispering, "Our Lady Zaynab, you understand how great my need is. I want to wear these earrings for a bit and you have such a lot, bless you. Let me owe you this vow, and next time I promise you I'll make it two."

My grandfather had become like an addict needing his fix, or a prisoner pacing his cell waiting to hear his sentence, when Juhayna reappeared, taking her time, her hair down and the gold belt in place around her waist, the top button of her blouse undone, and an air of affected simplicity. "I've been busy," she remarked casually.

My grandfather tried to be sarcastic but his sarcasm turned to anger, then when he was angry his words sounded pitiful because he was so full of reproach, and he swore that he would not let her out of the house. Their voices grew louder and louder. They were standing on the porch and he was shouting and swearing at her, forbidding her to go. He sounded like old men do when they've completely lost their memories, and he certainly seemed to have forgotten our existence, even yours: you had been publicly humiliated and I felt scared for you and for what you were thinking. Surely it hurt you to be in a weak position in front of the other women in your own house. We took refuge in our rooms like bees who had discovered that the meadow air was polluted. Juhayna's voice filled the porch. "Go on, ask your granddaughter. She wants to see me well and truly screwed. What are you going to do? I need to know where I stand. What are you going to do? I want action, not talk."

Perhaps this was a storm which had to happen before calm could be restored. It was replaced by one of another kind: a whirlwind of perpetual motion. My grandfather, the child, began to refuse his food or to criticize it: he would have liked to stop eating altogether but his love of food wouldn't allow him to. The air was filled with his shouting when he went into the kitchen, stirred whatever was on the stove, tasted the broth and burnt his tongue. He slaughtered a chicken even though there was already food cooking and came in with it dripping blood everywhere. He began yelling threats at the occupiers all the time instead of just when Juhayna wasn't around, and prayed to be made blind and deaf so he wouldn't have to see or hear the lorries transporting hashish. I persuaded him to come with me to visit Ruhiyya. "Give us a bit of a song," he said to her. "But not about death, for God's sake, or Husayn's martyrdom, or your cousin, or how God made you a widow."

Then he asked her to dance for him. He seemed absorbed for a few minutes and chuckled and called out, "You bad girl!" But after a bit he got up and went out, oblivious to his surroundings. Juhayna is a snail leaving a sticky trail behind her for my grandfather to catch his feet in. I think about a substitute for her day and night. I used to imagine that I'd found one as I lay in bed, but as soon as I woke up in the morning my search began all over again.

This was how I began writing to you. I was thinking about what I'd inherited from you and my mother and it gave me the energy to embark on my task. I can't believe I ever studied philosophy and logic and I return to books you read to me or made me read which I still remember by heart. What I see now is a girl, a woman, in the porch, by the washing line, in the kitchen with the pot for making camomile tea in her hand, and my grandfather happy at the warm sound of her footsteps and the familiarity of her presence.

7

My Dear Jawad

I see Ruhiyya surrounded by bedding and a mound of cotton filling from a pillow which she had emptied on to a straw mat to air. "My darling little cousin is coming, there's so much to do."

Her voice fills the tiny dried-up garden, and the self-sown pomegranate tree waits and listens.

"Yesterday Jawad phoned the family we don't mention. 'France has taken you away from us, has it?' I said. 'And you've forgotten Ruhiyya except to send her perfume and silk scarves. I suppose you think they'll make up for not seeing you.' And the son-of-a-bitch said, 'What do you want me to do about it? Shall I come and visit you?' 'Of course,' I said and he said, 'Sorry. I can't come straightaway. I'll be with you in a few days.'"

I didn't know what to reply, but I felt a sudden glow of pleasure as if this news concerned me directly. I thought I sensed Ruhiyya's eyes on me and tried not to let her see the pink in my cheeks. But she was engrossed in her fight with the ants, beating the bedding with a stick and asking why God had created them.

I laughed, covering up my excitement at the idea of this Jawad, whom – as far as I knew – I had never seen in my life. But I'd seen your book in French in pride of place in her "display cabinet" among the glass tea caddies and sugared almond boxes she'd collected at weddings. When Ruhiyya was absorbed in frying aubergines and courgettes, I used to try and amuse myself by looking at the things around me, including this book. I was usually content to hold it in my hands and flick through it, as I didn't know much French, but today this wasn't enough to dispel the boredom I felt in Ruhiyya's gloomy house. My emotions were aroused as if a man direct from Europe was suddenly with me in the room.

I put this down to the loneliness I had begun to suffer away from Beirut, which appeared to me now as a place seething with life. I wished Ruhiyya would take me with her to meet you, for besides being curious to see what you were like, I wanted to go to the airport, even if it was Damascus. It was ages since I had met someone coming from abroad or seen the inside of an airport.

But Ruhiyya didn't pick this up, although she read my coffee cup and saw money and letters and people. She interpreted this as meaning a cash transfer from my mother, and the people were obviously the occupiers of the land. Then she repeated the story of the doctor who had heard you talking on a radio programme broadcast from France. "He said Jawad was a genius. He suggested giving me a check-up, and examined me all over and gave me pills for nothing."

I didn't question my eagerness until I was walking home over the dry plain where the poppies jostled brightly together, swaying in the hot breeze. My feet knocked against the stones, I waved a fly away from my nose, and the silent mountains seemed to be looking surreptitiously down on to the plain. I saw myself standing in front of you, then I wondered how your lips would taste, if you knew what a kiss was, if someone who originally came from round here would understand that a mouth was for passion and lust, not just eating and shouting. I tried to stop myself: it was probably boredom making me so interested in the new arrival.

Then I put the blame on Ruhiyya who was always mentioning you and making me feel that I'd known you for ages and wanted you. The most logical explanation was that I was desperate for a man, any man, in this drought. I saw an attractive blond-haired man walking along with a fighter. He turned to look at me and smiled. I stared back at him in disbelief and smiled too. Was it possible in this baked red land that I should meet such a man? I realized from the way he looked at me that he too had been surprised to see me here walking on these unmade roads. However, we both went on our way, although we kept looking back at each other until he turned off towards the hill where Juhayna's friends worked, and I knew he must be a foreign chemist who was in charge at the opium laboratory.

I knock on Ruhiyya's door, my heart beating so fiercely that I look down at my blouse to see if anything shows through. "Shh." Ruhiyya opens the door when I've barely begun to knock. "He's still asleep, bless him."

A suitcase is an unexpected sight in Ruhiyya's house and its presence transforms the place; I imagine it makes it look like a hotel room in Afghanistan. Then I see things which take me off on a different tack: trainers stuffed with thick white socks, and sunglasses on top of a pile of foreign magazines.

My thoughts stray far from here. I think of a life where there are universities, where people jog on beaches and wide city pavements. Ruhiyya takes me by the hand and leads me into the kitchen, and whispers to me, "I love him, this boy, you should see, he's so kind. He even brought coffee and tea and jars of dried milk like Nido, and tinned food. He says people are going hungry here!" She picks up an unfamiliar-looking jar of coffee and asks me if I want a cup. I nod, feeling expectant and happy in a way I haven't done for a long time.

I sit with her waiting for you to get up, and I distract myself by telling her about Juhayna. But Ruhiyya isn't with me today. Your arrival seems to have turned her existence upside down. She leaves the beans boiling on the stove and drags me out into the back yard again. "I told him to write the story of my life with his stinking brother," she whispers confidentially, "and he told me it had already been done and made into a film. It's true. It could have been me. He said it was about a girl who loved a man and thought he loved her. But she couldn't read or write like him and he got ashamed of her in front of his friends. She was fed up, but when he left her she went crazy and had to go into an asylum. She learnt how to make lace, and was never quite right in the head. When he saw her like that

149

he began to cry and realized how stupid he'd been not to recognize the worth of what he'd had – a pure, noble, sweet spirit . . ."

I stop her in mid-flow, telling her the last bit must have been her own invention. Two hours go by and I grow increasingly edgy waiting for you to appear. I make as if to get up, and to my amazement she doesn't stop me or insist I have lunch with her as usual. But I don't want to leave. I try to hunt up some juicy details to tell her about my fears for Ricardo because I heard on the news that the Syrians are hunting down the Hizbullah in Beirut, and I realize that I sound as if I am the only one taking any responsibility for him. I raise my voice, ignoring her reminder to keep it down. She is no longer paying any attention. I rise from the table, scraping my chair loudly along the floor. Ruhiyya looks towards her room and you appear in front of us in shorts and a t-shirt, barefooted, rubbing your eyes, as if you've just dropped through the roof. Ruhiyya rushes to put a hand on your shoulder and inquire, "Love, are they your pyjamas or your underwear?"

I laugh to cover my confusion as you are looking at me, obviously astonished to find me there. "They're shorts," you answer.

I laugh again, annoyed that she hasn't introduced me. "Asmahan, isn't it?"

I am tongue-tied. She asks you disapprovingly how you know me, then correcting herself says of course you must know me because she's talked so much about me. But you say, "Come on! She was always visiting you. And once that boy – what was his name? Abdullah. Once he followed me into the café with Asmahan behind him and told me you wanted to see me."

Your eyes rest on me for a moment, and you go on, "And you, Madame, said to me, 'Is it true you live in Beirut, and go to school near the university and you've got a car?' and I answered, 'That's right. I live in Beirut. I go to school next to the university and my father has a car.' And you said to me, 'OK, if that's true, Ruhiyya wants you to marry me.' "

I laugh awkwardly, feeling pleased, and then slightly let down. Your openness, your easy manner suggest that you think of me almost as a distant relative, and someone who isn't really part of your world any more. You'd teased me, telling me that I'd got myself a husband and asking about my family. When I told you who my grandparents were, you'd muttered something about that being awkward, and I'd burst into tears and run off.

Ruhiyya claps her hands together appreciatively and cries, "You monkey! I don't remember it at all. Do you, Asmahan? God help me! Has he got supernatural powers? And he still remembers the crack in the table. He asked me about it and said he had to make sure whether he'd dreamt it, or if it was really there."

I don't remember. It's all new to me. I try, now, I try and I see myself sitting before a plate of aubergines and courgettes and fried cauliflower, and hear Ruhiyya talking to her mother, affectionate and irritable by turns. One day the old woman asked why there wasn't any meat. Ruhiyya shouted at her, "Shall I cut off my thigh for you and make kibbeh? There's no meat in the shops today." She snatched the plate away from under her mother's nose, saying, "I'll feed it to the cats," and began to go, "Noo, noo, noo, noo. Come and eat this. My mother's full."

You loll back on the sofa and I feel uncomfortable as the two of you have obviously forgotten I exist. I wonder whether to pretend to occupy myself somehow or slip away. I want to join in your conversation but can't think of anything to say. You start yawning again and I decide that you are so much at ease because you have the impression that I am a confirmed old maid, or someone like Ruhiyya who sings to console herself, fries aubergines, mourns her husband and spreads bedding in the sun to air. Do you know I'm a trained architect?

All along the road home I blamed myself for having been so awkward. The crowning thing had been my surreptitious attempt at intimacy when I said, "You look as if you've just woken up."

I shook my head as I walked along. "Girl, you're not normal," I said aloud.

I was uncertain whether to go and see Ruhiyya as usual

the next day and decided not to, convincing myself that the monotony of village life would get to you before long and you would seek me out with Ruhiyya.

But then my preoccupations took a different turn.

I awoke to hear Zemzem shouting, "It's him. Yahya... Ricardo. Fadila's nephew."

Impossible, I thought to myself. I had been wondering what had happened to him and his aunt Fadila, when I heard that the Syrians were arresting everyone in Hizbullah, and all the time Ricardo had been making his way to our house, crouching down among the dead trees and the blaze of crimson blooms.

Ricardo, Ricardo, I repeated to myself as I jumped out of bed, pulling on jeans and a shirt over my nightdress. Ricardo stood shyly on our porch, while Naima inundated him with questions. Why had he come? Where had he come from? Was his aunt in Beirut? Who was winning? How had he crossed from the western sector?

Either Ricardo hadn't expected to see me there, or he was asking me to protect him from the onslaught. He turned to me with a shocked expression in his eyes and sat down on the edge of the porch, like most of our male visitors, with no pretension, still holding his suitcase. It looked scratched and battered enough to belong to a travelling salesman, or perhaps it mirrored the state of its owner. Ricardo spoke, as usual, without wasting words saying he had crossed the Christian lines by taxi. I felt sorry for him sitting there in his ancient trousers and worn shirt. He looked so hunched and dejected that Naima soon stopped bothering with him. I felt a growing desire to take him in my arms, but not like the time before.

That night he had stood at our garden gate in Beirut while the rain poured down on us both. All sorts of notions came rushing into my head as I took the heavy paper bundle he was handing me. Was it bombs, a gun, money? When I took my time to open it, he said, "I hope you like it. They told me my mother gave it to me when I was little."

I put my hand in and took out a metallic object. It was dark all around us, so Ricardo lit a match. It was a squat little gold-coloured man, holding a red staff in one hand and a shield in the other, with a mouth gaping open like the entrance to a cave, from which I pulled another man and so on like a set of Russian dolls.

Ricardo struck one match after another and I stood there stupefied, wondering if I was in a dream. Each figure was dressed in striped trousers to the knee and a matching cap. I no longer saw anything new like this in Beirut. If shops had new imports for sale, they tended to be shiny, vulgar, stainless steel goods. We were so taken up with our own war and troubles that we were hardly aware of the existence of other countries; and here were these African statuettes or chess pieces proclaiming that other countries, other cultures did exist and holding out the hope of escape to a new life. I felt an indescribable pleasure when I looked at them and asked Ricardo if I could keep them until morning so that I could see them in the daylight. I couldn't help wondering what had made him think of bringing them. "They're for you," he replied.

I flushed and said I couldn't take them because they were a reminder of his mother.

"They'll be safer if they're with you," he answered, to my astonishment. "My aunt would chuck them out, or give them away."

I sensed that his visits to us weren't only to complain about his aunt, or consult me about his life. I felt uneasy when I saw his eyes shifting from my face to my breasts to my hands. I noticed a vein throbbing in his neck, fit to burst. All the same I didn't pull my caftan more tightly round me or go in and change it for my street clothes. In the match flame I saw the sharp beauty of his face like an effigy, his almond eyes, his brilliant white teeth. But this wasn't why I let him embrace me; there were many reasons: in particular the fact that he didn't have a family and friends, and his desire for me which made him tremble the moment his body came into contact with my breasts. I pretended not to understand what was happening to him even though he remained frozen, scared, embarrassed by his heavy tremulous breathing. I waited until it had steadied before I extricated myself from the dead weight of his head and chest, thinking that if I had dreamt this I wouldn't have believed it could happen in reality.

Now I was worried that he had come to take refuge with us until things improved, for our village no longer welcomed strangers as it had done in the past. I smiled at him: "What is it, Ricardo?" Immediately the words came spilling out of him, fighting to be heard, as if they'd been imprisoned inside him for too long. He'd seen the Syrians entering houses, searching for members of Hizbullah everywhere. Under the beds, on roof-tops, in lofts. His aunt had made him and her crazy brother stay inside. Ricardo wasn't restless being confined to the house. He wanted her to hide him, or smuggle him out anywhere, as long as he didn't fall into Syrian hands. They'd arrested Kazim and the Modern Sheikh and he'd felt his turn was coming. And Bassam, who used to hang around with them sometimes, had appeared in his true colours as a Syrian agent and would be sure to denounce him.

I noticed the tension on Ricardo's face even though he spoke with energy. Looking down, he lowered his voice and said, "My aunt started to go crazy. She wanted me to go abroad and she was trying to find the money for a ticket. But I could only think of coming here."

He put his hand to his shirt pocket and took out a bit of paper which he proffered diffidently. "From my aunt."

I read Fadila's handwriting: "Please, Asma, get him out of the country any way you can. I'll never forget your kindness and trouble. I have two twenty-two carat gold chains. I hope you understand."

I folded the letter and thought of the two gold chains en-circling her plump white wrist. She had promised them to so many people: me if I got married, her aunt to pay for the best medical treatment, another nephew; the doctor in the mental hospital where her mother was.

While the whole household was gathered around Ricardo, a woman came with a message from the house on the hill asking if the Afghan was meant to come to them and had lost his way. We all laughed: the colour of Ricardo's skin confused the local people.

Ricardo stayed with us for two days before Zemzem accompanied him to Damascus Airport with a one-way ticket to Africa. With him he had two old shirts that had been my grandfather's, two cotton shirts of mine, some dollars, and a letter from the Syrian officer in charge of our sector in Beirut asking the Syrian authorities to facilitate things for the said Yahya Ricardo, who was known to him personally, and not to be misled by his non-Arab surname as he and his family were sincere supporters of the Syrian state.

As I watched him walk away across the orchard in his old trousers, carrying his scratched suitcase, I knew he'd think of me when he was next alone with a woman but he wouldn't talk to her. He would think that it was enough to have his eyes open, for in childhood he had kept his eyes shut day after day and refused to open them. Would he keep his mouth shut in Syria? My concern for him weighed on me like a mountain. As he disappeared, he took with him the assurance he had unconsciously given me, when he took me back into a world I had lost touch with after Naser and then Simon left.

Ricardo from Africa had led me back to the heart of Beirut, entering by a different door from Naser, since all the events took place in an area like a walnut, containing hollow chambers which interlocked but were sealed off from one another. Whenever I came back into the swing of things, I found myself filled with new life, eager to be in touch with the people in the streets. I felt sorry that he'd returned to join the ranks of the Shia and found them fighting one another, and was leaving and forcing me to turn a page.

I found I was wrong about you: you weren't bored; in fact you seemed to wish the day had more hours in it. You didn't notice the evenings dragging: they were for writing up your journal in thick black ink in a brown leather notebook. You sat and thought about the people you had met, recalling the exact sentences they had used, and the little side road you'd searched for in vain, unable to believe that the villa with its ugly stone had been built in its place. I found I was in the journal as the little bride who now smoked cigarettes and drank coffee sometimes, and liked wine and books. Asmahan, who had been so tidy and well-dressed when she came to ask for your hand in her youth, had become a gipsy. It was possible her hair hadn't seen water for months and her dresses were like kimonos or gowns in Italian Renaissance paintings. Ruhiyya, it seemed, even made kibbeh and cups of tea with soul! "I was surprised at the state of her teeth: they looked as if a woodpecker had been at them while she was asleep. But they are nothing compared with some people's teeth which are a rusty tobacco colour, and like pencils sharpened until there is almost nothing left. These teeth say more about the economic and psychological state of the country than statistical and social studies. I have made up my mind to have Ruhiyya's teeth put right by Brigitte Bardot's dentist."

We clustered round you, our eyes nearly touching the pen, and Ruhiyya was proud that she had done something which would help mankind for centuries to come, by making an active contribution to your literary career. Even I was delighted at the way you had described me and felt a desire to be close to you.

But as time went by your enthusiasm for everything from the past made me critical of your naïvety, and I hated the way you carried your camera around photographing everything. I felt we'd all suddenly become specimens under a microscope and regretted ever having looked on with pleasure as you wrote in you orderly notebook with your thick pen.

These feelings didn't last and before long I was wanting to be back in the gloom of Ruhiyya's house, circling around you, waiting eagerly for you to say something concerning me in particular, hoping you would touch me, or brush against my dress. I saw your teeth when you laughed and thought about your mouth covering mine, and your thighs rubbing against mine. Did you think I was still a virgin? Or that, like Ruhiyya, I had been in love with someone and was living on memories? Couldn't you see beyond the few tiny white hairs, the wrinkles on my forehead, the prominent veins in my hands which I'd recently taken care to raise in the air at intervals, like an Indian dancer or a geisha, so that the veins subsided?

It's Billie Holiday. I must stop listening to her. She fires my emotions with her wounded voice calling out to the man, like a cat in April. Then I blame the dry-burning flame rising up from the ground and penetrating right into the veins of the trees, making me cling to this country – I call it that because it seems like a place on its own, the high mountains, the plains extending indefinitely, the sky almost touching the earth. It's as if the city, the university, the buildings whose tiled floors I can remember exactly, and the sea where I learnt to swim years before, have ceased to exist. When I look about me in the morning and see the fig trees, unmoving, I wonder if it's possible that I only arrived in the village ten days ago. Perhaps I have never left, or never been here before and ridden my grand-father's horse and gone back to Beirut to school or university with my hair bleached by the sun.

I lie on my bed peering into a small mirror, trying to see what you would see if you lay beside me or on top of me: the veins at my temples, the little hairs between my eyebrows, the redness either side of my nose. When I try to halt the flow of my imagination, the desire to be with you grows. Whatever I am doing, I hear your voice saying what I want it to say until one afternoon you appear with Ruhiyya, and my obsession reverts to irritation as I see you descend from the porch with my grandfather and go off towards the orchards listening to him intently. You pick one opium poppy, then another and hold them up to your face, looking where my grandfather is pointing. I hear your laugh. I also feel estranged from Ruhiyya who looks different today, beautiful, with her hair newly hennaed, kohl round her eyes, a touch of pinkish-red lipstick, and in a suit which is old-fashioned but still elegant. This concern with her appearance makes her seem more remote.

I quickly learn that I'm not behind this visit to our house: it is my grandfather and the martyrs' portrait painter and the mourning ceremonies for the new martyr Muhammad. Putting her arm round me, Ruhiyya whispers that she wishes she hadn't told you about the mourning ceremony, as you are insisting on coming with her. It's only meant to be for women, and she doesn't want you to find a way of getting in to hear her. She's scared she'll laugh if there's a member of her family in the audience.

"You've got yourself up like this to go to a funeral?" I say critically.

"His mother made everyone promise not to wear black and not to cry. She said a martyr of less than twenty goes straight to Paradise."

I regret speaking so roughly and tell her jokingly that she looks younger and prettier than usual.

She kissed me on both cheeks. "Thank you, my dear. It takes a lot of time and trouble. I don't usually bother when only the flies are going to see me. You've got Beirut and people to see you and friends and lovers."

I saw you looking at the new maid, Suma, wherever she goes. As usual she is moving extremely slowly as if she's afraid she'll slip if she hurries at all. She is bending to gather dry twigs and leaves and flowering basil to put before the statue of Buddha which stands in pride of place in her room. She always has different flowers stuck in her long plait, most often the yellow hibiscus which close at night. Perhaps you find her strange: although she looks so different from us she has picked up the village accent.

Suma is the woman who has come to live in our house to provide my grandfather with his quota of touching, pinching and nibbling, and no doubt other things too. Juhayna and her bright hair have faded into oblivion with the arrival of Suma and her black Sri Lankan hair hanging well below her waist. A few days went by before everyone was accustomed to her name. Sufa, Sumana, Subya. But then the whole house became engrossed in her doings, starting from the time she chose to take her first bath naked near the water-pipe which extended snake-like from the cistern to the edge of the porch. She didn't use the soap which Zemzem had given her, but cooking oil and a stone she picked up off the ground. She pounded her flesh with it until her gleaming body seemed to call out and announce its existence. The women of the house crowded together awkwardly at the kitchen door, squawking like startled chickens at the sight of her nakedness, covered only by a pair of panties. Perhaps because she worshipped Buddha they didn't rush out to tell her about what was forbidden and what was allowed.

Instead they began watching her as if they were at a movie as she bathed, dried herself and did her hair, dressing it with more of the cooking oil, which she had decanted into a medicine bottle.

She doesn't object to my grandfather touching her, however suggestive his touches, but she hates the tweaking and nibbling. She finds it strange that he should want to hurt the submissive flesh and mark its purity, when it is ready to comply with whatever is required of it at work and play. Entertaining my grandfather has become part of her routine. As soon as she's finished lunch, she follows him into his room, carrying a cup of herbal tea, calm and confident, with no obvious desire to hide what she is doing even from my grandmother. In the evenings she waits for him to call her and smiles at us as she gets up, as if it is time for her to go to work. Who knows? Perhaps the smile means she knows she's going to sleep with him and sees this as an important part of her job.

I guess that Ruhiyya has told you about my grandfather since you seem to have been observing him and Suma. My hostility nips me like a scorpion's sting and I attempt to needle Ruhiyya to get my own back. "What's going on down there? It looks as if Jawad is interrogating my grandfather. Perhaps he's thinking of knocking off a book about us and the village," I say with a scorn worthy of Juhayna.

"He's desperate to go to the artist's house. I said you'd go there with him."

"Go with him?" I say bitingly. "So that he can broadcast gossip about us over the pine trees of Beirut?"

Ruhiyya starts visibly at my tone. Then instead of shouting back at me she takes her revenge by telling me that she's noticed how cold I am towards you, even irritable; if she didn't know me so well she'd be sure it was because you hadn't fallen in love with me; I seemed to find any old magazine more interesting to read than one of your books.

It isn't really spite, more an unconscious attempt to get under my skin and put a finger on what's eating at me. I was supposed to have had a brilliant future lined up one way or another. I had a good degree in architecture and made designs for buildings from here to Beirut. Ruhiyya had witnessed the enthusiasm with which I'd noted and recorded the instinctive knowledge of technique displayed in the local buildings. What was the result of it all? Cigarettes, coffee, sleep, silence, laughter, fits of resentment. I ought not to have bared my soul to her as I have since my return, visiting her every day and sitting with her for hours on end. I should have stayed at home, giving her the idea that I was engaged on an important project. Or perhaps I should have visited her dressed in something she would consider nice and expensive, the same kind of thing you saw me in when I was young, not in my "remnants" as she calls them. My grandmother is right: one should always try to cultivate a special aura and arouse people's curiosity.

I leave Ruhiyya on the porch and go inside. I realize after a few seconds that I'm not really annoyed with her, and have deliberately set out to hurt her. I go out again laughing, holding her close, crying. I don't stop when I hear your footsteps crossing the porch. If anything, I cry louder as it occurs to me that now you might think I'm like one of Chekhov's three sisters, especially as I'm wrapped in a blue silk embroidered shawl of my grandmother's. For the first time Ruhiyya acts without recourse to her voice. She says nothing in reply to my grandfather's inquiries, leads me inside to the washstand in the hall and washes my face and smoothes my hair with a little water. I submit to her rough hands and burst out laughing. I look at her and she joins in, remembering to curse Satan, the cause of our quarrel. But she wants to finish with the whole episode as quickly as possible and says, "Right, now let me go in and say hallo to your grandmother."

"I'll make some tea."

I take out the tea tray with a new feeling of confidence. I avoid looking at you and don't pay you the slightest attention. I sit listening to the water in the tank and look at the piles of sacks, the trucks, the distant winding roads. I visualize what is happening in Beirut, and look for distractions, forcing myself to feel anxious about Ricardo, wondering what he's going through. You are discussing the occupation of our land, inflation, the political parties. You ask my opinion a few times but sensing my coldness, you switch your attention back to my grandfather, asking him for the story of the land in detail, listening with total absorption and hauling in the catch you'd trawled for in the vast seas of boredom and vanity.

As I walk with you later towards the painter's house I find it's like walking on mounds of human flesh, so soft that I almost fall over. You have undermined my self-confidence from the moment you stood in Ruhiyya's kitchen rubbing your eyes and yawning. It's because of my sense of failure, of not having fulfilled myself, but how were you to know about that? Now I find I am trying not to breathe audibly even though people always do when they walk at any speed along these uneven roads. The village is humming like a city: girls walking alone and in groups, fighters in jeeps or on scooters watching the girls, or chatting and laughing together.

I am amazed you still talk in a village accent. Your city accent seems artificial, like Zemzem's when she makes a big effort to adapt to Beirut. I wonder what is happening to me; it is as if I have never walked around with a man before, and I take in the road and the passers by at a purely mechanical level, while the awkward progress of my feet mirrors my words and thoughts.

Why did I come with you when it makes me feel so annoyed?

We are approaching the road leading off to the girls' house on the hill where the drugs laboratory is: I wish I could see the blond foreigner so that we could exchange glances. Then the artist's shirt comes into view hanging on a washing line strung between two trees. The magnificent black car is gone from the entrance where it is normally parked.

As soon as they catch sight of me they come out to welcome me, which makes me feel more confident but as I begin to ask the painter's mother if her son's at home, she lets out a gasp of recognition. You receive much more of a welcome than I did, even the first time I went there. All the sweets and nuts which have been kept well hidden on my past visits are placed before us, or rather before you.

The painter isn't at home. "I'll send someone to find him for you," cries his mother.

You're impressed because they would never do that in France.
"You don't realize that they don't even do it in Beirut nowadays. But you're an important personality to them."

When they ask you what it is like in France I can't tell if the sentiments you express are genuine or not. For the first time for ages I feel acutely aware that I belong to the family which owns this land, and used to invade the cracks in the walls and the pores of their bodies uninvited, and provided them with oxygen or shut if off at will. I see myself alone now. They have forgotten who I am and have me where they want me. I sit with them as if sharing their admiration for you.

This feeling annoys me. It reminds me of my grandmother and is painful, even though I've always criticized her for it in the past. She told me off for accepting a lift in the brother's car; he has turned up now and is pumping your hand as if he'll never let it go.

"Do you know how many hens and cows that family used to have?" she'd asked me scornfully. "They're nobodies."

I felt like saying that those days had gone for ever, and the women who came to visit her now were visiting the past, perhaps because the memory made them happy in comparison with how they felt about the present; she had become a temporary consolation, like a visit to a graveyard when you're depressed. But she was one of them now, completely powerless.

I look at their faces again, unable to believe that my family is dead and buried as far as they are concerned. I feel like reminding them of our existence, but I stop myself and sit there with a smile of gloomy satisfaction of my face, comforting myself with images and scenes from the past. I remember these young men as children tagging along in the wake of the noisy celebrations my family organized for religious feasts or election victories. A big space was cleared outside to serve as the dining area. Around dawn the sheep could be heard uttering their last cries in the distance before they were slaughtered and I would rush to see the men skinning them. All hands and eyes were on the woolly fleeces, even though it was my grandmother who would have the final word on what happened to them. The women from the village would position themselves around the eating area lighting braziers, pumping primus stoves, grilling meat, chasing away the cats, dogs, flies and children. So it would go on for hours until they collected up all the hot stoves, whose flames fluttered wearily and went out, then extinguished the braziers by pouring water on them so that they made a whispering sound: "wish, wish". Then all the cooking pots were lined up in the yard by the kitchen, waiting for Naima and Zemzem to spoon out the rice and arrange it on the wicker trays, smoothing it flat with their hands, pinching a mouthful every now and then. When all the trays looked like pools of salt or brilliant white patches of snow it was my grandmother's turn. She approached in her finery, raising her eyes to the sky and saying a quick prayer, then rolled up one long sleeve of her dress anchoring it above her elbow and exposing her beautiful white wrist. She bent down, closing her eyes and saying a blessing and began reaching into the pots, braving the heat. Lifting out the pieces of meat as if they were made of glass, she arranged them carefully on top of the rice, having second thoughts when she'd all but finished and moving a piece from one tray to another. While she was doing this the buses had begun to arrive, decked with banners bearing the names of their villages. The female passengers moved straight up to the house and gathered near the kitchen yard, squatting over the trays of food there, while the men streamed out behind the house and threw themselves on the other trays spread out there and did not rise up until there was nothing left. At this point the victorious candidate arrived and made a speech which went on until a man on horseback waved a flag and blew a horn; this was a sign for the men and women to assemble ready to depart so that the passengers of other buses from other villages could take their places and celebrate the candidate's win. The newcomers were preceded by a small band, and the trays of food were replenished.

The horn blew and the flag waved and instead of the winning candidate they raised my grandfather up on their shoulders. He tried to struggle free, but I'm sure he was secretly delighted every time they hoisted him high in the air. In the evening he went over the day's events with my grandmother, criticizing the winning candidate, and they made fun of the self-conscious way he walked, and his pompous speech; on my grandfather's instructions Abu Mustafa had brought a wooden stool for the candidate to stand on so that he would be visible above the crowd. His father and mother had been there to watch, convinced their son was an important personality, and his mother had bent and kissed my grandmother's hand.

Suddenly the painter comes through the door like a hurricane. He shakes your hand, squeezing it tightly, and greets me: "H-h-h-hallo, Madame." He comes back with the paintings. I look at the floor, afraid I will laugh at your solemn remarks. The painter is trying to articulate the sentence on the tip of his tongue as he confronts the paintings, which are even cruder than the lids of chocolate boxes. "In France don't they have e-e-e-exhibitions of the art produced by the struggle, or Is-Is-Islamic art?"

You nod your head soothingly. "They might do. There's no reason why they shouldn't."

Then his brother says, "We'll let you loose on the world, you scoundrel! Soon they'll be giving you an exhibition at the Eiffel Tower!"

The painter laughs delightedly and I shudder with annoyance at his delusions and your dishonesty.

On the way back I am torn by conflicting emotions, longing to be close to you and to shout at you in almost equal measure. It is nearly dusk and the setting sun bathes the fields around us. White and red poppies, growing alongside beans and heavily laden tomato plants, stand motionless in the still air. There are patches of sand here and there. Dogs bark, as they form packs to roam the streets. Wires carrying stolen electricity trail from the telegraph poles. I inhale the smoke of thistles burning on an old bonfire and the smell tickles my senses. I ridicule the painter for wanting his work to be shown abroad.

"I really admire him. He ignores what's going on around him, the drugs, the spin-offs, and just keeps painting martyrs."

"D-drugs. S-spin-offs. God help anyone who t-t-t-tries to do secret deals with him," I say, finding myself imitating the painter's stammer.

You burst out laughing so I think I must have done it well.

The smell of you begins to reach me even though we are out in the open, and again I feel a warmth because I am near you and we are walking together over this land. We are both strangers to it and this brings us just a little closer even though our worlds are far apart. I point to the hairdresser's sign where "Cleopatra" is misspelt in French. "That's sweet," you say.

You seem unwilling to talk as you look at the sky, the speeding cars, the plains on either side of the road, and confine yourself to exhaling deeply as if you are smoking. I think sadly how a person ends up existing for himself, however hard he tries to be close to others or give himself to them. But your sighs grow more frequent and finally you stop and seize my hand and say almost in a whisper. "Look what they're doing to these plains. See how everything's calm and still on the surface, but underneath it's seething with intrigues, drugs and party politics."

You carry on and I listen, but remain unmoved by your lecture about drugs and corruption. You've arrived late with your theories. There's nothing wrong with a little enthusiasm here and there, because you will soon forget and leave our reality behind for the European way of life. Your diary is crowded with appointments: publishers, magazines, dinner invitations, parties, broadcasts; all of them written in your neat, clear hand. You prescribe laws as if you were in a normal country with citizens who still glory in that title and all it stands for. It's easy for you to propound these views, when you haven't hidden in a shelter, had friends and neighbours killed in bread queues, returned home to your apartment block and found it has vanished, and realized after a moment that the rubble under your feet is all that remains of it.

I must hurry home: I can feel this person beside me writing a novel as he walks along and it looks as if I'll have to provide the warmth I need tonight for myself. I'll go home and listen to Billie Holiday.

My grandfather is on the porch eating his evening meal. Suma stands at his side waiting for him to signal if he needs anything. When he sees who's with me his face brightens and he waves you over to eat with him.

He calls Zemzem and to my astonishment Juhayna follows her out. Again I compare her mentally to a cat who knows there is no longer any food for her here, but still yearns for the smell. Even more surprising, you greet her: "Well, Juhayna! You've moved up in the world! Where did you spring from, my lovely?"

I realize you must have met her at Ruhiyya's. My grandfather scolds her for disappearing and avoiding him even when she was still under his roof. Then he slurps his milk down noisily, spilling it on his moustache and chin.

Juhayna hurls herself at me and flings her arms around me, kissing me, and I try to wriggle free. She grabs hold of my hair, exclaiming, "Look at this! It's the first time I've seen you with your hair curled."

I go into the kitchen and spoon some food on to a plate for you, eager to look at myself in the mirror in the passage. When I take the food out and put it in front of you, I can see that Juhayna is entranced by you, and realize why her desire to have her revenge even on the earth and air surrounding us has diminished. The day after she found out that I had hired Suma through a domestic agency in the nearby town she sent a message threatening that her sister's Iranian fiancé was going to intervene on her behalf.

I've never seen her as she is tonight, laughing loudly, not remotely resembling the creature who was making our lives a misery only days before. I gesture with my head, indicating that she should follow me inside, suppressing a desire to remind her of her position by calling out to her in front of everyone that I must pay her the money still owing to her. She doesn't make it any easier when she comes up and puts her arms round me and inquires of the assembled company, "Don't you think me and Asma are like sisters?"

My grandfather gets to his feet and comes over and takes hold of Juhayna by the hair, pulling her playfully towards him. "Come on, can't we be friends?"

"Leave me alone. I mean it. My grandfather's younger than you. That means you're the same age as my great grandfather."

Is this a withdrawal, a rejection of her past history with him, or an attempt to recover her pride? It's a withdrawal; the face she turns to you the whole time, disregarding, effacing everyone round her, wears a radiant expression. She tosses her hair about and looks into your eyes. Even when you look at other people, her eyes never leave you. You seem to share a secret. Suma is the one person you both look at. There is a hint of collusion in your laughter. Has Juhayna shown you the bruises on her breasts, let you have the details of her relationship with my grandfather, and told you the story of my war against her and my inhuman behaviour?

You are standing at the sink in the passage when I come out of the kitchen, pointing inquiringly at the picture on the wall.

It is my grandfather as a boy in his father's arms, holding a gun. His father is sitting astride a black horse, a sword at his waist, his face exuding an awesome dignity, which is augmented by his keffiyeh and headband and huge moustache, and the stately saddle with its black tassels. He wears a brocade jacket, and the two of them are surrounded by men with guns and swords at the ready. Although my grandfather's little face wears a serious frown, it is round and generous, and his teeth are big and white, like a foreign child's teeth.

"Do you know what I'm thinking . . . I wish you'd talk to your grandparents for me and get them to tell me about their lives. As far back as they can remember."

I find myself adjusting my approach to you. Perhaps I should be like Juhayna. Laughing, I reply, "Why don't you talk to them? They might be pleased. Let them get it off their chests."

Just as I expected, Juhayna appears. She holds some basil leaves up to your nose. "Please! Smell these!"

"I prefer the smell of your hands."

I go outside, leaving you together. Before my fears have a chance to jell, Juhayna comes after me. "If only I could go to France and learn to be a beautician!"

Finding me less than enthusiastic, she tries again. "Well, I could help Jawad in the house too. Cook and iron and wash his clothes and keep things tidy, and then go to college a few hours a week."

My grandfather returns to you, as if what has happened between him and Juhayna doesn't need to detain him any longer. What concerns him now is to get back to talking about the bastards who are running things, and local and international politics. He wants you to help him write a letter to the countries of the world, to be published in the magazines with the highest circulations, complaining about his situation and what has happened to his lands. You are observing everybody, especially Zemzem who stands there in her new nightdress, delighted that it should be seen by someone outside the family at last.

Again you are trying to make my grandfather talk about himself while my grandfather complains with increasing vehemence about the occupiers and the families who he believes are secretly implicated in this occupation, since they are looking for a market for what they produce. His voice rises to a despairing wail, as he pleads with you to help him understand the world.

Only the sound of my grandmother's voice, calling to him and Zemzem, silences him. As soon as they have left the porch, Juhayna raises her eyebrows at me again, winding an arm round my waist.

"Juhayna wants to ask if you need someone to take care of you in France in exchange for board and lodging," I say to you, pleased that your efforts with my grandfather have come to nothing.

You smile at Juhayna. "It should be me doing your ironing and cooking you meals and making you coffee," you tell her. Then you add more seriously that you live in a small apartment, eat out, wear your shirts unironed and wash them without starch. At this point you turn to me and ask if Zemzem still uses blue in the laundry. "Ask her yourself," I say indifferently.

We can hear my grandfather shouting again as he re-emerges on to the porch and as usual we tell him to be quiet.

You turn to me, your eyes shining, as if you've just remembered something important. You ask me if I've ever talked to the occupiers myself. "Imagine what a story it would make if you were to fall in love with one of them!"

The blood rushes to my head. "Why don't you try it yourself?" I say disdainfully.

The gathering becomes muted despite Zemzem's incessant chatter, which you encourage, Juhayna's laughter, the sound of the radio from my grandmother's room, and the voice of Billie Holiday in my private corner of the porch. I think I am listening alone until I hear you humming along. A gulf seems to have opened up between us. You are mean: the fact that you know her robs me of the feeling of having her to myself. As the others drift away or become caught up in their own thoughts, and we are left with her voice, you say, "You know Billie Holiday. You dress like one of Chekhov's three sisters. You laugh because your grandfather still has a roving eye, but when he really falls in love with someone you chase her away and look for a substitute to take his mind off her. At the same time you get angry about absolutely nothing. I don't understand you."

I attempt to shout but my voice comes out calmly and quietly. Unconcerned by Juhayna coming up and sitting next to him, I say, "It's because you're self-centred. We're material for your books as far as you're concerned. You belittle our feelings. You want me to fall in love with one of the thugs occupying my family's orchards so that you have a story that's a bit different and can go back and tell them a piece of local folklore about the girl who fell in love with her enemy."

You get up and walk away, leaving me trembling. Juhayna follows and the sound of your footsteps fades and Billie Holiday sings on alone. I hear one of the men camped below shouting, "Give us a rest from that bloody wailing! Put on a bit of Fairouz."

I don't want to be left alone. I go into my room and sit in bed with the light on. The dead silence is broken by my grandfather calling loudly to Suma. The root cause of my annoyance with you is that you regard us with a foreigner's eye. I shrug my shoulders. You see us as folklore. You don't sense what we are suffering, our desires and limitations. After a few moments I retreat from this line of thought. Is the heart of the problem that you are not attracted to me? Am I jealous of Juhayna and her youth? Or is it that living away from here you carry a beautiful picture of your homeland in your mind, while I see only a disfigured image of it? Does it annoy me that your imagination is a peaceful plain planted with crops, which you water, prune and harvest, while mine has become an arid waste? An encounter with the past must restore a person's soul, give him new life, otherwise why are you so relaxed, while I dangle on a thread of smoke?

I close my eyes and see myself lying on the grass in springtime and think, "Once I lay down on the green grass and looked up at the blue sky and said to myself, 'Why am I scared of failing the baccalauréat when all this belongs to me, even the wisps of cloud and the butterfly darting and spinning through the air as if she knows she will only live for a day? Everything's mine, including those pale stars in the sky.' "

But this image fails to relax my face muscles or dull the rasping tickle in my throat. I long for a glass of gin but know I'll be lucky to find anything but arak.

I get out of bed and go to the glass cabinet in the sitting room and open the double doors. In the corner at the bottom are hidden the expensive glasses and the drink not meant for casual consumption: arak for toothache and my grandfather's heartache and an empty liqueur bottle. I hold the bottle in my hand with tears in my eyes. My grandmother used to call it Franca Branca, and to this day she thinks it's a medicine for stomach ache. She used to give it to her friends when they were suffering from women's pains, and gradually they would relax and sit around laughing and cracking ribald jokes. The arak bottle seems to be running dry too, but I pour the dregs into a glass and go back to my room.

I feel myself becoming light, my body floating above my bed, and I close my eyes and smile at the thought of you, taking you in my arms and trying to sleep. Thoughts go buzzing around in my head: what do I want from you? Only that you take me in your arms and press your lips on mine, and squeeze me to confirm that you're interested. Am I crazy or frustrated?

I have to stop this rush of desire. I'm getting like Fadila. A sponge ready to soak up any moisture; a bird taking a sand bath whenever it feels the urge, not minding whether the grains of sand glint sharply under the sun or cling together in a damp mass.

Though recently I've written off several relationships, having woken up one memorable morning and sworn by all that was holy that never again would I close my eyes and open my legs unless I was in love. That morning, when I woke, my body had looked so crushed. Wrinkles had appeared on its pallid flesh: there were little hairs on my thighs; and the sheets were grubby and worn. A single hair of mine lay coiled on the pillow like a snake. I picked up my clothes from the floor and the edge of the bed and dressed quickly. The sounds outside had woken me with a jolt. I had seen glimpses of normal life carrying on noisily through the curtainless door: a family shouting to each other, children playing; even the worm-eaten date palm was part of the bustle.

I had looked down at the man lying beside me. I examined the little bald patch which he was usually so careful to keep covered, arranging his hair over it assiduously throughout the day. Did I know this man at all? This schoolteacher? Did I love him? I wanted to run away from him and the memory of the previous night, even though I had listened to him avidly as he told me how he would like to teach maths and physics, anything rather than history and geography. He could no longer stand the hypocrisy of explaining with apparent objectivity how the administrative districts of Lebanon had been reorganized, found himself unable to ramble on about its snow-capped mountains and ski resorts when there were armed men at the top of the runs keeping the skiers in line.

The day before I had swum with him in St George's Bay and the blackened ruins of the hotel came into focus each time we wiped the salt water out of our eyes. Gunfire from the eastern sector rocked the foul-smelling water where raw sewage floated, and we joked and held hands. All the same, that morning I simply wanted to run away, because the street noise was interrupting my thoughts, showing me how the war had opened me up.

Now, safe in my grandfather's house, I'm thinking about you again, and I can see my room through your searching eyes, as the bed creaks with loneliness. You understand at last why this woman Asmahan still isn't married. She's hot-tempered; she derives her sense of superiority from the fact that her family owns almost the whole village. She probably looks down on men who fall in love with her, so she's been rejected and sleeps alone. There are her books all over the place: art, politics, fiction, silly magazines.

I picture you picking up a book and flicking through it saying, "Strange. I never imagined she would have seen that director's films; and how did she hear about this novel? She can't have chosen the bed cover intentionally – she wouldn't know what it would fetch in Europe these days, or this carpet. She went to university just to get a degree."

I can see you shaking your head as you look through my books. I don't like it when you behave like this; you remind me of a dressmaker who can't see someone else's dress without inspecting it and giving her opinion of the sewing. I think I'm being hard on you but it's just that I feel your mind is more alive than mine. I felt the same when I was looking at your books in Ruhiyya's house, and the things you'd collected: a little acorn, a dry branch, a decaying plant, a dried-up fig. I wondered why I didn't feel this tenderness for such objects or think of saving them and why I passed by them blindly every day.

I succumb willingly to sleep and dreams and when I wake up in the morning I'm still writing this letter to you in my head.

8

To The War

I won't write "My Dear" to you since I don't understand you.

It's as if you're dragging a Persian carpet from under my feet thread by thread and then weaving it together again from one moment to the next. Your air is warm: there is a stillness everywhere, even in the skies, during the ceasefires or the lulls in the fighting as the warlords wait for some tactic to take effect. Even the garbage heaps are quiescent, the midges and buzzing flies at rest. The streets belong to anyone who dares venture into them. When you return to violence, we inhabitants of the city approach one another, come so close that we breathe as one and no longer think of much outside ourselves.

You are not my dear, and yet when the situation was quiet, and there was a sense of the clouds lifting, those who'd emigrated or gone into hiding started to pour back, the lights came on again to the sound of their laughter, and your mood changed. I noticed the change even in the café: with their arrival it ceased to be an oasis in the devastation and darkness, and we no longer took pleasure in drinking a glass of water there; it became a place to eat, and a fashion parade.

I find myself hesitating now. Why don't I call you my dear although I talk about you so warmly? I am frightened of letting go of this odd feeling of intimacy. Naser would understand it: the fabric of my relationship with him was surely woven during successive wars. In the sixty-seven war the smell of freedom emanated from his house. I could almost see it like a fine tent of muslin put up for our meetings, but it protected us like armour-plating.

Now after all these years I've changed my tone towards you. I've begun asking questions. What am I doing? Is this the life I was meant to live, or is there another path I should take? I blamed you for this instability, for leaving me in a wasteland without a glimpse of the future. You had a part in destroying my ideas about a new kind of architecture which would allow people to live in harmony with their minds and bodies. When I saw ruined buildings hastily reconstructed with wooden boarding and sheets of tin I heard you laughing at my ludicrous ideas.

I grew used to this frustration, and then you went away. Like everyone else, I welcomed the peace and rushed off to the beach and the mountains. But I kept my eyes fixed miserably on a small corner of the car because when I looked out it made me realize how lazy I had been: building activity continued to flourish even though it didn't produce structures of any beauty, and I felt guilty and full of regret when I saw the architects' boards dominating the sites.

When I tried university teaching I could never escape the feeling that every word I spoke was pointless. All the buildings around us were threatened with destruction, including the class-room we were in. We looked at igloos and straw huts and discussed whether we should devise a new building material, or be content with bunker architecture.

I left teaching and joined an association dedicated to preserving old buildings in Beirut, the ones with red-tiled roofs, small round windows, stained-glass fronts, high ceilings and stair-cases with black wrought-iron banisters. We were supposed to photograph them before they were destroyed or dismembered by huge pieces of shrapnel. The work was hindered by com-munication difficulties between the eastern and western sectors, the worsening situation interfered with meetings, and then most of the members went abroad. Against my better judgement I began accepting advice, and as soon as I left one job I took another.

I seemed to be standing in front of a large chest, opening

and shutting the drawers one after the other, like a relation of my father's who imported watches, poultry, animal fodder, opened a restaurant, went back to importing sponge mops, and ended up doing nothing. Frustration visited me every day in a new guise, sat in a chair in front of me agreeing with me as I described how slow the pace of life in Beirut was these days, how people had no enthusiasm for anything beyond securing their everyday needs. But then it grew bolder, contradicting me and reminding me of the long days of peace ahead, when Beirut would be throbbing with life again, and people would be working and producing. I became active once more, but only in my head, and imagined opening an architect's office, starting up a playgroup or establishing a zoo. Then I made peace with my frustration, convincing it that existing in Beirut all these years had been a full-time job. Getting accustomed to you took a lot of effort, as did witnessing Beirut changing hands time after time and gradually fragmenting into smaller and smaller pieces. My work consisted of acclimatizing to the new and trying to forget the old, accepting what was in front of me even if it was ugly, hoping and then learning to live without hope.

Did I speak about these feelings in my previous letters? I don't remember. It seems that these somewhat odd perceptions of mine spring from the fact that you are a strange war. It's as if you let one eye rest while you look through the other.

I used to wake up in the morning still feeling the impact of distant dreams about what was going to happen in life. I stretched, happy at the daylight, a song, the colour of a blouse, some appointment I had. I was only robbed of this sensation when the fighting started up again. All traces of the old animation were erased until the broken glass was swept up, people clasped their hands together saying sadly, "It's a shame about the people who died," and eventually I stretched out in bed again happy at the daylight, a song on the radio, some appointment, even the colour of a blouse.

One morning I woke up to a tune being played on a car horn, and heard the sound of Ali's voice accompanied by shrieking and laughter; Zemzem was asking Ali for some chewing gum, teasing him. "I can see you've got a huge piece in your mouth," she said.

Was Ali here in the village? Had he got through in spite of everything we'd heard on the radio about the fighting, the Syrians, the hold-ups on the route? Or had I become distanced from the chaos and forgotten how life could change abruptly from one day to the next, how Ali had dragged us out of our lairs as if we were small animals who didn't know spring had arrived, and taken us on that tortuous journey to the village to wait for calm to return to Beirut? Clearing his throat loudly, my grandfather called, "When did you leave Beirut, Ali? You must have grown wings!"

"Yesterday. I was afraid of being held up on the way. Although I had four passes with me, one for each checkpoint, to avoid any trouble. I thought I'd spend the evening in the restaurants by the river in Zahle and then stay the night and be at Miss Asma's at first light. It was a night to remember! Did you hear I'd married again?"

My grandfather laughed. "Why are you so shy about it? Are you keeping it to yourself so that you can marry as often as you want? We've lost count anyway."

"This time it's for real. Her children have changed me and made me more patient."

"I was praying you wouldn't show your face," joked my grandfather. "I'm so happy with Asma here, and you're taking her back to Beirut."

I came out fully dressed, delighted to see Ali, and greeted him warmly. I turned to my grandfather. "Come with us," I urged him. "Jawad and Ruhiyya are coming too."

Ali didn't let this pass. "What shall I do with you, Miss Asmahan?" he said reprovingly. "Are you trying to put a jinx on my car? On top of that woman's miserable dirges she chainsmokes and stinks the car out."

Ignoring him, I asked my grandfather eagerly, "What do you say? Will you come with us?"

"And leave the lands to the Almighty?" Then, laughing, "I don't know if He'd fancy it. So, Ali, I hope you managed to get an iron door fitted in the Beirut house."

I called Naima's grandson. "Run to Ruhiyya's and tell her to get ready to go to Beirut. Hurry!"

Ali still hadn't recovered from the shock of finding out that Ruhiyya was coming back with us. He told the boy to take his time, then turned to me. "What's going on, Miss Asmahan? Please, spare me that!"

"Come on. You can take it, Ali!" I laughed. "Ruhiyya's made me swear to take her back to Beirut with me. She's scared what will happen to Jawad there and she wants to show off her friend's great big house!"

"Of course she wants to boast in front of her cousin," interrupted Naima. "He said their family's house is in ruins. Where's he going to stay? In a hotel?"

"What's it got to do with me?" interrupted Ali. "She's like the Angel of Death. Her teeth are even going black. Everyone wondered why her husband died so young. Because he was living with the Angel of Death! She's wearing sackcloth and ashes and lamenting the dead in a different place each day!"

The smell of eggs frying floated down from the porch where Naima was making breakfast. I tried to breathe more slowly and calm down, but I could hear Ali teasing Zemzem and Naima, and then calling me. I went over to him. "What's going on? Where's Juhayna?" he whispered.

Naima overhead him and said scornfully, "Have a look indoors. She's nothing like Juhayna. The girls are all too full of themselves these days, but this one never complains. It seems the cat's got her tongue."

"Do you think I'm stupid? It's not a serious question. I'm joking. Everybody's heard the news. She thought she was the lady of the house and began poking her nose into everything. She wanted to act as go-between with the occupiers, and said your grandfather had married her secretly. When I heard it, I thought it was women telling stories as usual. I couldn't believe your grandfather had actually gone off his head."

I went back into my room and tried to concentrate on getting ready, but I was haunted by a sudden fear that Ruhiyya and Jawad might change their minds about coming. I was amazed by the elasticity of my emotions. I had stopped dreaming about him since he and Ruhiyya had come to ask me for a lift to Beirut.

I hurried into my grandmother's room which had the same atmosphere as always. Nothing in it had changed, and there was no evidence of the upheaval beyond its walls. The dish where she spat out pomegranate seeds was carefully covered with a piece of clean white muslin. There were her novels, radio, vanity case, prayer beads, a brooch of her mother's, a lock of my hair when I was a child, a cutting of some material she was still trying to match, and a little empty perfume bottle. She had kept this for years and continued to inquire about the perfume in shops in Beirut and ask people going abroad to find her a replacement for it.

I rushed over to her now, regretting that I hadn't gone straight to her the moment I started making preparations for Beirut. She had thousands of lira ready for me. She thrust her hand into her caftan again and took a piece of mastic from a beautiful little box which had originally contained face powder.

I bent and held her close. Who would have thought of this, apart from my grandmother? I half understood why I had reached this age and was still in the same place. How could I leave her? I had never seen anybody to compare to her. She started giving me instructions. "Remember who we are. Make sure the larder and the fridge are never empty."

We had grown accustomed to our house becoming like a refuge during the war. Men and women were no longer segregated. Everybody slept in my grandfather's room.

"Jawad said he's lived with a woman in sin for years," added my grandmother with an indifferent air.

I didn't answer. It hurt me to think that she was worried about my future and had picked up certain vibrations from me when I preferred to believe I had kept my feelings well hidden. She'd guessed that my longing for a man had become tinged with a nervous desire to get a hold on the safety raft because the waters of spinsterhood were no longer simply lapping around my ankles, but had risen half way up my neck so that only my head remained above the surface. I gazed at her pale face and her hands which were smooth and unveined and looked like a young girl's waiting for a wedding ring. She moved the dish of pomegranate seeds aside, and I wanted to ask her to love my mother again and understand that she was the only child she had.

Zemzem and Ali were chatting. He was telling her about his wife's voice. "Someone from a recording company heard her singing in her father's restaurant and begged her to come to the studios but she refused." Then he noticed Naima's grandson. "There you are! Give me some good news. Tell me Ruhiyya's broken her leg and isn't coming."

But the boy shouted back breathlessly, "Ruhiyya and her cousin are both coming. They're on their way. He said mind you don't go without them and sent his hand luggage with me to give Miss Asmahan."

I came out quickly and took Jawad's leather bag from the boy. Hurrying back into my room with it, I held it against my body and then up to my lips, thinking with trepidation how feelings change from one moment to the next and here I was longing for him again.

"How will I survive having Ruhiyya in the car all the way to Beirut?" cried Ali. "I always remember when my sister Safiyya set fire to herself everyone came to the graveside weeping and trying to throw themselves in after her. Just a young girl and she burnt herself to death and Ruhiyya came to mourn her and do you know what she sang to her? 'Do you want something to eat or drink? They're coming to bury you soon.' "

He told us what had happened since we left Beirut, who'd been killed and wounded, which buildings had been destroyed, and said the war between Amal and Hizbullah was really between Syria and Iran, who I thought were allies. He told us that a youth had fallen in love with Fadila's step-daughter in the shelter and married her the same night. "They sent for the sheikh and he was in such a hurry to get away, they hardly heard what he said."

I was once more engrossed in my appearance. I put on cream, foundation, powder, then took the mirror close up to the window. Once I looked as if I hadn't put anything on my face, I smiled with satisfaction. Juhayna used to creep in and watch me, because she'd noticed me looking different when I was ready to go out. I had this secret way of making my face look like ivory even though the make-up didn't show and I looked quite natural, as if I'd just washed with soap and water.

I heard the voices of Jawad and Ruhiyya, but instead of rushing out to them, I decided that it would be better to keep a distance between me and him for we had hours ahead on the journey and in Beirut I had all the time in the world. These thoughts evaporated when I heard Ruhiyya shouting, "The bastards forced their way in during the night and said they wanted to take Jawad away to interrogate him."

"Who? Who were they?"

Ruhiyya waved a hand dismissively. "Who do you think? I went for them with a knife and one of my clogs. I said, 'Let's have you', and one smartarse came towards me and Mr Jawad here began to shout at me to move. He shoved me out of the way and said he wanted to talk to them. Why should we have any truck with them? They were probably only there because they had their eye on his watch or passport or return ticket. God alone knows! They were pretty quiet when I asked them why they wanted to question Jawad. Then they began giving out this twaddle at the tops of their voices, like wild dogs baying. One asked me what he was going to write about. Our village is a sensitive topic now because of the coke, and another started asking him directly. Stupid bastards! I chased them away and told them not to show their faces again or they'd be sorry. It's good we'd already arranged to go with Asmahan, otherwise they'd think they'd intimidated us. I'm not letting them get away with anything. I'll show them."

Jawad took a breath as if he was the one who'd delivered this diatribe, then he sighed deeply and said, "There's no problem."

War, you're back, dressed in clothes to suit the village, coming into our house, assuring us that of course you exist, despite the sense that the villages are self-contained, isolated behind the barriers they have put up to keep you out. Everything was quiet here except for the shifting branches of a tree, the faint scrabbling of rats. We'd come to accept the idea that my grand-father's lands were occupied, and this occupation seemed more like an act of revenge or envy than anything to do with you. But you've struck at the foundations of Ruhiyya's house which used to smell of frying oil and a more secure past and echo to her verses of love and sadness. You came along and changed its history in a few moments, taking its silence by surprise, making it aware that it was now at the mercy of young minds whose only experience was of violence.

Even Jawad was different that morning because of you. As he sat on the porch wall, I felt he had become one of us. Somebody's son I'd played with as a child. He'd had a taste of the harshness of war, and come to enjoy our support and commiseration even though he seemed still to belong to a different world with his sports shirt and striped socks. I felt reassured by what had happened to him. It cast him into this furnace of doubt, made him a player in these shaggy-dog tales, put him within range of the magnet which drew everything towards it, even the breeze. Seeing Ruhiyya resisting them armed with a knife and a shoe, although she talked with the same accent as them, would change the nature of what he wrote in his notebook.

"Well, it's good you're safe," joked Zemzem. "God forgive you, Ruhiyya. You should watch your tongue. You were criticizing everyone under the sun for not visiting you to welcome Jawad and, you see, even complete strangers heard he was with you."

Nobody laughed, although Zemzem was only trying to dispel the tension. Neither my grandfather nor my grandmother made any attempt to change my mind about going back to Beirut. They seemed to know how set I was on making the trip, especially after hearing Ali's stories. As usual Ali took the opportunity to demonstrate that he had connections in high places and was back in favour, whereas what had happened made me realize again that we were all hostages, whatever the apparent signs of peace.

"Come on, let's slip away from the village without anyone noticing," urged Ruhiyya.

My grandmother consulted her prayer beads to find out the best thing to do, just as she used to in the past, when she wanted to see if I could go to the cinema with Zemzem in spite of my cough, or if she should make the trip to the village in the rain. Ali was the most realistic of us all. "They may be lying in wait at this moment. We must think of a secret route."

My grandmother observed that perhaps we should stay to find out who they were, but Ruhiyya objected with a shriek and insisted that we should go to Beirut and put Jawad on a plane.

In the midst of the general commotion surrounding the preparations for our departure, a woman appeared. I didn't recognize her even when she came right up to the porch. She looked deranged and was shouting, "Are you really going to Beirut?"

Her scarf had fallen down on to her shoulders uncovering her white hair, but she paid no attention to it. "Please. Who's going? My grandsons are in the fighting and they say one of them's been wounded. Can I get a lift?"

Ali took command of the situation. "No. What would you do in Beirut? Leave it to me."

He promised her he'd look for her grandsons and contact the village that night.

I noticed Jawad whispering something in Zemzem's ear. Then he asked the newcomer, "Is it you, Qut Al-Qulub? You used to do a lot of damage in your time. What's happened to you?"

The woman looked at him, uncomprehending. She had grown old and was hard of hearing. Everyone else understood. This woman had acted as a kind of bank, especially to women on their own; she used to make the first few interest payments on the money they deposited with her, then deny all knowledge of it.

He didn't want to let the opportunity pass. "Is it true you've got a belt stuffed with gold?" he teased.

She shook her head. "God be with you, love," she said.

Ali took us his "devils' route" over the plains, through the hashish, twisting round apple and cherry trees. Jawad marvelled at the colours of the rocks, which were different from anything he'd remembered. Ruhiyya was touchy and nervous, and tried to silence him, appalled at what she saw as his coldbloodedness. To me he seemed completely serene, absorbed in his surroundings. I had seen many people with their features jumbled and their senses thrown into confusion as a result of the fear you imposed upon them: the mouth which saw, the eyes which screamed aloud, the veins which smelt panic. I understood this in Zemzem and the mothers clutching their children as they waited for the school bus, but I felt only contempt for those who lost their sense of proportion and tried to wipe out what they had believed in for years the moment they faced danger, swallowing tranquillizers and tearing up personal papers and photographs.

Ali announced to our surprise that we were about to meet his wife, and we realized that the "devils' route" which he had chosen went by her village. My eyes met Ruhiyya's and we exchanged smiles. "Is it true your wife's a bedouin?" Ruhiyya asked him.

"What are you getting at? Yes, she's a bedouin. Not a gipsy."

Jawad asked him about her in his serious way. "Her family came to work on the plains," answered Ali shortly. "They're still cheaper and better than the Pakistanis, Afghans, Palestinians, Kurds, you name it. And they're given a roof over their heads and a wage they can survive on."

As we penetrated the calm of the small back roads, the rocks in their varying colours and formations rapidly buried all traces of you. The roads appeared as if nothing would disturb their tranquillity except the rutted asphalt and sharp bends, and an overwhelming sense of reassurance filled the car; I felt like a child being rocked gently to sleep. I smiled to myself because I was no longer dominated by Jawad; I had begun to think again, to be pleased or annoyed by things as if he didn't exist. Seeing the plain, so vast that it seemed to fill the world, obscured the episode of Jawad and the militiamen, and its changing colours blotted out the unwelcome novelty and violence. Driving along, it was difficult to be aware of anything but the colours of the plain flanked by the bare mountains whose foothills were dotted with greenhouses for growing flowers and vegetables. Women bent over the cannabis plants in their gaily coloured clothes, their heads covered by keffiyehs and scarves.

Catching sight of a blackened mountainside, I decided I was

right not to address you as my dear, for you are destruction and your atmosphere has imposed itself upon me, deluding me into believing that you exude an intimacy where relationships can flourish freely and that there is an enchantment in you which works on souls and bodies so that nobody feels alone, but it is a lying magic, aware only of the moment: a drug.

But then I feel happy again, even loving, because I see trees which have escaped you. Tall trees with green, spreading branches where crickets chirp, they stand in clumps on the verdant mountainsides like hermits who have tired of the clamour of life and wrapped themselves in cloaks which change colour with the changing light.

Ali took a fork in the road and we almost came to a halt. I don't believe it was a public road; nevertheless we carried on and it was as if we had boarded a lift which carried us into the sky. When we climbed out in space, the plain looked like a knitted patchwork blanket, red, yellow and green, and the road like a long zip on a dress with no checkpoints or obstructions, long expanses of road seemingly empty of people. You disappeared, no longer even a spectre in the memory, and it was as if stability had not ceased to be a concept and the dark winds of misery had never stirred. The moment the car came to a halt we heard the noise of children and saw them running from the only breezeblock building still standing. Young women surrounded Ali, disregarding us; our presence did not stop him replying to their jokes. Jawad was the only one to be delighted by all this, his face beaming with pleasure at what was going on round him, while Ruhiyya and I felt distinctly restless, knowing the coffee would be bitter, the cups dirty, the bread unappetizing.

Ali showed us into the sitting room, then returned a few moments later and introduced his wife; she was strikingly beautiful and I was amazed how young she was, as I knew she had been married before to a cousin who had died and left her with two children.

The room, bare except for mattresses on the floor, was frighteningly hot and the heat was exacerbated by their rough fabric which rubbed against my skin through my skirt when I sat down and made me feel as if I was being bitten by insects. Ali's wife drew back the curtains and opened the windows. "It's too much," she declared. "Ali won't let us open a thing."

"Someone as beautiful as you should be hidden away in a trunk," commented Jawad. "I see what Ali means."

She laughed, covering her mouth with her hand, and the colour rose in her cheeks. "It's a pity. We used to be beautiful once. Now hard work has ruined us."

When Jawad stood up apologetically and went outside, I could have kicked myself: I had ignored the heat rising like a wave of fever and breaking over me because he was sitting opposite me. I wanted to follow him out but Ali's wife continued to heap kindnesses on me, repeating that I was like a daughter to her, because of Ali. This delighted me, of course, as she was younger than me, and I forced myself to relax, and slumped down on the mattress. I must have overdone it as she asked me what was wrong and I answered untruthfully that I always felt sick in a car because I had low blood pressure. She rose and went to the window and shouted at the top of her voice, "A glass of water for Miss Asmahan," then asked me if I wanted an aspirin.

"She'll be as right as rain in a couple of minutes," interrupted Ruhiyya.

When the glass of water didn't appear, Ali's wife went in search of it and Ruhiyya turned to me and said reprovingly, "Come on. Pull yourself together. Who's going to entertain me if you don't? There's nothing here but these flies buzzing in my ears as if they're screwing non-stop."

I laughed. "I will. Don't worry. Do you still remember how you mourned Ali's sister? Whatever was her name?"

"Safiyya, God rest her. Are you planning to entertain me by raking up stories of people who've died?"

"Can't you remember what you did? Ali is annoyed about it to this day."

"Why would I forget? It's all written here," pointing to her head. "As God is my witness."

"Good. Tell me about it."

"Here? They think I'm cursed. They'll say I bring bad luck.

Don't you see how much Ali hates me? Do you want him to strangle me?"

She closed her eyes then opened them again and whispered, "I don't know why he misunderstood. I swear the trees and the rocks wept when I sang a lament for her."

She shut her eyes again and sang softly:

"My beloved, your eyes will never blink again
My beloved, these lips will never drink again,
My beloved, you'll never eat again and thank God for the
    food he has given,
My beloved, keep your hands outside the sheets
Because they're coming to bury you in the ground."

Then without warning her mood changed and she sang in a different voice:

"O Asma, Asmahan, your name is always on my tongue
I love you blindly
I see you before me in a sky-blue dress."

"I don't like blue," I interrupted. "And why the sudden change?"

"Sorrow and joy are two sides of the same coin, Miss Knowall. There are things to make you laugh and things to make you cry in this world and the next."

We stood up simultaneously to leave the oven-like room, and found Ali's wife waiting in the dusty yard for someone to bring lemons for my stomach. I looked around for Jawad but there was no sign of him. Ali's car had disappeared and I assumed the two of them had gone off to buy roast chickens in the nearby town, as I'd heard Ali and his wife discussing it when we first arrived.

She said her husband would soon be back and I wished I had the courage to ask about Jawad, but then a cry rose from a nearby building.

"The gentleman's taking pictures in the factory and they all think he's a magician," she remarked, gesturing towards the building, which was white with brown-painted windows and a tin roof propped up by a tree trunk and some rocks.

"Let's go in and have a look," I said to Ruhiyya.

Ali's wife intervened. "If you're still feeling unwell, don't go in the factory. The smell in there at the moment is enough to kill you."

"Smell of what?"

"They're making cannabis resin today."

"I'm fine now. I don't feel sick any more. Please don't bother with the lemons."

Jawad was taking pictures with his Polaroid of Ali's mother-in-law, who looked my age, and a lot of other women and some children. When he saw us he asked them for some of the photos back. "Just for a moment, so I can show them to Asmahan."

He approached me eagerly, clutching photos in both hands. "Have a look! See the modern light switch there, and then their clothes!"

The sound of shouting, coughing and talking filled the large room, which was crammed with women of all ages with only their eyes showing. Some rubbed black balls of hashish in their hands, others stirred it as it simmered over the fire. There were those who weighed it and inspected it for colour and consistency while the dust was scattered over the metal containers and the pumps which worked away noisily.

Jawad's smile revealed teeth which looked as though they had never had to chew food, as if they existed to smile. The women laughed delightedly at him. "What else do you want to take a picture of, dear?" said one. "You've got nearly everything except me, and I'm too old. If you like, you can have one of my granddaughter."

A tractor drew up outside the building overflowing with cannabis plants piled on top of one another under transparent plastic sheeting. Next to the driver was another man almost sitting on the wheel. A car stopped behind the tractor and three men climbed out, bristling with arms, obviously guarding the tractor's cargo. The men from the tractor unloaded it and put it in the corner of a small enclosure. The cries of the children announcing Ali's arrival, the sight of these men in their motley outfits with cigarettes dangling from their smiling mouths made me convinced that what had taken place in Ruhiyya's house the evening before was a bad dream. The men around here spent most of their time laughing together, drinking arak and showing off their fast cars, while the arms they displayed so prominently seemed more like a fashion, like the craze for growing one fingernail long. They were supposed to belong to different parties and carry weapons to wipe each other out or dominate one another. But on this plain they aimed their guns to protect one another: here each party, each sect needed the other. Who would distribute these sacks of hashish apart from the Christians with their connections with the outside world? Who would plant the cannabis, irrigate it and harvest it, other than the Shiites? Who would handle the cocaine if the Druzes didn't?

"Don't be fooled, Ali," remarked Jawad. "Money, not national unity is what binds people together, from the informers, to the militias, to Israel in the skies."

Ali's wife entered slowly carrying a glass of lemon juice, despite my earlier protestations, and warning everyone not to jog her. I rushed up and took it from her, thanking her, and then drank it without enthusiasm as the salt which had been added to it overpowered even the acidity of the lemons.

We went back into the stiflingly hot room and still managed to demolish the roast chickens Ali had brought, dipping our portions into a bowl of garlic. Ali's wife urged everyone she saw surreptitiously glancing at us through the window, especially the children, to come in and join us. Nobody dared take up the offer except her son. "I'm not surprised. They're probably scared we'll eat them," said Ruhiyya. "Look! We've stripped the carcases bare."

We all laughed and I started to smell garlic everywhere, even in the water I was drinking. Jawad spread the photographs before us as he tried to choose which to keep for himself and which to distribute to their subjects. Looking at them from a distance as they were handed round, Ali asked Jawad to take one of him with his wife. When it was ready, he seized it, gazing at it admiringly and remarking on her beauty. As we left she promised to visit me when she joined Ali in Beirut at the end of the season.

While Ruhiyya and I began to feel drowsy again, the visit, especially the food, had fired Jawad's enthusiasm and he questioned Ali eagerly.

The car drew up at a checkpoint. Half asleep we heard, "Would brother Jawad kindly accompany us?"

In a split second your spirit reigned supreme again, and it was as if it had never gone away. Ali turned to us and the militiaman had his face inside the car studying us, while he kept a tight hold on Jawad's passport and the papers for Ali's car. Another man squeezed in beside him and looked at us too. "Mr Jawad, please come with us."

Ruhiyya screamed, clutching Jawad's arm disbelievingly. "We came a route which nobody knows. How did they track us down?"

Ali yelled at her to keep quiet. She must have begun to doubt him; I certainly had, but Jawad tried to calm her. At the sound of his voice we both went wild and began screaming uncontrollably at the two men. Ali shouted at us to be quiet. "Can I get out and have a word with you?" he asked them.

"Go ahead," said the man who still had his head in the car.

As Ali opened the door to get out, he turned towards us. "Don't be afraid," he said.

He took the man by the arm and walked a little way off with him. Another one stuck his head in at the window for a moment, then straightened up again, resting his hand on the car. We peered out and the sight of Ali with the cigarette still in his hand as he talked seemed to allow us to draw breath for the first time. He drew on the cigarette, and we took another breath, but when he slowly approached the window we realized that he hadn't managed to have his way. I guessed there was some real danger as he said in a resigned tone, "Mr Jawad, it looks as if the boys want to talk to you."

Jawad dismounted with difficulty because Ruhiyya was screaming and hanging on to him. Ali opened the other door and began pulling her away while Jawad put his arm round her in an attempt to soothe her. "Take me instead," she wailed. "Kill me. Do what you like to me. Isn't he the same religion as you even if he does live abroad?"

I got out of the car too and caught up with them. One of the fighters was trying to talk to her as she grew more and more hysterical. "Listen to me," he shouted. "We just want a word with him. We'll give him a cup of coffee in the office and he'll be back."

Ruhiyya appeared to listen for a moment, then started to wail and shout and chase after Jawad again. She clung to him as he comforted her and patted her on the shoulder. Nothing would persuade her to stop until in the end one of them came up and asked me to calm her down, swearing they would have him back shortly.

They didn't take him into the little room adjoining the check-point but went off towards the jeep with him. At this Ruhiyya began shouting again. "See, Asmahan, they're kidnapping him. They've kidnapped him right under our noses. They think he's a foreign spy."

One of them was still sticking to us like a shadow and he started to reassure her. "He hasn't been kidnapped at all. There's nothing to worry about. He'll be back in a few minutes."

The sight of Ali climbing aboard the jeep ahead of Jawad set us off again shouting hysterically despite the militiaman's repeated assurances. "Don't be afraid. I'm with you. They'll be back very soon."

Our voices and his wove together in my head and passed into Ruhiyya's, then back into mine, so that we became like trees growing so close together that their branches intertwined and they no longer knew which fruit was whose.

"Please get into the car. It's better if you don't wait on the road."

We needed no further incitement to action. Noticing the keys were still inside I shouted at Ruhiyya to get in, started the engine and went after the jeep, which was still in sight. Ruhiyya was squirming uneasily like a thirsty plant but suddenly the life spread through her veins and she started encouraging me as I flew along, my hand never leaving the horn, until the jeep's passengers noticed us. Ali began giving us directions and the sight of Jawad's head from behind reassured us: I wished we were following the jeep to the bank of a stream which we'd never seen before, where we would spread out our picnic and put the melon to cool in the water. Then I found myself shouting and swearing. Crying, laughing. I've gone crazy living among these madmen whose sterile ideas provoke them into frenzied outbursts of noise and activity. What will their interrogation of Jawad achieve? Again I shout, swear, cry. Yes, we're at war. Gang warfare fought over religion, politics, money.

Once we had entered the small town where there were people and cars and shops the forlorn emptiness of the plain fell away from us and a sense of calm flowed slowly back. When the jeep drew up in front of one of the many-storeyed buildings, our optimism grew.

They dismounted one after another like friends on an outing. Ali looked towards us and gave a wave and a smile. Jawad did the same. Then they all went into the building. A pharmacy was tucked away to one side of the entrance, a butcher's to the other, and on the first floor were the offices of a big bank. The fighter whom we'd left behind on the plain suddenly appeared and put his head in at our car window, so that his face was almost touching mine, and reproached us for running away from him. Then he asked if we wanted something to drink.

I declined, but Ruhiyya answered eagerly, "Quickly, please! Something fizzy to cool me down. God bless you!"

He nodded and stared at me ominously. When he'd gone Ruhiyya turned to me and said irritably, "Let's be friendly to them. Please, not another word until our darling's back with us."

"That fool's stoned."

"I only hope the ones up there are too."

The youth returned with a bottle of water and stood there holding it. He asked why my eyes were the colour they were and pressed my hand as I took the bottle from him. I clutched the bottle, feeling its icy coldness spreading through me.

"Come on, give me a drink of water. I'm dying of thirst," said Ruhiyya as if we were two small children.

I loosened my grip on on it and passed it over to her. "Struggle. Heroism. Progress. Victory," the fighter said expressionlessly, like a recording which had been played again and again.

"That's right, love, God grant you victory, and victory to the people of Muhammad and Imam Ali, Lord," responded Ruhiyya. She assumed an air of affectionate concern. "Who wants to question him, dear? Get into the car, dear. It's better not to stand out in the sun. Who is it wants to question him?"

"The lads upstairs."

"That's obvious. I mean, what side are they on? We've got connections." Then she added in some agitation, "I swear we know people who'll kill anyone who touches a hair of his head. Who do they think he is?"

"Don't be afraid. Do you think we're savages or something?"

Fearing she'd insulted him, Ruhiyya backtracked. "Not at all. No offence. I still respect you with all my heart. Just go up and see what's happening. Please. We want to know."

"Okay," he muttered, softening at her tone.

He went off laboriously into the building. We both fastened our eyes on the entrance. Ruhiyya's seemed to have glazed over suddenly: she neither blinked nor breathed; her face was immobile. After a time I fidgeted uneasily. I looked at her but she didn't notice me although she wrinkled her forehead occasionally. I waved my hand in front of her face, but she ignored me or didn't see me. Her eyes were about to burst out of their sockets. Then Ali suddenly came out alone.

The moment Ruhiyya opened her mouth to speak, Ali cut in: "Jawad's coming. He's coming."

He smiled at me, exposing yellow teeth and a chin like a pit of thorns.

"Please go back to him," screamed Ruhiyya. "I know he's coming."

"Well, Miss Asma. You've got some admirers. There's a young man wanting to marry you but I told him you were already engaged."

"Why did you say that?" cried Ruhiyya reproachfully. "Say of course you can have her. Then when Jawad's back with us we can put one finger up at them and say that was your lunch and this is your supper."

I laughed, and Ali shook his head. "You're crazy," he told her.

"I'm not crazy at all. I brought you down from up there. Mind over matter. When my head began to buzz and hum I knew you were coming. And if I'd been alone without this ape Asma and all the noise in the street I could have told you to come much sooner."

"You're really crazy."

The minute we noticed Jawad we jumped out of the car and rushed over to where he was shaking hands with all the men who had escorted him downstairs. Ali took him by the arm. "Thanks a lot, lads," he said to the fighters.

Ruhiyya threw herself on Jawad and tried to drag him to sit next to her in the back but he went in front with Ali. When the car had travelled a short distance she burst into tears. "May God deprive them of the health and strength to do their evil work."

She embraced Jawad's head from behind, sobbing as if the enormity of what had happened had only just struck her. Instead of pushing her away, he allowed his head to rest on her hands. Then he turned round to her and stroked her head-scarf soothingly. I hesitated a little before resting my hand on his for a moment. He glanced at me and smiled.

Jawad made no comment on the events, even when Ruhiyya composed herself enough to ask him what reason they had for questioning him. When Ali had a chance to ask him what had happened, Ruhiyya interrupted, "You expect us to believe that you don't know, Mr Ali?"

Taking one hand off the steering wheel, Ali turned to face into the back of the car. "The Prophet Muhammad and Imam Ali are my enemies if I'm lying. Ask Mr Jawad. They made me wait outside. I stayed right by the door and didn't move an inch although the man in charge promised me Jawad was safe."

Jawad didn't want to talk about what had happened; they must have threatened him. A long time seemed to pass before we all returned to normal. Staring out through the car windows helped each of us to pick up the thread of calm interrupted by this episode.

We were still caught up in the snarls of your making, in spite of the calming effect of the rocks and mountains and neat stacks of firewood. There was a flock of sheep driven by a shepherd of eight or nine years old; when our eyes met he held up a black-eared lamb in greeting. A woman sold melons by the roadside. I opened my eyes wide like Ruhiyya and gazed at everything, then closed them so that the sound took over, and when it grew regular, I went over what had happened step by step and arrived at the questions and answers. They were always there, and yet I never paid them any attention before.

Why do people go on doing your work even though they have discovered that it involves nothing but death and destruction and that the politics is not about parties but symbols? I know the answer: because people have a desperate need to enter any conflict which has become familiar and acceptable to them to save them searching further afield and investigating the mysteries of life and death. Therefore they let your conflict take them wherever it wishes. In spite of the danger, they find they have stopped being uncertain. You give them confidence and a kind of serenity; people make this precious discovery and play your game.

What shall I do with these ideas? Expose them to the light so Jawad can latch on to them and publish them for all the world to see, or discuss them with Kazim and the Modern Sheikh and Ricardo? I recalled the desire in the eyes of the young men, Ricardo, Kazim's brother and others, some less than twenty, as they passed round an M16. To them it wasn't an instrument of death, but something they'd always wanted, like a woman, and now they were in her presence even if they hadn't all held her.

I confess that I'm living an anxious life in a city of anxiety because of you, but haven't you exposed and strengthened the core which was so hard to find when the country turned around itself, glorying in its glittering protective shell?

But there I go again describing you as if you are water which has been filtered until it is pure despite all the germs at the bottom. How can I connect the way I have arrived at the essence of things, thanks to you, with my friend whispering to me as I studied her husband's sculptures, "It's all a lie"?

I didn't understand what she meant until she told me the tale of how some militiamen had attacked their neighbours. The man's wife was hacked to pieces and let out a cry which shook the building. When she had called out for help, my friend and her husband, the sculptor, had hastily switched off all their lights and crouched behind the door. She said the sound of the woman's screams tore at her flesh, but at the same time the desire to save themselves prevented them from doing anything to help.

Jawad talks with his face almost flying out through the car window. I see the pulse in his brown neck. I have never felt as close to him as I feel now. He'll continue to be ignorant of what's happening, even though he has heard and read about you and tried to suffer with those who suffer at your hands, but his imagination can't grasp the ruins and the deserted shops he's passing now and he seems to swallow his sentence: "As long as there are people there is no ultimate destruction."

His words trail off and he catches his breath with the rest of us at the sight of houses without doors or windows, apparently inhabited only by the cry of birds and the sigh of the wind, although a vine trellis, a television aerial, a washing-line suggest otherwise.

We approach Beirut. Jawad reads on a wall, "No bread. No fuel. We're going to die."

I seem to see Beirut with its soul and guts hanging out, then I see it strong and unyielding and am filled with affection for it. Life appears normal, despite the collapse of its outer trappings. A couple of days before I left I started writing letters to Hayat and the kidnap victims, not only because most of my friends had gone, but because I and those around me no longer talked or listened to ideas which would shake us out of our stupor.

I wonder regretfully now how you managed to make us hang on to you like a baby's dummy and allow you to divert our attention from what was going on in the rest of the world. We crouched listening avidly for news of you from one day to the next, waiting for you to collect your belongings and move on.

9

My Dear Beirut

I've realized that you have two skies, because I've begun to see
you through Jawad's eyes: a sky of telephone wires and electricity cables coming from every direction like a spider-web
tent, and another high above where there are stars shining. I
don't remember stars like that in your sky before. Is it because
the damp weather has cleared, or is it the darkness which hides
wrinkles and makes bright stars visible? The moon, bigger and
fuller than ever, appears to be doing its job properly for the
first time, moving away from the sea to light up the streets.
The buildings are in darkness, apart from the occasional lighted
window. Jawad says, "Once upon a time, Clever Hasan saw a
glimmer of light in the distance . . ."

The darkness had the effect of making people's voices quieter
and deadening the constant blare of televisions. Jawad wanted
to go to the Italian restaurant to see if the waiter with arms
nearly to his feet was still there. There was a huge pile of
rotting garbage at the door but the waiter was inside and a
handful of tables was occupied. Much to Jawad's surprise the
women had handbags with them, instead of the usual water
containers. We went on to the Corniche and sat on two chairs
belonging to a mobile café facing Jounieh and the dark mountains. The sound of the waves drowned out the noise of the
generator, as we drank tea and watched the mist rising up off
the sea and advancing towards us. Jawad gripped the grey
chain railing. The mist grew thicker, cocooning us, drawing us

close in to you, and Jawad, affected by the surroundings, remarked that cities never die.

He sits, absent-minded and removed from my desire for him. I feel closer to him tonight. The car was different in the dark as we waited at checkpoints. The buildings change at night, the streets are empty of cars and people and at dawn the sound of invisible cats and dogs reaches a crescendo, to be replaced by the shouting of soldiers on their morning exercises.

I realize this night isn't going to go anywhere; Jawad sits silent and distracted, then says he wants to go to bed early. He asks me if I'll drive him around the following day or if he should hire a taxi. Hire a taxi, as if he is going to the seaside or the cafés up the mountain! I laugh, shaking my head and saying nothing.

The next morning I took him "downtown", the word he repeated constantly until he saw the ruins, when he held his breath in case he missed a single detail and looked up into the sky, perhaps to confirm that life went on. I was shocked by what I saw, even though I had visited the ruined markets several years before with Hayat. Silence hung over the long grass and monstrous plants, which would have looked less strange had they been trees with thick roots, growing individually, but they were springing out of the floors and walls and up through the roofs of the melancholy shops and offices.

Jawad closes his eyes, wanting to believe that things are as they were and that he's merely gone deaf or has distorted vision. Images buried in the convolutions of his mind rise to the surface. The top floor of the building like an elephant lying on its side used to house an eye clinic. There his mother had shown him two photographs of his grandmother, displayed to encourage prospective patients, before and after an operation to her right eye. The occasion of the operation had been the old lady's first time in the city and as she went to get in to the lift she had turned to her daughter crossly and said, "For goodness' sake, what have you been giving me to eat if you need to bring me to scales like these to weigh me?"

"Paloma" was the hairdresser's where they put a wig on my mother's head to encourage her to buy it. The smell of hairspray and the beer they used to make the hair lie flat and smooth as paper seems to linger in the air. The narrow lane is still there and the rooms overlooking it where I'd dreamt I was destined to end my days. A taxi had dropped me and Zemzem near here, between a repair garage and a bakery, close to the taxi rank. I clutched Zemzem's hand as she protested loudly to the driver who refused to go on to Sahat Al-Burj. "Lord, what a disaster!" she cried.

Instructing me not to look to right or left, she wrapped her scarf round her face, almost covering her eyes, and shouted to me to hurry; as I ran I was looking about me to try and find out why she was afraid, but all I could see were the garage mechanics covered in oil from head to foot. "Why? What is this place?" I asked, smelling the newly baked bread.

"A market where respectable people work."

I didn't realize that she meant the opposite until I heard her telling my grandmother about it, trembling, raising her eyes imploringly to the ceiling: "Lord, I hope nobody saw me," she moaned.

"So what if they did? Asma was with you, wasn't she? What's all the fuss about?" my grandmother had replied scornfully.

When I first thought about sex and love, instead of dreaming of a boy of my own age or a movie star, I began to have nightmares about being in a room in the red-light district and not daring to escape in case one of the men of the family killed me. The dream comes back to haunt me and makes me more frightened than ever of approaching Sahat Al-Burj from the direction of the market.

Jawad must realize why I laughed yesterday when he suggested taking a taxi. These ruins are bound to be shocking: you need to be prepared and be with someone you know. They're always shocking, however much you think you're used to their barbarity.

I remember when I was with Hayat a militiaman rising from behind a table in the emptiness and offering us a cup of coffee. Hayat hesitated, but I nodded my head gratefully. I was moved to be confronted by his kind, lonely eyes in the midst of this destruction; the tall plants all around created a sombre, slightly eerie atmosphere and I asked him if he was scared at nights. He laughed and tapped his gun. "How could I be?"

As we stood up to go he whispered in my ear that he was afraid of owls and there were dozens about. "And of crazy dogs," he added, like someone concerned to be as honest as possible.

To my surprise he asked if he could have a lock of my hair. As I was thinking that perhaps he hadn't seen a woman for a long time or was on drugs, he took out a Swiss army knife with a tiny pair of scissors attached to it. I held out my hand to take it but he came close to me and cut off an end of my hair, then tore a piece off an old newspaper serving as a table-cloth under a dish and empty beer glass, wrapped the hair carefully in it and put it away in his shirt pocket. I couldn't erase the scene from my mind for days and had visions of the lock of hair in the torn-off bit of newspaper hidden in his pocket each time I brushed my hair, and thought of that vast high-ceilinged room open to the street where there was a fighter who was afraid of hooting owls.

Now I am bored by these ruins, but I don't want to force Jawad to leave for it takes time to absorb it all. It's impossible not to have vivid memories of the past here, and then the ruins spring to life, with the temporary return of the imported palm trees, hurrying pedestrians, blaring horns, and distinctive smells of coffee, grilled meat, garlic. I remember my first visit to the commercial district after a gap of several years. I woke up one day in Simon's apartment and opened my eyes to see him picking his clothes up off the floor and pulling them on. He kissed me on the forehead and told me to wait for him in the hotel that afternoon. Simon was a press photographer who had a sad look in his green eyes, except when he was working. We had only dared to speak to one another the day before but we'd been exchanging furtive glances for the previous week. Although I was hung over I got up too and dressed hurriedly so that I could go with him to Sahat Al-Burj. Almost overnight this area had become a malign sickness affecting the collective mind. It had been the commercial heart of the city and now the roads had turned in on themselves and were known only as access and exit points. My breathless enthusiasm lasted until I saw a fig tree bearing a single fruit; it was bent double as if groaning with exhaustion, its broad, spreading leaves silent and covered in dust. I felt it was looking at me sadly, without reproach, but I knew I was a traitor because I had shown no aversion to the war.

From the roof of the Azariyya building I saw buildings collapsing like dominoes. The ones that resisted seemed to be waiting their turn, observing the splendid collapse of those around them; it was as if they preserved within them the memory of the past in the colour of their paint, the tiles, the electricity cables and the hoardings. An advertisement for a film surviving as a reminder of the city in the days when it used to swallow lights and spit them out like a fire-breathing dragon. The remains of a neon arrow pointing to Aazar coffee. The collapsing buildings like spotted leopards crashing to the ground. Strange colours for which people had no names, as they stood watching overwhelmed by the spectacle of the dismemberment of what had constituted everyday life. I found myself thinking of our house. Would it be like this one day? Then I rushed into the jaws of death with Simon and ate sandwiches with a group of snipers; a little end of the blue sea showed behind us, very blue. Simon wanted to make me understand that sniping was a military tactic, not a giant in the sky who regarded everything that moved on the ground as fair game.

There were three of them. One was staring intently through a pair of binoculars searching for prey. He said to the others quietly, "See the washing line. That woman pouring coffee. No. Next to the building with green windows. Yes, there."

"Yes, yes. I said from the start above the Pepsi Cola sign."

"That's right. The woman in a stripy dress."

Their sudden silence took me by surprise. I saw the gun recoil violently, then the man who had fired it laid it on the ground. "It was the woman in a blue dress," he said.

What I saw with Simon made me think about the war in a completely different way from those who didn't leave their houses and derived their view of what was happening from the radio, newspapers and the terror of the battles outside their windows. I hadn't simply grown accustomed to the idea of war; life and death had become realities embedded in the space before my eyes and in my throat, thanks to Simon. He was like two different people: one confident that he was protected from death by being in the thick of things, and the other suffering from a fear he couldn't dislodge, a chronic condition which set in as soon as it got dark, making him feel as if he was in a sauna bathed alternately in hot and cold sweat. He lit large numbers of candles but they only increased his feelings of isolation. His imagination gave birth to spectres and he felt that he was being watched. The moment he extinguished his candles his thoughts rushed in, confused and sick, and the night became an instrument of torture, bearing down on his chest with its leaden blackness so that he had difficulty breathing. He tried to shift it without success, for the air he breathed in the house was as heavy as if it was weighed down with tiny fragments of metal. Any moment now he was certain a bullet would lodge in his head, or flying shrapnel would burst through the walls and blow the place apart. He went to bed, but couldn't sleep; he wanted some affection. He wanted sex. He wanted to forget the violence. But even these sexual feelings couldn't erase the entrenched fear which had become synonymous with his soul, and which only departed in the morning, when he got up and light was flooding the room, and his clothes and the furniture and everything around him looked familiar and reminded him of the orderly routine of life. Out in the street, he liked the familiar disc of the sun, first red then yellow, which penetrated the fibres of his anxiety with a brilliant warmth, making him forget the night even existed and giving him the spirit to start the day afresh. The reality of the war re-established itself gradually and he rushed from place to place, with his camera slung round his neck, recording his fear and deferring it till night time.

Simon became the strength I drew on to carry me through my day, the news bulletin which, however unpleasant, was clear and activated my mind, bringing me closer to events. But Simon decided to leave. This didn't bother me at first, because he said he was leaving all the time. The first time we talked he told me how he decided to leave during the massacre of Karantina when he was certain he was going to be killed. In Karantina he had seen bodies piled up at street corners just like garbage. Bodies stacked in pyramids of assorted colours with irregular corners because of a random hand or foot or head sticking out. When he realized who was guarding one of these lopsided pyramids, not allowing photographers anywhere near it, he knew his luck was in. It was Abu'l-Zooz, the joiner who did work for his family and made all the wooden furniture they required. "I said to Abu'l-Zooz, 'I want to take a photo,' " Simon told me. "He was delighted for me to see him in this important position.

" 'Certainly. You can take everything except this,' gesturing at the pile of corpses.

" 'Fine. I wouldn't want to anyway. No one would publish it,' I answered indifferently, without looking at the human pyramid.

"I started clicking away, and managed to get a picture of it while he was busy offering me a glass of champagne and asking after my family. That picture was published in the world press and even though my name didn't appear on it I was terrified of Abu'l-Zooz. Only when things had settled down did he go back to his old trade. My mother invited him to the house to make sure that he was well-disposed towards me, filling up his plate each time he emptied it so he couldn't say anything about me."

But Simon wept, determined to leave the western sector. He had discovered how misguided he'd been to think the fact he was a Christian wouldn't stand in the way of him forming close relationships with the fighters, be they Palestinians, communists, Shiites or Druzes. All along he had remained convinced his name and religion were matters of chance and had nothing to do with him personally. He wouldn't even acknowledge that this could have been changed by the war. But, on a day when the desire for revenge reached huge proportions following battles and kidnappings on both sides, he was taken captive at a checkpoint and learnt that his name could be a matter of life and death.

In the end he hadn't been saved by the permits he carried nor by mentioning the names of important people in the resistance, since the militiaman holding him was impervious to reason and sense. All that saved him from certain death was the decision of the high-up official who came to inspect the hostages. Questioning Simon, he found he was wearing a bullet-proof jacket and this convinced him he had tumbled on a foreign spy, not a press photographer as the hostage claimed to be.

I couldn't help wondering, as Simon told me he had finally decided to go, how he would live away from the war, which had become his full-time job. His office was the trenches, the barricades and the empty buildings. I felt then that I didn't know him and hadn't experienced the taste of his lips, the weight of his body on mine, although sometimes we had been content just to hold hands in the darkness which was so powerful and so soft that it drowned out the sound of explosions. We derived warmth and tenderness from the sound of each other's breathing like two old people obliged to be together because they shared the same dentures. As I said goodbye to him I held him close, even though it was broad daylight in the hotel entrance lounge, promising to visit him in the eastern sector and stay with him for a few days every now and then. But as soon as I turned away from the hotel, Simon went right out of my mind; I thought about him from time to time when I wanted some affection, some physical contact, and crossed into the east as if I was walking a tightrope, swinging wildly between wanting to be with him and wishing I hadn't come. Eventually the thread that had joined us wore away and we rarely met because our city was divided in two.

After the duty-free market with its beautiful stone walls, the ruins and the jungle of monster plants, Jawad and I take a road which leads us by women with heads wrapped in black kerchiefs. One of them has a candle in her hand: I guess she must make regular visits to the remains of the church there.

One day I had broken free from my father's hand and gone into this little church. It smelt strongly of candles and incense and was lit by glowing chandeliers and the Virgin Mary's face ringed with gold and silver haloes behind protective glass. If you stuck a twenty-five piastre piece on the glass you knew that your prayers would be answered. I remember rushing outside to my father, who was buying vegetables, and pretending to be nauseous with hunger so that he would give me a quarter lira to stick on the magic glass in the church, then perhaps the glittering gold saint would exchange my father for a new one. But he wouldn't give me a quarter lira and dragged me from one market to another and through a narrow archway into a little place, gloomy as a rat's hole, which opened into another market smelling of roast meat; here we sat down with a lot of men at wooden tables. I heard one of them saying he could eat three camels. I asked my father if I had to eat a whole camel.

My father used to have a shop close by which my uncle had been forced to sell because it became obvious the losses could never be recouped once my father had decided to work for God; he refused to make a profit of one single piastre on his fine quality broadcloth, even though his brother and other members of the family took him to consult a man of religion, who urged him to return to buying and selling as before, limiting his profits in accordance with religious law. But my father renounced everything. He began selling off the Persian rugs in our house and my mother's jewellery, unknown to her, then donated the money to mosques in Iraq, indifferent to her wails of protest: she had been proud that my father's business was in the heart of a commercial area and well known to many people, and tried to make him do his duty again, threatening to leave him or devising ways to catch him out, but my father had moved into a world of his own, far removed from ordinary everyday life. He would have liked to be able to prohibit Isaf the maid and my mother from discussing mundane topics, so that they could spend their time and energy on praying. He stopped shaving his beard regularly, wore the same suit and pair of shoes every day, had his old red tarboosh repaired again and even shaved his head for the sake of cleanliness and purity. His relations gradually stopped visiting us, as all he talked about was repentance and Judgement Day. He advised one of them not to send his son to medical school, since God was the only true doctor, and said that instead he should go to Iraq to study Islamic jurisprudence and law. So it went on, until we found we had even stopped waiting for him at mealtimes. In fact it was a burden to us when he did appear, and my mother started up a flurry of activity in the house whenever he began to pray, hoping he would go to the mosque.

Jawad and I progress from the duty-free zone and Suq Sursuq to Al-Azariyya where the smell of old books still seems to hang in the air. His father had apparently insisted on bringing him secondhand books, in particular from a bookshop here belonging to a relative's family, and was never happy buying a new book, however cheap. Meanwhile I am thinking of the Capitol Hotel and Omar Sharif. I tell Jawad about going to the hotel with Aida who was thirteen, and on her way to take her father his lunch in the cloth market when she saw Omar Sharif going into the hotel. She caught up with him inside and told him about his admirers in her school. He was amused by this bright little girl who offered him some of her father's lunch. "You take care of your father's lunch, my dear," he said, "and we'll see you again some time."

Aida went back that same afternoon with three pretty girls from the top class and led them up to his room. He opened the door and looked embarrassed because he was wearing a hairnet to flatten out his crinkly hair.

Jawad responds to the mood of these memories, but proceeds to tell me of experiences as remote from mine as they could be. His thoughts had always revolved around phrases he couldn't get out of his mind, and feelings which pestered him to let them see themselves on paper. He wrote his first novel and hawked it round the publishing houses, who asked if he was prepared to pay the costs of having it published. As a result he stopped writing and put all his efforts into finding a way of leaving the country and going abroad, explaining to foreign consulates how vital it was for him to study in their countries, how much he longed to go abroad and experience a foreign culture, and describing his situation living in a house which was full of noise from morning till night.

I sit with Jawad in a café overlooking the sea with the ruins behind us. We hear the waves gently lapping against the wooden foundations and they seem to say everything's still the same. It's as if I've never left this chair, as if I'm still sitting in a group of students and we form a single network of thoughts and ambitions. Now I can erase from my mind the vision of myself naked in his arms, grateful to the circumstances which have prevented this idea becoming a reality. I find doing this gives me a feeling of strength which changes to happiness and makes me fly above the café table, at ease and restored to myself after a long separation. I study my fingers and the palm of my hand which seem important again as they did in the past.

As soon as we get up to go, the destruction is there in front of us again in spite of the sea, the sky, the sun, the leaves on the trees, the distant birds. We are uneasy too far from the sight of the war and its trail of refuse. Even the groups of soldiers, whether they are Syrian or Lebanese, arouse vague feelings of affection.

Everyone says "The eastern sector" and "The western sector", and your divisions have become a fact of life.

The eastern sector and the western sector. The old names have faded in importance, names that seemed to have been there for all time: Jounieh, Jbeil, Al-Dawrah. New names have become prominent: Tariq al-Franciscan, Sudeco, the Museum with its mud and water, the smell of urine and the people crossing from one sector to another with sorrow in their faces, a heavy weight on their shoulders, and the sense of frustration which escalates if this route is suddenly closed. People are always uncertain whether to choose the Sudeco route where there is sniping or the route by the Museum which is more difficult and requires advance planning.

Jawad is studying the roads again, no doubt trying to recognize them. His silence, punctuated by deep sighs, speaks clearly to me, his thoughts burn straight into my mind and interfere with my memories. As I look towards Sharia Muhammad al-Hout he shouts, "That's the racecourse! Would you believe it? The main entrance of the racecourse!"

The black iron gates have split right through and are covered in spots of rust like leprous scabs infecting even the gold whorls adorning the top of them. At Jawad's insistence we go into the racecourse. People are dipping through a hole in the wall as if escaping into a green oasis between the trees. Despite the strong smell of urine they pour through in their tens and hundreds, walking silently. They must be calculating the risks to themselves, hoping to reach the other sector without hearing a shot, and so they move as if they are on an urgent mission.

Jawad is thinking, "If they allow people to cross here, why don't they allow them to cross anywhere?"

I'm thinking, "I'm sure these people are wondering if they'll find anyone to give them a lift when they reach the eastern sector."

Jawad says aloud, "They are rushing through a bare landscape, between two sections of a city. Where are they going? Are they escaping from an ogre or congratulating themselves on winning their own personal Battle of Hittin? Or are they thirsty tribesmen who know where there's another oasis with plenty of grass and water?"

I laugh at Jawad's comparisons although I'm irritated at the way he continues to look at everything as if he is turning it into a work of literature.

Some people are going to their jobs in the other sector carrying their papers and food. An elegantly dressed woman bends down and puts on a pair of plastic overshoes. She must have got them from Europe. Two girls strut along unconcerned, in high heels that plunge deep into the mud, on their way to keep a date. One puts a bit more lipstick on and the other rearranges her hair.

Jawad used to go to the racecourse with his family and play in the big gardens. There was nothing to equal the smell of the racecourse gardens: pine, camomile, wild rose. He remembers Ruhiyya lighting a fire of pine twigs when he had whooping cough and making him inhale the smoke.

I have to strain to see the top of Sharia Muhammad al-Hout where I was born. It branches off Sharia al-Sabaq where we are now. I look at it, and at Sharia Hiroshima and see an image of myself walking along the pavement where the restaurant was, following my father. I see my mother wearing a hairband like a twenties hat, right back off her forehead. I see her laughing eyes. She gasps and says to my uncle, "Did the fortune teller really say that?" My uncle is reading her the biography of the singer Asmahan. "You were born in water and in water you will die."

I can see my mother, but not myself. For I am Asmahan and Asma. I see my mother, the beautiful child-woman, who suddenly turned and saw me there in her life. I call "Mama" and she remembers I'm not the singer Asmahan as a child, but her own daughter and what's more the daughter of a man whom she doesn't want to recognize as her husband, because he doesn't look a bit like her favourite stars, croon the latest songs, flirt, or even belong to the same epoch as her.

So when he lay motionless and Isaf's scream reverberated through the house, my mother, assuming he was dead, rushed around burning everything which reminded her of him so she could return to the present. Asmahan. My own voice is calling now. Asmahan. Asma. I see myself in the street where a car is revving its engine ready to try and cut across into the eastern sector. Nowadays the street looks like part of a film-set, with its façades built of cheap wood and stone and most of the shop signs removed or worn away. I can hardly make out the bakery, the Banana Bar and the dry-cleaner's. My father's building is occupied by squatters, except for our apartment, where I used to position myself before the hallstand, hands on its cool marble, gaze into the mirror and repeat, "I am Nadine, daughter of the famous actress."

I stood on the opposite pavement watching my father search intently through a pile of garbage, then make his way to the restaurant. I bought a bar of chocolate and stood sucking it slowly to make it last. I heard someone in the restaurant calling to my father, "Hallo there, Haj Mustafa."

I bought another bar and stood sucking it until my father came out of the restaurant, but I didn't run after him and plead with him as my mother had instructed me to. I said over and over to myself, "Who are you? I don't know you."

A woman and her daughter were looking at me, whispering together, making up their minds to talk to me. They must know

I'm the daughter of that man clutching the rags he found in the rubbish. I had my answer ready in a flash. The haj is a neighbour of ours. His wife sent me to fetch him back home. And if he called me "baba" as if I was his daughter I'd wink at them and say he calls everyone "baba".

So the girl's question took me completely by surprise. "We were saying you look just like that actress. You could be her sister."

"I'm her daughter," I answered immediately, with complete conviction.

The girl's face beamed with joy. "See. It's true. I told Mama: the resemblance is uncanny."

"Do you live around here?" interrupted her mother in amazement.

I knew at once what she was thinking: stars and media people don't live in this part of town. "Me? No. In Hamra," I answered confidently, in an accent which surprised even me. "I come here for private Arabic lessons." And I gestured to a building on the corner of the street.

We stroll around the racetrack. Signs of life persist there, but like a tree partly uprooted by a storm whose fruit continues to ripen and change colour from yellow to red. The pine trees are burnt and dead. We see a jockey in an Al Capone hat, sitting like a pasha behind a wood brazier with a pot of coffee boiling on it. He smokes, aware that Jawad is looking at him and avoiding his gaze. But Jawad goes up to talk to him about the racetrack and tells him how glad he is to see him, for the presence of the jockey flies in the face of the war's existence, and life around the track seems to go on much as usual. Horses look out of their loose boxes. The trainer sits near the jockey in a short-sleeved shirt drinking coffee. Everyone still treats the jockey as king. He sips his coffee. Steam rises from his cup as he watches the horses, their tails and manes unclipped, roaming idly in the enclosure unattended by a groom.

We went back to the car where Ali was waiting patiently and drove to Sharia Fouad I. I stared intently at it as it flashed past. We stopped once more, this time at an official roadblock. The man said our names weren't on his piece of paper. Ali got out of the car to see what the problem was, and although we were uneasy at not going straight through we began to study the shattered remains of the houses and villas and the trees on either side of the road with leaves like green lace and an orange tinge all year round.

A few minutes later we were at the last checkpoint right beside the Museum. It looked just as it had in the past, as still as the statues inside it. There was always an air of coldness about it, as if it had been forgotten opposite the Hospital for Boys and Children which only had two letters of its name left.

Jawad said that every time he went past in the bus as a child he wondered why it wasn't just called the Hospital for Children. He used to want to be a patient there, surrounded by toys.

Ali said goodbye to us at the Museum crossing and I told him to expect a phone call from me, and urged him not to lose my list of phone numbers. Jawad's eyes rushed ahead of his memory, feeding it material as we walked away from the car. The buildings and the policemen's uniforms were the colour of sand. He used to come here at the end of every month with his grandmother to see his uncle who was a policeman stationed here. They would ask for him at the police post and after a few minutes he would emerge with his mother's medicine which he obtained at a reduced price. Jawad always envied his uncle's police tie and had once asked if he could have it.

I noticed I was no longer so eager to visit the eastern sector. My heart used to pound in my chest like thunder and lightning until I could see someone waiting for me with a car. Even though I had telephone numbers and addresses with me, I used to entertain all sorts of notions, of which the main ones were along the lines of "what if the fighting suddenly starts up and they've forgotten to come and meet me?" or "what if the man at the barrier decides to stop me crossing? It would be like holding a flower up to my nose and having it snatched away."

Here there were official checkpoints and others which came and went according to the changing situation, and whether you got through or not sometimes depended on the mood of the people manning them, the views of the militia, or the politics which were different from day to day.

On my previous visit here when I was only a few steps away from the eastern sector, I had been stopped. The soldier manning the checkpoint looked through my papers and asked me why I wanted to cross.

"I miss the sea at Jounieh," I joked.

"If you miss it why aren't you living here where you can see it, and showing them how wrong they are? West Beirut belongs to Iran now."

I said nothing, but smiled, and to my astonishment he wouldn't let me through.

Even though he had withdrawn the flower before it reached my nose, I kept smiling. He was angry that the city was divided, just as I was. He wanted to express his anger. There was no harm in that; we were both young. He wanted a discussion and so did I, but it wasn't going to work. A taxi-driver drove up to me when he saw me going back and opened the car door for me, cursing the militiamen. He seemed to have taken it upon himself to get me across whatever my reasons for wanting to go.

He said they'd been just the same when his son was trying to cross in the other direction. Even when he'd told them his journey was vital, they'd refused to let him through. At that point there had been a sudden burst of gunfire from the western side of the crossing and the militiaman had called him back. "If you want to cross, go ahead," he'd said smiling.

"Did he go?" I asked the driver.

"Just to spite them, the fool."

The taxi travelled at speed along winding backstreets, across crowded thoroughfares and down deserted roads until we reached a piece of waste ground. He told me to get out and walk across it. "When you see the Pepsi Cola sign, it means you're in the right area. There are plenty of taxis there and they'll take you wherever you want."

I wasn't afraid when he left me on the wasteland. The sight of the sunshine and a distant building with washing hung out to dry on its balconies gave me courage and I set off, sometimes sinking into the sand and sometimes walking on hard dry earth. I was glad to see a few olive trees growing there. They had roots like faces which had been through the war. Even though the main road appeared close I found myself walking and walking. Was this really happening to me or was I walking through the vines to have a picnic with my grandmother and Zemzem?

When I got near the Pepsi Cola sign, it seemed to be saying, "You're safe now. You've arrived."

Would I find my friends, or would my stumbling progress through earth kneaded with urine turn out to have been a waste of time? Just thinking that I was alone in this sector of the city made me sad and a little uneasy, for this was my city too and I had begun to forget its familiar landmarks.

I spent that night in Jounieh in a room overlooking the sea and was plagued by mosquitoes, as the coil went out for no reason. I got up early and went out on to the balcony and leaned over the railing.

Facing the distant mountains, which listened and watched, I wondered why I didn't live here. But I had the niggling feeling that my friends were strangers even in their own apartment and weren't aware of what the road outside looked like, of the trees that grew round about, or the cocks crowing.

They were refugees living alongside other refugees, and had endured the woes of war and been driven from their homes, so that their vision had become clouded, their humanity a little blurred, and they began to pounce on opportunities of work and elbow out the original inhabitants. I went into the living room. The sight of the empty dishes brought a lump to my throat, reminding me of yesterday's dinner when my hostess had brought together people who had been at university with us, the majority of whom had moved in around here over the past months, when their life in the western sector had become impossible. I reproached one of them for not visiting me as he had promised. "Have you severed all your links?"

"God forbid. But I've had to wait around, had some problems. You have to get used to life in this sector."

I called my grandmother and she sounded far away. She asked me if the eastern sector was really the jewel they said it was, sparkling with nightclubs and restaurants. I turned round to look at my friends' chilly expressions. "I'll tell you about the jewels later."

My presence among them must have reminded them of the reality they were trying to forget. Everything was new: their addresses, jobs, homes; only their cars were the same. They had recognized what was going on in the country and settled in these new homes which they cared nothing for, even though some of them had grown up here. For them the heart of the city was in Sahat Al-Burj and Hamra, in their memories of the rumbling of the tram, the neighbour's voice and the low warm gurgle as she smoked her hookah, the frangipani opening overnight. They tried to hang on where they were, scared of what would happen if their patience ran out, but there was a lot of pressure on them from either side of the divide. Sometimes they rushed back to the bosoms of their families where they felt a sense of security, for there are times when a person only feels safe in his own surroundings where he doesn't have to watch what he says, or apologize, or justify the activities of individuals from his own community.

My friends still took a keen interest in the news that reached them from the other side. When it was sad news they chose to believe that the people they knew had escaped unharmed, but they were less discriminating when it came to the reports of how the streets were crammed with men in beards and women enveloped in black, how Iranis were thronging in, new mosques springing up all over the place, Quran recitations droning on from morning till night; the streets had all become alleys, sheep pens, chicken runs; at every corner, in the garage of every building was a prison for foreigners and Christians; every Christian who entered the area was pounced on by two men like Solomon's devils who impaled him on a fork from hell; aircraft only landed to disgorge weapons and fighters. The gulf between the two sectors was widening, not because the access points were being blocked with rubble and iron fencing, but because they were each going their own way.

Where I lived they thought the eastern sector was a jewel suspended between heaven and earth, connected to both by beautiful white bridges, where everything was magnificent: the restaurants, swimming pools, shops. Gesticulating and using their French words the people there referred to the western sector's inhabitants as if they were dirty, ferocious animals. The phalangists' cedar-tree symbol was on every breast, a gun on every shoulder. Sports cars and armoured vehicles raced through the streets. Ships unloaded gold and arms in the ports. The sea, the mountains and the streets were protected by high walls, reaching to the sky.

Jawad draws my attention to the white gardenias everywhere; even the chewing-gum vendors have them, and the beggars hovering around a little table in the middle of the pavement where men sit playing backgammon, a few feet from large piles of garbage. Drivers have them stuck behind their mirrors and they quiver with each blast of the horn. Street traders' barrows are decked out with them. There are solemn groups of people at intervals, buying and selling around once elegant shopfronts, poring over secondhand books and magazines, queuing for cut-price fuel at a mobile gas station, waiting at the cinema. Jawad says they look like mourners at funerals, and many of them, too, are carrying gardenias.

Jawad points to the open sea, and the peerless sky, and exclaims sorrowfully over the tall concrete buildings which block out the view. He searches for the old houses with red-tiled roofs and wooden windows painted red and green, wondering why they always stuck to those two colours. "Goodness me! A ghoul has eaten a bit of the sea!" he cries suddenly. "Goodness me! A ghoul has swallowed a big chunk of mountain!"

I laugh at his imitation of a village way of speaking which reminds me of my grandmother, feeling warmth and love towards him and wishing he would rest his head on my thighs.

"They think they're making a riviera," says Jawad scornfully. "A riviera coast! And over there they're creating Karbala! That shows they're both the same. And yet the place is divided in two. They both suffer in the same way, whether they talk about the war or not. Chasing here and there armed to the teeth to secure flour, fuel, medicine, wasting their time and destroying their nerves in all this instability and chaos. Look at them!

Their cars are falling apart. And the refugees aren't happy whichever sector they're in."

I smile, pursuing my own thoughts. The expressions on their faces are the same. Their children, like ours, are only aware of the country's historic monuments from pictures in books, and all they've ever known is sandbags and toy guns. People here justify theft and petty crime just as we do, attributing them to poverty and need, while the old people sigh over the past, and take present events as a personal insult.

On our way to the Cedars we went along the coast. I looked out on the left and told Jawad I was looking for the Tzigane restaurant. He didn't ask why or seem surprised that I'd caught his disease. It was more as if he had handed me very clear photographs which had lain untouched in a cardboard box and kept their original brilliance and colour; as if the accumulated layers of the past had not been buried under years of war, and the present had accepted its wounds and recovered enough to bear fresh ones.

I stared out at the salt pools where we used to turn bronze after one day's bathing and where I could swim without any effort. Jawad still wondered, just as he always used to do when he was a child, why there was nobody guarding them. He asked me if it was far to the army checkpoint where Simon was supposed to meet us.

Simon was sitting behind the wheel of a car, waiting for us. My thoughts flew on to the green meadows and the bare pale hills. Did the bus really leave from here with us chanting, "Hurry, hurry, driver. Yours is the best bus ever. Put your foot down and go fast. We're the cleverest girls in the class"?

When I was getting ready to go on a trip and Zemzem was boiling eggs and potatoes for me, Haja Nazar used to visit my grandmother. These visits annoyed her, especially when Haja Nazar cried, "Don't let your granddaughter go up to the snow. It buries human beings."

"Come on, Haja Nazar," replied my grandmother brightly. "Asmahan is much too clever to let the snow hurt her. They're all girls from good families at her school. The Sursuq girls are there."

I didn't want to take the eggs Zemzem had boiled: they were a strange colour because she'd boiled them together with the potatoes. She gave in to me and made me some more eggs, clattering the pot about and swearing.

The sun set in a flood of colour when we were still on our way to the Cedars. At the Syrian checkpoint I felt suddenly anxious. Simon had said we would follow a car sent by a relative of his high up in the army, and it was true we had taken an unexpected route to reach the checkpoint. A Syrian soldier appeared, glanced towards us, then signalled to us to go through. After a while we noticed that in every village there were only a few houses with lights in them and the rest were dark or lay in ruins. Music played from a balcony amid a buzz of talk and laughter and Simon told us that if a house had lights on it meant its politics fitted the current climate; those in darkness or levelled to the ground were the ones with the wrong politics.

As night descended on these villages, we were able to discern the inhabitants' political inclinations. Tranquil village life, when people had disputes over simple things like the rights to a well or a tree, was a thing of the past. I felt blissfully happy to be here with Jawad, seeing things through his eyes, and I was grateful to him for scraping the rust away. But I still hadn't decided whose room I would share that night.

A little before dark we reached Besharri. We drank arak and ate and laughed. I felt drawn to both of them and pictured myself lying between them. I was happy. The Cedars were visible in the darkness. I thought about them for a while then put them out of my mind. We went to the disco; it was almost empty and I noticed a group of men discussing politics in a corner. From time to time they whispered and debated earnestly, their heads close together, or one of them raised his voice angrily. They were guardians of the Cedars and the ski lifts. In the hotel reception hung a photo of the Shah of Iran and Soraya when they visited the Cedars. Although I was alone I slept well and woke up the next day entirely happy. We walked to the Cedars, which looked from a distance like animals huddled together for protection. As we drew nearer we noticed the fence which had been erected around them. Were they afraid that someone would dig them up, since there had been thefts from other national monuments?

"The trees are decaying, and they're trying to do something about it."

"Why? Are they teeth?"

But trees die standing up. They are normally struck down by some disease which nobody notices at first. Once, our oak tree in the village began dropping a sticky deposit on the washing underneath. My grandparents were concerned for months and talked about it as if it was human.

"I first touched these trees when I was a child, but I still don't know what you call these things; they're not leaves and yet they're not pine needles."

"There's someone who wants to poison the cedars so that they won't be a symbol of Lebanon any longer."

Jawad's whimsical notion seemed to strike him suddenly and he continued, "You know, that's not impossible. Maybe they're trying to wipe out the heart of Lebanon."

Simon shook his head and laughed. "Don't get carried away. It's easy to imagine your opponents have long-term plans, when in fact they do things on the spur of the moment just like you."

There were plants growing on the mountainside, all alike and strangely familiar. Simon laughed and put his arms round me. "You need glasses, darling. Where is it you come from? You should know. It's cannabis."

"Do they have it here as well?"

"Why shouldn't they? The Bekaa, here, everywhere. See, they know how to care for cannabis, but not the Cedars! You in the western sector know nothing about us!"

"Visit us more often and tell us," I laughed.

"We can't live without you. You have everything in the west – wheat, flour, fuel, spare parts for washing machines and fridges. We're being strangled economically without you."

"You've forgotten the most important thing, Simon," remarked Jawad. "What about Asmahan? You only get her in the western sector."

I knew why Jawad had come out with this: because Simon

had called me darling and put his arms round me. I looked at Simon: there was nothing between us any more. I let my eyes rest on the silent cedar trees and the mountainside where the hashish sprang green from the hard earth, thinking how things can change.

We returned to West Beirut, leaving the mountain breezes behind us. In no time it was as if we'd never been away from the damp heat, and Jawad seemed to consider himself under my protection again. I wondered if he was like the rest: the moment they landed in Beirut they adopted me as their barometer, observing my tiniest movements and taking comfort from them or reading disturbing signs into them, especially when the atmosphere grew more tense and rumours overshadowed the untroubled days which suddenly seemed like borrowed time. There were sporadic outbreaks of firing, and Ruhiyya was behaving as if we'd been away for ages and were ignorant of the realities of life there. She took hold of Jawad's hand just as I did with visitors to Beirut. "Come on, my dear," she cries. "Leave now, before it's too late. They'll start fighting again soon."

"Okay," answers Jawad, trying to be casual but his anxiety shows him up. "What do you think, Miss Asma," he says to me, "should I be worried like my cousin seems to think?"

I was always shocked by visitors but these last few days had brought us closer together and made him seem less like one. But here he was now treating his own life as if was more precious than any other in the country. Perhaps he and the others who had left were perfectly entitled to do so: they had escaped to protect the precious gift of life while we persisted in walking carelessly over minefields.

"You're more scared than she is," I wanted to say.

"It's for you to decide," was what I did say.

We went into a café, almost the only one where we could observe people like us. There were two girls sitting alone together and it was obvious that the other customers were wondering if they were easy meat, as they laughed and smoked and drank gin and tonic.

I felt a pang of regret for the noisy cafés of the past, when it was impossible to hear what your companions were saying, and freedom hung in the air with the steam rising from the coffee machine. In those days there was too little time to absorb all that was going on, and even men and women from the Gulf sat together in pavement cafés. The atmosphere here wasn't what we wanted, and we hurried out, intimacy flowing all around us, setting us apart from the rest of the street.

We walked along, holding hands with bravado; we were afraid of losing each other; the streets themselves appeared hostile to beautiful, uncomplicated faces, or unusual clothes. Men and women alike stared at us, making me hold Jawad's hand tighter. I didn't know what he was thinking about me at that moment, but I was wishing that he wasn't leaving, because getting used to life here without him was going to be hard. We wanted to sit together in a quiet place and made for the bar of a nearby hotel to join others who like us had taken refuge in the gentle gloom from the brightness of the day.

"I'm going soon, and I'm starting to feel so close to you."

"Don't go then," I laughed.

He ignored my laughter. "I want to take you with me. I want to make you come away with me."

"You'll come back to visit us?" I said anxiously.

"I don't know when. Not for years maybe."

I seize his hand suddenly and bend over to kiss it, then hold it in both my hands and press my face to it and kiss it again. I love the feel of it and want to put it on my hair and neck and throw myself into his arms and let him stroke me like he strokes Ruhiyya.

I raised my head slightly, wondering how to avoid looking at him and the other customers in the bar. As soon as I looked up he brought his face close to mine, put his arms round me and kissed me as if he was going to pull my lips off. We only stopped to take a little breath, like two expert swimmers.

I fidgeted and stared at the table before I looked around me. We were sitting in a corner and the barman was polishing glasses.

This happiness turned to confusion because the kisses had triggered off that other feeling in me. But this time I knew it was an extension of my affection, even a response to his voice and the things he said. I was scared nevertheless that the instinctive feelings would become more and more powerful and I would give in to them and think only of the moment. I wondered why I shouldn't let myself go. Was it because there was no fighting just then, and in the lull I couldn't justify urging my feelings on to the limit? Or should I banish such thoughts and enjoy this sensation even if our relationship was temporary?

We sat in my car, with him at the wheel. The sun had begun to set leaving a red glow round the edges of the sky like pieces of watermelon. I looked around me wondering, as the noise of the city showed no signs of abating, why these people weren't like him and me.

I told him to drive along to where a tall pine tree sheltered the balcony of an old building. We stopped there and got out and went up the steps. "Where are we going?" he asked.

Barely pausing to introduce him to my friend when she opened the door, I hurried him past her and up on to the roof: "A few more steps and we'll be in an oasis. You won't be able to help thinking of the past, peacetime, normal everyday life, when you see the washing hanging out to dry, the old water tanks, and the city looking calm and familiar, like somewhere with soul, where children live, where there's night and day, sunset and dawn: it's still our city from here."

Beirut, you looked composed. The colour of the sunset put a veil over the destruction and made you a friendly place with the voices of your inhabitants floating gently up from a distance, as if the war hadn't damaged you at all.

He takes my hand and brings it up to his mouth then puts it in his pocket. "I know why you've brought me here. You want me to stay."

"Not at all," I lie. "When you come back to visit us, it'll be just like feastdays when I was a child."

He squeezes my hand. "I want to be with you on my own."

"Who's stopping you?" I reply gaily, although I long to hold him tight and rest my head on his chest.

We are drawn together, our limbs and desires intertwining.

"Who's stopping me? Madame Ruhiyya, Madame your grand-mother, the martyrs' portrait painter, Fadila."

"Isn't there someone from your side?"

"Yes, there is. But I can't help myself."

"I've seen a picture of her. Ruhiyya showed it to me."

We went down the steps into my friend's apartment and found her trying to get through to her office in New York via Cyprus. Assembled around her were the Arabic books and oriental accessories which she exported. As she shouted the customs numbers down the phone, the feeling which had been there for a few moments on the roof was erased, and we were brought back to the reality of the city which had been reduced to a connecting link, your beauty for export. As we made our way home I hoped Ruhiyya would be there so that I wouldn't be alone with him. When I heard her voice as we climbed the stairs I wished the opposite. Eagerly she spread out a caftan which she'd bought in Al-Dahiya for Jawad's girlfriend to repay her for the bottle of perfume she'd sent.

"Look at that colour. She'll be wild about it. Do you think it's her size?"

No. I didn't have a fit of jealousy. She'd got there first. I had to be cheerful about it. What vexed me was Ruhiyya's acknowledgement of her existence. The caftan looked as if it had been made by a seamstress who didn't know what she was doing, and the cheap material and nasty colour didn't help.

I had resolved to keep our relationship just as it was so that the sense of satisfaction didn't leave me. If you wanted someone who wasn't there your imagination could take control and mislead you and you could think you were in love.

"I've got a caftan I can do without," I said.

I hurried to my room before I changed my mind or they noticed my confusion, opened my wardrobe and chose a caftan from among the many there: old, threadbare ones made by hand bought when they came into fashion in the late sixties, and new machine-made ones.

Jawad examined it and exclaimed over its beauty.

"Think how much it must have cost," said Ruhiyya, disappointment written all over her face.

"That's not relevant. I'm paying for it." Then he turned to me. "I'm not taking your caftan. Go and put it on. Let's see how Lebanon's Joan of Arc looks in it."

"Asmahan, head of the tourist section. Asmahan, hostess, guide and interpreter," I finished for him.

I went into my room and put it on and didn't fasten the opening with a brooch like I used to. How sensible I must have been in those days! Or was it the fashion then to cover your breasts completely? I'd stopped feeling embarrassed, perhaps because I'd decided that our relationship wasn't going anywhere, and was looking forward to getting letters from him. That's what I needed in this country, to receive letters, to sit down and write letters and get replies instead of composing them in my mind. Like a heroine in a novel I'd tell him about what went on in the atmosphere of war and ceasefires, I would be a martyr or a witness; he was right to call me a Lebanese Joan of Arc.

I rushed in feeling suffocated and flung open the window and leant right out. He didn't comment on how I looked in the caftan. "You should wear a different caftan every day. Don't give any away," cried Ruhiyya. Then she added, "Look at you – you're two mature people. Why don't you get married? Wouldn't that be better, Jawad? You know what they say about marrying someone of a different religion. It brings you a whole lot of problems you're better off without."

"So you're thinking of him and what's best for him, not me?" I teased.

"No. Of course not. Of you," she cried. "I feel a pang every time I look at you and see how beautiful you are, and get to know you better and better, and I say to myself, why hasn't somebody had the intelligence to step up and pick that flower yet?"

"Asmahan doesn't want to marry me. Go on, ask her."

She rebuffed him angrily. "Get out of here! Only foreign girls call out their wares in the street."

Our eyes met and we laughed at the thought of how I'd grabbed his hands and kissed them a few hours before and buried my face in them and sucked his lips greedily and let his leg touch mine and his hand rest on my thighs as he steered with one hand.

Ruhiyya pounded the raw kibbeh then sat waiting for Fadila to bring her fresh basil and marjoram, because the herbs had all withered in their pots while we were away. She sang a funny rhyme as she waited: "Take me in your suitcase, Jawad, roll me up in the wink of an eye."

"There's not much room in it," responded Jawad drily, but he asked me to go to the sea. "We'll look at the sea and buy some wine."

Look at the sea? He wants to see the sea, get a spoonful of it before he goes. It's only tourists who feel guilty if they don't see everything, if time doesn't permit them at least to cast their eye over the places they haven't seen.

Embroidered Palestinian cushions were on Jawad's list, although it was the folly of the massacres in the camp which interested him more than the beauty and colour of the work. The shop where these cushions were sold was still there at the camp entrance. When we went in, there was a smell of coffee and the woman in charge sipped from a cup and knocked the ash off her cigarette as she showed us the cushions. The voice of an Egyptian singer on the radio rose from one of the shacks nearby.

I thought the time Jawad had spent in the city might have erased the traces of the visitor left in him, of the person who would have liked to record the whining of the gnats when he was in the village. But it seemed I was wrong: he was still recording.

"The people of Beirut are hemmed in. They don't have any-where to go but the sea."

This must have been provoked by the five boys leaning on the sea wall, staring despondently at the waves. I don't believe they could see them in the darkness but it was as if they were turning their backs on the reality which awaited them.

"Do you know those people from the golf club?"

I had taken him to the summit of contradiction in the city: to the golf club, the place – after the American University – where a person finds it hardest to believe where he is: from the distance it looks like a green dot on a brown manila envelope. There were birds twittering everywhere, hopping from tree to tree, plate to plate, ground to table, in pursuit of crumbs, asserting their miraculous freedom. The trees there were green, the sky a deeper blue. Even though from time to time we heard gunfire close by, the atmosphere was only disturbed briefly by the mothers jumping up to fuss over their children and the golfers coming in with their bags to sit in the café until all was quiet again. People sheltered in the corridors inside the clubhouse until life gradually returned to the fairways and swimming pool. When the birds went back everybody followed, including the Syrian soldiers who watched the players with a disparaging air.

We got back into the car and went looking for a shop selling wine. In a narrow street, where the pavements were eaten away and overshadowed by rubbish and irregular broken stumps of trees, we found ourselves alone except for our desire for one another and embraced fiercely, trying to reach each other's souls, as if squeezing harder and inflicting more pain proved the strength of the emotion.

We only stopped when we heard a car engine behind us and I switched on the ignition, wishing I didn't have to steer and could let the car take us where it wanted. I don't know how we reached home without crashing into any shadowy street lamps or piles of rubbish, since our fingers were firmly intertwined.

We went into the garden, and when I saw the row of containers standing there I knew Ali must have brought water for us and I let out a cry of delight. As I poured water over myself in the bathroom, I longed to be with Jawad naked.

I heard his voice in the hall where the bookshelves were and felt pleased because he would see me with only a towel wrapped round me. I rushed past him into my room, wondering if he was waiting for me or was genuinely interested in the books.

"Aren't you going to give me your books?" I called from my room.

"It's difficult to know with you. You might not like them."

"There's a young man asking for you," called Ruhiyya.

Had Kazim been released? I didn't really care who it was and put on a caftan while drops of water ran down off my hair. I spun round in a circle elatedly, watching myself in the mirror, went right up to it, mouthed a word then stepped back and studied myself. I held my hair up and sighed, imagining Jawad watching me through a hidden lens.

Kazim's brother, who had become a nurse to some wealthy old people, was waiting for me. Before he could say anything, I asked him about Kazim. "The Syrians released him a few days ago. Would you expect them to pay for feeding and guarding him for more than a month?" he said.

He'd come to ask for my help. He wanted my friend Hayat to send him fifty chicks. I laughed, trying to understand the joke or the hidden meaning behind his request. But Kazim's brother was entirely serious: he flashed a magazine in front of me, European or even American, and I looked through it and saw an odd-looking, garishly-coloured assortment of roosters and chickens worthy of the martyrs' portrait painter.

Kazim's brother took my apparent interest in these strange birds, coupled with Ruhiyya's enthusiastic declaration that she would buy some of them too, as meaning that I agreed to help him. "I knew you'd do it," he said happily. "The eggs have begun to break when you pick them up. The shells are like cigarette-paper. You don't know what might hatch out of them!"

I didn't laugh, not wanting to fall into his trap. Summoning up my courage, I said dismissively, "I don't know when Hayat's coming, and anyway it's not reasonable to ask her to bring chicks with her." Then the whole thing struck me as ridiculous and I gave a shout of laughter. "Have you gone mad? You really want me to make her carry a load of chicks in her luggage?"

When he saw that I was determined not to help, he didn't pursue it. "I'm not mad yet, but the guy who brought fifty on the plane nearly went crazy with the noise. All the way from London to Beirut. The passengers thought it was the aircraft's screws working loose. And on top of that the wind got up. Some of the chicks died on the journey."

What a lot of time I used to spend sitting in this kitchen, enjoying the conversations interspersed with shouting, laughter and outbursts of anger. Here it was, familiar but diminished, with its walls cracked and spirit gone: it no longer wrapped me in its arms as tenderly as Isaf or my grandmother; now it was there from necessity, somewhere to prepare food and a cause of trouble, starting with the tap which whistled emptily instead of producing a kindly flow of water. Once the tap had stopped fulfilling its function it began to look like an ugly rooster's crest, rather than a king with a crown. The big gas cooker, the pride of the kitchen, which Zemzem had insisted on buying to be like the Beirut neighbours' daughter who baked cakes in an assortment of tins, stood silently waiting for the gas supply to return. If we switched it on there was a high-pitched, grating whine, and the cooker looked increasingly dirty, as Zemzem had stopped buying the special expensive powder for cleaning it. Meanwhile we had left the hole in a corner of the room made by a missile and replaced a broken window-pane with plastic sheeting when we'd repaired it once too often. The kitchen was no longer a spacious room with a generous expanse of tiled floor and high walls, against which bundles of green moloukhiyya were piled, never reaching more than half way up, however much there was. Everyone except my grandmother would sit stripping the leaves off the twigs and piling them up on a pale green sheet. Our kitchen no longer caught the sun in the winter as we sat on low chairs, eyeing the strips of orange peel which Zemzem always hung to dry from the window bars to burn in the stove with the coal. Although the fridge had taken over from the pantry as a place to store food before the war, the pantry had now resumed its previous role. I wished I could go back to being as I was in the past, and listened to Ruhiyya and Fadila talking, hoping their lively voices would reassure me, while the smell of kibbeh filled my nostrils and spread throughout the house.

"Your hair's wet. Don't get in a draught," Ruhiyya's voice interrupts my reverie. "Where does Madame Zemzem hide the oil?"

I dashed to the pantry, still dominated by my desire for Jawad and my need to act nonchalantly. As if I was on a difficult assignment I flung myself down on my knees to open the bottom door of the pantry and found only an empty oil bottle. I began taking out bags and jars so that I could see better, not knowing that I was revealing a secret: Fadila, who was telling Jawad about her husband the sheikh, let out a shriek and fell upon the things I had just taken out. "Zemzem's a liar. She swore blind she hadn't taken any handouts from the Iranis."

"Perhaps she was scared of my grandmother."

"Why should she be? Is Iran that bad?"

"Worse than anything you can imagine."

"Why do you say that, my dear?" exploded Fadila. "We got a maternity hospital from them. Beautiful! So clean you could eat off the floor. And they had women doctors. Not any old male doctor coming and scrabbling about inside you."

"Is that what happens, Fadila? The doctors come and scrabble about inside you?"

We all laughed at Jawad's comment, and I pretended to find it immensely funny, although I was really picturing what it would be like to be pregnant by him and have him taking me to the doctor.

"It's not fair to the Iranis," persists Fadila. "They haven't done us any harm."

"Really? Have you forgotten what they did to Ricardo?"

"What did they do to Ricardo? He got what he wanted. To become a pilot and join Hizbullah. It's the opposite, Hizbullah's on the side of learning. They've opened schools and they're educating people."

"Great schools! They give the children exercise books with a picture of Khomeini on the front."

"Why not? The government hasn't come up with anyone better."

"God help the government. Do you still call them that?" interjects Jawad.

"I swear, the boys from Iran asked me if I wanted money for my mother. I said no thanks, but they paid part of the next door boy's school fees. And they do house repairs too."

Ruhiyya ignored our conversation. She was engrossed in

kneading the faraka, tasting it from time to time on the tip of her tongue. "Not enough marjoram and basil."

"If only they'd given me the key," observed Fadila petulantly, "I would have watered the pots with clean boiled water."

Scorn appeared on Ruhiyya's face, making her wrinkles more pronounced. "You mean we'd be eating faraka with scabby sea-water in it?"

Fadila sighed. "Why don't you put cream on your face, Ruhiyya? Your forehead's gone like a lizard's skin, like my skin was before. Ask Asma what it used to be like and how it changed after I started using cream. It was like the Sacred Night – God forgive me! – it worked magic on it and all the wrinkles vanished."

Jawad laughed. He had become like an extension of Fadila and Ruhiyya in spite of his European clothes, discovering in Fadila the type of creature he had been searching for, and taking great delight in her conversations. Fadila moved on from face creams and talked about her brother envying his mother in hospital because she was given French bread and butter and jam to eat.

Then she told us about the Syrian soldier who fell in love with her, even though he was so much younger, and had to be transferred as a result.

"He loved you for your stuffed courgettes in yoghurt," interrupted Ruhiyya.

"That's rubbish. The courgettes were for all of them manning the checkpoint. Anyway, what time are we going out tonight?"

Fadila was scared her evening would be spoilt when I suggested Ali should come with us and, as I'd anticipated, Ruhiyya wanted Jawad to take us because he'd pay for us all, since visitors don't count their cash. I tried unsuccessfully to convince Ruhiyya that we'd feel more at ease if Ali came with us, while Fadila despaired of me and directed her conversation to Jawad: "Night time in Beirut is out of this world. You stroll down the street, taking in the sights, and dance and enjoy yourself any way you like."

Jawad looked at me as if seeking my advice. "Don't look at Asma," objected Fadila. "She's the last person you should ask.

She's against going out. If you go by what she thinks you'll be in your room all evening. Come on. We'll take Musa with us. He's easy going."

"Musa? The one you were in love with?" interrupted Ruhiyya.

Fadila didn't reply, but took out a jar of cream from a plastic carrier bag and put it down in front of Ruhiyya. "The proof of the pudding is in the eating," she declared pompously. "Five dollars to you."

Then she danced around in a circle, ending up in front of Jawad and pinching his cheeks enthusiastically. "You kill me! I adore this face and body. Tonight I want to dance and sing for you."

"She's crazy, poor thing," remarked Ruhiyya, as soon as Fadila left. "It looks as if she's going the same way as her mother, and her mother took after the grandmother."

"And her brother's well on the way," I added.

"And her brother's well on the way," muttered Ruhiyya to herself.

Fadila was supposed to come back once she had changed her clothes, so that we could all go touring the clubs together. When it started to get late, Jawad suggested we should go to her place. She received us with everything jingling and clanking: the gilt chains around her neck which hung down to her waist and knocked against her belt and her long earrings which almost reached the whole length of her short neck. It was as if she'd been expecting us, in spite of the rollers which bounced on her forehead, for she said nothing about being late, but welcomed us, especially Jawad, and called out to her brother Hasoun to go and buy Seven-Up. His voice came back to us: "You just want to get me out of the house so you can all go off and leave me here."

Fadila cursed him, then raising her voice she assured him that she was sending him out for Jawad's benefit: Jawad loved Seven-Up and would take him back to France with him and find him a French wife.

Jawad suggested we took him with us tonight, before he came back to France with him and even Fadila spluttered with laughter, although she was plainly horrified at Jawad's idea: "We can't possibly take him."

Her brother's aggrieved voice came from the other room. "What do you mean, you can't possibly take me? Are you afraid people would talk?"

We were waiting for Musa: Fadila described him as her son and said he treated her like a mother.

Fadila ignored Hasoun's insistent pleas, then disappeared into her room and came out with a photo of herself and Reagan which she stowed away inside her handbag with her passport; her bag and her winter coat go with her everywhere when the fighting starts. Conspiratorially, she told Jawad how she had her photo taken alongside one of Reagan when she was visiting my mother in the States some years before, and how she was afraid the Syrians or Hizbullah would see it and think it was a real photo and accuse her of spying. Jawad asked her why she hung on to it if she was worried. "I show it to people for fun and they believe me and say talk to your friend Reagan for us about getting a visa."

Fadila's house was different; the tiled floors, sofas, low tables and wooden pillars were still there, but the pictures of movie stars had gone from under the glass on the tables. It was empty without her mother and mine, and the rise and fall of their laughter, the smell of coffee, and the avid gossip about the men they knew who looked like movie stars.

Musa came in, a big man with a thick moustache. When he stood by Fadila she scarcely came up to his waist. If she had embraced him like a mother she would have heard the squeaking of his stomach instead of the beating of his heart. He shook hands all round and asked her if there was anything he could do. "Aren't you coming with us?" she exclaimed. "Who's going to take us? Why aren't you coming?"

He offered to take us to where we wanted to go and come back for us at the end of evening, but Fadila and Jawad both insisted that he should come with us. It didn't take him long to have us feeling that he really was Fadila's son, and since she was like my mother, that I was his sister.

"Excuse me for saying so, Asmahan," he said to me, "you're

dearer to me than a sister, but are you really going out for the evening in that dress? People will think you're a bedouin."

"What's wrong with that?" I laughed.

Jawad asked him why he'd adopted Fadila as a mother.

"It's amazing, we're very close. Just as if we're related."

I was secretly grateful to Fadila for thinking of sending for Musa, as he knew all the places and who their singers and dancers were and how much they charged for dinner, starting with the hotel on the seafront which was pathetically empty in spite of the band wearing sombreros.

We were told the place filled up after one, but when Musa wanted reassurances the manager looked at his powerful frame and lost his nerve. "You'd be better to come back on Saturday night," he said.

So on we went to another club which we found bolted and barred, and a third which had been booked by a family related to a warlord. These clubs were far apart and Jawad offered to pay Musa for the petrol. "It's all paid for," he said to an uncomprehending Jawad.

Musa's job must have been to protect the rich and famous from the rats of the night, not the ones which bounded off the garbage heaps every time they heard a car, but those loafing around the club entrances and street corners.

He had ambitions to be like Ali, bodyguard and protector of important personalities, not so that he could eat and drink well, but in order to become more powerful. These conditions suited people who knew their way around. Being an escort meant that doors opened up for you; with your car and gun you could cut through the confusion and delays. You were the one in charge, even more important than the person you were protecting, as he became the ring on your finger, his fate dependent on your strength and intelligence. Through your position you got to know who had their hands on the purse strings, who were the key players, the warlords, the owners of the wealth. Once you had this knowledge you began to have access to easy money, and as things progressed you came to occupy a powerful position and attract a retinue of followers, some of whom might even act as your bodyguards in time. Such a chance for profit had to be seized with both hands. Musa's aim was to be an important strongman, not somebody employed by a rich, anonymous emigrant to frighten off thieves. It was clear that Fadila had exaggerated the status of the people I knew, but Musa must have thought that if he got access to Ali through me then Ali would pass on the jobs which he didn't have time for and gradually Musa would rise to Ali's level and overtake him.

We went into the fourth nightclub where there was a lot of noise and Franco-Arab music playing, women singing along and men swaying in their seats. It was only minutes before our table was heaving with noise, dance and song like the others, Fadila, Musa and Ruhiyya swaying in time to the beat of the songs, while Jawad and I sat, overwhelmed by what we saw. Who would think that the world was turned upside down and people were frightened?

Musa pointed out a man dancing and said he was a nobody before the rise in the dollar. The people at the tables ate, danced and sang along with the young performers, whose names showed that they came from villages in the south. The city's legendary night life was being undermined. The man with paper bags stuffed full of dollars danced, shaking his stomach in the direction of his veiled wife whose gold earrings swayed to the music. She moved the wine glasses out of range as soon as the photographer came to take pictures at their table, while Fadila sat happily next to Musa, tugging at her glittering silver scarf every time it slipped back off her head, looking with envy and admiration at a female customer climbing up and dancing on a table where the dishes and glasses had been pushed to one side.

Why the decor – the artificial bunches of grapes, the loud colours on the walls, the awkward, ugly chairs? What I saw provoked powerful physical sensations of rage and bewilderment. What was the relationship of taste to the war? Why did the songs sound as if they were composed by someone in his bath?

The people make a city, and these were strangers. Although they filled the room, I could only see empty spaces.

Jawad and I felt we were in constant communication through what we were thinking, and had no need to talk over the uproar. Some of these rowdy men dancing and shouting had opened businesses with stolen capital and precious artefacts taken from shops and houses. Some of them mixed with well-known people who had active roles in the parties, and longstanding businessmen who had found religious loopholes allowing them to charge interest to their hearts' desire. There were plenty of drug-dealers among them: pre-war exiles coming back with capital, eager for status and prestige now the arena was empty of those who deserved it. Musa pointed out a man who worked as an intermediary between kidnap groups and hostages' families. "His life's in the balance," he remarked laconically.

At some of the tables were people like Jawad and me who'd come to see what had happened to you and your inhabitants, and others, like Ruhiyya and Fadila, eager to belong to the world of the rich, if only for a night.

After a while Jawad and I wanted to go home: what we saw was making us miserable. "Rats in fancy clothes," was Jawad's accurate description.

We were dependent on Musa to see us back, as you no longer gave us our freedom for nothing, so we left Ruhiyya and Fadila alone, on condition that Musa would come back for them; they couldn't understand why we wanted to leave "when things were really humming".

We stood in the garden. What was going to happen between us when we went up the steps? We breathed to a single rhythm; our words anticipated each other's thoughts. The need for close physical contact generated by your atmosphere was affecting us both now. We were an island surrounded by heaving waters full of crocodiles. The electricity was off and everything was in darkness. Thought was paralysed in such an atmosphere; I was like a witch leading an innocent stranger to her castle and working her magic by isolating him there for days on end until he was dependent on her for his survival.

For a while Jawad had been immersed in his fascination for the past, his desire to find out about the old ways, and blind to the present. Then one day he opened his eyes and saw the dark streets and heaps of garbage, the sound of the generators penetrated his carapace of tolerance and the noise and murky fumes started to get him down. He began listening to the news and found it didn't make sense. Even the television irritated him, because of the clothes the announcers wore, the ideas expressed or the banal songs. The newspapers no longer provided him with a hunting-ground for his sarcastic jokes; it almost seemed to cause him physical pain to read of the senselessness of what was happening.

"Do you remember, Asmahan, I told you about the girl I used to be in love with before I left here, the time I grabbed hold of her by the hair when we were visiting an old fort and said, 'Don't wait for me. I don't want to stand in your way. When I come back, we'll see if you still love me.' "

He takes hold of my hair and says, "I grabbed a handful of her hair and put my mouth on hers and kissed her so hard I almost suffocated her."

He puts his lips on mine and kisses me hard and doesn't suffocate me; I kiss him back.

We stand by the garden pond breathing in the diesel fumes from the generators. He asks me why we've filled up the pond with stones. I remember how I never used to be able to get to sleep unless I could hear the sound of the water running from its little tap. I can picture what the tap looked like; the neighbours' son Bahij who was about twelve broke it off; metal was his obsession and he took away anything movable made out of metal and sold it; he was known as Bahij the Metal. Jawad puts his arm round me as I tell him about the pond and Bahij the Metal, and presses my shoulder. I seem to have been expecting it. I want to throw myself on him, I don't care where, just throw myself on top of him with all my weight. But I remain frozen, even though I haven't felt like this since my first dance with an adolescent boy.

He is going in two days. Why do relationships require a physical contact to develop? Why can't this continue when we are far apart? I picture myself writing letters, waiting for his. When I try to imagine what I would write I can hardly think of anything. For he has already preserved his days here: the plains reaching to the horizon, the vine trellises, the blackened landscapes, the rocky hilltops. He found out about the contradictions when he called his girlfriend in France from the post office in the neighbouring village. He didn't believe that on a hillside in this devastated land a post office had been built, fully equipped and staffed. Up above it was a beehive where the bees still returned to swarm. Nobody dared to go there but Hashim who launched a surprise attack on the hive, roping himself to the rocks above and swinging down the rock-face to reach the honeycomb.

I drew my lip from between his, and went into my room without a word. I threw myself down on the bed, picking up the mirror which I left there before dinner, when I was trying to see what he saw in my face. But it didn't bother me any more; the electricity was off and I wasn't going to switch on the generator because I couldn't stand the thought of the noise. What's more, I was trying to be like a mole, and pick up every movement Jawad made. The neighbourhood generators had gone quiet because of the lateness of the hour, although the noise of the nightclub was still loud in my ears. I chased away the images and tried to make myself indifferent, saying out loud, "People have to live a little."

I didn't think about the nightclub for long, because I was wondering whether my body was alerted by love or wine. Why didn't he knock on my door? Why couldn't I hear him in the kitchen or the living room? I jumped up suddenly as if I was supposed to be meeting him and had forgotten about it. When I opened my bedroom door, I heard his voice from the living room asking me how to make the electricity come on. The thought that Ruhiyya must be coming back any moment flew out of my head the moment he came near me, so that the darkness entered us both and we vanished like the things around us, of which only the vaguest outlines were visible, or perhaps we just knew they were there, but couldn't really see them. I was losing my self suddenly, losing the thread which tied me down to life and flying like a bird. Our conversation became bolder as if it didn't really count, because we were in the dark. My body took me by surprise as usual and I felt it begin to throb, and I smiled because Jawad couldn't see what was happening to me. We both became bolder and our breathing was like the light suddenly being switched on to reveal everything. His fingers reached out to touch my face, and I knew they were what I'd been waiting for all those years; they blotted out the music and noise, the faces with too much make-up, the mouths full of food and the gyrating stomachs; this tenderness was all that was left. As we moved in close together and I felt his breath on my face where his fingers had been, he asked me in a whisper if he could go on, and how I was feeling. I liked this hesitation, which I had never encountered in the others, this circumspection, this strength of will. The war here and his life in Europe hadn't given him the feeling that everything was permissible, all the barriers down. The fact that I was lying here like this had no connection with the war and the lack of permanence. I had moved far away from the living-room floor, my grandmother's house, the western sector. The desire to hold on to him wasn't like a drug, or because life went on and there was always someone somewhere being born or dying or having sex. I was lying on the carpet where I used to play as a child, and which I used to race across to go to school or meet a friend in my adolescence. For the first time I wasn't shutting off my feelings of love and desire as I entered the house, or transforming them into daydreams.

I discover that making love isn't as easy as it used to be. I'm far away despite my desire for him, expecting far more than this kissing and touching and holding. I take hold of my mass of thoughts and it's like picking up a heavy bird which has begun to walk rapidly along a piano keyboard sounding a jumble of different notes. This closeness has put a bubble in my veins and started to shift the sluggish blood along and make me breathe more deeply, restoring some spontaneity where before was only grim determination. I crave his lips, my hands grip his shoulders, his chest crushes me and his face is immersed in mine, but more than sex this is a way to great calm, as if existence had been poised on one foot and has at last regained its balance. Jawad's eyes look into the distance then focus on me. I pull him to me and call out aloud, "I love you. I love you."

He must be wondering why I'm not trembling with pleasure, what's stopping me even responding to him if I love him as I cry out that I do. Is everything in me blocked and sterile like my work, my future, my car engine which cuts out as soon as I turn the key in the ignition? Do I breathe like a spinster? Have I got the body of a dried-up old maid, although I feel as slippery as if I've oiled myself inside? Of course I was talking to him as I chased the bird which hopped over the piano keys, shifting from black to white; I talk to him in my head as he continues to crouch over me, embracing me, marvelling that despite all the heat I'm giving off, I'm not in time with him. I wish I could tell him that I can really feel him, not only inside me but to the very ends of my body and all around it, but I want more than this cohesion of muscle, tendon, bone joint. "More, more, more," I mumble and he gets up and walks about the room.

After a long silence I put on a shocked voice and say, "Imagine if the electricity came back on now and Ruhiyya saw you."

"I wish I could understand what's the matter with you," he says.

I used to be certain that I would be all over Jawad like ink on a white sheet, spreading out and running in every direction until I was part of the fabric, so what is happening to me? Has seeing life diminished by the terrible dancing creatures in the nightclub made me wither like a flower snapped off a bush?

We couldn't begin a discussion: it was difficult if I didn't know what was wrong with me; but he took my face tenderly in his hands again and asked if I wanted him to carry me to my bed.

I clung to his neck as he picked me up and almost dropped me again. I remembered Naser's back pains then quickly drove the thought from my mind as I usually did when it concerned Naser. I smiled to hear Jawad saying, "Good heavens. How heavy you are. Like a lump of concrete."

"Is she as heavy as me?" I tease.

He says nothing.

"Soon you'll be carrying her around."

He throws me on to the bed. The metal springs bounce me back towards him. A wave of happiness rushes over me. My bed is different, laughing as it receives me with the one I love. We are in the house which thinks it's there for everything but lovemaking. It witnesses births, marriages, deaths, people moving in and moving out but not love. It's not used to lovers joining in the room of childhood and adolescence; they go far away so that they can let their bodies do as they please.

As I think these thoughts, I feel the house embracing me suddenly, giving out its warmth to me. The furniture watches and greets the union with gladness, breathing softly around us. I have not felt this relaxed with any man before. My roving encounters with Naser hardly made our relationship secure; there was no bed which we used habitually, no sofa whose colour stuck in my mind, no room which brought back certain words. Terror lurked constantly at the back of my mind and in the corners of my lips at the thought that his enemies might choose these intimate moments to attack.

Jawad touches my lips again, my arms, and releases me from the throng of thoughts and images and makes them lie dormant.

I followed him seconds after he had left for his own bed, and he was waiting for me; he made a space for me when he heard my footsteps, put his arm round me and asked me, "Do girls here leave things to nature or do they use something?"

I just laughed, and then he began to breathe regularly so that I knew he was asleep. I studied his face; I was a little girl and this was my grandfather breathing reassuringly beside me, and everything was all right: the top window had been broken by local boys with a sling, not by sniper fire. Then I hear Jawad's voice as if in a dream, telling me that I'm just like my mother and that's how he recognized me after all these years.

He was a child when my mother visited them, in a long brown split skirt with a fox fur round her shoulders and dark red lipstick. She smoked a cigarette which she hid each time she heard footsteps, sang songs and laughed loudly. This image of her stayed in his mind for a long time afterwards.

He puts his arms round me. "It's incredible," he whispers. "Here I am with her daughter. It must be fate."

I lay without moving. I wanted to turn over as usual but I was afraid of disturbing him. I must have fallen asleep in the end, because I woke up and the light was streaming into the room and I heard Ruhiyya moving about in the kitchen. A feeling of sadness overwhelmed me when I saw his suitcase. I tried to extricate myself from the embrace of his arms and thighs but he held me tighter. "You can't go," he muttered, his eyes tightly shut.

"Ruhiyya," I said, pretending to be flustered.

"Let her see us together. She can make up a song about us."

As I try to get up I want to ask him if he loves me, but I can't bring myself to, then the sight of our limbs entwined under the cover gives me courage and I wonder how I could have felt shy.

10

The Last Letter

My Dear Hayat

Although these long days passing have created a gulf between us you're still my friend, Hayat, the wall off which I bounce my thoughts – happy, painful, immoral sometimes – and yet I never detect any scorn in your eyes. Do I? I think I see only love. How wrong I was when I convinced myself that we had set off along two parallel tracks which would never meet again: the very fact that if I feel uneasy about something I can only dispel it by analysing your circumstances in relation to mine means you are still there.

You are with me now in the departure lounge of Beirut International Airport. Do you remember the word 'International' huge and black on its walls? The point is, I'm trying to ask your advice, but you disappear just as I'm about to hear your reply. Or is it that I don't want to hear it? I'm sitting here now, a mass of confusion, uncertain whether to focus on Jawad, myself, the waiter, or the other passengers, and I see you pushing them all aside and coming towards me. It's strange, you who are far away occupy my thoughts now, and not those I have just left who must be somewhere around the airport, waiting for my plane to take off. Is it because I always connect you with this airport, as I normally only come here to meet you or see you off, and it sometimes seems as if people only leave here to take things to you?

You never let slip an opportunity to urge me to leave too; I hear your voice, read your letters: you're like a school head-mistress trying to rustle up business with an enthusiasm which can be troublesome, and make me feel sometimes I am being hounded by you, although I never need to ask why. I know you can't understand why I stay in the flames while where you live even the sound of people's voices is calm and reassuring. I know you're afraid for me but this fear must be accompanied by some pangs of conscience and the flames spread to create a dense wall between those who have stayed and those who have left. This feeling must have disturbed your stays here and made you wish you were far away from all the commotion, enjoying an atmosphere where the biggest disturbances were caused by thunderstorms.

Even during periods of calm in Beirut, when the sky was closer to its original blue, you were telling me to leave. I realized then from the tone of your voice that you weren't afraid of my dying or missing out on a husband or a future, but you were scared for yourself. Your life had never led you into dark labyrinths before: you were born into an exemplary family; from an early age you were aware that you were being fed with a silver spoon, which had been your mother's before you and which you were to preserve so that your own children could use it one day. So you went on dates with boys to compete with other girls, to find out whether your face was pretty and your body desirable, not to find a husband. Even education was not for the sake of knowledge but simply so that you could get a job which would give you a certain status in society.

You used to believe that the world consisted of the earth and the sky, and that everybody lived in beautiful houses, which they made beautiful if they were ordinary, then produced children for ever and ever. Death would never dare enter the solid walls of your family house, disrupt its order, mar its beauty. So as soon as war broke out you packed your bags without stopping for a moment to ask what was going on or who had unleashed this violence. You were more concerned about whether the airport would be blown to bits. Now, my dear, the people mix ash with water because soap is so expensive, and water is scarce. When I think how I used to wash my hair with clean water every day not so long ago, ignoring

Zemzem's instructions to be sparing and only use it for vital washing.

I used to listen to you insisting that you were really happy, and so were your children, and repeating your invitations to me. When I tried to find out what your life was really like, you seemed at a loss and I drew my own conclusions.

"My life?" you would say after a bit. "It's the same as usual. Yesterday I went to an exhibition and was introduced to someone in the art world here, then I went to the cinema in the afternoon, and enrolled in a yoga club."

As time went by the tone of your voice changed. You'd been in exile longer and you must have found out that you were only on the fringes of life in this western country: its politics didn't concern you and its social problems had little effect on you. The weather was about the only thing you remarked on to its inhabitants; it brought you closer to them, although you couldn't handle it the same way they did; you were still tied into a four-season cycle and if a heatwave struck in early spring, you were thrown into disarray, for you'd put your summer clothes in trunks like you did in Lebanon. Only when you got a job did you become part of the place, but it didn't change you or even affect the tone in which you spoke, except for the note of weariness creeping in. "What am I doing? The same as usual. Work and more work. The cinema, galleries, yoga."

But then you began to sound more discontented, asking me enviously if I'd had kibbeh in yoghurt recently, even though you'd told me before that you'd met Olga, a Lebanese cook, who came to you once a week and cooked everything you wanted. You began telephoning me, telling the Lebanese exchange when you booked the calls that it was a matter of life and death, and writing disjointed letters as if you were a doctor trying to take the pulse of an anxious patient without him noticing. You would ask me about daily life in Lebanon, the state of security, the electricity, the schools, and I guessed you were seeing how the land lay before you decided whether to return, like a bird poised above an island reconnoitring the terrain before it descends. I try to dampen your enthusiasm. "You? In Beirut?" I gasp. "You wouldn't last a day. And your children? Not a second. Things are still very difficult. Don't come now."

By reacting like this I gave myself an aura of superiority, as if I was better equipped then you to bear the upheavals and disasters. At the time I didn't know why I wasn't encouraging you to return, even though conditions were fine and hopes were emerging that the war might be a thing of the past. It seems to me now that I really believed we existed like two parallel lines, and I wanted to be free in the new Beirut, at first with Naser, then with others; I needed to be certain that the old ties which had unconsciously dominated me in the past did not carry on into the present. I blamed myself for not encouraging you to come back every time I sat by the sea and watched the swimmers enjoying the waves and the sunshine, every time Beirut seemed like a city doing its proper job. I felt your distress when you left but all the same I did nothing to persuade you to stay; in fact I probably made you more determined to go saying, untruthfully, "You're so lucky to be leaving."

Your desire for familiar company increased daily. You wanted me to drop in on you so you could enjoy your life, warm yourself as if we were around the stove in your village. Do you remember the Feast of Pentecost when you took me with you to the church and there was a fair set up in the churchyard with swings and stalls and the man they said was a bedouin with a complete set of gold teeth, calling, "Buy your sparrow for the Feast. It's not a feast without a sparrow"?

We picked bitter oranges and ate biscuits and Turkish Delight and when I went home I spoke like the people in your village.

I don't think it occurred to you that my presence in your life in exile would only warm you for a short while because I would soon start to feel the cold like you. It would be a like a local anaesthetic – the effect would wear off and the syringe would be empty.

You wrote to me once words that remain engraved indelibly on my mind, like a tattoo. "It seems to get more difficult as I and my children grow older. Life is harder here, even though you've got the war at home. What gloomy future lies in store for us? Abroad you get along with other people on a purely superficial level, but to take it any further is asking for trouble. The days don't cut a groove into your memory – it's as if I get up in the morning and do what I have to do, but never feel more than the faintest glow of pleasure or excitement, and that's not enough to make life bearable."

For all that, here I am sitting in the departure lounge of Beirut International Airport. If I told you that I hadn't thought much about leaving and had decided under Jawad's influence, you wouldn't believe me, or if you did you'd reproach me in your heart, wondering how our long friendship had never prompted me to go, while for the sake of a man, and one attached to another woman, I was sitting on this airport seat with my clothes sticking to me. You'd say to yourself, "Asma was waiting for a man. So that was her problem, and we got it wrong when we were convinced she couldn't leave Beirut because she wouldn't survive away from the place for long."

I know I should have told you about Jawad before. I thought about it, but how could I? For that kind of conversation you need to be face to face in some private corner away from prying eyes and listening ears. Do you remember when we wanted to make sure that Zemzem or your mother couldn't follow our conversations we used to talk in riddles and put feminine endings on and change the boys' names into girls' names and collapse into fits of laughter? Could I possibly have booked an international call and sat there in the queue with all those sad and bewildered-looking people? These calls are expensive nowadays and people use them in emergencies – to say someone's died or is getting married or going away, or to ask for money. Imagine when my turn came, I'd be shouting from the booth, "Hayat, I'm in love with someone called Jawad. When he takes hold of my finger, picture it, just one finger, it blows my mind. When he holds my head it's as if he's putting his hands on everything – the ideas, the confusions, the past, the beauty, the ugliness. When he holds my breasts I see flashes of light and become as hot as an oven. I think he's the first to hold my breasts. The others didn't notice I had them because they're so small."

Secrets between friends are ageless. I heard from Zemzem

that old Zaynab told Naima how her husband once beat his own head in distress when he found ten liras missing from his pocket. Zaynab had said casually, "What's all the fuss about? I took it to buy a bundle of mint."

"What are you telling me?" he roared back. "You put your hand in my pocket without so much as a by-your-leave and took my money?"

"I've never once heard you ask permission," answered Zaynab as casually as ever, "when you put your hand in my fanny."

I know you'll think of Naser when I tell you about Jawad. Don't ask me how love finds another branch to thrive on when it seems so dead that thinking about past loves no longer hurts or even makes you feel happy. Recalling what happened with them is like watching a film: you feel detached from it and if it moves you at all it is to make you surprised or horrified that you could ever have loved them.

I'm stopping this letter here, my dear Hayat, because the last bit is private and you won't be able to understand it all. Not that I doubt your intelligence or your ability to take in situations and ideas, but this is leading me deep into myself, making me turn the matter over and over, leaving no aspect of it undisturbed. If I keep writing to you it will distract me from my course even though it has brought hidden things to light: he is the reason why I'm sitting here now. I feel like a pupil preparing for an exam, trying to recall the words and visualize what the pages look like.

When there were only two days to go before he left Beirut I found myself talking to him in a dry, cold voice. I wasn't acting: I had gone over things in my mind and concluded that since he was leaving so soon I might as well consider him already gone instead of putting both of us through this torment. The subject of his departure had taken over and the more we tried to push it aside the more we found ourselves right back at the heart of it. When we tried to lose ourselves in each other's bodies we ended up clinging to one another in apprehension. His leaving ate up the hours. The slow-moving time, which had always lagged behind any other on the earth's surface, began spinning us round, and the moment we started on anything it alerted us and sent us whirling off again. If I tried to pretend he wasn't going I was reminded of it by the evidence of his hurried preparations all around me and the things piling up in my grandfather's room: his papers, the things he used everyday, his navy suitcase, his airline ticket, his shirts ironed by Ruhiyya, the photos he'd taken of us in the country: me by myself, with Juhayna, with Ruhiyya: and Ruhiyya picking pomegranates, smoking, singing, crying.

Now that he was preparing to leave I could no longer see what he had enabled me to see in Beirut: the memories of the past, even the squalor and sordid things. All I could smell, all I could see was rotting garbage. Along with the embroidered cushions, turquoise glass, patterned rugs and Ruhiyya's wicker tray, he was taking all that his visit had restored to me and made me cherish again. Although I tried not to give in to these negative feelings, reminding myself that this always happened to me when my friends left Lebanon, and I would be depressed for a few days and then get back into my routine, it was different this time. He'd knocked on my door, instead of just pushing it open like Ruhiyya and Zemzem, but then he'd come in without giving me time to get off the bed and look down at the floor. "Give me Hayat's telephone number and anyone else's you like. What shall I tell them?"

I'd asked him to call my friends when he arrived in France. I searched through my drawers and found my little red note-book. As I flicked through the pages he said, "Isn't that an old one?"

"Five years old," I laughed. "Do you think I'm like you?"

For five years I'd written down special days and dates and phone numbers in Lebanon and abroad. I turn the pages, read-ing the names and numbers. Hayat. Naser. Iman. Suham. My mother. Other numbers in Cairo, Tunis, the United States. The people pass through my head, jumbled images exploding and scattering like fireworks. All of them are far away, living their own lives.

"Five years old?" questioned Jawad. "And you haven't

bought a new one? So the future doesn't exist as far as you're concerned?"

"The past is important to me. As it is to you."

"It doesn't seem to be, otherwise you'd keep the notebook with you so you wouldn't lose touch with your friends. You took ages to find it. You don't take anything round with you. If I lost my notebook, you know, it would be like losing a piece of myself."

"I preserve things in my mind. *You* have to write everything down to remember it."

Ignoring this, he lowered his voice. "I can't leave you and go away." The words reverberated inside me, making me tremble, but I answered coldly, "You'll soon get used to it."

"I'll be anxious about you if you stay here."

"It's the best place to be! It's you I feel sorry for!"

He took hold of my head, pressing both hands to my temples so that I couldn't open my eyes. I felt as if I'd drunk litres of warm wine. When he let go I was light-headed and ready to burst into tears.

"Why are you so cold towards me? Do you regret what has happened between us? Or do you want me to stay here? Or do you want to come with me? Which is it?"

All the arguments I'd used to convince myself crumbled away at that moment.

I don't want to be separated from him and that makes me feel unburdened like children who enjoy the present and live only for the moment because they don't know the past and the future is simply the name of a tense which they forget the moment they close their grammar books. So I become a little girl: he can tuck me under his arm and walk off with me or hoist me on to his shoulders so I can view the world from up high. We allow ourselves to be swept back into the current – and regardless of whether it is day or night, there no longer seems to be any need to wait impatiently or panic or pray that time will pass more slowly or more quickly. Night is melting into the pillow, into his body and into his voice as he tells stories of the past, before the long slow years of war. Day is springing through the streets with him, busy with my thoughts, visiting places and contradicting him at once when he whispers that I have to come to France with him.

"Never. Never, I can't ever. I can't possibly leave. I want to die here."

But it seems I didn't mean what I said, because when I saw his things everywhere I began to think about new places, places with horizons. I pictured myself in his apartment: French songs drift in through the window; I'm in that caftan with his foreign friends around me and we're listening to old Moorish songs and Umm Kulthum. I hurry along in the rain as I used to in Beirut in the old days with my umbrella up, drawn to the lighted cafés, smelling of warmth, coffee and cigarettes. I walk through the streets at night, feeling as if something exciting is about to happen. In the day I stroll the pavements and wear a hat, or put a purple streak in my hair. I see films I've read about, buy magazines and the rust of years falls away.

I looked around me. How could I leave all this? And all this was only the house, with the paint almost peeling off before my eyes.

"Give me one good reason."

I nearly laughed: my decision to stay in Beirut was regarded as more or less unassailable and people had stopped suggesting I left, even when everything was in a state of violent upheaval. And he was asking me for a reason?

"Just a minute. If you're so sure, you shouldn't be afraid to discuss the ins and outs. Give me one good reason why you don't want to leave."

"My life's here."

"Your life's here? With your grandmother and Zemzem and Fadila and Ruhiyya? Even Ricardo's gone. I forgot. Kazim will show up soon, and his brother of course. Who'd look after his chicks for him?"

I laugh, then prolong my laughter to give myself time to think of an answer. Whenever I'm about to say something it sounds too vague and doesn't do justice to my feelings.

"I don't have to give a reason."

To my surprise he didn't insist. Instead he took my hand. "Imagine the day after tomorrow. When I've gone. Imagine what it will be like without me. Remember what a nice time we had together, even when we fought in the village. We were angry with each other, and we comforted each other. Do you think it's easy to meet someone who feels with you just as though they were part of you? Think about it."

My words tumbled out strangely fast. "I can't go the day after tomorrow. Let me think about it. I have to organize things."

"Pack straight away and telephone to make a reservation. Then we'll go and get the ticket. If you don't have the money I'll pay for it."

"I need time to organize myself."

That is, I want to back down. No, I want to go, but I want to prepare myself. Suddenly I began to cry. My emotion took me by surprise. "I don't have a visa," I said, and burst into tears again as if I had been planning the trip for ages and had just had my passport returned without a stamp in it. But at the same time I felt like a thief trying to escape before I was arrested. To escape from the place I had believed myself tied to for ever by the strength of my feelings. Ruhiyya came running from the kitchen at the sound of my convulsive sobs, while Jawad tried to calm me, taking me in his arms in front of her. Although I was embarrassed by her presence, I rested my face on his chest, still sobbing.

"Stop. Please," he urged. "I'll postpone my departure and wait till you get a visa."

I found I'd left mascara on his shirt when I took my head away, scared of what Ruhiyya might be thinking. I didn't have to wonder for long. "What's going on, Asmahan?" Then to Jawad: "Why are you going to wait? What's going on? Please tell me."

But he ignored her and held on tightly to my head when I fidgeted. I could hear his voice rising in his chest. I'd never been so close to anybody's voice: he was assuring me that Ali or Musa would see to the visa for me.

"Sending people to talk for you doesn't work with the embassies any more."

"You and I will go then. I'll take my passport with me and talk to the consul."

"What is it? What's wrong?" cried Ruhiyya again. "You'll leave your passport in the embassy and it'll be blown up or something. Then what will we do? Are you trying to kill me?"

I dressed quickly and put on my shoes, trying to hear what Jawad and Ruhiyya were saying to each other. I splashed rosewater on my hands and face. They were talking about me. She was asking him questions and he was replying. I don't know what he was telling her, but I heard her calling me and before I could go to her she was in the middle of my room.

"Do you want to make sure I go to hell? Your grandmother will roast me alive and your grandfather will have me for dinner."

"I suppose you're thinking if I go away with Jawad it means I'll be living with him. He's already living with Catherine, in case you'd forgotten."

"Good God!" she interrupted. "Is this how we talk now: I'm going to live with him; she's living with him. Aren't we going to get married any more . . .?"

"Let me finish," I cut in. "I'm leaving, like most other people. Maybe I'll go to my mother or my friend Hayat. I don't know."

Because Jawad wasn't taken aback by this, I decided I would never leave him. Laughing, he gestured towards Ruhiyya. "Anybody would think you were at a funeral!"

I couldn't contact the village. How could I be sure of leaving? I'd dreamt that there was a snake going after Hayat's daughter, and my premonition that I wouldn't be able to get a visa turned out to be accurate. There was no reply at Ali's and I tried to contact him on about five other numbers and left messages for him and always met with the same response: "Asmahan. How could anyone forget the name Asmahan?"

The morning passed and the rest of the day, and evening came and I hadn't heard from him. Instead, Fadila contacted me to ask me what was happening and whether Musa could help: he had been with one of the people I'd talked to when I was trying to track down Ali.

"I don't understand why there's still a war on when

everybody seems to have supernatural hearing," remarked Jawad in amazement.

He was telling Musa about the visa before I had time to think, and Musa listened attentively as if he was being briefed for a military exercise.

"If you'll excuse me," he said to us, going off into a corner with his mobile phone, and we could hear him muttering, chuckling and cursing good-humouredly. When he'd finished he asked Jawad for his passport and a letter confirming that I was a relative of his and that he'd invited me to spend a holiday in Paris.

The hours crawled by. A day passed, then another. My hand was on my heart, Ruhiyya's at her throat, ready to do away with herself if Jawad's passport didn't come back to him. Jawad tried to convince himself that even if it disappeared, the embassy could supply him with a replacement. All the same, he eventually succumbed to the same fears as Ruhiyya and I, but used them to get closer to the city where people were always worried. He told me how he'd begun to be plagued by the idea that he ought to leave me in these troubled waters where I'd learnt to swim so well, as I must derive a special feeling of confidence, even delight, from confronting the risks, and then he'd found that notion evaporating into thin air as we waited for my passport; he realized that people here had no freedom of choice, even to travel: the closest they could get to another country was to touch the lines and colours on a map. I told him foreign countries no longer really interested me and that he should try to look at life through other people's eyes sometimes. I was caught up in a tangle of thoughts: I felt guilty about Ali, who would find out that I'd gone through Musa instead of him, but mainly I was indifferent to what was happening round about – the generator breaking down, the noise of gun and rocket fire in the eastern sector, the kidnapping of an engineer – and kept coming back to focus on my passport and whether I'd be given a visa or not. My thoughts were like a flock of sheep herded together and driven along a single track, egged on by heightened emotions which made me think I saw Musa coming every other minute with my passport in his hand, or heard the sound of his car horn, and his cheerful voice telling the tale of the James Bond-like exploits which had accompanied his successful quest for the visa. I had been used to Ali telling us stories of his unique skill and ingenuity in procuring visas until we'd caught him out one time and found he was telling a pack of lies.

Jawad began asking why the embassy was taking so long, and looking for their phone number. The fact that he was thinking of calling them meant he no longer understood the mentality he had left behind him. But this discovery didn't make me halt the game of wishing for the opposite of what I really wanted, which they had taught us in childhood. I had disliked Jawad and here I was in love with him; I hadn't wanted to leave with him and yet I was waiting impatiently for my passport. I heard a car horn, the voices of Fadila and Musa, and Fadila's heels clicking along the path.

"Here's your passport, Asma."

Fadila announced this with pride, as if to say that Musa could do anything. "You need him from now on. He'll keep an eye on you. Ali doesn't have the time these days."

Ruhiyya trilled for joy and was about to burst into song, but then she paused to examine Jawad's passport again to reassure herself that it was really there. Musa interrupted us all to tell us how interested they had been in Jawad's passport at the embassy, how the official had decided to give me a visa within an hour of him going there, and claimed that even the President wouldn't expect such good treatment from foreign embassies in the current situation. I reflected that times had changed; it was those living abroad who had the power to influence things now.

Jawad thanked Musa who was eager to get to the point. "Mr Jawad, will you do me a few letters for emergencies? And we'll photocopy your passport in case Fadila or her niece want to leave."

I examined the French visa stamped in my passport, seeing it as a return to a normal life, where we would have valid passports, obtain visas without trouble and travel by air whenever we wished. I turn over the pages of my passport: visas for

Egypt, Spain, Tunisia, Jordan, all places I'd gone to because of Naser. The French visa stood out beside them, bright and new. Is this one for my sake or Jawad's, or for both of us?

Fadila was right to think that I'd be in debt to Musa. He accompanied me to the bank, to say goodbye to a friend, to the Artisanat to buy olive oil soap and to the airline company, since I had given up being patient and wanted to leave quickly, terrified that the airport would suddenly be closed. Such hasty preparation for a journey was unnatural, but rather than being on edge, I found myself saying, "It doesn't matter. I'm leaving everything behind."

I want to hurry up and go before anything happens to me, for in my mind's eye I can see newspaper headlines: "Stray bullet kills woman as she prepares to leave the country."

I try to keep my head down in the car, and walk close in to the walls. I jump in beside Musa and drive swerving from side to side, so that any bullet coming in my direction will miss its target.

I rush into the house and kiss Ruhiyya. "Jawad's not here," she says.

My hand goes up to my heart and I see more newspaper headlines: "French author of Lebanese origin struck by stray bullet."

"Did he go out alone?" I ask desperately.

"I wish he had. Fadila took him to see a relation of the artist Unsi. When he heard that they were selling off his work he was mad keen to buy some."

I stood in the garden, opening the gate and looking along the street from time to time, then went back into the house, my anxiety growing by the minute. I decided to call my grandmother, however long it took, and dialled the chocolate factory in the village. I asked to speak to Zemzem or Naima but the line went dead while I was waiting. When I phoned back a quarter of an hour later, Zemzem answered and I told her I was going away. She sounded apprehensive and I tried to reassure her, promising her I wouldn't be gone long, telling her to send my love to my grandmother and assure her I wasn't going to America. "Ruhiyya will shut up the house and give the key to Fadila and she'll give it to Ali. The house is lovely and clean and tidy, and the garden's looking beautiful," I finished lamely, lying through my teeth of course, to Ruhiyya's amusement.

I didn't begin packing my case until Jawad returned. I picked out a lot of clothes then put half of them back, feeling completely confused, and consulted Ruhiyya and Fadila, who wanted me to take letters for my mother and Ricardo. Jawad preferred locally made traditional clothes, caftans, my grandmother's old clothes. About modern clothes he would say, "That's not in fashion any more," or "The colour's not nice," or "That's like something from a sale of synthetics."

Mountains of clothes accumulated around me; some leapt out at me, compelling me to take them, but all of them carried such powerful associations that I didn't want to leave any behind. I looked around me in confusion: I was really going away, leaving this, taking that, and going. I wished I could change my mind. I loved everything I could see and if I couldn't keep things as they were, I wanted to take all the clothes I owned, even the ones I'd put away in plastic bags and never wore.

It wasn't only the clothes; there were numerous other objects I desperately wanted to have with me: an ashtray, a picture, some of my grandmother's old things. When I thought about it, I wanted my grandmother with me. I went frantically round the room like a dog chasing its tail, touching one thing after another. These inanimate objects took me back to my mother and father, Isaf the maid, and my childhood; I had a vision of an aircraft, a scrawl of orange writing on the blue sky, gone in a minute. How could all this fit in my suitcase? How could I leave it behind? I was like a cat in the fish market, disoriented by the overpowering smell. I didn't know where to begin. How could I pack the cracks in the ceiling whose changing shapes I had watched for hours? When I thought I was all ready to go, I found myself magnifying the hitches I'd encountered on the way and envisaging others. Jawad would be kidnapped next day because he had a French passport; hadn't they'd interrogated him on the road to Beirut? When I told him of my apprehensions he drew me close and put his arms round me reassuringly. "How could you live here all these years and not be afraid?" he asked, as if I was a small child who wouldn't take in his question because she was surrounded by distractions on all sides.

"I used to think I was part of the war. Like a fighter at a checkpoint unafraid of the bullets flying round him. But now I feel as if I'm running away to save my skin."

Suddenly more sombre, Jawad began to tell me what had happened to him on the road. He said he prayed that his few hours as a hostage were a sort of welcome, as his interrogator had put it, an acknowledgement of his literary talent and the name he had made for himself in Europe and the rest of the world. He wanted to draw Jawad's attention to the lengths Syria had gone to on Lebanon's behalf, and to the way the Lebanese were prejudiced against them. It was Damascus who was getting the hostages released, and was intent on restoring Lebanese sovereignty. The Syrians had entered West Beirut to stop the bloodshed between the political parties because the devil had been in charge there. People hadn't dared stick their heads out of their windows or over their balconies, and now even foreigners were coming out of their hiding-places in broad daylight, and still the Lebanese wouldn't admit the truth: that Syria had given them back the fresh air of freedom.

"In other words, they wanted me to tell this to the world."

"You mean they wanted you on their side?"

"Exactly. I said to him, so everything you're doing is for their sake, for the Lebanese, because you love them so much? What about local and international politics?"

I was at a loss to know how to answer him and made no comment. He leaned forward to kiss me on the lips, while I wondered whether we would be leaving the next day after all. The last thing I wanted was for him to kiss me; I would have liked to hear Ali responding to the message I'd left and promising to take us to the airport, for I wasn't sure how much influence Musa and his friends had there. I fidgeted, trying to breathe, like a whale looking for the little air-holes in a sea of ice.

"My mind's somewhere else," I whispered.

"So's mine," he replied, and put his hand on my breasts and bent his head, looking down inside my blouse almost furtively. He said I had nice breasts, then added in a low voice that my nipples reminded him of the nipples of the women in his family, large and pink.

"Did you look at them secretly?" I asked.

"How did you know?"

He told me his mother fed him for five years because he was greedy and used to call her when she was sitting in the house with the other women.

We remained silent for a while, preoccupied with our own thoughts. The room grew steadily darker then all of a sudden it brightened again. The darkness in the daytime must have brought on this drowsy, reflective feeling; the dark of night etched its thoughts into the mind and the soul so fiercely it almost dissolved them. He seemed to have fallen asleep and I could hear the sound of his light, regular breathing. I slipped quietly out of my grandmother's room. Ruhiyya was lying on the sofa smoking, and as soon as she heard me she called, "Haven't you had enough of each other? I swear what you're doing is wrong. If he wants you he should go and ask your grandparents now, before you leave. Watch he doesn't suck all the goodness out of you, then spit you out."

I smiled: even though she was more progressive than the other women in the village and many in the heart of the city, she was still Ruhiyya, who lived her life in the belief that men were not to be trusted. She came with me to the neighbours' house, having urged me to try and contact Ali again; she too was reluctant to believe that Musa would have any dependable acquaintances in the airport, and wanted to make sure Jawad was safe until his plane had taken off and she could watch it in the air as it left the skies of the city far behind. I picked up the key and a jasmine in a pot and we left the house quietly and went and knocked on the neighbours' door.

"Who's there?" called a voice.

"Your honest neighbour coming to tell you your house is on fire," whispered Ruhiyya sarcastically.

"Asmahan from next door," I called back.

The door opened at once and the whole family stood ranged in the doorway. I put the jasmine down for them to look after till my grandmother came back, and felt a pang of nostalgia as I looked around the half-familiar room. Through the window I could see part of our wall and one of the trees in our garden. The young children observed me boldly, with affection in their eyes.

At a certain period my existence had been important to them, as I used to help them procure fuel, water, bread, doctors, even transport, and yet they never connected me with any particular side. The husband and sons returned to the dark balcony. I could hear the boys shouting across to friends in the building opposite, arranging to swap bullets and pieces of shrapnel, just like we used to swap stamps and silkworms. Their father was giving advice to a rebellious young man, evidently a relation, mentioning various members of the family and their situations. "The family is the most important thing. Don't let anyone tell you different. If you think about your own situation and what's going on out there, you've had it. You'll only make matters worse for yourself and others."

"Ali. What about Ali?" said Ruhiyya, afraid I might have forgotten why we'd come.

"Can I use your telephone?" I asked the wife.

"Of course, my dear." She went towards it and we followed dutifully behind her, as if the telephone was a person we owed respect to. It was surprising that it still worked, and to my astonishment Ali answered.

"Of course I already knew," he said.

He was the one who had pulled strings to get the French visa, he'd get his own back on Fadila very soon, and Musa didn't deserve a penny from me.

I was delighted influence could still be wielded from the inside, and also pleased that I hadn't yet paid Musa. But then I told myself how mean and ungrateful I was being and felt ashamed and sorry for Musa, who was only trying to better himself and make life more interesting.

We returned home, where Jawad had woken up, and was

258

stretching and yawning. "Tomorrow at this time we'll be in Paris," he said. "It'll probably be raining. I remember before I came to Lebanon this time I thought, tomorrow night I'll be sleeping in the village at Ruhiyya's, but I didn't really believe it was happening until I got stung by a mosquito."

I wasn't thinking of the next day, or the next night and where I'd be. I felt as if I was inside a car engine with noisy parts moving frantically all around me yet failing to start the car. Paris was far away and didn't concern me. Jawad appeared to interpret my silence in another way.

"Are you wondering whether we'll be together like this tomorrow night? It could be difficult."

"Not at all," I answered hurriedly.

I realized with sudden clarity that we were never going to spend the night together, and to my surprise this didn't bother me. I thought, perhaps I don't love him, but he's my means of escape.

"I don't want to shock her the first night," he went on in a whisper.

It was his voice, rather than what he said, which made me dismiss the idea that I no longer loved him. I didn't sleep, or perhaps I slept with my eyes open like a wild rabbit, and I dreamt I was in the university café with Jawad sitting opposite me. There were people I used to see around, who must have left Beirut a long time before: a photographer; the owner of a record shop; a barber; a lecturer in the university; the chemist who used to sell me eye cream and the breast-firming cream he made up especially for a friend of mine; Wafa who was always around the campus when we were students – in the cafés, under the trees, waiting outside the exam halls – although we found out later she was never registered as a student. All of us were weeping and hugging each other. Although this dream scared me, I didn't keep going over it in my head as I would have done normally, for I was rapidly becoming drawn into the last-minute rush. I was woken by my own heartbeats and the moment the light banged against my eyelids I was up and into the bathroom, quickly dressing and doing my hair, while Jawad took his time. The voices of Ruhiyya and Fadila distracted me and I hunted unsuccessfully for my passport, ticket, phone numbers, bag. I went around the house leaving behind things I needed, as if Zemzem was going to clear up after me and send things on. I noticed my toothbrush on the table where I must have put it for a moment while I opened the door with my arms full of other things, and decided I must focus all my energies on packing my bag. Time was running out and I would soon be leaving this house far behind. As I came down the stairs I didn't feel any final wrench. I got into the car and waved goodbye to the neighbours but the lump I'd imagined coming into my throat as I set off on my journey failed to materialize. Fadila's kisses left no trace on my cheeks; when I took Musa's letters to post in Paris, I felt bad that he was under an illusion, as I couldn't imagine ever sticking stamps on them and posting them in a Paris street. I began to feel I was really on the move when I saw quarters of the city I had forgotten all about, buildings which I could remember only vaguely lying in ruins, burnt pines and vegetables and ugly curios for sale on the street. The familiar world returned with the road blocks. The first one was to examine our luggage. Ali took delight in giving them permission, then showed them an identity card. The soldier smiled at us and gave each of us a bar of chocolate.

"The day before yesterday they were giving out bananas," said Ali.

The airport appeared in the distance; the dull ochre façade was stamped on my memory, its familiar clock had lost its hands and looked like a dead insect stuck on the wall and there was a cluster of concrete stumps – the remains of a building or unfinished bridges. Cars stopped some distance from the airport to deposit luggage, and passengers and their friends and relatives.

Angrily Ali asked Ruhiyya why she had to come with us as he wanted to accompany us through security and customs.

She didn't answer, but embraced Jawad fiercely, laughing and crying, cursing him, wiping away her tears. She pinched his cheeks, then hugged him again, calling him her heart's love. She held me close and only let me go when I disengaged myself. Ali parked the car and took my case, brushing away the men and boys who clustered round us, wanting to earn a bit of money by praying for our safety or carrying Jawad's bags. My heart was in my mouth but the soldier hardly looked at Jawad's passport and our cases weren't opened. Money had talked, and Ali knew everybody. We caught sight of a group of men in civilian clothes, carrying beds.

"Do you think they're for the Syrian intelligence?" said Ali.

There were a lot of cages of poultry about and Ali assured us that it was a thriving business.

The airport seemed neglected, despite the crowds. The tiles were dirty. There were signs everywhere, indicating different tour companies, announcing destinations all over the world, giving information in other languages and advertising the presence of the major airlines: Aeroflot, Interflug, KLM, Alia, British Airways, Air France, Pan American.

All this had been there before the war, and we hadn't seen it. We didn't need it because it belonged to another world which had nothing to do with us. Our world was Lebanon and Beirut in particular. Now there were long queues of passengers ahead of us, large groups with their luggage and children. This time we had to open our cases; Ali whispered something in the Lebanese soldier's ear but he indicated a Syrian soldier nearby, then gestured as if to say it was nothing to do with him and searched our cases, thrusting his hands among the fine loaves of marquq bread, the packets of thyme, even into the boxes of pastries. The Syrian soldier gave back our passports and said, "Why are you together?"

"We're relatives," I answered.

We stood there in the turmoil of baggage and people. Fadila and Ruhiyya screamed at us from behind the barrier where they stood with Musa and others who had been given special permission to come in and see people off. They looked as if they were waiting for food and water to be distributed to them. The people travelling weren't going on holiday or business trips like before the war, or even emigrating in the way people did in the past. They were setting out to begin again in a far-off country with new minds, even new bodies, and seemed to grow less substantial, like people turning to smoke before they disappeared inside the djinn's bottle. The people seeing them off feel simultaneous pangs of sadness and envy, and are mystified by the behaviour of those inside the airport who seem already to have forgotten about them and be too taken up with the various transactions preceding their departure to give any display of affection.

The airport floor used to be light beige-coloured like sugar, sixties design, reminding you of those times. Now it had dark patches on it and there were cigarette butts everywhere as if the floor was a giant ashtray. A cloud of cigarette smoke hung permanently in the air, or was it just dark? Is a human being only acceptable, in harmony with himself and his surroundings, when he is in the country or the desert and has no need of artificial light or decor? There was no electricity in the airport building, and the low ceiling was made of plastic squares, some of which had been torn out. The architect evidently knew he was designing a temporary structure. On a miserable wall there was a portrait of a man with no name, no title, only the cedar to indicate who he was. Portraits of Lebanese presidents used to leave a lasting impression, the medals slashed across their chests giving an air of strength and determination. There were pictures of Hafez Al-Asad everywhere, with his name underneath.

Ali pointed out that we were standing in the first-class queue. Then he said, "Wait. I've got a contact here. I'll fix it for you."

But Jawad insisted on paying the difference himself so that I could travel with him. He looked over towards Ruhiyya. "Don't let her see. She'll have a heart attack."

When Ruhiyya had found out that Jawad always travelled first class she begged him to go tourist and give her the difference. Jawad told Ali not to mention it to her, well aware he was tempting fate. Ali laughed, delighted that Jawad understood him so well. "What does it matter to you?" he said.

He attracted Ruhiyya's attention and pointed to the first class sign but she didn't understand and gestured frantically asking him what he meant. The two men turned away, laughing.

The airport seethed with bobbing heads, like a pot of maize on the stove. There was uproar everywhere. Ali said goodbye to us at the security, but stood waiting to see us come out through the passport control. My heart stopped again when Jawad handed his passport to the Syrian in plain clothes.

"Jawad. Born in Lebanon. And you're French."

Jawad laughed. "What are we supposed to do? They give us the nationality with the passport. Do you expect us to turn it down?"

Then the soldier took my passport and looked at me. "Your hair's better now, young lady," he said.

In my passport photo it was short.

We waved to Ali, then to the other three before we vanished from their sight.

As we entered the departure lounge I shrank back in surprise: I'd got used to houses being dark, but hadn't expected quite the same murky gloom in the airport. A blown-glass chandelier hung from the ceiling, reminiscent of the Phoenicia Hotel, the colour of the sea and calm days. I felt as if I was meeting the Lebanese face to face for the first time. Travel exposes people and they appear as they are, without trappings. I discovered how short they were. Perhaps that was why the architect had designed a ceiling so low that the heads of the tallest almost touched it. The country is ordinary. There's no war going on here, but it's poor. Old people, young people and children mill around between the old-fashioned stainless steel tables and ashtrays. The green and blue carpet is full of holes and has seen better days. I order a coffee without sugar.

We heard a cat miaowing but paid no attention and went off to the duty-free shop. It was like somewhere in the back of beyond, the goods on display all looking old and tired. We stopped at the shop selling local handicrafts, a shining oasis in the dull desert of the airport. Jawad bought keyrings with blue eyes hanging on them and we went back to wait in the lounge.

A litter of kittens like little balls of wool were playing there, hiding under the chairs to tease their mother, jumping on to the seats and pulling at the frayed wickerwork. A little girl was playing with one not much bigger than her hand. Suddenly she looked around and slipped it into a bag, closed it and took a few steps with it before a woman, presumably her mother, swooped down on her, opened the bag and gave the child a resounding slap. The kitten fled like a demented creature, with an expression of terror in its eyes.

I couldn't relax. I felt uneasy without knowing why, as if I didn't believe I was really free to go.

Something white approaching distracted me: a large doll with reddened cheeks and lips. It was human, a bride in a long white dress and veil. She didn't look around her, but kept her eyes fixed on a large overnight bag which an airport employee was carrying for her. She sat down, drawing the bag close to her white high heels. In the crowded, smoky atmosphere she exuded a damp warmth. Everyone was looking at her.

"Poor thing, she'll suffocate," I said, seeing her take a plastic wallet from her bag and start to fan herself.

"You're always so negative," said Jawad. "She's glad to be the centre of attention. I'm beginning to be sorry you're dressed so casually. It would be fun if you landed at Charles de Gaulle in a white wedding outfit!"

I laughed irritably. "She's like a lamb ready for the slaughter. Does the whole world have to know she's an unsullied virgin going to meet her future husband?"

"You personalize everything. She can do what she likes. And we can watch," he added, taking a film out of his bag and starting to load the camera.

The planes were running late, and an air of impatience began to build up. The temperature rose and the bride, sweating, swigging lemonade and wiping her face and neck with Kleenex had become the barometer of the place.

The waiter, dressed in a rusty black uniform, gathered up the empty glasses, pocketed the tips, took orders, interspersing his sentences with French and saying "Merci" and "Pardon" as politely as could be.

Why am I here waiting for a plane? Why do I want another life when life is all around me in the laughter of the passengers, the bustle of the airport employees, and the waiter bringing the orders with an air of precise decorum?

"Can you believe that a month and a half ago there was

fighting and all hell was let loose?" I say to Jawad. "And see how normal everything is now!"

"Normal? Look at the people around you. They've become strangers in their own country. Look at the way they're buying things and hear how they're talking, just like tourists. They even talk to their children in foreign languages. People from the same country normally stick together until they reach their destination. But not here. See how curt they are with each other, how critical."

"In the shelters and buildings under fire they stick together," I think to myself. "They must do abroad too."

I'd seen Assyrians in front of a church doorway in Beirut: young and old fused into a single being. And Lebanese abroad as well, on a television news bulletin. The ship docked at Cyprus and a group of Cypriot women was there to welcome it, demonstrating their solidarity with the Lebanese women, whose tearful eyes and tremulous mouths worked in unison. As they were given sweets and drinks, my anger grew and I lay there on the sofa reproaching them for not being at home as I was, with friends or relations, or squatting in an empty building, instead of crying in front of the liner which had carried them away and was tossing fretfully on the waves in the background.

Jawad was the warm bait which had drawn me out of my idle stupor, enticed me away from the gentle ease of my calm existence and my indifference on to this airport seat, where from time to time I interrupted my attempts to picture the life I was going to lead, by jumping up to make sure my passport was safe, or listening intently to the announcements. I progressed no further than thinking that I would wake up in a different country and need to make a physical effort to adapt to the way of life there, before sinking back in my seat again. I would see nobody until I had bought some clothes and gone to the hairdresser and I wouldn't leave the house for two days. I wanted to become acclimatized to the different atmosphere. Would I have a bed from the start? Would Catherine meet us, or would we arrive in the early hours of the morning? Would I stay in a hotel or would they take me home with them and leave me grinding my teeth as they said good night and disappeared into their bedroom? I would lie down on the sofa under the woollen blanket they'd given me and try to cry, but find I was too tired and close my eyes and give in to my thoughts which would inspire this song:

> You brought me to France
> And for the sake of this blonde
> You deserted me
> And left me cold on the sofa
> Ask her what I'm singing
> See if she understands
> I'll slit my wrists if she knows
> Museitbeh from the Sphinx
> Or bileela pudding from fool beans

The sense of waiting hung over us once more with the disappearance of the bride in white. Then we heard Jawad's name over the loudspeakers. My heart sank. I knew that from chaos springs order and order produces chaos. How had they found him in the middle of all this? It was always the same here: they would suddenly be concerned with the most trivial details, and just as unexpectedly at other times they overlooked important ones. Did they want to scare him, or say goodbye to him and remind him to talk about the Syrians and their role in Lebanon?

"Mr Jawad. We apologize for this delay. The VIP lounge is at your disposal."

Jawad relaxed visibly when he heard this, but the gesture was a nuisance to him. He began to make his excuses but the official insisted, implying that it would annoy the Syrian intelligence officers scattered around the place and thereby give deep satisfaction to his fellow countrymen, if he accepted the offer.

"Really, I can't be bothered," repeated Jawad warmly. "They don't need to feel bad about it. I'm comfortable here, thanks."

Despite the fuss this offer caused, I couldn't help thinking how the world was changing; writers were on a level with politicians and media stars. They obliged us to go into one of the two VIP lounges. The low leather sofas were cracked and split, there was a layer of dust on the carpet and the glass tables were covered in sticky stains. I noticed a dead cockroach in a corner. This was different from how I'd imagined such places; they should have bright lights, not spiderwebs and cockroaches, and the people invited to use them should feel they were privileged to be shown the country's human face. People came in here as a result of interventions on their behalf by "public relations", militias, politicians or the Syrians. Things which I had thought of as fixed and unchanging were in as fluid a state as I was. Then we found out that we were there because of Ali, not Jawad, when someone came to give us Ali's best wishes for a safe journey.

We found ourselves relaxing suddenly. We weren't going to fail Ali: we'd drink the lemonade and behave as if we were used to VIP lounges.

I watched the women in the latest European fashions, and felt like an outsider. The world seemed to have entered a new era without me.

Jawad insisted on us going back to the ordinary departure lounge to inquire about our flight. Everything looked far away, colourless, and the sky was not blue but grey, behind a thin covering of mist. The mountains rose in the distance beyond the red sandstone hills whose beauty seemed to take Jawad by surprise.

I felt dislike for everyone I saw. All I could hear was people talking about visas and Canada, Canada. Jawad came back and pointed out a thickset man who was leaving Detroit for Canada. His brother had already left and gone to Switzerland via Italy and was working as a waiter. Emigrating. He's emigrating. Emigration.

I wanted to guard against a sentimental view of this emigration. Most of them were leaving in search of work, not to escape the violence. They looked healthy and many were smiling. It wasn't the kind of exodus we read about in history or were used to seeing on documentaries: people fleeing as aircraft droned overhead, pouring along roads and on to troopships, their faces wretched with hunger. Ours was different. We packed cases. Shut up our houses. Reserved aeroplane seats and cabins. It wasn't how we emigrated but where to which was surprising. Leftists went reluctantly to the States because Arab countries would no longer accept them. Intellectuals lived in the Gulf whose people and way of life they had always criticized.

The firm ground beneath my feet is starting to shift uneasily. I am afraid of the lost-looking old couple, because I sense a fellow-feeling, although they talk anxiously and in loud voices, whereas my speech is subdued. They will transfer their worries to their sons who'll be waiting for them at the other end, and I'll take refuge with Jawad who thinks it is such a straightforward, normal thing for me to leave Beirut. I'll throw myself on his mercy, if only for a few days. As far back as I can remember, I haven't made anyone take responsibility for me except Isaf when I was a child, and it's been other people unloading their troubles on to me. That was how I liked it, and this dependence on Jawad makes me feel naked, as if my body is light and empty and will break up and blow away at the least puff of wind.

The seat was uncomfortably hot and my clothes stuck to the worn leather. I began to think seriously about what sort of life I would lead in France. I felt as if I was gradually emerging from a dream. What was I doing there? Was it really enough that he said to me, "Don't worry. Things will sort themselves out"? Would I look for a job in some boring Franco-Arab establishment? At the start I'd have to rely entirely on him. Why had my family put their trust in their lands and possessions instead of ready money?

I remembered a friend of mine who had gone to the States to study during the war. She was so keen to be independent from her family that she shared a single damp room with another student in a street whose buildings were collapsing from the misery and poverty and violence they witnessed. In exile, everyday things did not just exist alongside the people or as part of the structure of the house. Even drinking water cost money, and tea bags were used more than once. After a few months she was forced to move in with her sister in another state to save money, but of course this had its own price. Her sister criticized her for sleeping till ten in the morning and my friend claimed it was because she hadn't slept properly for so long in Beirut. Really it was because she stayed in bed trying to put the pieces of herself together again and forget the destruction and disillusion she had left behind her against the background of competing television channels. She couldn't get used to spending her days in shopping malls, or staring idly through the window watching her nephew kicking a football. Her sister told her she was too fond of herself, and she wondered where this self was to like or dislike. One morning she woke up to the sound of hammering: her sister's husband was making a worktable for her. She was delighted; she would take up drawing and painting again, although the view from the window only made her think of old age and loneliness. On either side of her sister's garden she could see elderly Americans mowing their green lawns. But more than anything she was pleased because she thought her sister and brother-in-law had at last realized what she was going through and were trying to encourage her back to her art. The feeling didn't last: she found out that this table had been made for her so that she would start being realistic, as her sister said, and set up a stall in the Saturday market, selling Lebanese pastries, just like the Mexican neighbours who made tortillas to sell.

Jawad looked at his watch. "She'll be getting anxious now."

I smiled at him, wondering how he could love two women at the same time. Would I have put up with it if I hadn't been old currency, obsolete but still around, with faint traces of its former charms clearly visible? I took out my handbag mirror, examined my face and abandoned my idea of myself as old currency.

I felt the tiredness spreading into my joints and, although I tried to stop myself, I wished I was in bed at home or lying comfortably on the sofa listening to the neighbours' cat miaowing. The passengers I had been watching for the last few hours must have contributed to weakening my resolve. I wouldn't let them do this to me. I told myself I would know what I had to do once I got to France. I would start caring what happened to me again, work, study, learn about computers. I'd find a room that suited me. I asked Jawad who he socialized with there.

"Nobody much. A few artists," he replied.

I would refuse to get to know other Lebanese. I didn't want to become like them, missing kibbeh with tomatoes. Like Hayat.

I have to stop wavering. I don't have any alternative but to leave now. Why am I allowing myself to forget that I felt like a stranger even in my own house? Didn't I begin these letters by saying that I was a hostage in a place where I no longer understood what people were saying? What's changed? Why do I think my fellow passengers look like stupid sheep?

When Jawad goes home to France and draws back the curtains he will find it difficult to know where he is, seeing that he lives in the past and spends his time writing about it. He will walk along in the cold and see suns everywhere hanging from bunches of grapes and lamp-posts fixed to militia points and coloured leaflets floating down through the skies; people he's forgotten he ever met will pop up like jack-in-the-boxes. Even if the war hadn't happened, he would have felt this nostalgia for the past.

"Why go back to places if they're preserved in your memory?" I asked him once in the shadows of the garden.

"I visit them in the flesh to see how much they've changed and how much I've changed. Even if I tried I couldn't live here any more and I feel the places themselves don't want me, but they're always in my mind and they stop me being content. They won't let me rest."

"But they're one of the main reasons for your success, aren't they?" I said consolingly, delighted to hear that he suffered a little.

"I know. I pick the bitter fruits of war and write in a western language about the emotions which lie between my language and my conscience. The more successful I am, the more my conscience troubles me, because I always used to long for this country to be destroyed."

For the first time I seemed to see Beirut as it really was: a ball inside a ball inside a ball. Dark halls and passages opening into one another endlessly. Unlike most of us, Jawad had chosen his life, or rather gone racing down the path which had opened in front of him. Chance decides how we are inspired to choose one course of action over another. I was conscious that I had reached middle age without noticing. The war was like an express train hurtling along without a stop, taking everything with it. It had deprived me of the opportunity of using the past to live in the present and give shape to the future.

Jawad is scared that the plane won't take off, and I am scared of admitting that I want to go on providing nourishment for his sentences. He only sees what is in his camera lens and recorded in his notebook. I don't want to become like him, collecting situations and faces and objects, recording what people around me say to give my life some meaning away from here. I don't want to keep my country imprisoned in my memory. For memories, however clear, are just memories obscured and watered down by passing time. There are many empty corners between remembering and forgetting. I want things to be as they are, exposed to the sun and air, not hidden in the twists and turns of my mind. For the first time I wonder if Jawad is insisting on taking me with him, as Hayat wanted to in the past, to be a link with his home, for him to hang on to when he needs it, like a baby's dummy.

But what about these war years? If I go they'll flow away like waste water. And if I don't go, but connect this moment up to the distant past, ignoring the long years of war in between, the burning streams will rise up around me demanding: "What have you achieved? How did you live?"

Jawad is afraid that the aircraft won't take off; I'm afraid that it will, scared to own up that I feel sad because I'm about to put the war behind me; as if I am not a witness to those who have come and gone and those who have stayed: Maronites, Druze, Shia, Palestinians, Syrians, French, Ottomans, Crusaders, the Lebanese army, the Sixth Fleet, and the Israelis wanting "Peace for Galilee". How can I put years of patient waiting, fear and astonishment behind me? Naser made me greet the war gladly like him; Simon showed it to me at close quarters and now Jawad is trying to take me away from it.

What is peace? I carry my war with me wherever I go. I can hear bullets spraying around us now, although the sky is quiet, the mountains are peaceful and the airport is full of cheerful noise. I want to go back to the house and garden and familiar faces, to the pleasurable feeling when the fighting stops of getting dressed at last and doing my hair. If I try to pin down what made me happy, forcing myself to look back, I have to acknowledge my hypocrisy: I see myself trying to hide from the noise of the battles which pounded through my head until I wanted to scream for help; lying in bed in the darkness able to make out the peeling paintwork, the furniture from my father's apartment building piled up against the wall, the broken mirrors, the books going back to another age. The house was no longer as it used to be, alive and waiting, with a presence as real and distinctive as our faces.

It upsets me to think I can even consider staying behind, and I want to put my arms round Jawad. When I look at him all the little physical details I've come to know so well crowd in on me and I have a lump in my throat. The dimple in his chin, the single white hair in his eyebrow, his collarbone where it sticks out slightly. How would I be able to sleep soundly ever again, or wake up without feeling the pain of losing him? Deliberately I picture myself walking around the streets and quays after Naser had left, when I couldn't get his features out of my mind, and he seemed to have left traces of himself in so many different places. I followed him to the cities by the sea, and when at last he sat opposite me I was still searching for him. Losing him had split me in two and I had to find the other part of me to believe that he was really there before me. I let my hand pass over the individual pores of his skin, without actually touching him, gazing at the little hairs between his eyebrows, the purplish mole on his neck, the thick eyelashes, stained teeth, brown hands. His wrists were surprisingly slender for someone of his build. Looking at it all set me on edge as if the dentist was probing around in my mouth, and yet I felt detached. Even the voice which used to caress me had become a hollow echo of my memory, bouncing off the lemonade glass, not the voice which triggered off passion when it said, "My darling," and desire when it murmured, "I've missed you. I've missed you."

I knew from the pen in his shirt pocket, even from the colour of his shirt, from the portable phone, the way he glanced down the bill before paying it, the tone of voice in which he asked about Beirut, that it was over between us, and that I should have decided this for myself when he left the first time, when the Israelis entered Beirut and Lebanon became a different place, and the Palestinians were thrown into disarray. Inside me I suppose I had known it was finished, but needed to weep over the corpse before I could make a new start.

Jawad comes up and announces irritably that the flight will be postponed if the aircraft doesn't take off within the next two hours, because the airport in Paris won't accept it after a certain time of night.

Unlike me, he hadn't remained nailed to his seat waiting, but instead seemed to have become hyperactive; the war hadn't taught him, as it had taught us, either to be in a state of readiness, forgetting everything but trying to stay alive, or to be grateful for the calm periods and make the best of them.

The announcement of a flight to Amman rekindled his enthusiasm. "What do you think about taking any plane out?"

"I've only got a visa for France and Lebanese need them for everywhere these days." Then I added to comfort him, "They told you the flight might be cancelled so you wouldn't keep asking them. They'd lose a lot of money if they didn't fly."

I gave him my hand and felt myself relax. The warmth of it distracted me from the thoughts which had been pitching me to and fro like waves on a turbulent sea, and all I wanted was to be close to him – and how close I was going to be in Paris! He fidgeted restlessly, drew his hand away and stood up. Perhaps if I'd been able to read his mind I would have seen that he was wishing he was alone so that he could take any flight out. I would never know what was going on in his head.

As I look around me now everything seems normal. Even the sight of my shoes reassures me. Medium heels, navy blue: an indication of how peaceful life has become here. However hard I try to summon up the sounds of the fighting, and the fear, isolation and despair they create, I can only think that the violence won't return, that the past has really gone for good, leaving behind this pleasant numbness which is rising up from the tips of my toes and spreading all over me. I yawn continually and wonder if I'm too relaxed and peaceful to pick up my suitcase and make my way out to the aircraft, never mind endure the trials of the journey. I rise to my feet with difficulty and stand facing him. Gently I take the camera from him and put it down, then take hold of his hands and bend my head over them, indifferent to the crowded airport, kissing the palms, and pressing them to my face. The tears come however much I try to hold them in, and splash on to his hands. I wipe them away before I stand face to face with him, and tell him that I've changed my mind and I'm not going with him.

I see another face, unconnected to the man with the camera, out of place in this airport; the face of the one who walked with me over the stony ground in the village, who took me in his arms on the floor of my house. His eyes are affectionate, angry and bewildered at the same time. Then anger takes over as he looks right through me, repeating a single incredulous word: "What? What?"

He collapses on to a seat and takes his head in his hands, muttering like a child who's lost his toy, "I'm not going to let the plane take off till you decide to come."

I hadn't pictured he would react like this; it seemed to have slipped my mind that I hadn't let him take part in my dialogue with myself, this rag doll hauled to and fro by its arms, as my feelings started playing tricks with me like shadows cast on the ceiling. Throughout my internal debates I had treated Jawad as nothing more than a travelling companion.

He comes close so that his knee touches mine and puts his arms round me. "What's wrong? Are you angry because I said she'd be starting to worry? Do you want me to choose between you? Shall we get married? Just tell me."

I wriggle free of his arms, embarrassed because of the people around us, but manage a smile and even a nervous little laugh. "I can't leave. I can't."

"What are you afraid of? Perhaps it's my fault. I didn't do

274

enough to set your mind at rest about how you'd live. We didn't discuss the details. We were preoccupied with the visa and Musa, then with the bride and the airport. You've got to tell me what's happened to you in the last three hours."

He looks around him in confusion, trying to concentrate on what's being broadcast over the loudspeaker, then resuming his attempts to make me explain myself, incomprehension and fear in his eyes. "If you've changed your mind about me, never mind. But don't confuse the issues. It shouldn't stop you leaving."

I don't feel the pressure of the war like he does but I begin to cry, swaying my head from side to side.

"What's this for?"

I'm crying because I don't know how to stop myself. I lift up my head to look at him but as soon as I notice the pulse in his jaw, and the trembling of the faint growth of stubble on his chin, I can't bear the thought of not seeing them again, not hearing the voice which has become part of me, like a skin I'll never shed.

"I love you very much, but I want to stay in Beirut."

"You love me but you want to stay in Beirut. Do you mean you want me to stay in Beirut? Perhaps it would be better for me. Who knows?"

Stay here and live in the same conditions as me? He'd even lose his delight in words. That's the effect Beirut has on those who haven't witnessed its war. It rips the smiles off their faces, then removes their safety helmets, covers their eyes with grimy gauze, daubs their noses with black paste and their tongues with castor oil and leaves their bodies for the birds to peck. Then the circle shrinks and the wide expanses of land are reduced to a few metres.

"Perhaps you'd like me to stay?"

"No." And I tell him what I am thinking.

"Why do you want to put up with it yourself?"

I had read what he'd written in his notebook when he'd left it lying on his seat:

"I've discovered that my nostalgia was just because of being a foreigner in France. How I longed for the self I thought was somewhere else. Well, I seem to have spoilt the dream by coming back. I feel as if I've never seen this land before and never knew the people. Instead of mountains I saw concrete in a country which has become as black as night: the walls are black, the soldiers are dressed in black. The countryside is charred and burnt, and the population is living on top of the biggest arsenal in the world."

"What do you do here apart from gossip?" he asks me now. "Your whole life's focused around making sure you have a supply of electricity, water and food and avoiding the bombs. It's as if you can only live in this twilight world between war and not-war. This doesn't have to be what life's about, you know. There's a whole big world out there."

"I don't want to turn into one of those pathetic creatures who are always homesick, always saying I wish I was still in Beirut. I don't want to become like you, split between here and there. I know I'm not happy here, but why should I be unhappy in two countries?"

"Why are you thinking of all these things in advance? Try it and then decide."

"It's easier living in the middle of what upsets you than running away from it and worrying at a distance. Things seem worse from a distance."

"I don't understand why you're anticipating being depressed in either place. Come, and see how you feel in a few weeks or months." He pauses wearily, then seems to feel compelled to go on speaking. "Beirut's an excuse. You hide behind it because you're scared to begin a new life. I want to help you think about something else besides electricity and water and rediscover the world beyond this place."

Beirut International Airport. Beirut. I seemed to hear the word for the first time and I repeated it several times. Beirut. I saw it written. I saw it on the map, on postcards. Zaytouna. Ma'rad. Martyrs' Square. Riad Al-Solh. On photographs and pictures in foreign books. I saw it written, the letters forming a child's cart with big wheels or the collar of my school uniform.

It was as if it had been branded on my mind in the course of the war. Beirut at war takes on bulk and shape. I can hold on to it, whereas in peace time life was like a garage full of spare parts and broken-down vehicles and I didn't know where to begin with it. Now I picture Beirut as a big pit in the ground, all small furrows and hollows and cavities, barren except for clumps of green grass clinging to its sides. I began my letters saying that I was a hostage and now I'm trying to see little plants growing, as they are all that my land produces. My life is here and every country has its own life.

"You've become addicted to this war, you know."

I say nothing.

"You're afraid that if you leave here, you'll no longer be a queen like you were in Beirut, with the neighbours and Fadila and Ricardo. You're forgetting that your experiences will make you much more interesting than anyone who left at the beginning and has stayed in Paris ever since."

"They say that to travel is to die a little death. In any case, I'm not in the least curious about life in Paris."

"Why do you think that is? It's because you're lazy, and afraid."

"Maybe if I'd left before I'd think differently, but each country has its own way of life and my life is here."

"What about me? Where do I stand?"

I gather all my hair to one side and chew on my lips and say nothing.

"That's a stupid question. It's probably not the right time to ask," he says.

I saw everything I had left behind in Beirut through a fine veil of nostalgia, perhaps because of the distinctive atmosphere of airports, although I knew I would soon view it once more as a tawdry, rundown circus.

Whenever the pulse in his hand beat faster, I felt the beads of sweat breaking out on me and smelt it mixed with his smell and began to have second thoughts and wonder if what I'd been saying amounted to nothing.

Jawad stops trying to persuade me and just looks at me, then kisses my hand from time to time, punctuating his actions with a shake of the head. He touches my cheek and says he's already missing me, then takes my hands impulsively in his again and I'm holding them out eagerly like an orphan to touch his lips and feel the currents of desire running through them, and then he's saying imploringly that I must follow him tomorrow or the next day.

I'll follow him now. As soon as our flight is announced I'll stand up and we'll go together. I can't envisage staying here alone, watching him go off without me.

I'm happy to have made this decision and want to surprise him and I'm the one to take his hand this time and bring it up to my face as if I'm telling him what I've decided. He, meanwhile, is trying to recover his composure. "What do I have to do to make you leave?" he asks. "Perhaps if you had everything running on batteries, even your hairdryer, you'd find your life here suddenly had no purpose."

"The case!" we both shout at the same time, suddenly remembering.

"What do you want to do about it?"

So I don't tell him I'll come with him after all – as a matter of fact, I relax because he's accepted the fact that I'm staying, and he seems to think he made the decision himself.

"I'll leave it – otherwise you'll be here all day."

"Good. If you leave your things with me, you'll have to come and get them." Then, as if he has caught sight of an image gleaming at him through his camera lens: "Now what shall I do with your clothes when I get there? I'm going to keep them all mixed up with mine."

His delight at the prospect of having my things with him annoys me; it seems as if they are a substitute for me, although at least remembering my case has stirred me into action. His face brightens again at the thought of taking it with him, while I try to conceal my regret as I whip through its contents in my mind.

I let them go grudgingly, perhaps to be the silent link between us, their effect on us only becoming clear later. Our conversation seems suddenly to have died. I remember myself as a little girl in my grandmother's room in the village. My grandmother put me in a new dress and shiny leather shoes and spent ages doing my hair. Then she tucked an artificial rose behind my ear: it was one I'd seen her wearing on many different dresses. To my amazement she passed a finger over her lips, taking a bit of lipstick off them, and dabbed it on my cheeks. Finally she sprinkled me with cologne from her vanity case, then clapped her hands: "Now go out and show them how pretty you are."

I went out and stood before the children who'd come from all over the village to see me. They stared at me from a distance, none of them daring to approach the porch. I knew what I thought of them, but not what they thought of me. When my grandmother appeared and smiled encouragingly at them, they scattered. She called them back and warily they drifted closer, but we didn't talk, just looked at one another for a while, although judging by their fixed expressions and unblinking eyes, they saw nothing. I stared at their bare feet, the spots and scabs on their legs, their unkempt hair.

I also remembered how Jawad came out of the village café with Munjid's son and I was waiting for them by the door. He asked me what Ruhiyya wanted him for and I said, "She wants you to marry me."

Everyone I love is leaving, and also those I don't love; even the hostages will go one after the other. Jawad asks if he can kiss me on the lips. I refuse, but he gets up from his seat and kisses me fleetingly on the mouth and I reproach myself, wondering how I can let a man like that go.

When the flight was announced I left him standing alone in the queue with his camera and hand luggage. Energy flowed back into my limbs and the blood surged through my body, and once more I went to confront the city which had made its war die of weariness.